A DARKER MAGIC
This Way Comes

A DARKER MAGIC This Way Comes

by

CARMEL NILAND

published 2016 by Shimran
Suite 10 Lauder Court, Milborne Port
Sherborne
Dorset DT9 5EL
UK

set in Dante 11pt and Dante Italic 11.5pt

Worldwide distribution by Filament Publishing Ltd
filamentpublishing.com

ISBN 978-910819-65-4

For John,
my Merlin

About the Author

Carmel Niland has lived two lives. In public, she has been on the firing line working for a state government in Australia, leading agencies on gender and racial equality, human rights, child protection and disability services. But what few people know is of her endless fascination with historical legends, particularly the tale of King Arthur and of his famed magician, Merlin.

For decades Merlin captivated her imagination and has seen her create her first novel based upon these ancient stories. With a passion for Roman British archaeology mixed with a keen interest in the Arthurian legend, Carmel Niland has devoured every piece of literature she could get her hands on, and climbed every Iron Age and Roman Fort in England, Scotland and Wales if it is in any way associated with Arthur. This passion and knowledge about the once and future king compelled her to use her research to reimagine his and Merlin's story and to write the first book in the series of five for readers, who like her, love secrets, mysteries and something strange.

Contents

Acknowledgements

Many helped create this book.

My friend, Austin, who shared his vast knowledge of Arthurian legends and murmured Merlin's secrets to me.

My nephew, Jack, and my niece, Emily, who stimulated me with their knowledge of worlds unknown to me.

My sons, Adam and Josh, always Knights of the Highest Orders who model how to be noble, and their children whom I write for.

My friend, Robert, who typed drafts before I learned how to, and critiqued them as he went, and Karen, my reality check, who took over from him.

My sister, Joan, who read my tedious first draft and gently made suggestions.

My niece, Charlotte, who allowed Emily to borrow her Australian long-necked turtles, Roget and Winston, so there would always be a bit of the New World in the Otherworld.

And the Cornwall Archaeological Society that generously shares and spreads their knowledge of the Cornwall of the Romano-British.

And the countless who whispered to me unseen around midnight.

Thank you.

Many people helped transform my words to bring them to you. There was Susan, my entrepreneurial agent from Shimran; Viv Mainwaring who produced the You Tube video, Susan's Glastonbury team of Ranchor, who created the covers, drew maps and illustrations, and laid out my text, and Aashi who built the website.

There was Julian who edited and Chris who printed and distributed this book. Thank you all and I am looking forward to working with you again on *The Curse of the Dragon Kings*.

"By the pricking of my thumbs
Something wicked this way comes."

Macbeth, Act IV Scene I

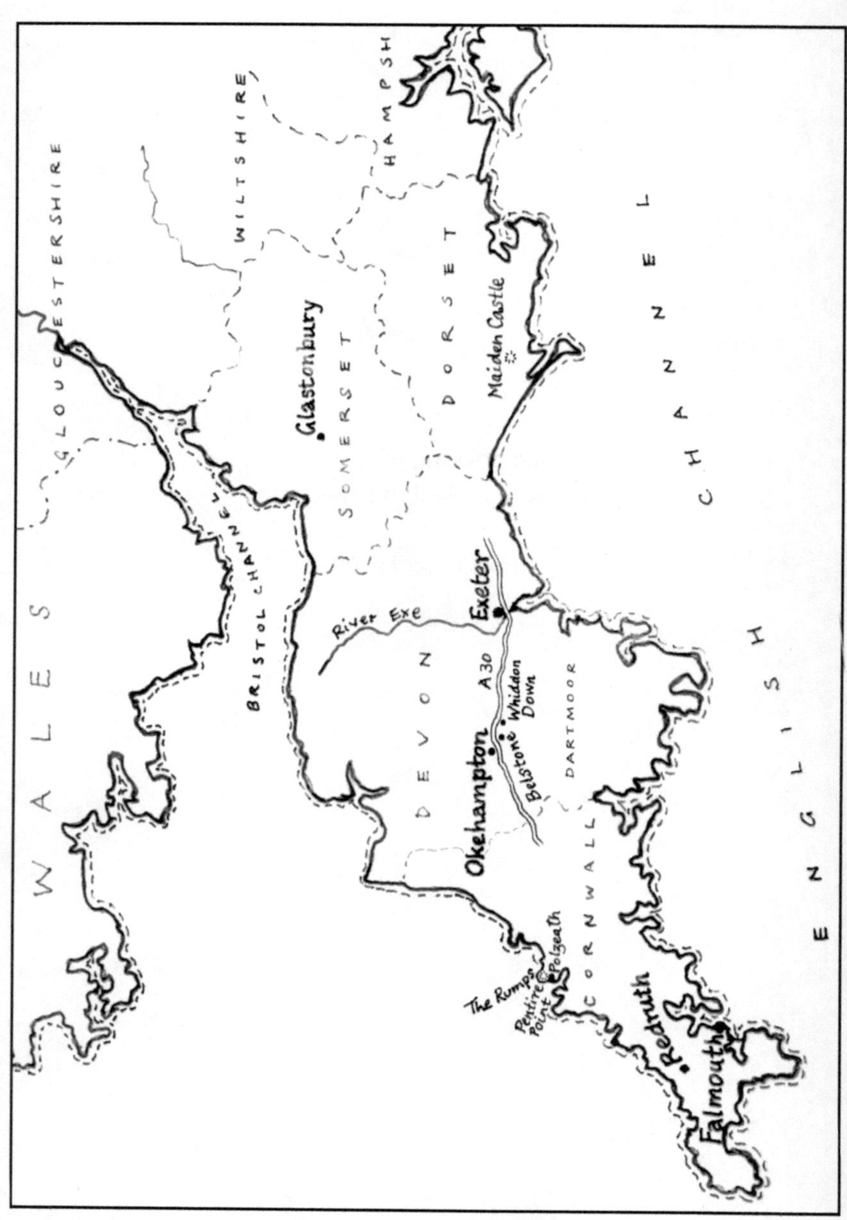

Map 1: Present-day South West Britain

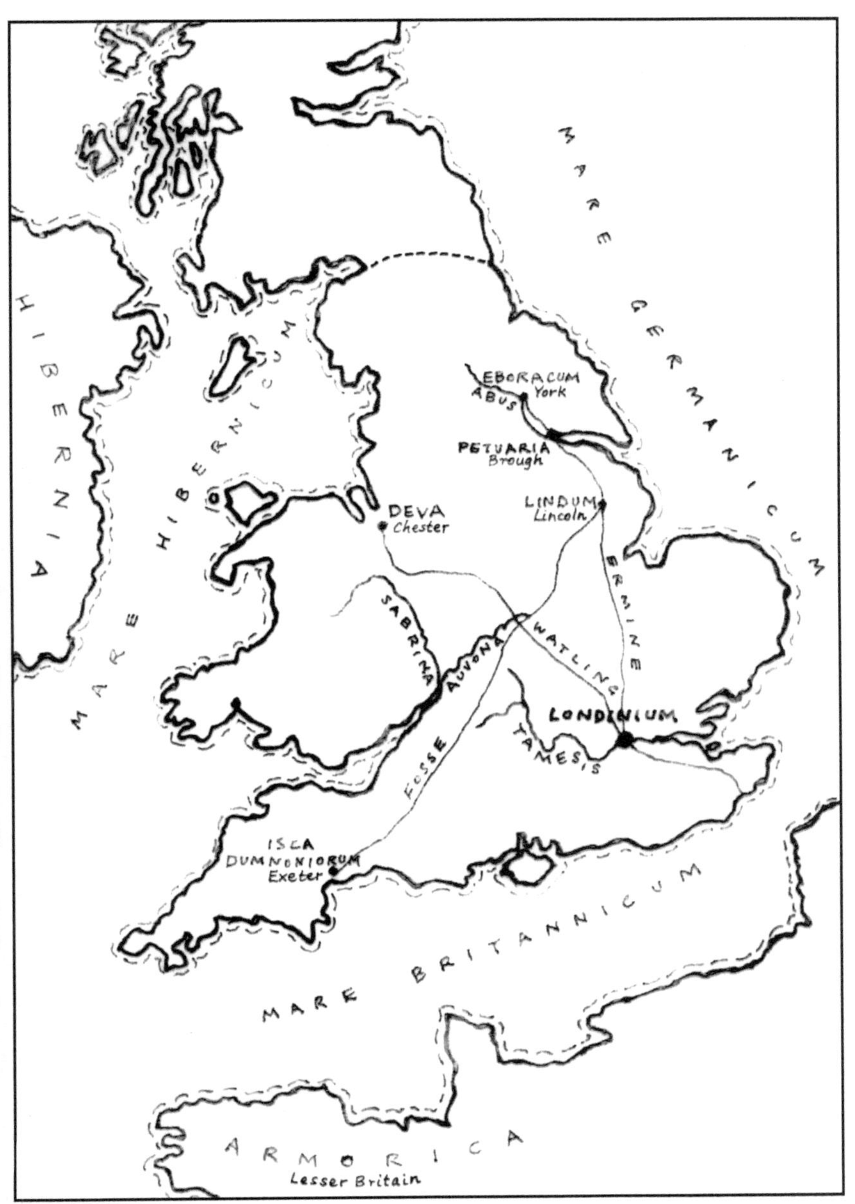

Map 2: Roman Britain in the year 451

XV

I AM MYRDDIN.

I weave magic.

I engineer battles.

I remember the future.

I toy with the laws of nature.

I fly with my lady-hawk on the sky tracks of the air.

I am a smith of strangeness.

I speak from silence to weave tales of the valour of our knights and the nobility of our ladies. It is easy to sing their praises and I cannot see any reason why I should not because they were simply astonishing.

Yet this tale is not only their story and that of the Pendragons, Uther and his son Arthur, it is also the story of a nation blessed by God: Britannia.

And some of you may find my stories hard to believe because you have become used to the romance of our legends, many of which are my own outrageous invention.

Most of what I will say to you is true, but let me warn you, I can never resist a flash of mischief.

Before I die I will teach the bards of Wales many beautiful poems about Arthur and Guinevere to be sung in the royal courts of the Franks, but for now I will reveal to you something else.

I will expose you to long buried secrets and I promise you they will not be what you expected because I have deliberately hidden my origins and those of many of the knights in a web of fantasy.

I Myrddin, Arch-Druid, warn you that my chronicles are not for everyone.

There are dragons in our waterways and gryphons that carry us across the abyss, and sometimes there are Archangels, Michael and Raphael, who when they appear will frighten us with their skies of swords and thumping vanes even though they only want to play; for such, I have found, is the nature of working with angels. And there is the wondrous Arianrhod, a weaver of dreams and goddess of the Northern Lights, who spends most of her life spying in the guise of a spider.

I want to pass on my knowledge to you who bear the swords of Light that you earned healing, and teaching, and fighting with us; then we will be able to celebrate our own history. But why should I share the secrets of the battle of Britannia, one of the world's great battles between Light and Darkness, with someone whose mind is closed to how things were and still can be?

I have lived for more than a hundred and ten winters and my face is brown and wrinkled like a walnut. Yet still my eyes can see the wonders of the future and the past. These are not earthly powers, these are gifts from God.

My memory, schooled by the Druids, can recite every word of the poems of Homer and Virgil. Therefore, it is easy for me to recall their passionate loves and their brutal wars, their intrigues and their betrayals, their code of honour and their experiences of the Holy Grail.

What I want to forget, but cannot, are the limits of my magic against the darker magic, and the cosmic clash between the Light and the Dark. I also loathe having to settle that perennial question the Druids always ask me: did we win? Of course we won and I will show you how.

The secrets of our Dark Age are yet to be opened to your diggers of the past. Although I know the answer to every mystery, I will reveal to you just enough to make you wonder and be hungry for more. They will help you understand how my times and your times blend.

You do realise, I hope, that the purpose of this chronicle is not just to entertain you. It is to inspire the warrior king, Arthur, who will return in your lifetime to deliver us from our enemies. When he reads my Secrets he will know the truth and what he must do to help Britannia. But he will not return alone because Guinevere and the Grail knights, Kai, Borholt, Lancelote, Galahad and their ladies Cassandra, Clare, Elaine and Angharad are reading this chronicle at the same time as you are.

So am I.

You must know that I have outlived most of my friends and foes. My love sits beside me and constantly elbows me about what I should tell you. She wrote much of this manuscript because, as you can see, I am a bard and can be quite a florid and clumsy writer and mawkish in the matters of my heart.

So my scribes sit in front of my charcoal drawings of scenes from my life and patiently translate my mouldy old Briton words into your English to ease the passage of my story.

I came to this blessed priory in the woods at Betys y Coed to tell my tales and die. The love of my life is a fairy from the Otherworld, who will lay me out on a rocky shelf in a cave overlooking the Swallow Falls. There I will lie at peace until the land slips and you start to sort through my bones. But you will know it is me.

Our story begins in Britannia in the dark and desperate times of the fifth century after the birth of Our Lord. It is over four hundred years since he walked here with his uncle, Joseph.

Most of the Roman legions have left for Gaul to fight the barbarians; taking our gold with them. Now our towns and harbours bereft of their labour, fall into decay.

Here in Britannia there are only two powerful Roman leaders left and they are close friends. Constantine Maximinius is the dux of the Legion that guards the Emperor's Wall in the north. He married Elen, a Welsh princess, and exhorted his friend to find a Welsh princess too because his marriage brought him many blessings and three sons.

Marcus Cotta, his friend, is a retired general of the Third Italia Legion and lives on the edge of Dartmoor. He married a Welsh princess, Ingraine, an Arch-Druidess of profound beauty and accomplishment who was schooled by the priestesses of the Avalon Isles. He named his only son Ambrosius Marcus Cotta. My mother called me Myrddin. You can call me Merlin.

These two leaders fear the discord as our life collapses, but mostly they fear the slaughter of the invading Danes and Saxons. They draft a letter on behalf of our people to the Commander-in-Chief of the Roman legions in Gaul, to plead with him to return here with his troops. But before they dispatch their letter, they need to convince the squabbling British kings, split apart by grudges and mistrust, to sign it with them. So my father called a Moot at our villa in Okehampton to win their agreement.

Ours is a treacherous and divided world where kings and strong men ready their sons and villages for war. The Jutes and the Saxons were invited into Britannia by a petty king from the north, Vortigern, who is known to us as the Great Betrayer. Cotta invited him to the Moot too, to unite the kings through their common loathing for him.

Yet there is gold that glistens in this gloom.

There is magic and myth and music and rhyme. Our oak trees guard the sacred groves where fairies dance and our bards sing. Our animals and people talk to each other in friendship.

There are many people who know how to ride the energies of the earth and fly above our land to soar like falcons. Our Druids help us with their knowledge of calculation and medicine, and their spells and enchantments. Our priests christen our babies and remind us of the Feast Days and how to beg forgiveness for our sins.

And your realm of the twenty-first century, and mine across the fifth and sixth centuries, are merely a whisper apart if only you know the gateways.

When you finish reading my secrets you will possess knowledge not known in your world. It will be like re-entering an ancient tomb, buried in a hollow hill, where you can rediscover what you knew long ago. My secrets begin.

1

Dartmoor

1.00am, Wednesday September 8th, Merlin's time

THE DARKNESS HAD WAITED LONG ENOUGH.

In the gloom, they are almost unseen like wisps of smoke, and only their voices echo in the cave.

"Stay out of it, Morgana, I will deal with him!" Moloch orders before he roars his invitation: "Enter!"

And who should swagger in but Vortigern? He is a very handsome man, with his pale hair and his beard carefully trimmed and wearing a leather breastplate moulded to exaggerate his muscles. It clings to him above his short kilt. At his left shoulder his scarlet cloak is fastened with a gold and ruby brooch. In his eagerness to impress he pushes the sorceress aside until he glimpses her beauty, and then regretting his missed opportunity, he turns to leer at her instead.

Moloch is annoyed. "I am over here, Vortigern!" he snaps. When Vortigern turns towards him all he can see are two pricks of orange flame piercing the gloom.

"Sit here and give me the details."

In the dim light, Vortigern wonders whether he should leave while he has a chance. Above him hanging from a trapeze is the giant bat, its head merely a breath away from his, its serrated teeth as long as his jewelled fingers. But it isn't its teeth that unnerve him. It is instead the memory of last time he was here, when Morgana warned him that her bat was rabid and a drop of its drool would bring him terrors and a thirsty death. He strains to see Moloch because he has no idea what he looks like. But he is just a puff of smoke, a stench, and those two flickers of flame. Vortigern swallows uneasily and begins the story he rehearsed over many weeks.

"I hid behind their wall hanging until they were asleep. I cut the king's throat first. When the queen stirred she murmured my name, 'Vortigern'. I smiled and kissed her."

Vortigern pauses wanting their approval, but Morgana just stares at him blankly. Her lack of interest perplexes him because everyone that she knows loves a bloody tale of murder. Nevertheless he continues,

"Her blood mixed with his. I left their bodies on their marriage bed, and after stripping the richest of their treasures, I rode to Petuaria on the Humber. There my ship was waiting to sail to the white fens of ice in the land of the Jutes. I haggled with them until I had the cheapest price, and I hired three hundred soldiers, six smithies, three cooks, twenty-five slaves and five war boats. It was a deal of absolute brilliance for the gold you gave me because these men are savage warriors who will guard my back against the Picts."

There is a long silence. He taps the table with a bone; annoyed… No one keeps Vortigern waiting. Slowly he realises he is not in command here, and as the silence lengthens he grows anxious. Eventually Moloch asks in a silken voice,

"Vortigern, why do you lie to us?" Vortigern's chair rattles under him and a current of foul wind encircles him. "Where is he?"

"I am up here, Vortigern. Don't you know that we know what really happened? We watch you constantly. You are a bragging fool. You did not slaughter your parents like animals; you poisoned them years ago. Now who is left with royal blood to crown you and give you legitimacy?"

This thought had never occurred to Vortigern because he crowned himself. No one, except Moloch, had ever doubted his power.

Where was that voice coming from?

"And we agreed you would invite the Jutes into Britain as mercenaries to stop the invasions of the Picts across the Emperor's Wall. This was to be our deceit. We agreed it was the only explanation the other kings would swallow. How will you ever gain their trust if you are not truly a king but a murderer of one? How will you gain their trust if you betray their best interests by bringing enemies into their land? And there is one more issue. You say you got a brilliant deal? So what did you do with my change from the thousand gold pieces? Horde it? Bury it? Spend it?"

There Moloch pauses for full effect to watch his quarry bead with sweat until he suddenly reveals himself as an inhuman shadow with two pulsing vermillion eyes.

"Vortigern, I am a Prince of Darkness, I am the author of all confusion and lies, but I can assume the most pleasing shapes. I thought I was unique until I met you. You lie to me. You steal from me. While I agree these are highly commendable qualities when done to someone else, they are not when done to me, because when they are done to me they are unbelievably stupid! And there's more. I have been told that the general of the Roman Legion, Constantine, had a son who died suddenly under mysterious circumstances. It was a poisoning that has your sticky fingers all over it, but you never reported his unexplained death to us."

Moloch pauses and lowers the giant bat closer until Mot's face hangs a hair's breadth from Vortigern.

"You lie to us and think you can get away with it. You steal from us and dress yourself in jewels. Let me warn you, Vortigern, I am the Prince of Lies. If I lie, you will not know it. When I steal, you will not notice it. When I strike, you will not survive it."

Vortigern opens his mouth to reply, but Moloch persists: "I want Constantine and his spawn destroyed too. Find someone whom you can teach your art of poisoning to and secrete him into the service of that family. You are dismissed."

As Vortigern staggers out, Moloch called forth a thin man with dark lank hair who balances a huge rack of antlers on his head. His face is covered in woad, the blue war paint of the Picts, and his face and arms are tattooed with writhing serpents.

"Report, Doone!" Moloch commands.

"The digger is above us and she is close to breaking through into our villa. The Roman Lord is north with Coel in Chester, seeing what he can salvage from the abandoned fort there. The house is preparing for the Moot when the kings will gather to groan about the invasion of the Saxons and petition Rome for help against them."

Morgana speaks:

"Keep the Roman's son close to you. Train him well. Later he will have to teach me all he knows. Report everything to us each night." There is silence until Moloch adds menacingly,

"One more thing, Doone, I wear the horns around here. Do not let me see you in that rack again."

Once Morgana has sent Doone away, she says to Moloch,

"If we do not act now, the digger will break the seal between the realms and Merlin will squirm through to do whatever he wants and keep interfering with everything. Once Merlin's out, there's no controlling him. Yet, he will create a path of silver slime that will guide me to cross over into their time where I can be heard, but not seen. As long as his 'mummy' allows him to play in the digger's time, I can wriggle through and can come and go with ease."

Eventually Moloch agrees she could cross over but he is unhappy. He calls up an image from the digger's realm.

"I can see her daughter in Dartmoor going to our sacred place, the stones of Baal. Soften her up. If Merlin is already there he will watch your every move. Unchain the mastiff, Morgana, and give it her scent, and let us have some fun with this Chosen One until I can see the way ahead to finish this."

12.00pm, Wednesday September 8th, Our time

"It's time, Emily!" Casey called out urgently. Her watch said twelve noon on the dot.

"I don't really want to do it," Emily groaned as she peeled hair from her face where the bitter wind had plastered it. She was freezing. She had dressed for show in her skinny jeans, a light top and a single sparkly glove. The glove was for Jack, a Jackson fan, and she would flash it for the best effect in the photo as the proof of their dare.

"Hey, we took this dare," Casey argued. "And it is a healthier option than getting down on our knees and licking the Castle floor or trying to cut Jack's putting green with scissors or—yuck-yuckedy- yuck—making out with Toby, or any of the other vile things they thought of!"

"It's still a dumb idea to skip around a pile of old stones." But she knew they had agreed to dance around the Nine Maidens on Dartmoor at noon, at the very time when the legend promised that all the standing stones would dance too. Now she regretted it. It was really a very weird thing to do. "It's blisteringly cold and windy and I don't know who's looking at us."

Casey scanned the deserted moor.

"There's no one looking at you," her friend reassured her, "there are only some sheep, and a helicopter over there doing a fake rescue. Otherwise there's no one here."

"How do you know?" Emily demanded.

"Well, I can't see anyone."

"The hairs on my neck are twitching, Casey, so I know," Emily insisted,"someone's watching us."

"Where are they, Em?" She was becoming exasperated and she just wanted to get on with it and get out of the wind.

"Over there!" At the very moment when she pointed up to Belstone Tor, a natural seat of granite that overlooked the stone circle, a shadow of a dark-haired woman faded away. A fox squalled.

"There's no one up there, just some old fox. Maybe it's the Belstone fox," Casey smiled, remembering the favourite movie they watched as kids.

"All right then," Emily sighed with resignation. "Why don't I leap around the circle, and you can take some photos? When you do it I'll take the photos and we'll send them off quickly to Jack and Toby. The sooner this is over the better, because I think this place is spooky. Did you know," she continued, pointing to the centre of the circle, "that the ruined cairn in the middle is an old grave? It's a wonder Mum hasn't dug it up already. Okay, let's get it over with."

When Emily took off and jumped around the standing stones, she showed the natural grace of a ballet dancer who had her first lesson at three. Casey stood admiring her.

"Come on KC, shoot it!" As Emily finished with three perfect cartwheels, Casey took the photos on her phone.

Now it was Casey's turn. The two girls could hardly look less alike. Casey was very tall and long-limbed, ice-blond, blue-eyed, and utterly flat-chested. She sprinted like the athlete that she was. Everyone said her ancestors had to be Vikings, she looked so Norse. Her best friend, Emily, was an elfin, casual beauty with pale skin and green eyes and her copper hair gave her the tawny look of a Celt. But it was her laugh that almost tinkled that everyone loved. They just wanted to be around her because she made them feel happy.

Suddenly Casey stopped. "What's that noise?" The wind whipped around them moaning. "Is that a baby crying?"

"You said there was no one here!"

"Well, now I am hearing something. Can't you hear it?" Casey insisted. "It's coming from that grave."

"It's just the wind."

The baby's screams grew louder.

"I'm moving those rocks in the cairn because that really could be a baby. Come on, give me a hand!"

Carefully Emily took off her sparkling glove and knelt down beside her friend.

"Who would bury a baby alive?" Emily was appalled. She shook her head saying, "Nobody would do that."

"I think I can see some light in there. Let's move that big rock."

"Careful, we don't want the whole thing to collapse."

They were both kneeling, their bodies straining to lift, when a shadow moved behind them and grabbed Emily's glove.

"Just one more rock, my lovelies," Morgana breathed, "and you'll see…"

There was a swirl of air around them and a putrid smell. Emily shuddered.

"What is that? What's that awful smell?" She screwed up her face in disgust. "Is it coming from the grave? I think something is dead in there."

"It's not unusual to find something dead in a grave," Casey replied tartly. "Could we just give this rock one, two, three, heave ho?"

Emily tried and let the rock go.

"It's just too heavy, KC. It just won't move." A fox squalled again, this time right behind her. Startled, she turned around, and with a laugh asked, "Where did you come from, Mr Fox? Hey look at this!"

The fox was well groomed with a luxurious reddish-brown pelt, and as she spoke to him he flicked the triangles that were his ears and sniffed at her. The spot on his chin where his fur melted into the white made his black nose and fine long whiskers look even more prominent and elegant. He examined her closely, seriously and unafraid.

"Aren't you one handsome animal? A fantastic Mr Fox! Hey, he is so tame. I bet he was hand-raised, Casey."

Then there were three more foxes behind him, their brush tails up, the white tips of them waving like flags in the wind.

"He's brought the family," Casey cried. "Over there, look, there's three more, and two more over to the right!"

For a few minutes the foxes enjoyed each others' scent, and when they were satisfied there were no threats, they sat down behind the stones. Their amber eyes seemed fixed on a ringmaster or someone invisible to the girls, awaiting their command.

"The baby's stopped crying!" Casey didn't know whether Emily had heard her because she was so enraptured with the fox. 'Em and her animals,' Casey thought, 'she's probably crawling all over with those bloody turtles right now! Casey sensibly preferred her animals at arm's length.

'Do you think we're taking stones from your den, Mr Fox? This could have been his burrow, Casey, and it could be one of his kits that is crying!"

"Em, it's autumn; kits are born in early spring. That was a baby, not a fox, but the crying has stopped now. Did you notice?"

"What should we do about it? Should we call the police? Do you have any phone coverage out here?" she asked, checking her phone. "I don't. It's gone."

Before Casey could answer, the foxes took off and loped around the outside ring of the Nine Maidens. They let off the occasional high-pitched yips as they went faster and faster around the stones.

"They don't walk and they don't run, they trot. Fox trot," Emily giggled. "They're dancing for us! Aren't they beautiful? I wonder what would happen if we danced too?"

Cautiously at first, Emily moved slowly like a fox, trotting playfully around the inner circle before she leaped into a dance. She pulled her reluctant friend up to join her. Now, when Emily was not obliged to dance, it was all she wanted to do. Wild, feral and free, she forgot her fear of being watched and the strange baby cries and she imagined she was the vixen to Mr Fox. She laughed and sang as she danced with them.

If you were standing on the Tor above the Baal stones where I stood, you would see three wheels in motion: the round of the foxes, the circlet of the Stone Maidens, and the two girls dancing, all of them a-shimmer in the autumn wind. Yet my eyes are on the dancer with her russet hair that swings when she moves. I knew that girls went secretly into the woods to dance under the moon, and once I hid there to watch them, but never have I seen anything like this or a

girl as wildly beautiful. She flies with the grace of a fawn, leaping to her own internal music, and I watched her, mesmerised, until I had to pull myself away.

I whistled my appreciation to my fox and the friends he rounded up to help me. They had done well, not only by distracting the girls from the trap of the sorceress, but in dancing as if they did so every day. I signalled them to stop. Dolossus rose onto his hind legs and caught something mid-air. The others followed, each catching a morsel too small for anyone's eyes to see but mine.

"Who is doing this?" the dancer demanded. "Come on. Show us who you are!"

No… I had no intention of meeting her when anyone else was present. If you had just seen the most beautiful girl in the world, a girl who is graceful and free, would you not want to meet her away from the stench of Morgana? Somewhere where you could be safe to dance with her alone?

"Who's there?" she demanded again.

I breathed my voice on the wind, whispering something that sounded safe but inviting:

"Later."

"You heard that! A man with a deep voice just said, 'Later!' Creepy! Absolutely creepy! I told you someone was watching us. I think we should leave now. It's all spooky!"

"Hey, it's just getting interesting," her friend protested as the foxes slunk away and blended into the moorland.

"Where's my glove?" The dancer turned this way and that, looking worried. "I took it off before I lifted the stones. I threw it just there," and pointing at the spot, she added in dismay, "Jack gave me that. Now it's gone!"

I knew where it was because I saw Morgana steal it. But what did she want with that dancer?

"Perhaps Mr Fox took it," her friend laughed, "when you weren't looking, as a souvenir of your foxtrot. Come on, let's go, I'm hun-

gry! We've got to pick up our bikes in the village, and then it's a two-mile ride to Okehampton. Let's go!"

As soon as they left, I whistled to Dolossus and followed him to the ancient grave at the centre of the standing stones.

"Over here and smell this… there's a good boy! What do you get?"

He looked up at me with his eyes half closed; it was a squint of warning. I moved the stones carefully to determine the source of the cries. Nothing there! When I heard Morgana crowing, full of menace, I knew I was right. She was after the dancer, but now I knew she was after me too.

2

Okehampton Castle

2pm, Wednesday September 8th, Our time

O KEHAMPTON CASTLE stood on the edge of Dartmoor, a gaunt and haunted ruin. Pungent smoke from an autumn fire twisted over the site of the excavation of a Roman villa. It was worked by students from Exeter University and volunteers from the local high schools, and the wraiths of smoke smarted their eyes.

Professor Julia Hughes, sunglasses pushed up on her head, knelt in a trench of river silt that was in parts deeper than a grave. Underneath her was a tiled edge that could be the roof of a cellar, or even of a large hall. She was excited. If it was a hall, it would be inside the enclosure of a villa, but if it was a storage place it would be near its gates to allow delivery carts easy access. While her mind puzzled over the layout below, something swooped at her, she didn't know from where. But the flash of a silver white eye, the black, crow-like body with a nape of grey and its rattling attack suggested it was a jackdaw. It flew straight for her face before darting off with her sunglasses in its beak.

"You…!"

Julia stopped herself from swearing in front of her students and jumped up from the floor of the trench. Grabbing the rope, she climbed out to try to retrieve her glasses. But as she jumped she heard a crack and the floor of the trench dropped away and the earthworks around her rumbled and crumbled. She rolled away from it trembling and gasping.

"Help! Over here!" she yelled to her team. "It's a cave-in!"

Jeff Hoskins, a bulky man and slow at the best of times, hauled the pale Toby out first before he came to her rescue.

Everyone else ran. They scattered across the river field and climbed up the castle's hill, crying out to one another. The last thing Julia Hughes saw through the cloud of dust was her shade cloth disappearing into the maw. The last thing she heard was a dog howling from the castle ruins.

"What do you think happened?" Jeff panted as he flopped on the grass beside Julia, and unaware of how anxious he was, he started making a feast of his fingernails. Students flung themselves around them and held up their phones to record what they could, to send their friends the proof of their lucky escape.

Under normal circumstances Julia would give her godson, all flash and dash with his spiky blonde hair, a hug to reassure him, because she had been there when his archaeologist father was buried alive in a cave-in. She had known Toby since his birth, the only child of her close friend, Karen, but she never saw through his jokes, nor did it ever occur to her that the last thing Toby—now nearly seventeen—would want was to be hugged by a professor. Julia drew a deep, calming breath.

"Professor," Toby interrupted, grinning with mischief, "there's supposed to be the ghost of a dog in that castle. I can hear him howling now."

"Toby, there are no such things as ghosts." But when the dog howled again, she was the first to shudder and doubt it.

Jeff tried to explain what happened.

"You could have been standing on the roof of an old mining shaft; we know there's some iron ore around here. Or it could have been the roof of a stable…"

"Or of a tomb!" Toby interjected, his diamond earring sparkling almost as much as his eyes.

Julia's professional training took over, and assuming the tone of someone used to being in charge, she began her instructions.

"The aerial photos and geophysical mapping clearly show the outline of a large, Roman villa below the castle ruins. It faces the river with possibly a village of round huts close by. Now, we'll have to cordon off the area because we don't know how far this subsidence has spread. Jeff, can you call the university? Let them know what's happened and that everyone is safe. And then get onto the air base. It's nearly time for the chopper to go to Bristol and Bath. It leaves at 3.30pm. Offer the pilot a hundred quid to detour over the castle and take as many shots as he can of what happened here."

"But," Jeff protested, "we don't have a spare hundred!"

"We will when I sell the photos to the Okehampton and Exeter papers. Send all the volunteers home. But can you wait, Toby?" She waited until everyone dispersed and spoke to him quietly. "Our abseiler has left for Egypt. Do you know if anyone local could climb down through that hole and have a look around for us?"

It was only a year before when the Principal of Exeter Academy, a Jesuit school for gifted students, sidelined Toby as 'useful for nothing'. Ever since that time, in his eagerness to be loved, he had tried to make himself useful at everything. So he replied,

"I'll call my climbing instructor. He may have some ideas. Otherwise, I can ask Jack and we could do it. I've got all the equipment except the headlights."

"Thanks!" She turned to Jeff who was roping the area off. "In the meantime I'll review all our photos to see if we can dig thirty metres or more from here where we think the round huts of the villagers were. Otherwise we'll have to up tools and head for our next dig at the Rumps in Cornwall."

She paused and in a much softer voice, with a hint of tremble, added,

"Just between you and me, and don't say anything to anyone about this, if that bird hadn't stolen my glasses, I'd have fallen down that hole. God knows what would have happened to me!"

"We all had a lucky escape!" he agreed, checking his nails again before he pulled out his phone.

7.00pm, Wednesday September 8th, Merlin's time

"Myrddin, my son, shhh, shhh! Be attentive to me… listen!

A darker magic this way comes, and with its clearer sight of the future, it knows more than you will ever know. When it followed you to Dartmoor today it almost trapped the Chosen One. Did you not realise who she was? She is the one!

You just sigh. Your sighs will not be any protection from their wickedness.

A silver cord links you and me. It has never been cut.

Any attack on you is an attack on me, and no one can force you to come or go without my agreement.

This is your protection.

For these three days and three nights you are to go far away, but do not leave our land.

In other realms, they will know your future. Do not ask about

your future or you will become inflated with your fame, and you know our charms only work from humble commands.

As you have seen, the maiden is lovely and headstrong, and you already know the Darkness is drenched in blood. They will kill her, Myrddin, if they are given the slightest chance. You must promise me to protect her. Please do not overwhelm her with your learning, or scare her off with your magical powers. Take her something sweet-smelling from my garden and be graceful with her if she does not understand you.

Morgana will never understand you. She will try to defile your innocence, your valour and your grace, and she will do that to any other who crosses her path.

If you want to deliver the future the Darkness fears, you must use all those spells I have taught you; you must enchant with your art and command all the elements. If you have to battle him, do not defile the earth by allowing him to walk his treachery there; instead choose the sky which Lord Michael can always purify.

Return to me when your father gathers the kings to petition Rome. Return as a master of our arts and my falcon of the sky. And when you return, conjure, if it pleases you, the red dragon of our country to delight my brother and me.

May the Lord Michael protect you and keep you safe from every harm!"

3

Night Visitor

10.00pm, Wednesday September 8th, Our time

EMILY SAT CROSS-LEGGED ON HER BED in her pj's, her bronze hair still damp from the shower. She played nervously with her phone. She'd already told Casey Madigan all she knew about what happened to her mother and revealed to Jack Devonport, her closest friend, all that she feared as a result.

Curled up on the bottom of her bed was her orange and white Brittany spaniel, one eye open, one eye shut. Kelso startled her with a deep growl, only to beat his tail against her coverlet, and Emily knew that meant he was alerting her to the arrival of someone who smelled safe, like her family.

"Who's there?" Emily whispered.

Out from the shadows stepped a very tall boy, about sixteen or seventeen, with clear white skin, a prominent nose, overlarge lips and coal-black, shoulder-length hair.

"Who are you?" she cried. "What are you doing here?"

He smiled sheepishly, jiggling the stolen sunglasses.

"This is for the woman with the pate of beaten copper," he

said, offering them to her with one hand behind his back. She jumped up to grab the sunglasses.

"Where did you find Mum's glasses? This is a security building! How did you get in here? You have to get out, you know… because this is my private space."

He ignored all her questions and protests, and asked instead, "Are you alone?"

Her eyebrows flew up in mock alarm.

"That is a dangerous question for an intruder to ask. I could pull out a gun and shoot you!"

"I regret I appear to you as an intruder and someone dangerous to your welfare because I came here as your friend. I have a gift for you. Here, I picked this posy from my mother's garden."

And this was the moment, Emily knew later, when her life changed. If she had screamed at the intruder, her mother would have come running and called security, and who knows how this strange boy would have reacted. But she did not scream because she never felt really afraid of him. Instead, from the first time she saw him, she knew him, she just knew him, and because she felt no threat she smiled at him with her whole body, and that meant her eyes danced, her lips parted and her hands fluttered and she nervously hooked her hair, her best feature, behind her ear with her left hand while with the other she reached out for the wilted red and white field flowers. Every protest she made after that moment was undermined by her delight at seeing this graceful man in her room.

"Didn't you hear what I just said?" Emily protested weakly. "This is my bedroom and you're very rude barging in here!"

Very shyly he smiled back at her and bowed.

"I beg you to excuse my lack of manners, my lady, I know I should not be in your chamber uninvited because it is rude, but could you kindly tell me what you're doing?"

"I'm texting Toby; I'm letting him know I have this strange

man in my room. My mum doesn't allow any boys in my bed-room. So you'd better get out, now!"

He threw his head back and laughed because he had no in-tention of leaving without her. Emily thought to herself, 'He thinks only he can give orders around here and full of charm refuses to hear mine.' It was then she noticed his eyes were the brightest blue and they darted around her.

"By your leave, will you show me 'texting'?" he asked.

"Hello," Emily replied, "you must live on another planet!" She held out her phone. "It's sending a message long distance through a mobile phone, and you don't have to talk. You type in using letters to make words of what you want to say."

"What's that?" He pointed to a glass box, partly filled with water, on the floor beside her bed.

"It's a terrarium. It's for my long-necked turtles, Roget and Winston."

"Will you please show me?"

"I don't think that's a good idea. You have a mouse on your ear and another on your neck. My God, my turtles will eat them for supper!"

She knew that they wouldn't touch mice, they really liked spi-ders, but he was annoying her by not reacting. 'He is almost ig-noring me,' she thought, and so she asked him:

"Would you like me to call mum's cat? One mouthful and your mice will be gone!"

Finally she got a reaction, he looked alarmed.

"I'll put them in my pouch," he replied hurriedly.

"What's that?" he asked, pointing to the flat-screen television. He moved his hand before it to see if it was reflected on the screen, and when it was not he rushed out into the next room to check whether those coloured figures he saw on the screen came from there.

"Listen. It talks, too!" Emily released the mute button and

hip-hop music filled the room. "I'm dancing to that music to-morrow night with Toby." And when she moved with its rhythm, he too swayed to the music, transfixed by the images, laughing.

Emily sat down on the bed holding Kelso to steady herself and watched him closely. He paced back and forth examining her silent computer screen, her digital clock radio, her school back-pack and the coloured blue glass of her water jug before he returned to the flat glass of the television screen that he measured with his wrist to elbow, shaking his head in wonder as if it was a biggest sheet of glass he had ever seen. But it was the phosphorescence moving across it that intrigued him most of all.

"I am remembering everything I see so I can re-examine its science and mathematics and its source of power later." Until something new caught his eye.

"And what's that?"

"That is a statue of Mary holding her baby son, Jesus." On hearing her reply, he bowed his head reverently at the statue.

"I have never seen one of those. My father has one of Mars, the god of war. His hero."

His eyes flicked around the strangeness of the room and stopped with a jerk.

"But what is that?"

"That's my telescope. Well, it's Dad's really; he's just parked it in here." The silver cylinder on a tilt base was tall enough to reach her chin. "If you sit here and look through the eye-piece you can observe the craters of the moon. It's very clear, at the moment, because there's a full moon tomorrow, you know."

"I know, of course. Can I, if it pleases you my lady, look too?"

"Yes. I'll adjust it for you."

Once he was settled with the scope's barrel between his legs, she leant over him until the focus was clear.

"There you are. That's called the Crater of Copernicus."

"Are you sure this is on the moon? It looks very flat and desolate."

"Move it slowly to the left or to the right and you will come to its curved edge, and beyond the rim you'll see the dark of the night sky behind it."

"This is as close to heaven as I've ever been on earth." But he said it in a way that implied that it was her closeness that made it heavenly. "Can you see all the planets too?" And when Emily nodded that he could, he asked, "Is Mars really red?"

"Let me adjust it for you, I was looking at Mars before I went to bed." It took her a minute until she found the planet. "Here, look at it yourself. We discovered from sending probes into space that its surface was a weathered iron ore and it gets its colour from that. So yes, as you see, up close, it's a ruddy brown."

"You have so much to tell me. Can I come back to use this again?"

"Yes, if you like."

Looking at his elegant but odd clothes and the gold band around his neck, Emily was puzzled. Was he outfitted for a costume ball or something?

"Are you dressed for bed?" Emily asked, curiously. "Is that your night shirt?"

He laughed. "No!" and he flung his crimson cloak off his shoulder and fingered the finely woven cloth of his garment. "My apparel proclaims that I am Roman. This is my tunic. Do you like it?"

"Well, I suppose cross-dressing can be cool. Who are you anyway?"

He turned back towards her with the telescope still between his legs, and when he realised he was merely an inch away from her face, he started, blushing as he bumbled to his feet. After a calming breath he bowed again.

"I am so sorry, I should have announced myself properly. My name, my lady, is Ambrosius Marcus Cotta."

"What kind of name is that? It sounds like it's Italian or Latin."

"It is a Roman name, but I am gentle born. And what, may I beg, is yours?"

"My name is Emily Charlotte Hughes. It's just a plain old English and Welsh name." And she lifted up her toy red dragon to emphasise the Welshness of her name. "There's no gentility here."

"I will call you Emilia because then I can use it properly whenever I think in Latin."

"I'd prefer you not to. My father speaks Latin and he likes the English version of my name, not the Latin version. That's why he called me Emily, and because he loves Emily Dickinson—the poet, that is! And I like my name. Don't you like yours?"

"You know, I have lots of names. My mother's Welsh too, and she calls me Myrddin. My father calls me Ambrosius. My Pictish slave calls me Bryten, meaning Britain. My mice call me Squeak. My jackdaw, Crook, calls me 'Kak-Kak…'"

"I thought a jackdaw cries out 'tchock'," Emily interrupted, giving a very good imitation of their cry. He was impressed and his mouth turned down with a shrug of approval.

"With all those names, Ambrosius, it must be very confusing!" And she continued with a playful laugh to ask, "Was it your jackdaw that stole my mother's sunglasses?"

He patted Kelso's head and spoke to the Brittany spaniel in the strange clicking language of Cornwall and Brittany, then plunged his hand into the terrarium to allow Roget to plod up his arm.

"Your mother is the woman who is digging down into our villa and we would like her to stop. She has broken into the roof of our granary and that has let the rats in. Winter is coming."

"My mum's an archaeologist. That's what she does. She digs ancient sites of Roman forts and villas, but actually, that's not all she does. If there are any humps and bumps in the countryside like barrow graves or old bones anywhere, she's into them, too."

"I live there." He pointed through the window across the river towards the ruins of the castle. "I was born there."

"You're weird, you know. It's like we're on different wavelengths having parallel conversations."

"My father is the Decurio of Isca." She noted he used 'Isca', part of the Roman name for Exeter. "My father retired there after he was the Dux of the Third Legion in Germania. Now he oversees the old soldiers' camps and their deserted marching areas, and sends reports for the Emperor. He is like a Consul."

"Well, that's Okehampton Castle where you're pointing, and it's a Norman ruin built hundreds of years after the Romans were here. But below it, according to my mum, there is a Roman ruin if that's what you're talking about. It's on the land that belongs to my friend Jack and his family and she got their permission to dig there. No one lives there now."

"I live there, but only for a few days more because I join the legion in Gaul. I am going into the architectura—to learn how to build bridges, roads, camps, bread ovens and sewers."

She turned up her nose. "Lucky you!" And then she added quickly, "Thanks for bringing back my mother's sunglasses, and thanks for bringing me the bouquet. It was very sweet of you. I love wild flowers!"

He was smiling all over his face, obviously delighted. "Would you keep my visit a secret and not tell Tobias or your mother?"

"You don't need to worry. If I said a strange boy came into my bedroom before midnight, a boy I suspected of owning a jackdaw that saved my mother's life, a boy who thinks he's Roman, and who wears a dress... they'd think I was a weirdo and they would laugh at me. Yes, you can be sure I won't tell them a single thing."

"Good! Can I come back here soon?"

"Why? To use our telescope?"

There was that beautiful smile and laugh again, he thought. What a question! Why did he want to come back? How could he explain what caused this flutter, this mysterious spark the first time he saw her? After what seemed like a long time, he blurted out,

"Yes, I would love to see the heavens again, but I really want to see you again too. I like you, Emilia. You look straight at me and you do not avert your eyes, and that is so strange for a girl. You like animals too, and you are persistent and answer my questions clearly like one of my tutors. And you wash yourself like a Roman and you smell of the breath of flowers..."

She knew she was blushing. "You're getting very personal... Okay. I think, that will be reason enough to visit again."

"No it is not, because there is more. You did not scream at me for intruding into your sleeping-chamber, you almost laughed like we are playing a game. You are forthright and you say what you think. I feel you will make a very good companion."

"I'm only fifteen, Ambrosius. Well, in two sleeps I'm sixteen. My birthday is on Friday," Emily replied, her face burning pink, and when she remembered that fourteen was the marrying age in Rome (or was it thirteen?), she felt more embarrassed. He was staring at her as if he was committing her face to his memory. She looked down and fiddled with her phone for something to do. When she looked up again, he was still staring at her.

"What?" she demanded. Then her strange boy disappeared as quickly as he appeared.

"Ambrosius, hey, where are you?"

"Look up!"

He was standing upside down on her ceiling.

"Hey, you'd better come down or you'll get hurt!"

He leapt to the floor and waved his hands slowly across her face.

"What was that all about?" she demanded.

The insight came to him clearly that he was showing off, but he was sure she had not noticed.

"I thought I would get a different view on things," he laughed. "Watch me!" And he drew a frog from her nose.

'Very funny, Ambrosius! You're a magician, aren't you! I think you just hypnotised me. But you're probably a figment of my imagination, a dream. Now, give me back Roget because soon I'll wake up from all of this and you'll be gone."

"Good night, Emilia. If you ever need me, call Merlin. It's the name of a bird, my bird, my lady-hawk with the orange eyes. You are entitled to my service." He drew his crimson cloak close, spun around, his coal-black hair glossy in the light, and he was gone.

And the very first thing Emily did was Google 'Merlin'.

"Shit, a squillion hits! I'll be here all night!" She was sure that the Merlin her father went on and on about was Welsh and not Roman, and that his father was a devil and his mother was a nun!

4

Flying to Merlin's World

11.30pm, Wednesday September 8th, Our time and Merlin's time

B UT EMILY COULDN'T SLEEP. She was too excited. She could hear her father downstairs singing 'my brown-eyed girl' to her mother and she knew that meant she was crying—she was such a wuss, she cried no matter what, and he was always consoling her. Casey, who wants to be a psychiatrist, says women who cry a lot have buried pain and who knows, she could be right, for all Emily knew. But one thing Emily did know for sure was that Merlin's jackdaw saved her mother, and her question was why. It could not be a quirk of fate that he suddenly appeared in her bedroom. And why did he actually visit her tonight? Couldn't he have left Mum's sunglasses at the front door? How did he get in? Would he ever come back? Imagine going to the movies with Merlin, he'd never keep still!

Every time she closed her eyes she saw his handsome face saying, "Look up!" and there he was walking on her ceiling. She was sure he created the illusion of walking on the ceiling, but the sheer magic of it all made her heart race. She Googled 'Merlin' again. Yep, there were thirty million results... there was no doubt he was a celebrity. When she Googled her name, there were two hundred and ninety-three thousand results, but none of them were hers. 'Oh, my God. He's out of my league. Completely! A national treasure to be sure, but with one major complication... he is dead. So how come he was just walking around my room? Was he a ghost? More likely he is an angel because he was so polite and handsome—almost ethereal. Anyway, whatever he is, he said he wanted to see me again and I want to see him. I wish I could phone him. What if I call his name? Will he come?'

"Merlin?" she murmured, but nothing happened.

Roget scratched the side of the glass, wanting a cuddle.

"Come on, handsome, I was just being stupid thinking he'd hear me."

"Yes, I heard you," Merlin replied. "I never left you. I was waiting and hoping you would call me. And it's not the volume of your voice I hear; it's the vibration of your intention."

"What on earth does that mean?"

"It means I know when you think of me and I know the emotion behind it." And when Emily looked at him incredulously, he tried again. "You set up a connection between us like a thread of glass that allows me to watch you and to know how you are feeling."

"If you don't mind, where's my privacy in that?"

"I will turn my gaze away from you if it's an indelicate time. I would be honoured if you come out with me. I'm going to a grove near the river with Doone. He's a shaman from Alba, the place in the far north behind the Emperor's Wall. He's testing me on techniques I may need if I scout for the legion."

"I can't sleep, anyway. I'm too churned up." Then, fearful that she had indicated an interest in Merlin, she hurried to add,

"Casey and I had some weird experiences on the moor today and I've a big day tomorrow. Our dress rehearsal is on. At the Exeter Phoenix." Emily was babbling and she knew she was talking to fill in space and he was just smiling, enjoying every moment of it. She desperately wanted to go with him, but didn't want to seem too eager. "If I go with you, how long will it take?"

"In your time, only a few minutes. Here, take my hand..."

"Wait, I can't go out in my pyjamas, I'll need to put on some clothes. Can you come back in a minute?"

What to wear on a date with Merlin? God, he is hot! Emily, mumbling aloud, ran through her checklist: skinny jeans, yes, riding boots, yes, warm hooded top, yes, perfume, yes; mouth spray, yes, for you never know but you can always hope; and lip-gloss—perfect! 'How is it possible,' she thought, 'to ever smell sweet enough?' Phone, yes. Roget, yes. Winston, no. Kelso, no.

"I'm ready," she whispered. She was so excited she could barely talk.

"Take my hand." And Merlin led her through a window onto the roof, and before she had time to worry about it, she was enveloped in his crimson cloak. Her head spun, an icy wind blasted her face so she turned towards his chest for protection and his arm tightened around her and her hair smelled of mown grass and camomile. And she knew she had just crossed a line where her world ended and his world began, and Merlin knew he had crossed over the edge into the abyss.

The only question Emily wanted to ask him was, "What other super-powers do you have besides flying?" But the very thought of what he might say made her break into giggles.

"Are you ticklish?" he asked, and Emily nodded.

"And I laugh a lot!" she replied, because rather than discuss the powers of superheroes with him, it was easier to admit to being ticklish. But what do you say to a magician? 'How do I talk to him?' she wondered. 'Talk about what he knows,' she concluded... Magic!!

"Flying through the dark like this is magic, isn't it?"

"It seems like magic, but there is good science behind it and I could tell you how it works."

"I know you are a magician, but I don't really know what that means. Can you can do things like spells?"

"I can. I used a form of spell yesterday with those foxes."

"Oh, so that was you on the moor! Now this will seem like a silly question, but the Welsh in me loves the magic; but most of all we love dragons. Have you ever seen a dragon?"

"Besides yours, do you mean? Sightings of them are quite common. Would you like to see one?"

"Yes, I would. Dragons are not in our fossil record and therefore we don't know what they look like because they only live in our legends."

"You only find what you are looking for. So let me describe them for you and that should help. You will be pleased to know that dragons lived in Wales. They grew as long as ten to twelve feet and as high as five feet and as wide as six feet. They have four clawed feet and a rough, tough skin."

"They sound a bit like crocodiles."

"Do crocodiles have wings?" And when Emily shook her head saying 'No', Merlin continued: "Dragons have wings up until five years of age, when they lose them and their body seals over and leaves a useless flap like an ear-lobe that does not serve any purpose. They have a reddish tinge to them, like Mars. Look up... over there. Now, it is not a dragon exactly," Merlin smiled," but it is a cousin of one." And Emily saw a violet sky hung with diamond-bright stars so close she could almost touch them, and flying across it there were strange birds. One responded to Merlin's call, and suddenly it swooped at them, screeching.

"What is it?" she gasped, clinging to him. "It's scary, Merlin!"

At first, she thought it was a prehistoric creature because from the front it looked like a giant white albatross, but towards its rear she was not sure, because it turned to gold. He soothed her saying,

"It is only a gryphon, and they guard the empty space that we have just passed through. Don't worry about her. She is just doing her job." And then he could not help boasting: "You'll be safe with me!"

They bumped to the ground into a climate very much warmer than the one she had left, and into a chorus of chirping crickets far louder than she had ever heard before. She thought that if she was really in his world, it was a world where no one sprayed the bugs. The night noise was deafening and the stars were so bright she might have been in the desert.

"Master Bryten." A sinewy man spoke to Merlin, his arms, neck and legs covered in fierce blue tattoos of snakes that wove up and down his bare legs in cruel patterns like varicose veins. He stood aggressively, clearing one nostril, then the other, by blowing his snot hard onto the ground. "Master Bryten, are you ready?" he demanded, ignoring Emily.

"He cannot see you," Merlin explained, "but he can sense you, Emilia. This is Doone." Emily nodded to him and tried, unsuccessfully, to hide her distaste.

"He is a remarkable man who taught me the ways of the wood—how the deer talk, where the otters hide; and about the rhythm of tides and floods and the colour of the winds. He is my guide, a man of few graces as you can see, but a good man."

"Why can't he see me?"

"We have crossed the abyss and you can't see people from the Otherworld unless you are advanced in magic like an Arch-Druid."

"Okay." *Maybe he sees me but does not let on*, she thought. "So am I invisible to everyone I see, except you?"

"And there is my mother, because she is an Arch-Druidess, and my nurse, Angharad, because she is a wise woman."

"Okay. But it is weird to be in a world where only three people can see me." She could hear a man singing to a lilting harp. "Where are we?"

"We are at our villa, but time is different here. It's bent and twisted from your time and we have moved across in a tear in its fabric. For the moment it is the same day, the same month, but a different year."

"So what year are we in?"

"It is difficult to say because you count the days and we count the nights, and we divide our years differently. Valentinian III has been our Emperor for twenty years, so I suppose in your dating it is now somewhere around 450-452."

"But that's over fifteen hundred years ago! It is past and finished. Gone!"

"The past is not finished, Emilia, because it still lives in you and beside you, and you can reach into it if you know how. Otherwise how could we be standing here together now?"

"I don't know. But I know one thing: if it is really that date you said it is, then you should be dead, and because I can see obviously that you are not I've got to work out what is true and whether I am dreaming or not."

The night was lit by a hundred flares that flickered in the wall sconces, and in front of her Emily could see an elegant cream and crimson villa, one and a half storeys high like the model her mother displayed in her university staffroom that she built for her Master's degree. 'It is beautiful,' she thought, 'just beautiful!' Towering all around the villa there was a forest of trees that groaned and roared in the slightest breeze. They were not in any of the models. Why was this villa different? The building must look, she believed, towards the river because she could hear it rushing nearby. 'That is interesting,' she thought, 'because that means it faces south east. Strange! Mum is adamant that when a Romano-British building faces towards rushing water it was a Druidic hospital. So what is this place? Does Merlin live in a hospital?

She stood in a long and wide courtyard. To her left, there was a continuous roof tiled in pale terracotta, and under it there was a barn full of hay and a shed of hutches for rabbits and ferrets. Coming from behind her, there was the warm smell of horses, and turning towards it she saw their stable, and next to them there was some kind of storehouse with a collapsed roof. Mum's work, no doubt. She took a photo in the dim light only to be disappointed when the screen was black. 'No coverage,' she thought, 'I suppose that made sense.'

She turned back around and saw that behind the villa, which was directly in front of her, there were gardens on one side, and on the other what looked like a bathhouse. Next to it was a small forge with a furnace to heat the bathhouse and the floors of the villa. The wooden gates in the brick walls behind her were closed and two men in metal helmets and tunics guarded the entrance. 'If only Mum could see this, she could write fifty papers about it and give them at conferences in exotic locations, and I could go to cheer her brilliance and see the world. If only, if only...'

The guards marched over to Merlin, punched their fists across their chest in salute and gave him two swords sheathed in holsters on a long belt, a polished wooden staff, and a shorter one with a soft leather pouch. He checked the contents of the pouch carefully, and arranged the weapons around his waist and crossed the belt over his chest. Emily stared at the staff.

"I can see you are looking at this." He held it up so she could touch it. "My staff is my most precious possession."

Merlin twirled the long rod, hopped over it, and pointed it at her for her to examine more closely.

"It is made of oak, as you can see. I stained it with walnut juice and polished it with bees' wax. But it's this knobbly end where it is most functional. See how it has controls here, like the ones on that silver tongue that told your talking window to hush up." It took her a second or two to translate and to realise that he was talking about the remote for her TV, and when she got it she giggled. "These control whether you want to go up, or down, or stop. Inside that knob there are special little minerals and crystals that govern where you want to go."

"Show me how it works," Emily asked with her best smile.

"Later, when…"

As soon as she heard him say 'later', she knew she had heard it before at the Nine Maidens. And that confirmed it was Merlin who was watching them. She wriggled with delight.

"My lady, if you please, could you excuse me while I attend to some business?"

He bowed and walked over to thick forest behind the villa. There he moved his hands across his face and placed his elbow and his ear on the trunk of a towering oak. The roar of the trees slowly subsided until it was only a murmur. He bowed and raced back to her looking worried.

"I have saddled the ponies." Doone interrupted her thoughts and whistled a command and two jackdaws swooped in response, one to his shoulder. The other, with a crippled foot, flew onto Merlin's hand and hopped up to his shoulder to nuzzle his ear.

"You can ride behind me, Emilia," Merlin said, attaching his staves onto the side of his horse.

Because Emily knew her horses, she knew these ponies were sure-footed, with rough, dark coats and big liquid eyes, quite like the ones that still roamed Dartmoor. But Merlin's leather saddle was very odd. It had four pommels, one at each corner, but no stirrups. 'How on earth will he stay on? My God,' she suddenly realised, 'they haven't discovered the stirrup yet! That means they cannot fight from the saddle of the horse or play polo or joust in tournaments.'

Emily used a stone block to climb on to his pony's back, and pressing her thighs tightly around the pony's middle, she reached behind her to grab the two nearest pommels to help her balance. Staring into his back she saw that the silent bird with the crooked foot and diamond eyes was now sitting on his shoulder and chewing his ear. She wondered where his mice had gone. Lunch?

"Is that jackdaw your pet?" she asked, and reminding herself of her own turtle, she felt under her top to check that Roget was all right. "Is he a pet like my turtle?"

"No, this is Crook, named obviously after his distinguishable feature. If you ever see him, you will know I sent him. He is a working bird like my merlin: he guards, he spies, he attacks and he defends. My pet bird, however, is a blackbird—the bard of the forest. He just sings for me. He is my music..."

"...If you don't mind me interrupting?" They were riding to-wards the river and he turned in the saddle to look at her. "Do you also have a pet fox?" she inquired.

"Yes, you met Dolossus yesterday at the Baal stones."

"How did you do it?" she asked him, and she laughed as she remembered the experience. "How did you get those foxes to dance?"

"What, and spoil my mystery?" he teased her, and turned to look ahead. "And reveal my secret spells?"

"Come on, Merlin, tell me!" She put her arms around his waist and squeezed him and laughed easily as if she'd known him for years. "How did you get wild foxes to dance?"

"I put them in a trance and took the spirit form of a fox my-self and directed them to do what I wanted. It is all shaman trickery I learned from Doone."

"It was so cool! Can you do the same stuff with birds?"

"Yes... I have been many things: foxes, wolves, birds, fish and deer. Tonight you will see us working with birds. I will use my jackdaw because I find it is easiest at night to see the landscape through his eyes. The bird of my totem is a small falcon, the merlin; and sometimes I work with her, but not much at night because her eyesight is poor in the dark."

Merlin found he loved explaining things to her, and what was even more amazing, she seemed to like listening to him. So he kept talking.

"Occasionally my jackdaw will talk and repeat something I say. If that happens, and if it pleases you, do not be startled because he does not really know what he is talking about. He is just repeating the sounds he has heard. But others do not know that and it can help me gain a tactical advantage."

"Does he swear?"

"Only in Greek."

"I bet he stole my mother's sunglasses!" she laughed. She poked him in the ribs. "He did, didn't he, and on your command?"

Merlin turned back in the saddle again, smirked and nodded.

"Okay, but why?"

"When your mother was digging above our villa she broke a seal that allowed Crook and me to wriggle through time."

"You know, we have this saying: If something smells like shite, looks like shite, then it is shite! I find this hard to believe, and if I wasn't here with you... I wouldn't believe it, I'd say it was shite. But my real question is still, why? Why now? Why us? Every time my mother digs, and this must be her third Roman villa, someone from the fifth century doesn't come wriggling through some wrinkle in time to invite me to go on a pony ride!"

"Later," he said laughing, "not now!" And, Emily accurately concluded, 'He's dodging my questions.'

After fording the river Emily knew as the West Okement, they reached a glade in the forest where Merlin and Doone dismounted quickly. She slid off and watched in silence.

"Ready, Master? Tonight, on your father's instructions, we will survey the barbarian camp yonder," and he pointed in the direction of Exeter, "and gather intelligence. You are to tell me how big the camp is, how many animals there are in it, and how many men; how they are dressed, what weapons they have and, most important of all, what frightens them. We will begin with our exercises."

Anticipating what he would say next, Merlin had already positioned Crook when Doone said:

"Put your bird on that stump, sit in front of him and move your thinking into his body and answer these queries. Is Crook hungry? Is he tired? What can he see? What can he hear?"

Merlin nodded after each question because he had already checked the answers with his jackdaw. Doone paused there before he commanded:

"Bryten… Be the bird! Once you and the bird agree on all those things, ask him if he will allow you to fly with him to the river at Isca."

"Ready, Master Bryten. Let us fly away!"

But Merlin didn't budge. Instead he sat cross-legged, peaceful and silent beside Doone, motionless as if in a trance, although every now and then he jerked and smiled. Minutes passed.

Suddenly Merlin sneezed and Emily jumped. Doone sprang up and shook him roughly.

"Listen to me, young Master. You answer this riddle: What has glossy black feathers, puffs himself up and leaps into the air sneezing and making a spectacle of himself in front of his hen. Is it a black grouse or is it a merlin?"

"It is the black grouse doing his mating dance and showing off."

"Well, tonight it is the merlin." Shaking his head sadly, he continued: "Our art needs strong purpose and strength of concentration. It is not for fools and…" he added glaring at Emily, "it is not for girls. I have called the jackdaws back. We will start over."

Showing off, his jackdaw repeated, "Kak-kak!"

'Maybe that bird really does know what he is talking about,' Emily thought, smiling. 'Maybe Merlin is showing off. Awesome! I just love it!' She shivered with delight. But she wasn't going to show him how much she enjoyed every minute of being with him. Instead, she climbed back on the pony, and stroking Roget, she asked him,

"What have I got myself into?"

And Merlin was not to know then that he would come to regret making a spectacle of himself.

It could have been fifteen minutes, maybe more, before the birds returned and Merlin and Doone stirred into life again. Merlin began his report immediately.

"The Saxon camp is nearly twenty miles away. It is built on the old Army marching ground up from River Ex. I saw five men, five boys and two bound women. There were four white and five brown ponies, all local ones. The men wore metal skullcaps, which went down to their noses, and short tunics of wool. They had small round wooden shields—perhaps ten of them—that lay on the ground. And each man had a metal sword and an axe on a metal pike close by him. In the distance towards Isca I saw a burning farm. I suppose they could have looted it earlier in the day and torched the farm and captured the women from there. Beside their fire was a large, bulging leather bag, which could hold their booty. Their long ships are beached five miles further on the River Ex in the sand below Isca. The boats are big enough to hold at least twenty men per boat. So this raiding party could be just the first. I believe they are a threat to my father's farms. And you asked, what did they fear? When my jack-daw dropped a stone into their water jar they jumped instantly for their weapons. They're skittish. And like everyone, I suppose, they fear surprises."

"Well, Master, what do we do?"

"We will surprise them. I have a plan."

Ever since Merlin was six he would sit with soldiers playing games of tactics, or he would shadow-fight with them, brandishing wooden swords and knives. Later in the day he would sit with his father and they would dissect all he learned. Marcus Octavius Cotta hero-worshipped the great Caesar. But most important of all, Caesar's mother, herself, was a Cotta. All reason enough to venerate Julius Caesar and all reason to know why the Cotta's were of noble blood. His father, who had read everything Caesar had ever written, had learned from his tactics four things: you spy, you plan, you surprise and you attack. So when Merlin planned to attack, he too based his plan on Caesar's strategy.

But he had a unique advantage because Doone had trained him well. He knew how to convince any animal that he, too, was exactly of the same kind, just as he did with the foxes the day before. He could weave his hands in front of their face before using his hundred-mile stare to put the animals in a trance. 'Hypnotised' Emilia called it. His jackdaw, Crook, would obey his commands, and daily Merlin exercised with agility his attack and defence skills and increased his upper body strength by smithing at his forge. He was in peak fighting fitness. He could use all this against the invaders.

"I have a plan," Merlin repeated with confidence, although he did not reveal what it was. His father said the walls have ears, and Doone had taught him that even the trees listened too. He should assume that the Saxons had men trained in Wyed, too, who understood the ways of the wood and the language of trees. He calmed himself doing the square root of 1760, the number of yards in a Roman mile. Once he had calculated it to the thirteenth place, 41.9523539268061, he felt happy with himself. Everything would go well!

Doone asked him in Greek, "Does your plan involve that girl?"

Merlin looked at him surprised, assuming that he could see Emilia. Doone wanted to let him know that he not only saw her but did not like her, because he continued saying:

"That girl who is over there and who is silly-smiling all the time; the one who smells syrupy-sweet like a whore. Because if it does involve her, Master, you will need a new plan."

"Silence!" Merlin snapped. He didn't need a slave insulting Emilia or telling him how to protect his father's farms.

Then Doone thrust his face towards Emily and slowly closed his eyes to show her that, tattooed on each of his eyelids, was the outline of a blue eye, so that even when his eyes were shut it seemed he was wide-awake, seeing all.

'He is warning me,' she figured. Annoyed, she pursed her lips, distorted her face and stuck her tongue out like a gargoyle thinking, 'Two can play this game, Doone, just watch me!'

But the shaman only saw her as a whirl of sharp red light and concluded that the sooner this angry fairy was gone, the better.

5

Raiding the Saxon Camp

Just before midnight Wednesday September 8th, Merlin's time

THE STENCH OF FEAR *and long unwashed bodies was so foul that it made Emilia gag. That and the whimpering that came from the distressed woman and girl. I could not begin to think about what they had been through that night. In that moment I questioned whether I should have brought Emilia with me. Doone was right, this was not a place for a woman.*

We had travelled swiftly to the Saxon camp, leaving the ponies by the river and using our staffs like pole-vaults to cover the distance. Doone and I knew all the points to land on and how, using our staves, to spring from one to the next. I carried Emilia while Doone carried our weapons. Our birds flew beside us. Within fifteen minutes we stood on a ridge looking down on the embers of a fire and on nine sleeping men. A boy, younger than Emilia, stood guard. I took the charcoal from my pouch and rubbed it all over my face and arms and hands. It was only then that I listened, standing like a statue, for any sounds that did not belong there.

"So what is the plan?" she whispered.

"It is surprise, attack and capture. I will begin. 'Ab igne ignem capere'. Light a fire with a fire. Just watch."

"I've been watching you and sitting on the sidelines all night. Can't I help you? If Doone can't see me, those poor wretches and the Saxons can't see me either. That gives me an advantage. Couldn't I free that woman and the girl?"

I was surprised. Ingraine warned me she was headstrong but I thought she was wrong. Unfortunately, Emilia did not seem to understand that the invaders were savages and as such brutal fighters; they did not care who lived or died and they would bludgeon a woman to death without blinking. I knew too, because Emilia's fragrance was so strong, that they could easily find her and blindly slash her to ribbons. While I had promised to protect her, I would have to use all my ingenuity to keep her safe.

"Those women are best left where they are for the moment, Emilia. Even if the Saxons cannot see you, there is a chance they can smell you because Doone can. You have a fragrance of springtime. And because it is now the autumn and all our flowers have gone to seed, your fragrance is not in its right place and that could alert them that something is wrong."

She looked at me in disbelief. She must not know that we train our noses to read the wind. I had to think of something to keep her out of the way. So I tried again.

"There will be sudden noise and tumult and that will startle the horses and they will try to escape their pen. If you please, go over into their pen to calm and sweet-talk them until the fighting is over. Yes? Good! Here's my plan!"

Once Emilia was inside the horses' pen, it would only have taken her a moment to realise that every horse in there was already securely hobbled and that she was standing ankle-deep in foul manure whose odour was strong enough to envelop her and protect her. It was the perfect hiding-place. She stood there glaring at me and I read her lips as she murmured to herself: 'This can't be happening to me!'

Everything was still. Minutes went by. I waited until the noises of the night had restarted their regular drone and buzz before I counted with my fingers held aloft for Doone to read them. Then suddenly the camp was rocked by our blood-curdling yells. The jackdaws mimicked each of our yells, calling out from the opposite direction. Startled, the barbarians snapped awake and grabbed their weapons, absolutely sure they were surrounded. When I plunged my short staff into the fire a white blinding light flashed through the camp, followed by a series of loud bangs.

The young lookout fell to the ground in shock. The Saxons ran around in terror, swinging their axes wildly, blinded in my white light. Doone, his naked body blue with woad, took advantage of their confusion and swung his club smashing the heads of four men. Their blood spurted in a high arc towards Emilia and sprayed all over her. He caught another boy who tried to escape and went to slit his throat; but what are we? Savages? I flashed a spell to immobilise him because, although that little chap was capable of killing us, he was still a child. With the two screeching jackdaws, I terrified...

But I am going to stop my dictation there because you do not need to know what devils I conjured in their minds to produce such terror until the rest of the raiders lay cowering on the ground. Once the living were tied up, I went over to assure myself of the safety of Emilia. Although she had not told me that she had not seen death before, I could read it by the vacant horror in her eyes. And despite seeming moved by their loss, she was not really engaged. She was in a daze. What seemed to divert her for the moment were my battle techniques.

She spoke to me strangely, as if she were talking to me under water.

"How did you do that flash of light?" she asked.

"It was magna—I scraped it from the bottom of a cave—I used it to light the fire with fire."

"It must be magnesium." And jerking her head in the direction of the dead men, she asked bitterly, "Do you do this every night? I can only think of one word to describe what happened tonight, and that is… gru…" She paused and added shakily, "… awesome!"

Of course I knew what she really meant… Gruesome… And she was right, it was gruesome. And being anxious to explain why I left her in manure, I mumbled,

"I could not risk you getting hurt, Emilia. I did not think you had any idea how savagely and fiercely these Saxons fight. Those captured women know. They would have seen the worst. But this was the farthest those women have ever been from their homes and you, unseen to them, would simply have terrified them even more."

"What I saw, Merlin, was Doone, who was more savage and fearsome than any of the Saxons. And so were you! Those poor Saxons did not have a chance. Some of them were just kids. But if I were ever in this position again, I would rather be behind you, watching your back with a sword, than on the sidelines, like tonight, having to watch your slaughter."

"You cannot mean that! I have a bird to watch my back. Be careful what you wish for, Emilia, because this is not a spectacle at the circus, this is war. These people are invaders, and because you are not battle-hardened you must stay out of it. And now I have a difficult night ahead of me. I have to get those men into a prison where they can be interrogated, and I have to organise comfort and shelter for those women."

I briskly spun my cloak around her and grabbed her by the waist; and as we lifted off, my mood softened somewhat and I whispered, "But I do like that new word, 'awesome'."

She gave me the faintest of smiles and asked, "Why are you so protective of me and my mother?" She spoke as if she was demanding an answer, and although I had already rehearsed my response, I still felt unhappy with what I eventually said. Holding her tightly, I began,

"*My mother, Ingraine, tells me our times are sealed, and you do not really know whether I ever lived or not because I only exist in your fairy tales and not in your history books. Your mother's plan of digging up re-used ancient forts and Roman villas will give you a very accurate picture, I am told, of my whole life.*"

Pausing there, I considered whether I should warn her of how I saw Moloch under the fort at the Rumps, but I realised that what I had to tell her would scare her enough, without giving her details of the whereabouts of the Prince of Darkness.

"*Your mother's work will be very important because it will help her uncover our secrets, and we want her to uncover them. But others want the past to remain sealed so you can neither study it, nor learn from it, nor repeat it. They plan to stop your mother by frightening you both and, if given the chance, kill you. It has been agreed that I will protect you from harm and make the future they fear possible. But I have only been given seventy-two hours, that is only three days to do this, and nine hours have gone already.*"

Before she could ask another question, I put my finger gently on her mouth.

"*Sleep on what I have said and save the rest of your enquiries for later. Do not tell anyone unless you absolutely have to. They will not believe you anyway, as you said; and remember, I will protect you.*"

"*I get the uncanny feeling, Merlin, you're only telling me a tiny fraction of what's really going on.*"

She was right, of course, and I am the one who is used to being right.

When we reached her chamber I could still hear her father singing about a brown-eyed girl, so I bowed to her stiffly and said, "Good night, Emilia."

"*Good night, Merlin.*" *And she rushed away, gagging, into her water closet. I stepped into deep shadows to listen to her while she sobbed and retched and threw up.*

It was, at least, a night that had begun well. Flying into my realm I held her so close I was giddy with excitement. I demonstrated my arts before her and she seemed to admire them, and it was at that moment, I realised, I should have brought her back home. Instead, because I was eager to show her all my spectacular techniques, I took a young woman from a future realm into a Saxon camp. I brought Emilia, who I am sure had never even seen the butchering of a lamb, to a place where I could parade the butchery of warfare. And I made her stand in shit to watch it all. 'Awesome,' she had murmured shakily, and I pretended to believe her. Later, when I should have complimented her on her bravery for wishing to fight behind me, I lectured her on her inexperience and went on to describe the desire of the Dark to kill her.

"Hail, Myrddin, all hail!" I said aloud to myself. "You are a fool! Listen to her; she is wretched and now you have lost her."

And being too embarrassed to go back to console her, I just stood there. Like a fool!

And when her retching finally stopped, I felt hopeless.

I wonder what she thinks of me now. Will she ever take this hand of mine again?

I could still smell her perfume on my fingertips.

6

Trouble on Dartmoor

6.30am, Thursday September 9th, Our time

LESS THAN SIX HOURS LATER, the September mist was still clinging to the valley mire when Emily saddled up her white polo pony, Jerry. Rhys was already cantering around on his brown mare, Tiger, whistling and singing 'Morning has broken, like the first morning, Blackbird has spoken, like the first bird…'

"Hey, Mr Rock Star, I heard you singing Brown-Eyed Girl last night too. Can't you sing anything written after the dinosaurs?"

Emily was not a morning person. She felt tired after a night of throwing up and replaying in her mind everything that went wrong. Was that man's blood still on her jeans? She gagged again at the thought of it. She would wash them all over again tonight. In the few times when she slept she saw the moment when the light went out of their eyes. Should she have screamed them a warning? Maybe then Doone would have killed her instead. And if all that wasn't bad enough, Merlin warned her about the threats to her life and she felt scared. It was unbelievable! How was it possible that a death sentence hung over her head? Who had sentenced her? What had she done?

Now Jerry became skittish because horses always know. Yet, as she squinted at the morning, it looked so completely normal with the slight autumn nip in the air.

"Let's go, Wonder Woman!" her father yelled as she finally mounted, and he resumed his hymn to the morning: 'Praise with elation, praise every morning, God's recreation of the new day'.

Kelso danced gracefully around Emily well out of the hoof range of her horse. Whenever her dog saw Jerry, his excitement would build because that horse meant one of two possible adventures: either a wild run—or a wild run with birds.

Once they were clear of the stables, Dartmoor offered them acres of grass that were perfect for galloping, and there were hundreds of collapsed stone walls that were perfect for jumping. It also offered an endless choice of prey to an orange and white dog that lived for bird hunting.

"Race you!" Rhys called.

The first smile of her day lit her face.

"You're on!" Emily yelled back.

But it wasn't until their third jump that she saw any birdlife. Some snipe, early arrivals from Sweden, pecked with their long, straight bills in the boggy patches, and curlews with their melodic cour-lees were being mimicked by Rhys, until they became so confused by this man invading their territory that they flew off. Autumn was here already, Emily thought, and that meant winter was just lurking over the next hill. 'And it is not even my birthday yet!'

As they crossed the rise a clattering flock of jackdaws chased and tumbled above them in the thermals. 'Do you know,' she told herself, 'I think they fly like pigeons?'

Racing underneath them, she felt exhilarated and called up

to them, "Good morrow, Merlin!" knowing he would hear. And so, despite everything, she sensed he was close, and felt better for his protection.

And her father, on seeing her usual, beautiful smile spread across her face, sensed he could let go of his anxiety about yesterday's accident with Julia. He was sure it must have been the cause of the distress earlier that he saw in his daughter's eyes, but after a shaky start to the day, Emily seemed back to her sunny self. His relief did not last long.

Because when he saw a black dog in the distance, a dog that stood out menacingly from the heather and gorse of the moor, he was worried again. There was something very strange about its coat because it dazzled far too brightly for that gentle morning light. 'This is peculiar,' he thought, 'I am seeing a huge mastiff with fiery eyes and it's alone on the moor. It must be over one hundred kilos and there is something glittery in its mouth. Is it a doll or a ball or even a glove?' He hoped that slobbering fool of a dog Kelso kept well away from it. He wheeled Tiger around to check on Emily.

The mastiff was racing towards her, snarling and snapping, and before she even saw it she had sensed she was in danger. Jerry skittered.

"Sh, Sh, Sh..." She soothed him like he was a squally child. "It's okay, really it is, and Merlin will look after us!" But Jerry knew better than to rely on a man with birds on his shoulders, and he reared up and whinnied and tried to change his direction because he knew he had to get her away. And Emily, hanging on for dear life, was prepared because she knew exactly how to handle a startled horse. Even as Jerry sprang away and bolted for home, she remained calm and in control. She sat back in the saddle and shortened his reins to pull his head up while she soothed him with gentle murmurings. Merlin was right, her life was in danger; but she was going to swallow her panic. But all she could think about was her dog because she knew that no one got anywhere near his Emily without his agreement. And Kelso never backed away from a fight.

She turned in the saddle to see the mastiff leap on her spaniel's back, and its sheer weight collapsed him to the ground while its jaws sought out the soft pouch under his neck. And when she saw Kelso squirm nimbly a few feet forward, only for the mastiff to pounce on him again and again, she cried out in disbelief:

"This isn't happening to us!"

All Rhys could do was circle Kelso and whistle the sharp sound of the cracking of a whip but, at that moment, all he wanted was a bloody big gun to shoot the thug. Emily knew there was only one thing she could do and that was to allow her horse his head and race away until she could reach the stables and get some help.

"Merlin, Merlin, I need you Merlin!" she pleaded to the sky. "Please help my Kelso…"

When Rhys first heard the noise he thought it came from thunder in the distance, but once he saw the sky darken with clouds of screeching jackdaws and snipe and curlews, he was overwhelmed. What the hell was happening? He clutched the reigns of Tiger as hundreds of birds circled and swooped him and forced him out of their way before they swarmed over the animals. The wading birds used their beaks like needles to pierce the neck of the black dog, while the jackdaws favoured his eyes. Although the mastiff growled and snapped, the birds were relentless. When a jackdaw pulled out his eye with its beak he screeched in terror and rolled off Kelso and skulked away. The army of birds followed and dive-bombed him with brutal accuracy. Rhys would swear later that the attacker had not lost one eye but both of them. At that time, though, he was too distressed to know for sure. He dismounted and lifted the bleeding

Kelso onto his saddle and raced his horse back towards the stables.

"Hey," he soothed the whimpering dog, "I take back all I ever said about you, Kelso. You are not a slobbering fool; you are strong and smart and you are one brave dog! You are the bravest dog in Devon! And do you know what I'm going to do? I'm going to write to the Queen and nominate you for the Victoria Doggie Cross…" And so he blabbered on, incoherent. Yet at another level he wanted to know what was causing these unprovoked attacks.

"First Julia, then Emily, and now Kelso," he added it up. "It's time to leave Okehampton and move back home to the safety of our home in Exeter. One jackdaw rescue could be a quirk of nature, but two jackdaw rescues hours apart has to be something other than a coincidence."

And somehow Rhys sensed that Emily knew more about this than she was letting on. It was time to find out what was going on.

9.00am, Thursday September 9th, Merlin's time

"My Lord Moloch, the Great Baal—he who rides on the thunder clouds—will surely deliver us from these problems. The mastiff is a quivering mess. He is swollen with poison, one of his eyes has been plucked out, and the other has no sight. I cannot heal him."

"Useless. Don't slit his throat, Morgana. Put him in a warp and let him forever howl in Okehampton Castle. Report, Doone!"

"The daughter is under the protection of Merlin and Merlin is under the spell of the daughter."

"How can his power work outside his time?"

"*Ingraine, his mother, is in a deep trance and she holds his spirit.*"

"*How is she defending herself when she is in a trance?*" he asked.

"*She has woven silver thread around her that cannot be touched.*"

"*Report again soon.*"

As soon as Doone departed, he asked,

"*What do you think, Morgana?*"

"*The power of Ingraine has limits. She may be able to protect herself, but she cannot protect him, my Lord, from all your spies.*"

"*Nor can she protect her from all your poisons,*" Moloch replied, "*nor from your disguises nor from your silken wiles. I want to know all I can about him.*"

"*But why? Is it Merlin who is our quarry? Later I will need him to teach me all he knows. I can smell his musk now and when he smells mine... But that will come.*"

Morgana paused, looking dreamily to the future before she began again.

"*Is not our quarry Emilia? Will not her death stop the work of her mother? Will not it stop her future plans? Doone says the heart of Merlin is engaged with Emilia. Therefore will not her death weaken Merlin's sense of his own importance and add new meaning to her title 'the Chosen One'?*"

"*Merlin uses birds. Let us use them too.*"

"*I do prefer bats,*" Morgana persisted. "*Our bats are better.*"

"*But like you, my alluring one, they are only useful at night.*"

"*Then birds will have to suffice.*"

7

Dartmoor Castle

9.15am, Thursday September 9th, Our time

I T IS A TRUTH UNIVERSALLY ACKNOWLEDGED among fifteen-year-olds that most parents are created to embarrass their children. There are some who are so perfect that they constantly surprise them.

The Marquess of Exeter, the eldest son and heir of the Duke and Duchess of Dartmoor, always knew his parents were perfect. He flopped into the ornately-carved oak chair, stretched his long legs, pulled out his ear buds and demanded of no one in particular,

"Where's Emily?"

She had promised to meet him here at Dartmoor Castle at nine sharp for breakfast, after her morning ride. Now she wasn't answering her phone and his frantic texts were bouncing right back. Their art installation, spread across the library table, was due next Monday at the start of term and the Marquess—'Oh please, just call me Jack'—was anxious.

By thirteen hundred hours he was due to attend his next flying lesson. Afterwards he had to present the trophy for rifle-shooting at his father's regiment in Exeter before inspecting the regiment's new helicopter. He did not have another moment.

Jack burst into the gilded dining-room, a room reconstructed, panel-by-panel, by his ancestor from the château of Madame de Pompadour. It was so ornate it needed no further decoration, but there was one exception… the painting of the ruins of Okehampton Castle by Turner, a wedding gift from his mother to his father. He went straight to the sideboard and lifted the silver lids of the tureens until he found the scrambled eggs, bacon, sausage and blood pudding.

"Would your Lordship like vegetable juice this morning?" Alfred, his butler, asked.

"Yes, and some builder's tea, please."

His phone vibrated. Emily. Finally!

"Where are you?"

"I'm at the vet's. During our morning ride Kelso was attacked by a vicious dog. It was a two hundred-pound, bull-baiting bastard that went for his throat. Kelso's been sedated and stitched up and the vet is keeping him in for observation. If you don't mind me in my riding clothes, Jack, Dad can drop me there in fifteen minutes."

"All that's truly awful, Em, are you okay?" Shakily, she assured him she was, but he didn't believe one word of it. He knew she had to be very distressed because she loved her animals with a passion. He would make her laugh again. "I am in the Pompadour Room. I've just started breakfast."

Each room of Dartmoor Castle made a statement like this one, because it showcased the decorating eccentricities of long-dead dukes. This was Jack's favourite room; it was magnificent. He loved the pale green and gilt panelling, sculptured but still delicate, with glimpses of his father's formal rose-garden through its doors. Jack's appreciation of art and architecture came, however, from his mother. His father wisely chose a duchess of fine taste and strong bones from a ridiculously wealthy family, who had made their fortune in chocolate. His choice allowed him to renovate and rewire fifty-three rooms with the latest technology, and create eleven new bathrooms and four kitchens; but most important of all, it allowed him to install one hundred and seventy steam radiators.

His mother's business activities constantly surprised him. He got used to society weddings and tourists viewing their vast collection of art celebrating King Arthur and his Knights of the Round Table, but did not get used to Jolly Roger flags and finding Captain Jack Sparrow applying his makeup in his bathroom. The autumns were always quieter. It was then she converted the barn into a chocolate factory for busloads of northerners, who came down south to enjoy the warmth of Devon and her melting moments.

Jack, who looked just like his father, was tall at six-four, golden-headed, with ruddy cheeks and a smile showing large white teeth. Despite his obvious artistic and musical talents and his mother's Quaker beliefs, he would go straight to Sandhurst Military Academy to train as an officer in the army as soon as he finished at Exeter Academy. He was sixty-sixth in line for the British throne—and family traditions were strong; and some things, like his future career, were unquestioned. There was a suggestion that his red hair came from the Welsh Tudor line and stretched back to King Arthur himself. But every day of his life, Jack passed through the hall outside the library and admired the Edward Burne-Jones' painting 'The Last Sleep of Arthur in Avalon', and he never saw a hint of the red in Arthur's hair.

When Emily arrived, pale and dishevelled, the pristine butler bowed her in.

"Dear one, you look terrible!" cried Jack, bear-hugging her. "Have you been getting enough sleep?" And when Emily stared at him blankly, he concluded she had not and he asked, "What can I get you?"

"Just tea and toast, thank you."

"No, no. You need a sugar hit! It has to be one of Mum's special chocolate milkshakes."

She laughed in agreement. His mother's special had full cream Devon milk with two scoops of her dark chocolate ice cream and a wallop of chocolate sauce… all that on her ravaged empty stomach. It would either make her or break her!

"Jack, I didn't sleep last night. Maybe it was a premonition!" And she blurted out the story again of the huge mastiff, her missing glove, the bolting horse, the bloodied dog and the bird rescue. "What do you think we should do?"

"I suppose you know that The Hound of the Baskervilles story was written about the wild dog of Dartmoor, and the Park's rangers are quite rightly suspicious of any new sighting of it. They fear it's a prank, but I'll tell you what I'd do. Did you take a photo of Kelso's wounds?"

Emily pulled out her phone and showed him, and Jack grimaced, clamping his teeth together and sucking air through them.

"He looks terrible, Em! I'd take that with me for proof to the Park authorities and demand a permit to shoot the bloody thing!"

"'Do you think it could be the hound of the story?" Emily was serious and Jack could not believe that the girl who topped Science at Exeter Academy could ask such a question.

"Of course not! That's just a yarn from Conan Doyle. But I have an idea: why don't we just leave the earth for a while and stick our heads up in the clouds? How would you like to go flying with me after we finish here this morning? The sky gives you a different view of things."

"Jack, I'd love to go on a quick flight! Toby and I have the dress rehearsal tonight for Gotta Dance. I'd have to be home by three to practise with him."

"I'm coming to see you two perform. Casey told me all about your dancing at the Nine Maidens. Okay, you won your dare! And Tobes told me all about Professor Hughes' collapse near the Castle and asked if I could abseil with him into those ruins where she is digging. 'Righto,' I said, 'but it'll have to be tomorrow. I don't have a moment today.' We're governed by the clock, so we have to get moving. Into the Library now, and we'll take our brekkie with us."

8

Triptych

10.00am-12.00pm, Thursday September 9th,

Our time

IN THE DUSKY LIGHT OF THE LIBRARY, a sense of calm came over them. Jack usually worked in the studio of the barn where the light was good, and whenever he hit a bare patch in his creativity he could turn to his drum kit and bang away.

This morning early he had moved their artwork, Layers of Self, from his private place to the library table. Laid out and assembled in order, the three pieces were starting to make some sense. In the work they used their own self-portraits to explore the set examination topic: 'The passage from adolescence to adulthood'.

Jack's self-portrait was almost as complex as he was. It showed him photographed on a throne of carved and twisted dragons. 'Where did that come from?' Emily wondered. He digitally separated the tonal layers of his portrait, printed each one of them, and after mounting them on very thin cardboard, he laboriously cut them by hand. He painted the background canvas as an oil of Dartmoor Castle. On top of this canvas he sprayed on his layered self-image.

Emily's self-portrait was more conventional. She painted her portrait in a mirror of herself painting a portrait of herself painting a portrait in a mirror. Each picture was slightly different, and she based them on her photographs of herself over a year in as many different emotional states as she could enact.

Today they agreed they would work on the centrepiece of the triptych. Emily had already sketched Jack playing his drums at a gig in Exeter and, in a contrasting mood, playing his cello on the bluebell walk. Now it was his turn to sketch Emily, and he knew she was not in the mood. 'Somehow,' he thought, 'I have to lure that fear out of her eyes and get her laughing again.'

"How should I pose?" she asked playfully, sipping her milkshake. "Oh my God, Jack, this is bliss!"

"Feeling better?" he asked with a smile; maybe his Emily was coming back.

"Yes. I am feeling a little better. What if I posed like your relatives?" And she jumped from one grim ancestor adorning the library walls to another, and mimicked their dour faces.

Jack laughed at her antics and took a very deep breath before he said:

"I would like to sketch you as a girl in love."

And then he held his breath waiting for her answer.

"What! Me? Oh, no! With who? With you?" She was laughing as if she was delighted at his suggestion. "A sketch of me? Sitting adoringly watching you play drums? Oh no, that wouldn't be any good! If I were to sit adoring you, it would be listening to you play whatever it was you played out there in the bluebells. That is one of the most beautiful memories I have. What was it you were playing? Bach's Prelude or something?"

"Sadly I know you are not in love with me or my cello," Jack smiled wistfully. "But maybe you could pretend to be in love with one of those mythical persons that you girls always have crushes on. Like a Mr Darcy or a Sir Galahad."

"But why?" Emily laughed again but this time a little nervously. "Why are you taking this approach?"

"Because we have not yet explored first love and it is a rite of passage… between adolescence and adulthood…"

"…Hey, there's a very good reason we haven't explored it, because I am not in love!" Emily heard herself speaking with an emphasis far louder than her normal voice, as the scene from the Saxon camp came back to her. "Are you?" she demanded. "Are you in love?"

Jack ignored her question because, surely, she must know the answer to that by now.

"Why are you looking so alarmed?" he asked, standing beside the easel, with a paintbrush in his hand. "What's come over you? Looking at you now, all I am seeing is fear. It's almost as if being in love is what you fear most!"

"Don't you?"

"No. I fear losing my honour and degrading my family name in some way. That's what I fear."

"Well, I fear embarrassment or being laughed at for doing something nerdy or stupid like dancing around old stones." And she laughed at the thought of it.

"Well then, if it is not love you are frightened of, this should be easy."

'But it isn't easy,' thought Emily. 'If only I knew what being in love felt like. Is it like being giddy? Or feeling like the flutter of butterflies inside? Or is it like the exhilaration of surfing on the curl of a wave? Or this feeling I have of hopelessly drowning in the deep like the song I loved?'

But Jack was on a roll. "I have a painting of Sir Galahad here." He pulled a piece of velvet off an easel to reveal George Frederick Watts' portrait of him. Emily did not doubt it was the original.

"Where do you get these pictures? Galahad looks so perfect and pure," she said dismissively. "He's too saintly for me. I think I'd prefer something more edgy, like a Merlin."

As soon as she said it, she realised she had given herself away. And by mentioning Merlin's name she had called him in, and that would mean that even her gentle teasing of Jack would stop being fun if Merlin was a silent party watching over them. And then a crazy thought came to her. Let him stand in his own manure and watch her! Smiling, she said softly,

"Hey, on further thought, I would prefer to be in love with you, Jack. You could draw me gazing at your picture!"

Flushed with embarrassment, Jack turned away. He didn't believe her. What was she up to?

"Well, my backup plan is simply to photograph you as you are, and imagine you in love and draw you from the photo."

"Why don't you do that, and I'll try to behave." Instead, she did the opposite. She and Casey had been coaching one another on how to flirt. Casey was always Googling self-help sites like How to find your own Mr Darcy or conversation starters like the ten best Hollywood kisses. Her latest was How to flirt. They had practised on one another. The first step was for the girl to look into the boy's eyes and hold them fast for a count of two before gazing down and then slowly looking back up to peep through her eyelashes. There she was to smoulder for a count of three before she looked down again with a secret smile for four beats. After her second run-through Jack was so puzzled at her behaviour that he cried out,

"Peek-a-boo, Em! Come out from under your hair! What is wrong with you, have you got something in your eye?"

She laughed, wondering whether her flirting had managed to prick any jealousy from Merlin. But you never know when you act on a light-hearted impulse, how it may impact back on you later. And Emily would regret her five minutes of fun.

A shadow fell across her face when she smelled something rancid, and for some reason it reminded her of the Nine Maidens, until her thoughts jumped back to last night and Merlin's words: 'They plan to stop your mother by killing you.'

So despite her playful attempts to distract herself with flirting, all those questions rose again:

'Who wants to kill me? Why do they want to hurt me? Did they make the baby cry yesterday? Was the black dog sent by them? How did the dog get my glove? Was he given it to know my scent? And if so, was I the real target and not Kelso? I'll have to warn Mum about the threats to her. But what can I say? She won't believe me. She'll want to know who's doing this. She'll think the attacks are a coincidence. But Dad, he'll listen. But Merlin said, Don't tell anyone". Well, he can't set the rules when my life is at risk.'

Jack broke into her thoughts.

"Hey, you've become all gloomy again. Are you going to tell me what's going on in that head of yours?"

"Sorry, Jack, I'm really worried about that baby crying on the moor, and the attacks on Mum yesterday and on my horse and dog this morning. Maybe they were not so much attacks on my animals as on me. I'm worried each incident was not just random, but linked in some way."

"The Professor wasn't attacked. A cave-in is an occupational hazard for her. But this morning was a savage attack, and that dog should be put down. As soon as you're up in the air, you'll forget all about it, and when I loop-the-loop…"

"Hey, remember, I don't have a cast iron stomach like you or Toby! It is very tender at the moment and I'll throw up my chocolate milkshake!"

"Charming! In that case you'd better go home now! Seriously, I'll ask Alfred to drive you if you want."

"Dad's just texted me and asked if I want a lift. I'll sit for you for another half hour and see how I feel."

"Now look at poor Galahad here. He cannot believe you do not find him the sweetest hero alive! Did I tell you that in the third grade pageant I played the jester, Sir Dagonet, in the court of King Arthur? There's this joke about… Sir Lancelot and King Arthur…"

"Okay, I'm listening," and she smiled, and he clicked away with his camera as he told her the joke.

"King Arthur was readying for another round of battles against the Saxons, and before leaving he locks Queen Guinevere into a chastity belt and gives the key to Sir Lancelot. 'If I am killed,' he says, 'unlock the belt so she can marry again.' He kisses his queen goodbye and sets off with his army. Just outside Camelot he turns around for one last look at his shining castle where winter is banished, and he sees Lancelot racing towards him on his white steed. 'Wait, your Majesty,' Lancelot calls out, 'wait! You've given me the wrong key!'"

"That's good!" Emily is laughing again, her eyes dancing. It is just what Jack wanted so he could shoot away again. "Hey, I've got a King Arthur joke," she offers. "Guinevere was blond and beautiful and brainy, but Arthur just had muscles for brains. Guinevere wants a night with Lancelot so she asks Arthur to go up to the round tower and find her tapestry in the corner room. He searches all night."

"That's not in the least funny, Emily." And she started laughing again because Jack was so sure and serious. "But that joke reminded me of this one that is really funny. Okay, why did King Arthur have a round table?"

"I don't know," she answered, shaking her head.

"So no one could corner him!"

"That's bloody awful too!" she groaned. "Okay, my turn. What's Camelot famous for?"

Jack pulled a face and pretending to look helpless, shrugged.

"You don't know do you, you dimwit! It's famous for its knight life!"

"Well, I can beat your juvenilia. Who invented the round table?"

"Merlin, of course!"

"No, Sir Cumfrence." And although Emily groaned, she kept on laughing anyway.

"Now here's one about Merlin, and therefore it is more intellectual so you'll have to put your brain in gear to get it. Okay? It is Merlin's first job and he is hired as an astrologer and a prophet working for the dangerous King Vortigern. The king is always asking him about his fortune and about his future, and he is driving Merlin mad with his anxieties. So one day Merlin prophesies that the King's favourite mistress will soon die. Sure enough, this beautiful woman dies the very next day. Vortigern is furious at Merlin, because he is certain his prophecy willed her death. 'Merlin,' he says, 'if you are so great a prophet, tell me when will you die?' Now Merlin knows the king will kill him no matter how he answers, so he replies, 'Your Majesty, I don't know when I will die, but I do know that whenever I die, you will die three days later.'

"Emily, now you are really laughing! I'm finished here now, and the last photo that I took at the punch line was smashing. Let's go flying!"

At that moment her phone rang and she signalled him to wait. It was her father.

"No, I'm not coming home now," she protested, "I'm going flying with Jack."

"That's not on, Em," Rhys said. "You've got to rehearse and perform tonight, and you and I have got some things to talk about."

"Like what?"

"Like what really happened this morning, and what really happened yesterday."

"What's the use of talking about it?"

"That answer convinces me you know more than you're saying. So apologise to his lordship. I'll come and I'll pick you up in ten minutes and we will have a little chat."

Emily stopped laughing.

9

Avalon

1.30pm, Thursday September 9th, Our time

"R IGHT, YOUNG LADY, WHAT'S GOING ON?"
Rhys returned with his daughter to their rented town-house that was across the river from Okehampton Castle. Emily stood in the kitchen squeezing an orange juice for her father, and she told me that whenever her father asked her a direct question, she asked him a question in return.

"What do you mean?" she requested quickly.

"I mean two attacks, two rescues, and both by jackdaws in two days. It's against the law of probabilities... What's going on, Em?"

"Why do you think I would know the answer to that?"

"Because, my darling girl, you've got that silly strained look on your face. And your darting eyes show your mind is searching for an escape route that will allow you to avoid this conversation."

"Since when have you become a psychologist?"

"In the olden days I took out two firsts at Oxford, one of them in psychology, the other in classical languages. However, I am not going to be diverted, Emily. What is going on?"

Biting her lip anxiously, Emily asked the expert: "Ever heard of

Merlin?" She thought twice about mentioning my name, only to conclude that if ever she needed me it was now, because she felt miserable and could not lie to her Dad.

"Yes, of course I've heard of Merlin."

Rhys looked at her incredulously before leaning back on the kitchen cabinets and crossing his arms.

"I'm Welsh and he's ours. He's one of my heroes. He aids the birth of Arthur; he teaches him kingcraft, and fights the Saxons before it all ends in sorrow at Avalon. Merlin is a kindly old man with a long beard and a pointed hat. We Celts mourn him and await the time when he and Arthur and his knights will return to us. Now don't divert my attention onto one of my favourite subjects!"

"I'm not. But the Merlin I've met doesn't have a long beard. He's young and cool and he is the one who sent the jackdaws to help us. They are his birds. He works with all the creatures of the air and he flies with them too. The Merlin I met is tall and strong and bright and plays tricks on me, like a magician. And he protects me. Well, Mum and me..."

Rhys's eyebrows shot up as she spoke.

"Okay, Em. This is not the answer I expected." And he seemed genuinely puzzled by what she said. "Aren't you a little old for an imaginary friend? Do you claim that you've met the real Merlin?"

"Yes, Dad. He came here last night just before midnight. He came right into my bedroom, uninvited by me, I assure you, and returned these." She pulled some sunglasses out of her bag. "See, Mum's sunglasses. These are the ones his jackdaw took yesterday."

"Are you sure they are hers? They could be anybody's!"

"They are Chanel, Dad; they are real Chanel, not fake, real! Cost a fortune, and I had them monogrammed inside. See, J.M.H...Julia Madigan Hughes."

"Okay. Now you have my attention. But how do you know your Merlin is my Merlin, and not someone in fancy dress playing a trick on you?"

"Oh, he's real enough. He wore a Roman tunic and a cloak and he dressed like a real dork. He showed enormous curiosity about all the technology in my room. There can't be anybody in Britain who hasn't seen a TV before, but he hadn't and he wasn't faking it. He said his Welsh mother called him Myrddin, but he used Merlin in English after his falcon, which is also a merlin. He showed me tricks and pulled a frog from my nose, and I took his photo on my phone when I thought he was an intruder. See!" She held up my photo and showed it to him.

"It's very blurry, it could be anyone. Why weren't you terrified at an intruder in your room?"

"I was asking myself about that at the time. Merlin wasn't scary, only a little bit weird, but still fun. I liked him straight away."

"Okay, let's assume you are right, just for the moment. Why did he send a jackdaw yesterday to steal your mother's glasses?"

"So Mum wouldn't fall down into the hole that he knew was just about to happen. He also knew that she would climb out to get her glasses back. The hole is in the roof of the granary of his house that is buried near the castle. That is where he was born, and it's beautiful, like a palace!"

"Sadly, I thought he was born in Wales, not England."

"Hey, be consoled, he speaks with a Welsh accent."

"What happened this morning? I heard you call out his name and saw you smile."

"I saw the jackdaws and I thought of him, and I spoke to him as if he was there, and when I did that I brought in his protection even though at the time I didn't know I would need it."

"Why is he protecting you? You know that's my job, I'm your father!"

"Dear Sir, and you do it well!" Coming out from the shadows of the pantry, I spoke in Welsh. "And as we speak, you are saving her again, you know, because by your insistence on bringing her home you have saved her from a stalled engine in the dragon king's flying machine. It is happening as we speak. It is you who rescued her dog this morning and you who consoled her after her horse bolted. It is you who sang her a lullaby each night, like the true bard that you are. Greetings, I am pleased to meet you. I am Myrddin," and I bowed deeply.

"Step out of the shadows where I can see you," Rhys demanded in Welsh.

I towered over her father. His eyes moved over my rust-coloured tunic and the gold snake torc around my neck, as if he was checking every item for its historical authenticity; but he laughed when my mice emerged to sit on my shoulders and groom their whiskers. Then when I caught Emilia's eye, she was staring at me in surprise and delight, and there was nothing in her face that showed she hated me as I feared she would.

"Thank you for your help this morning," Rhys stammered, momentarily distracted by his daughter's radiance on seeing me, and by his own realisation that if ever he were looking at a Roman, he was now.

"Could you two speak English, please? I want to hear if you're talking about me." Emilia always pretended she could not speak Welsh to encourage her parents to make secret asides in the language in front of her, while she followed every word.

"Myrddin, what's going on?" Rhys asked me, in the obsolete Greek of Homer. "Where did that vicious dog come from this morning? Poor Kelso is still in hospital and will be there for days."

"I have brought this special physic for him," I replied in the everyday trading Greek I spoke with my father, as I handed Rhys a small clay pot. "Put this in his drinking water. Kind sir, there are some people who want to stop your wife's work here and what she plans to dig up in Cornwall. They do not want our past uncovered. They want to keep it buried. And particularly anything that is in it to do with me."

"So who are these people?" Rhys switched to Latin and left me wondering what game he was playing with me, changing languages. I just shrugged and answered him in the Latin of Virgil,

"I really do not know. They leave no footprints; they are just echoes in caves. Yet I know that part of my father's lands, the parts where Emilia went yesterday for her dare and near where you rode this morning, they are still used by Carthaginian traders for worship of their god, Baal. The local people will not go there, especially after nightfall, because they are dark and dangerous places." I found it hard to concentrate with Emilia staring at me. Perhaps because it was the first time she had seen me in the light of the sun. "Now, dear Sir, have I passed your language tests?"

"Yes," said Rhys, switching to English, "I am now the only person alive on this planet who has ever conversed with a native speaker of Latin, or to someone, for that matter, who speaks the trading Greek, and there will be no point in boasting of it because no one will believe me. But back to the subject at hand, what can we do about these attacks? Obviously I can't go to the police if I don't know who's behind them. I suppose I could hire a bodyguard. Or I could simply ask Julia to stop her archaeological excavations…"

"Dad, you know Mum doesn't even believe in organic food or natural healing, let alone that a wizard called Merlin the Magician saved her from the unseen dark forces that caused her cave-in!"

Rhys shook his head and asked me in Welsh, "What can I do?"

"Work with me. Hire me as a bodyguard," I almost pleaded. "I am not a man of twists and turns, driven off-course by any breeze, but constant in my attention."

"That is interesting, Merlin." Rhys smiled at my reference to Odysseus, the inconstant hero of the Odyssey. "Do I take your quote to mean that unlike Odysseus, the slippery adventurer, you are like Achilles who is steadfast and locked into his destiny? If that is so, then you need to know that my Emily is also like Odysseus but only in three regards: she is an adventurer, and brave, with the quicksilver dazzle of his mind. No doubt you saw that this morning watching her handle her bolting horse. Now you are forewarned, just how much would you cost as a bodyguard?"

"My fee is that you accept my one request: that you will allow me time to get to know your daughter in order that I may court her." 'What am I saying?' I ask myself. 'I am locked into my destiny and I am not free to court her.'

"Now, Merlin, that's a strange, old-fashioned request. Have I anything to be worried about in what you are asking?" Rhys looked at his daughter who was looking at me amazed, and he realised he had a lot to be worried about. "So you want me to pay you for something you were willing to do for free? Okay, I'm willing to keep playing along with this."

"What on earth are you two talking about?" asked Emily, the pretence of curiosity written all over her face.

"A gentleman's agreement, Em," her father explained, "between Merlin and me."

"So, Dad, do you believe me now?"

Rhys still looked doubtful.

"He looks like a Roman, and he speaks like a Roman when he uses the Greek of the bazaar and the polished Latin of Cicero. As well, he has read Homer and he's passed all my tests; not cum laude but good enough."

I have never been dismissed as 'good enough'! So what else could I do? Win his praise using enchantment? No, because this man is a scholar. I will have to appeal to his area of speciality. But what? How could I make this scholar of language piss in his pants with excitement?

Swiftly, I recited the first twenty verses of the Iliad, alternating each and every verse between old Greek and new Greek. Then just as fast I recited the first ten verses of Virgil's Aeneid in Latin before I switched it to Welsh. When Rhys's face was covered in amazement, I allowed myself a slight smile because next I had a special *treat for him. I was going to bore him at breakneck speed with the first book of Caesar's 'Gallic Wars'!*

"Gallia est omnis divisa in partes tres, quarum unam incolunt Belgae, aliam Aquitani, tertiam qui ipsorum lingua Celtae, nostra…"

The scholar of languages waved a white cloth over his head moaning and laughing at the same time:

"I surrender, Merlin. Stop, please. Please stop!"

He was not getting away from me so lightly, because there were still thousands of words left to recite. When I saw, however, that even Emilia's face was wilting I knew it was time for some of my real magic. Beside me lying in a dish there were golden balls of a soft fruit that called out to me that they wanted to fly. I obliged, and once freed they jumped into the air. But when their window blinds raced up and down, their water taps turned on and their pot boiled, Emilia and her father laughed with tears running down their faces.

Maybe I had won her back, but I do not doubt it was Julius Caesar who had ultimately intervened, because every member of my family knows he was the greatest lover in the history of the world. So I asked him for inspiration, and as I lifted her into a slow dance and before she had a chance to say anything, I apologised:

"I am very sorry about last night Emilia. I should not have taken you on a bloody Saxon raid only to abandon you when you were so sick and distressed. I beg you to accept my apology and forgive me?" With that plea, I kissed her hand and she glared at me from the corner of her eye before slowly, very slowly, a little smile spread across her lips and she lifted up my hand and kissed it saying:

"If you set out, Merlin, to achieve the world's worst first date, you could not have achieved it any better." It sounded like she was not pleased.

"What is a date?" I asked.

"It is when a young man or woman asks someone they like to go out with them to have some fun together."

"And I asked you to go out with me and I made you wretched!"
She laughed at my embarrassment and playfully hit my hand.

"Hey! You can't catch me!"

Bewildered, Rhys watched us as we chased one another up the walls and around the ceiling. There we were, a strange girl frolicking with a stranger boy, and both of us drunk with delight while dancing in the air. I could see Rhys feeling an acute sense of loss at no longer being the most important scholar in her life and at being unable to protect her from the inevitable hurt heading her way. For now I know that no one knew my story better than he did, and my foreboding about my future had always led me to believe that my story, and that of the unborn King, were tragic ones. And Rhys could see his daughter playing with an ancient magician and becoming entangled in those tragedies. It had to be a perilous course. And like a true bard, all he could think of was a song; a song he told me he never knew the meaning of until then. Emilia described it as a haunting melody from his childhood, a song full of grace and wistful sadness. As he watched us, he sang:

> "Would you have me dancing out of nowhere,
> Avalon?
> Avalon
> Avalon
> Avalon
> Without conversation or a notion, Avalon
> Where the samba takes you out of nowhere
> And the background's fading out of focus
> Yes, the picture's changing every moment
> And your destination, you don't know it, Avalon.
> Dancing
> Dancing
> Dancing
> Dancing

When you bossa nova there's no holding
Would you have me dancing out of nowhere, Avalon?
Avalon
Avalon
Avalon
Avalon
Avalon."

10

Bird Strike

3.30pm, Thursday September 9th, Our time

"WHAT'S THIS CRAP MUSIC?" Toby burst through the door, having just fallen out of the door of Jack's Bentley. His cap on, his sunglasses on, his red shirt and red shoes on, turbo-charged as usual, yelling: "Em, we can't dance to that crap!... Oh sorry, Rhys, I didn't know it was you. I thought it was Bryan Ferry. Where's Em?"

"She was just here." Rhys looked around for Merlin and was relieved he was nowhere to be seen. "She's probably upstairs changing; she was still in her riding gear."

Toby raced up the stairs to the landing.

"Hey, you decent? Because I am here," he stressed, in case she'd missed his entrance. "Did you hear what happened to us?" At breakneck speed he continued, "Hey, I went flying in your place with Jack. A twin-engine Piper Comanche. The engine banged out. Bird strike. It sounded like a bomb going off, like we were under attack. It was a Red Alert danger. I nearly shat my pants! The instructor took over the controls and banked us over the sea... using up the gas before we did an emergency landing in crash position with fire engines blaring!"

"Are you okay? Emily asked. "What did you do?"

"I immediately demanded a refund"—Toby was smiling—"and I asked Jack if that's any way to treat his dearest friend!"

"A cave-in and a bird strike in twenty-four hours, Tobes? That's scary stuff!"

"I'm twitching all over and I've gotta dance!" He started shaking his hands and break-dancing with his feet. "Gotta move my energy. Some back-flips, somersaults..."

"Is Jack all right? I'll just text him and check!"

"Nothing stops Action Jackson. He's going up again tomorrow, would you believe? Why don't you go up with him? On second thoughts, that's not a good idea. It's not lost on either of us that you were meant to be in that plane. You're a jinx! Don't expect to come in our car tonight. You'll be walking to the Phoenix, Exeter. And with an armed escort! I'm not joking, Em. Jack's coming with some of his father's armed bodyguards."

"Oh that's too silly for words! Let's get moving downstairs. We've got to clear the furniture."

When the house started thumping with hip-hop Rhys stepped outside to call Julia.

"I'm at the Castle getting wired-up for an interview about the cave-in," she said. "The picture in the local press did it. Channel 4 has flown down Tony Robinson to do the interview—can you believe it? You know, the fellow who used to be on Time Team. He'll ask good questions. We've got four minutes of airtime. It's on at five on Channel 4."

Having decided it was not a good time to fill her in on Jack's misadventure or Merlin's visit, Rhys wished her luck.

"Emily says the cave-in was into a granary."

"How would she know?" she said dismissively. "Speak later!"

"Thank you, Professor Hughes. Time Team will be back soon to follow up."

Julia stood smiling for the cut-away shots and then moved her head earnestly up and down for the noddies. As soon as they removed the microphone pinned to her blouse she switched on her phone. It rang. It was Rhys.

"They just showed a bit of the interview live on the local news. Marvellous publicity! You were concise and informative and unbelievably sexy!"

She laughed. "Thanks! How's Em's practice?"

"Unbelievably noisy. They're outside now practising gymnastics. You know, all that leap-frogging and back-flips. I told you Em said it was a granary, and Roman from the fifth century."

"How would she know? Lucky guess! Tell her I'll be there at seven. But when we put the miniature camera down into the granary, I spotted something strange on the floor. It could have been a skull."

"Julia, we have to talk about Em..."

"I have to go now. I'm being called over to see the video of the rerun. I'll see you at the Exeter Phoenix and I'll go straight there from work. I'll call you when I know the real answer."

And she was gone.

11

The Villa of the Cottas

5.00pm, Thursday September 9th, Merlin's time

I STOOD FOR A WHILE IN THE PANTRY, and as soon as Tobias went upstairs I walked outside and melted into the sunlight. I had an urgent meeting to attend with my mother, but first I needed to burn away this floating, airy feeling and plant my feet firmly on home ground.

Caballus was battering a bronze breastplate at the anvil, tap, tap, tap, with the rhythm of a drummer. His cross-eyed son, Motius, worked the bellows at the base of a circular brick forge, his face the colour of a robin's breast. Both of them were covered neck to toe with thick leather aprons and on their working hand they wore a leather gauntlet. Caballus' real name was Caius, and even though his nickname meant 'broken down old nag', he loved it because everything he did proved he was not. The smith had been thirty years in the army, mostly as a farrier for the cavalry. He specialised in horses' feet; making horseshoes for the draught horses that pulled the heavy loads and fixing up ailments of the hoof in the cavalry horses. He now lived with his family outside the villa, happy to be still working with his general, my father.

"I will work on my sword, Caballus." The smith stopped his work and pulled the folded steel blade from under his bench, admiring its textures. He was an iron man himself, and did not understand my fresh method of smelting iron ore in my furnace to create steel. Nor did he approve of the way I poured molten steel into a one-piece mould for a sword. Everyone knew the sword's hilt and its tang were applied separately to its blade, but I am sure he appreciated that I knew what I was doing. I often saw Caballus' amazement at my skill with silver, copper and bronze and how quickly it had far exceeded his own.

Once my sword was red-hot, I worked it carefully; it allowed me to empty my mind and enjoy the heat and the thump of the bellows and the rhythm of the hammer. After a steam bath I would be ready to meet my mother.

6.00pm, Thursday September 9th, Merlin's time

Ingraine sat in silence, a shaft of dusty sunlight coming through the window from above her, and the purple rug of royalty stretched across her knees. The sweet smoke of Arabian incense burned in a visor on the floor and it curled around her feet. Her soul was an ocean of peace.

I crept in and sat next to her, waiting until my breath was in rhythm with hers.

"It is me, Myrddin," I said as quietly as I could, but she still jerked into the present, opening her startling blue eyes. "Can you give me more time?" I asked.

"Why? Is this because of your dance? Her father has a fine voice. I watched you dance. It was beautiful."

"I loved dancing with her. Did you see her dancing with the foxes yesterday? I felt my soul change colour when I first saw her. Is she not beautiful? I want to show her the isles of Avalon—the Dragon's Tor, the tree of the Holy Staff and the Church of the Mother... Do you know she has a statue of the Mother in her...?"

Ingraine held up her hand to shush me. "I hold your energy, Myrddin, and now I hold hers too and I see all and know all this. Nearly one day has gone already and I know my energy can limit you to our land. Perhaps it is not more time you need, but more distance."

"Perhaps. Can you give me the freedom to move past father's land, much further away?"

My mother did not answer immediately. Instead she observed, "I am pleased you have protected her from their attacks."

"It has not been difficult to outwit the Dark Ones, whether it be below the castle, on the moor or in the air. They are very predictable, you know."

"Do not become blind to their mischief, Myrddin, or it will move you into error. You missed why the Dark One stole Emilia's glove, and today, just before you danced with her, her friends could have died in their flying machine. I held it up for the few seconds it took before the flying teacher could react and you could help.

"There were other times when I smiled. The foxes' dance was so charming, Myrddin. When Emilia dances she is graceful, and I smiled when Doone chastised you for showing off in front of her. Did he not put you in your place? But when you took Emilia to the Saxon raid and put her, indignant but sweet-smelling, in the horseshit, I held my head and shook it in disbelief. You have a great deal to learn about women, Myrddin. I was grateful when she accepted your apology. I do not think I would have been so forgiving.

"But let us not be distracted. The Darkness will now increase their assault. Their spies are everywhere and they know, as you do, you only have the forty-eight hours that I can spare. If you take Emilia to Avalon my power will weaken because Summerland is not our country. Or if she were ever taken by them out of our country, my power would weaken too and I would have to call in others to help. There will be greater risks. When do you plan to go?"

"I want to take her there tonight after her dancing competition. I can feel the Darkness creeping closer and I know war is coming. Only I do not want to think about it yet. Unless I am working at the forge, or fighting the Saxons, I feel weightless as if I am spinning in the space between her life and mine and I do not want it to stop. Yes, yes. I know it will."

"I saw you dancing on the ceiling. I can see the love light in your eyes, Myrddin. Now look at you, miserable, like a dove without its mate. My son, you have an honest heart, a cool mind and an easygoing nature... who could not love you? Shhh... shhh, Myrddin. I have got friends. Let me see what I can do."

12

Bruto's Command

6.30pm, Thursday September 9th, Merlin's time

OUR PEACE WAS BROKEN *by a deep, gravelly voice that boomed,*

"Ambrosius! Where the hell are you?"

The door was thrown open and there stood the towering mass of my father. His army nickname was Bruto, which meant ugly. And he was! Mother did not marry him for his beauty. His ears stuck out like the handles of a jug and his badly broken nose was spread across his face. He was a thickset man, bulky, tall and immensely, physically strong. His whole demeanour said, 'Don't mess with me, I am a brute force.' And you need to know that is exactly what he was!

Bruto was a general, who before he was briefly stationed here, was told that Britannia lies virtually at the end of the world and is inhabited by people who ungratefully rebelled against Rome. When he arrived he was surprised by its beauty. He loved it and decided to retire here. He was already filthy rich from investing in Iberian gold and from selling horses he bred for the army. He assisted as many of his legionnaires as he could to become colonists and they lived around him in our village. His First Spear, known only by his nickname Primus, became the foreman of his farms. On retirement, Bruto was awarded three hundred acres of arable land and five hundred acres of forest for hunting. He bought more.

He owned most of Dartmoor although, then and now, it was not a moor. I am calling it Dartmoor because that is what you call it. It was once a wood rich with oak, elm, beech, hazel and hawthorn, and in many of its stony outcrops there are strange sites of worship for Carthaginian traders. It has superb hunting. On his retirement, taking advice from Constantine, he searched for a Welsh lady to become his wife. Across the Severn (which we call the Hafren), the king of Davydd had a gifted daughter being schooled by the priestesses of Avalon, and although well past marrying age, she was still a maid. After months of negotiation, they settled on a maiden fee and Bruto procured his Welsh princess and British royal blood for his son. He loved her at first sight.

"Princess, greetings!" His giant mass, like a brown bear, hugged her tenderly. "I need our son now for an important mission." He kissed her brow. "Right now, Ambrosius."

I gave my mother a look of resignation.

"I will return," I said over my shoulder, going out with my father.

Slaves scattered before us like squawking ducks. We went into the main hall of the villa, whose walls were covered with frescoes of Mars, the god of war, and the stork insignia of his Third Legion. It was already garlanded with ivy and berries for the event on the morrow, and in the centre of the room stood a long oak board surrounded with new padded stools. The kings of Britannia would not recline on our Roman couches.

"Sit." He motioned me to a couch and lifted his feet, one after the other, for his personal slave, Maroc, to remove his boots.

"Let us drink a goblet of my good ale first."

My father learned to brew beer in Germania and built his own brewery below wind of the villa. Before he raised the drink to his lips, he clapped his hands to be left alone and then he spent a long moment appraising me. He wanted me to toughen up, he had told Primus, to get me away from the sticky, motherly warmth of Ingraine and used to the noisy, brutal battles of the Legions. I knew of his intentions but I did not know that even before I left for Gaul, he had immediate plans for me.

"Good trip?" I asked, uncomfortable under my father's scrutiny, and I began to sense Bruto was going to tell me something I did not want to hear. Something that would mean I could not take Emilia to Avalon.

Bruto checked we were alone before he lowered his voice and spoke quickly in Greek.

"I know you thought I went to Chester to see Coel. I didn't. Went to Verulamium to meet Constantine. There is bad trouble up north, just south of the Emperor's Wall. Constantine is threatened by those savages, the Picts; they come at him by land and by sea. The Jutes and the Saxons attack from the east and those bloody rebels, the Brigantes, at home still fight as if we had never conquered them. Now they are joined with the Saxons. But his real problem is just to his south in Petuoria, you know, with that crafty little shit, Vortigern. He lusts after Constantine's land, and it is vast land that stretches from the Carvetii on the west coast and across to the sea in the east and down to York.

"Vortigern is coming tomorrow but not to sign anything; he is coming to cause trouble. You know he is a calculating murderer. He poisoned his mother and father, got drunk to celebrate, and could not help boasting about it. He has bastards everywhere but he has no queen now. She died and probably at his hand; he abuses his daughter, a poor, neglected little wretch, and countless others.

"His daughter produced an inbred son, an imbecile, who mercifully is already dead, I am told, God rest his soul. And Vortigern's

bringing her too. How distasteful it is to have him in this same room as your goodly mother.

"Now Constantine says he fears he will be Vortigern's next victim. He is so fearful that he gave me his treasury and his ceremonial sword for safe keeping and I have locked them away and you know where. His oldest son, Constans, died suddenly. Constantine is very suspicious about his death. His two other sons were hidden away for years in Lesser Britain with Audren, his brother, so fearful was he about their safety. Constantine is not coming tomorrow, but sending his sons instead. They plan to ambush Vortigern somewhere near Isca tonight. It will be a minor skirmish, I am sure. Constantine and I want you to stop them."

I was smiling to myself. My father and Constantine were men who planned the futures of their sons with such precision, that years later they were still trying to manage how we spent every moment.

"Why stop them?" I challenged my father. "Surely everyone is better off without Vortigern. Why not allow Uther and Ambrosius to do the dirty work?"

"As a child, Ambrosius, your first word was not 'mama' or 'papa' like other infants, it was 'why'. So, why? The spies of Vortigern working in the villa of Constantine have betrayed his sons' plans to Vortigern and he has set a trap to kill them."

My father constantly surprised me. I had to inquire: "Dare I ask how you know all this?"

"My intelligence comes from my own spies. I have a spy in the inner circle of Vortigern. And many others strategically placed throughout Britannia."

"Does Vortigern have one in ours, here?"

"Probably. I always act, as should you, as if he does. Who can be trusted to keep our business a secret? Is not that why we are alone here and speaking the Greek of the marketplace? I hope you have examined all your staff?"

"On my sword," I declared, pulling my sword out and kissing its hilt, "I can swear to their loyalty. But why send me, father? You know I am trained as a Druid and exempt in this country from hand to hand fighting." I paused for a moment, overcome with the desire to please my father and the fear that I could not. "You are surrounded by many loyal veterans who could butcher Vortigern. Why send me?"

"Because, my son, you move fast through the old pathways of the air, and you know enchantment. As a Druid you hold the wood with its sounds, smells and its teaming life in your head. As well, you know this country; you know its landscape, and you can fight. But it is your intellectual sinew that leaves me in awe of you. And, in a few days, you will be called on to fight in Gaul."

"Unsoldiered as I am, I am honoured, sir, that you, a general, would choose me for this mission. Thank you." I bowed to him and sheathed my sword. "What does your intelligence gathering say?"

Bruto rose and motioned me to come to the table where he unrolled a map of the Isca area.

"Constantine tells me his sons and their parties are travelling up the river Exe disguised as monks. They have two boats, six men, six horses and two slaves in each; that makes fourteen fighters in all. They plan to ambush Vortigern, who has one boat, ten men, one daughter and four slaves as oarsmen, before he reaches the first cataract of the river below the bridge and the town. Right here." And Bruto stabbed the map. "Vortigern has sent a party of ten Saxon mercenaries by land on foot with one pack pony along the Fosse Way. I believe they should be here by now." And emphasising their position by thumping, he added, "Right here. Their orders are to get to Isca first through forced marches and to capture both of Constantine's sons as hostages. They plan to intervene right here," and again he thumped the map so hard the candelabra bounced and I was forced to hold it steady. "Right here at these warehouses on the river below the fort."

"*So, the two sons have fourteen men, and Vortigern has himself plus twenty men. We will not count his daughter. That means for every two of ours, they have three. Exactly when does Vortigern expect his mercenaries to reach Uther and Ambrosius?*"

"*As the full moon rises,*" Bruto replied.

"*That is just after eleven tonight!*" I exclaimed. "*Do you know for sure that Saxons were quick-marched for Isca? Unless they have good discipline, it would be very hard for them because it is said Vortigern only recruited them recently, so they cannot be Roman trained. They will not speak our language and they are in a strange land.*"

"*I agree with your view, but only in part.*" He paused to swill his ale and I feared a long story might be coming.

"*Remember, I had some Saxons in my auxiliaries years ago. They are very thirsty fighters for blood and for beer, and Constantine tells me he had them too in his auxiliaries at the Emperor's Wall—he agrees with my assessment of them. But that said, any Roman-trained Saxons will not come cheap, and where would Vortigern get the gold to pay them? It is very brazen and risky to march his mercenaries down that long toll road. It exposes them to plenty of witnesses and plenty of gossip. Any Roman soldier with a full pack could walk twenty-three miles; and if in a forced march, maybe he could cover up to thirty-two miles. But even in a forced march it would take nine days to come south from Lincoln along the Fosse Way. Consequently, when his men do finally arrive, they could be late; they could be exhausted; and they would certainly be confused and disoriented. This is all to our advantage, of course.*"

Bruto rocked back on his heels satisfied with his analysis and poured himself more ale.

"*Then, why send them by the Fosse Way in the first place?*" I asked. "*What is the point of that? Why not send your troops by sea like last night's raiding party? Seems odd, do you not think? What would you do, sir?*"

"*Remember, our noble family of Cottas gave to Rome the mother of Caesar. We must always think like him, Ambrosius; spy, plan, surprise, attack. We must know our enemy, my son, and know him well. So, first, I would verify every word of our intelligence, check it as only you can: their positions, their actual numbers and the routes they are taking. Second, you know the landscape. That will be your main advantage over the Saxons. Use the landscape and its animals and birds as only you know how. Third, I would alert the sons of Constantine as soon as possible so that you can plot and plan with them. Remember, the eldest will be used to being in command, but for reasons you will see for yourself, Uther is his eyes and he is an instinctive soldier and leader in a way that Aurelius is not.*

"*Fourth,*" *and he drew a slicing finger across his throat,* "*I would take out those mercenaries quickly. Finally, I would escort whoever is left standing back to Okehampton for interrogation so we can squeeze every drop of truth from them.*"

"*Thank you. I will take Doone and Caballus with me. I will fight with a tight team. Could you send your Primus with a cart to Isca for my prisoners, and send any others you can spare to act as escorts? And I will need some horses saddled for emergencies. Ask Primus to wait on the west side of the Isca Bridge. Now, I have one last question. What do you want done with Vortigern? Do you want him alive or dead?*"

"*Alive, for sure. Constantine and I agreed that our best chance of getting the kings to unite is for them to face Vortigern and let their distaste for him fan their anger at his betrayal. Then, I am sure we can spark them into action.*"

"*I take my leave, Sir,*" *I said bowing to him.*

"*Aspirat primo Fortuna laboris! But before you go, Ambrosius, I want just a quiet word on a completely different subject.*" *He took my arm and walked with me to the furthest corner of the hall. He spoke in a whisper.*

"When you join the army, you will be asked to join the secret Rite of Mithras and to select an animal as your protector. I have artoris, the bear, and Constantine has the lion. So, I believe, does his son Uther. Have you thought which one you will select?"

"Yes, sir, I will have a local animal: old broc, the black and white badger."

"The badger!" Bruto let out a low growl in surprised disbelief. "The badger? That is a slow animal, Ambrosius. It follows the same tracks its ancestors laid down, ones they could have travelled hundreds of years ago. As it is native to here it is not known in Rome. So why choose the bloody badger?"

"I have good reason, sir. Here, the badger is the animal most feared by all the other animals. He is the most ferocious, but he is not the most aggressive. He has sharp teeth and hind claws that surprise and shock because they are poisonous. I want to hold my own and surprise and shock just like a badger. It is said around here that any badger can hold his own."

"If you choose it because it symbolises invincibility, then I agree. But remember to teach your troops about its power. Have you got its skin yet?"

"Yes and no. Doone caught and killed one and its skin has been scraped and stretched. It will not be ready until I leave for Gaul. Can I borrow your arth, your bear skin, for tonight?"

"Good thinking—you will need all its strength and stamina tonight. It will be my honour to be present at your battles through him. A bear will be best under these circumstances."

Bruto, his dear face a map weathered by years of hard fighting and softened by his tenderness, put his huge paw on my shoulder and patted it.

"Hold your own, my son!" and he walked with me to the door.

"When you are in Gaul you will hear stories about me, they blame me for everything, you know, except the centuries-old Punic Wars, because I was too young to fight in them!" Bruto roared laughing. I smiled, although I had heard this joke ten times before. I would not bear the Cotta name in Gaul for many reasons, but one of them would be to avoid his enemies settling their scores through me. I searched my mind to try to find what there was about my father that reminded me of myself but I never found the answer.

"Mother, I must go. I am uneasy about this venture. I have to fight, and as you know we do not agree with fighting and I should be exempt from it, but father ignored that argument. This is not how I planned to spend tonight."

"No. I too was hoping for something else. The digger and her daughter are in Isca and both are safe now, but at midnight they will need us because Darkness has plans. I have been able to extend your protection as far north as the Summerland and as far south as Cornwall. You have not much time."

"Well, Morgana, well? Has my enchantress planned another failure?"

"Even you will be surprised. Meet me at midnight."

13

Hip-Hop

7.30pm, Thursday September 9th, Our time

THE BUZZ OF THE AUDIENCE CEASED as the auditorium went pitch black. Up-tempo rhythms swept across the sixty people who stood in front of the stage. The air was electric.

Der de dit, der de dit—the first six ultra-amplified chords pounded the air and purple lights strafed the dancing platform like thunder and lightning. They revealed two dancers. Facing the audience stood Toby, his white hair in stiff spikes and his leg tapping the beat. He wore skinny black jeans, red and white hip-hop Nikes and a red shirt sliced down its front with a red and black tie. Beside him Emily wore identical jeans and shoes and a black sports bra with a loose, sheer red top over it. Together, they counted out loudly: one, two, three, four, before turning sideways and moon-walking. They appeared to glide above the stage; the audience loved it and cheered.

"God, I miss Michael Jackson," Jack whispered to Casey. "Miss you, MJ!" he yelled out, but nobody heard him, the music and the dance had captured its audience. As the high beam of lights circled them, the dancers synchronised their back-flips. The song's refrain began:

> *"I waited years for this one time.*
> *To move with you on the dance floor.*
> *Dance, move. Dance for this one time."*

And during this chorus Toby and Em danced a house mix of head-to-toe flicks followed by gliding until the big moment for Toby came. He leapt into an inside turning kick perfected from his tae kwon do training. The audience gasped before cheering wildly. It was simply spectacular.

Next, it was Emily's turn. In a matrix of red lights, she loosened her hair, collapsed her right knee, popped it then bounced. She rotated her shoulders, punched down and undulated her body like a belly dancer, her arms supple and fluent. She followed these movements with three slow cartwheels and a three-point turn. She ended with a cheeky over-the-shoulder toss of her head. The audience roared.

Toby completed his final dance sequence full of complex break-dancing moves and leaps, before they came together again for the last synchronised back-flip.

It was Jack who was the first to whistle and clap and yell out, "Hot, hot, hot!" The dancers bowed deeply, all smiles, waving as they ran off-stage.

They ran straight into the arms of Jo Campion, their dance instructor.

"You were fabulous! We have some timing to work on but you're ready for the final. See if you can get some rest tomorrow to be in top condition for Saturday night. And by that I mean, take it easy, no late nights!"

"We'll be in bed."

And Jack interrupted Emily, rolling his eyes.

"Really?"

Emily blushed. "I mean in separate beds, you idiot, by eleven-thirty," she assured Jo.

There was a great buzz in the foyer as the dancers jostled to be seen by the talent scouts. It was Emily and Toby who were spotted by the manager of Battle of the Bands. He was a short, round man who flashed with gold, and he wanted to sign them as an act.

"That song never gets old!" he said, patting Toby on the back. "You could do the same for us. It's a hot act."

"I'm their manager," Jack announced. "Here's my card!" and he smoothly handed over something impressive with a gold crest on it. "Can I have yours and we'll be in touch?"

Once they too had clapped one another on their backs and Mr 'Battle of the Bands' had exited, they all collapsed laughing.

"Tell him, Jack, it's the two acts," Casey said. "Our band, Brick Street, with their dance routine. We're two for the price of one."

Parents of the other contestants crowded around Toby and Emily, saying: "Great work!" and "Good on you!" as they turned on their phones and thought about taxis and worried that their children were not half as good as those two.

Toby drank it all in. He was on a high, still dancing in the foyer when he came up to Jack and whispered,

"There's this beautiful moment when her breasts are close enough to... And you know what happens? That turtle head pops out of her cleavage and glares at me."

Jack roared, "Serves you right! I'm allowed to think she's hot. You're not. She's like a sister to you!"

Suddenly, very tired and very hungry, Emily had had enough.

"Let's get pizza," she declared. "Where are Mum and Dad?"

They were with Karen, Toby's mum, both standing back a little, almost in awe of the talent of their offspring.

"You were fabulous, fabulous!" they mouthed.

"Pizza would be good," Julia said. "Let's go over the road."

Toby started singing… "Dance, move. Dance for this one time"

Casey came in with: "So don't be scared,…"

Four friends, with parents trailing, crossed the road holding hands and spinning around in utter joy, oblivious to the menace of the man dressed in black standing in the shadows, waiting for the right moment.

14

Before Moonrise

8.00pm, Thursday September 9th, Merlin's time

I F YOU STRAINED YOUR EYES, *you could make out my silhouette from the motionless jackdaw sitting on my left shoulder or the restless falcon, with her orange eyes, side-stepping along my right shoulder, but you could not be sure it was me. I stood on the stone bridge that crossed the River Exe and surveyed the legendary fortress that the Second Legion had built on its eastern bank. Behind Isca's walls I could make out its skyline of temples and baths, its basilica, and the tallest of its timber houses.*

The night was noisy. Besides the loud chirping of the crickets, it was alive with the sounds of frogs and owls and the splash of jumping fish. There was a distant flute playing, and somewhere, outside the wall, I heard the whine of the axe. Underneath those night noises, I heard rumbles: one was the sound of the river rushing over the cataract upstream of the bridge and the other was from men getting drunk at the Fosse Gate. It was time to check whether the intelligence of my father was reliable.

My merlin headed out first, with my spirit in her. Together we flew downstream to a hamlet about three and a half miles away, just where the river Clyst joins the Exe. Above it in the tang of the salty air, my falcon scanned the tidal river, looking for the approach of the boats. Doone's jackdaw had flown in the opposite direction checking the Fosse Way for five miles, with all its taverns and whorehouses. Back on the bridge, the smith watched out for us, but all he saw were two silent men sitting cross-legged and upright, staring out at a world that only we could see. But he was so excited to be back in the action, he kept pissing off the side of the bridge, interrupting my concentration.

Eventually my falcon soared, her wingspan, fully stretched at twenty-five inches, was as wide as a woman's arm was long. I could see, through the eyes of my bird, that the brothers' boats were already beached and disguised under sails of animal hide near the wharf below the fortress. Vortigern was three miles downstream in an open Norse boat but with the tide racing against him; he would take a good while to reach the wharf. He had only twelve men on board, I calculated, two less than I was given in Bruto's intelligence.

When my merlin returned to the bridge, I instructed her anew and slipped a message scrawled on a scrap of parchment into the brass ring around her leg, and together we flew back to the town's wharf. She scanned the people milling there, searching for Uther's red hair. Uther was a tall man; tall enough to be known as a giant, well over my six feet three inches. He was lean, almost gaunt, with a rough beard, which was very unusual among the clean-shaven Romans. Fortunately, right beside him was the shorter, fair-haired Ambrosius Aurelianus, the elder brother and therefore the leader of the two. But like everybody else in my realm he was known by something other than his given name and was called Aurelius, the 'golden one', because whenever he spoke or sang, golden honey poured from his mouth.

When Aurelius turned towards the falcon I saw his impediment *immediately. He was wall-eyed. One blue eye looked directly at the falcon and the other turned out from his nose and looked to heaven. We swooped onto the railing close by them. Both men looked at us curiously because my merlin has strange eyes too. She has the bright orange eyes of a sparrowhawk and not the dark eyes of a falcon, and she was out well after her roosting time. In no time her comic antics had them laughing as she tried to draw their attention to the scroll I had fixed to her leg.*

"Over here!" It was more of a command than an invitation that came from Aurelius, and she hopped over to the scholar, who gently removed the message and read it aloud to his brother.

"Spies tell us Vortigern knows your plans. He is downstream with ten men. His Saxons plan to ambush you from shore at moonrise and take you hostage. The son of Bruto will attack Saxons. Send response with my merlin. Ambrosius Cotta."

"I don't like it," Uther sounded off immediately. "How do we know this isn't a trap?" And he continued talking to his brother in a language I did not understand, although later I realised he was speaking a curious mixture of Latin, Greek, Gaulish, and the Cornish spoken in Brittany, along with other made-up words. It was their own secret language invented by two boys frequently left alone in peril overseas.

Aurelius replied in an even tone, speaking Greek,

"Let's assume you are right and this is a trap, then who is trying to trap us? Do you think it is Vortigern who is using a bird to converse with us? Then how is he setting his trap? And if it is a trap, let's be ready. If it is not a trap, and truly we are about to be attacked, then let's be ready. Either way, it is the same course of action. Our father respects Bruto and has praised the brilliance and bravery of his son, Ambrosius."

"Will you write the reply then? I would say we need to join forces. We may have to fight a frontal attack from the land and a rear attack from Vortigern coming up from the river. We are here for one

reason: to capture and kill Vortigern and we should not get distracted from it. We have barely one hour to moonrise."

Listening to their continual discussion, I commented to myself, 'If I were about to be attacked, time would be critical,' but they chattered on in their own speech. I prodded my bird to flap her wings rapidly and squawk loudly to get the brothers to hurry with their reply. Eventually Aurelius wrote,

"Need to join forces. Will place slaves as guards at our boats and move to higher ground above the river path to support you."

Deo gratius! Now I was able to withdraw my mind, confident my merlin would return to the bridge with the message I had already heard. I was not overly impressed with their secret chatter, but then I have never had a brother. I could only hope they were faster in action than they were in analysis, although they did confirm their purpose was to kill Vortigern. That was a mission I would have to abort.

Doone opened his eyes at the same moment that I opened mine.

"Master, my jackdaw saw a merry troop of ten Saxons," he announced. "Eight were almost drunk and two were past drunk and falling down. They are camped near the Fosse Gate. Isca is buzzing with much fearful talk after our Saxon raid last night, and now this. So the mayor ordered the gates shut early and doubled the guards on the ramparts."

"Tell me, Doone, did it not occur to you why those Saxons did not light a beacon and announce their presence with drumbeats? They cannot be that dumb to think they can ambush anyone after they have made such a spectacle of themselves! But why would they do that? Because, I fear, the Saxons you have seen are only decoys, and that their real strength is lying in wait for us somewhere else. Doone, ask your jackdaw to circle the town and check the south side in particular, above the wharves."

After I scrawled a new message to the brothers, I told Caballus: "Tie this to my falcon's leg as soon as she returns. I will be busy.

Point to me and say to her, 'Fly back to the red-headed man and wait for reply'. Now take my mice and mind my staff, my ropes and other things. I need to be quiet now, so, for God's sake, stop draining your dragon while I am in a trance."

The wind had been gusting strongly off the river from the south-west, and that made it useless for my purpose because all its information came from the wrong direction. Winds were my messengers; they carry weather changes, soils, smells, sounds and vapours—they were rich in all kinds of intelligence. If, on the other hand, the wind came from the east, then the foul smells and the guttural growl of the Saxons would come my way and any movements would reach my ears. And there was a third advantage: an easterly wind would further slow Vortigern's approach up the river.

Sitting again cross-legged with my back to Isca, I dug my elbows into my ribs, held my palms together at my heart, and splaying my fingers into a V, I breathed in the purple west wind. I built my vitality by inhaling and exhaling swiftly until there came a point when I was ready to explode. I threw my arms in the air and swivelled to the east while forming in my imagination a smooth, cool, pale wind that blows from that direction. I called for the help of the Archangel Lord Michael, and finished with the command, "So be it," and in doing so I brought my vision into being. The wind bounced back off the city's walls to me. It had swung to the east. I gave thanks to God. Only then did I relax.

It was time to listen. I used my six ears; two of my own and the four ears I borrowed from my mice. We consulted one another and shared what we heard carried on the east wind. We heard men, men hidden from sight, snuffling and puffing above the river path and right below the south-side walls of the city. I waited until the jackdaw of Doone confirmed their number and position, because my plan of attack was taking shape.

I took a moment to become peaceful again and look in on Emilia. She was so close to me in the Exeter of the future that I could have run to her in minutes. Emilia was dressed in trousers again and doing movements I did not know were possible with her body in dance. I envied them laughing and squealing like children on a joyful spree while I was planning havoc.

15

Ambush

9.00pm, September Thursday 9th, Merlin's time

THE MAYOR OF ISCA WAS A REASONABLE MAN, *a man not prone to alarm, but the sight of a giant man with blackened skin and teeth and wild hair teased with goose fat must have scared the living daylights out of him.*

"Honourable Sir," I bowed. "Do not be alarmed. It is I, Ambrosius Cotta."

The Mayor sighed with relief. As his eyes darted, I could almost read his thoughts: 'A Cotta! A Senatorial family, and this is the son of the richest, most powerful and most noble man this side of Londinium. Some even said Cotta was the Consul, and here was the boy hero who only last night tricked and captured five Saxons and freed our people. How low should I bow? I will go down on one knee and kiss his hand.'

Satisfied that he had exceeded what courtesy demanded, but not by too much, he said, "How can I be of service, my Lord?"

It was then I heard my mother's voice offering me advice in my head. 'When dealing with anyone in authority, always "butter them before you batter them".' So I began gently and was very fulsome in my praise.

"Sir, you are to be commended for doubling the guard on the ramparts tonight and covering each gate. These are wise moves. I am here, Sir, to help you defend your beautiful city and its surrounds from two Saxon war parties, and from a very threatening war ship coming up the Exe."

As soon as the mayor looked suitably alarmed, I continued,

"These are dangerous times. We both know of the Saxon raid last night. Now, they have their party camped at your Fosse Gate in the northwest of the town. They appear to have been drinking heavily, but it could be an artifice... a trick. They could be cold sober. There is a second group of ten men below the southern wall on the edge of the gorse and grass. I intend attacking them just before moonrise. Could you move all your guards to cover those two sections of your walls? The first group to the Fosse Gate should prevent those Saxons joining up with the other party, and the rest need to be stationed above on the Southern Wall. Below is where I plan to attack. This way you can help me defend your town!"

"Son of the noble Cotta, you are most welcome. None of our people are sleeping tonight, worried as they are of an attack. I will deploy the guards as you ask. Secretly we placed five men in our tunnel, which allows us egress during a siege. It has one entrance on the western side just below the wall, and another down at the riverside. My men will block any movement of the Saxons along the front path to the river. You can see we are thinking along the same lines. My only concern about what you have asked, my Lord, is that it will leave our eastern wall unwatched and undefended."

"What is your eastern side like?"

"It is quite unlike our other lands because it is heavily wooded and inhabited by brown bears and wolves. That means you see few deer or boar. It is a wildwood. We do not even hunt there. It is too dangerous."

"It must follow, then, that it is too dangerous a place to launch an attack from. Thank you for your help, kind sir. But show me the tunnel, maybe we can use it too."

11:05pm, Thursday September 9th, Merlin's time

Just before moonrise our blackened bodies slid quietly down ropes on the southern wall of the garrison town. Unfamiliar as the Saxons were with the sounds of night in our land, I am sure they heard nothing at all. Once hidden on the ground, my ten hoots from the long-eared owl signalled to the town guards above that they should count to ten, before they let their arrows fly.

It was Caballus who blew a horn to signal the attack. Blazing arrows arched above the heads of the Saxons who were facing the river, while Doone and I with our birds screeching, rushed at their backs. Startled, the Saxons swivelled, their arrows drawn ready to return fire. Once they were facing the fort, I let out the bark of the owl and Aurelius' men emerged from the woods to attack their exposed backs.

Overwhelmed by surprise, they were easy meat. Uther was a fast and ferocious fighter, an expert with his gladius, that short, stabbing sword we Romans used. He dodged the Saxon axes coming for his throat and gloried in the bloodshed. Quickly, three men lay dead at his feet. Doone speared one Saxon as I stabbed another in the heart. I watched as his blood sprayed down my armour and his eyes glazed. 'God rest your soul, Saxon!' It was the first time I had killed a man and I felt sick.

Aurelius, with delicate distaste, sliced up another. The remaining four just stopped fighting and laid down their arms. It was all over in ten minutes.

'Father was right,' I thought, very pleased with myself, 'it was a minor skirmish! I will clean myself of my disguise and I will be with Emilia in a little over an hour.'

As I slapped Uther on his bony back to congratulate him, I felt he was a deceptively strong man, a man of iron muscle who could easily split a hefty oak. His face shone at my praise, and with his smile of huge teeth it was like looking into the mouth of a horse. Here in him, finally, I had found a man who was tall enough to look me straight in the eye and I liked him at once.

His older brother was a clean-shaven man of natural grace and modesty who shook my hand politely. I understood that this man was not a warrior like his brother, who gloried in a red sword, because I observed his distress at the dead who lay with their faces up and their eyes open. Dismay had spread all over his face. And when he thought no one was looking, and oblivious to my watchful eye, he sneaked a glance at his only kill of the evening. It was a headless torso of a young Saxon, maybe twelve, and he lifted the boy's head to position it reverently on his chest and made the sign of a cross over him. I was aware of rumours that Aurelius planned to be a priest and had taken the first orders but the times demanded otherwise of him, and his father had snapped, 'One son a monk is enough.' I knew Aurelius was a man I could respect. Yet given what I had observed, I was puzzled where his desire to kill Vortigern came from. I suspected there was more fuelling their mission than I had been told.

I nodded a command to Caballus who sprang into action. He roped and gagged the four Saxons who had surrendered, ready to be marched to the First Spear waiting on the other side of the bridge. But first Aurelius allowed his men to strip the prisoners of their weapons and valuables before they would turn with relish to plunder the dead men. The bodies of the Saxons were piled in the clearing and covered with branches cut from the scrub around us. Because they are not Christians they would not be buried, they would be burned, but not until the next skirmish was over and plenty more of their countrymen had joined them.

I asked Aurelius' permission to call all his men together and speak to them quietly.

"Good work!" I began and motioned for them to sit. While I knew it was not usual for soldiers to sit with their commanders to listen to their strategy for the up-coming battle when they would prefer to be stashing their loot in places of safe keeping, nevertheless I stressed, "Please be seated." And I waited until Aurelius repeated my invitation and sat himself on the ground next to his brother and Doone.

"We have now only a short time to moonrise," I continued. "That is when we believe Vortigern and his men will attack. There are two threats to us as we approach this battle. Vortigern to the south of us on the river may only be minutes away with ten men. The east wind has slowed his progress, but it also carries the sounds of his approach away from us."

"The second threat is the ten Saxons who are supposedly drunk near the Fosse Gate. Doone observed these men and they look exhausted. They seem to lack the energy and vigour we have just seen from these defeated Saxons. Those drunk at the Fosse Gate are being supervised by the Isca guards. If they make any attempt to move in our direction they will block them and we will be warned by a burning arrow."

Aurelius rose to speak next.

"I agree with Ambrosius, these are our threats. But let us also look at our advantages. We are here on the highest ground and we have an easy escape route around the riverfront into the fortress. The men of our enemy are split into two groups, and with two different commanders. They do not know our landscape, and although they do not realise it yet, they have lost their element of surprise." As he finished he tapped the shoulder of Uther, who stood up and prowled as he spoke.

"*Our disadvantages are also our risks,*" *Uther began.* "*Yes, we may be outnumbered and, yes, our intelligence about the enemy is patchy. But, everything we do carries risk and I love the thrill of overcoming obstacles, as do all of you, or why would you have chosen to be soldiers?*" *The soldiers hit their swords to acclaim what Uther said. He smiled and continued with relish.*

"*Risk and danger, with no flinching, that is what I like the most and that is what I know you like too. And while I never underestimate an enemy, I know these long-haired Saxon boys, with whom I have had skirmishes before up north, are not very bright. Truly, they are real dullards. Unlike you, they cannot read or write. They tell me their language is not even written down yet.*"

Uther was enjoying himself, and laughing he bent down as if to speak to one of the men privately.

"*Do you know,*" *he said in a loud whisper, holding up his hands,* "*the Saxons cannot count past ten because they run out of fingers,*" *and the soldiers loved this and laughed. Uther mimed passing his water.* "*And they cannot hold their piss. Whether it be this one,*" *and he mimicked gulping down a tankard of beer,* "*or this one,*" *and he mimicked spraying pee everywhere. His men laughed so loudly I started to worry they would give our position away. But there was no stopping Uther.* "*I doubt if those dullards over there on the Fosse Way are worldly-wise enough to carry out the ruse of being drunk. What you see over there is what they are: they are pisspots! Merlin and the Mayor have taken moves to neutralise them as a threat.*

"*Now the real threat is that slimy turd, Vortigern. Let us assume his party saw our flaming arrows from his boat down river. If I were in his position, I would assume my Saxon pussies had just been attacked by the garrison. Besides, the east wind would have blown the tumult of our attack to him down the river. So if I were him, I would now be very cautious and worried.*"

Listening carefully, I reassessed my earlier view of the brothers' ability to analyse. I was impressed, so I too stood saying.

"I would like to build on what you both said as we have two more advantages," but before I had a chance to finish my words I caught sight of movement in the corner of my eye, and saw Doone stealthily grab his jackdaw. It was then that I heard what Doone had already heard: a chorus of wolf wails. Because I once was wolf, because I spoke wolf, I knew what their howls were saying: 'Fresh meat... and plenty of it'. But what kind of fresh meet was it? Bear? No. Deer? No. Then what?

An owl screeched in alarm. It was the call she used when she sensed intruders near her home. And I knew what that meant, too. The fresh meat that was causing those wolves to salivate was moving through the dense undergrowth, and it was not woodland game, it was human. A few seconds later, when the east wind blew the guttural voices of Saxons towards us, it confirmed the owl's warning. I knew then I had miscalculated and should not have relied on the advice of the mayor. I should have investigated the wildwood below the eastern wall myself. I had underestimated Vortigern. I realised we had just ambushed his advance party. Now we had two, and possibly three more war parties to contend with. I hoped Uther's portrayal of one of them as drunken soldiers was right.

"Pick up all your weapons now!" I commanded. "Knock the prisoners on their heads and prepare for an attack!" Quietly I said to the brothers, "Doone and I will gather more intelligence."

To their bewilderment, Doone and I released our birds like game-hawkers before sitting down cross-legged and seemingly going to sleep. Uther assumed we were praying.

"Ambrosius and his slave must be asking God who is coming!" he joked to Aurelius, interrupting my trance.

"Shush, shush, they use birds!" his brother cautioned. "They use them the way we use scouts, and that way they get a bird's-eye view of everything. That falcon—it is a merlin I am sure—was his messenger to us. We can learn a lot from this!"

The jackdaw of Doone took off in the direction of the howl of the wolf pack, while my falcon headed down to the river and to the wharf. Minutes later we were back. Doone reported first:

"At least twenty-strong coming from the east, heavily armed in helmets and body armour, carrying swords, spears, axes and shields. Some are archers. With the east wind at their backs, once they are into that clearing, the wind will carry their arrows far."

"I have seen Vortigern," I began, "who has just moored at the wharf and left his slaves there to guard his boat. I watched him slit the throats of your two guards, Aurelius. Counting himself, he has eleven men. Doone saw at least twenty of them there in the east, so they have a minimum of thirty-one—and we have thirteen—that is more than two to one. We have twenty-three swords and fifteen quivers of arrows. So we are not exactly an overwhelming force.

"Earlier, however," I continued, "before the animals warned us of trouble, I was about to tell you about the tunnel entrance on the western wall of Isca. I suggest you withdraw your men through there and head up to the ramparts. Once there, you could give us some cover."

Uther broke in.

"Yes, if we stay here we will all be out in the open and too exposed, and those coming from the east will have the cover of the woods, but there is enough coverage for you and Doone to hide here and surprise them. From above we will have a good vantage before we rush down to help you finish them off."

"And the Mayor of Isca sees it in his best interests to cooperate with us," I added. "He has twelve guards on duty tonight and an arsenal of weapons, including huge logs soaked in oil if we need them. As you say, Doone and I will stay down here. I have a few ideas of my own with fire and wind to make life very uncomfortable for them."

Uther added very quietly to his brother, "And I have some ideas to make life very uncomfortable for Vortigern before I cut the turd's throat!"

I realised that to obey my father's command, that Vortigern attend the Moot, I would have to protect my enemy from my ally.

I signalled to Doone to sit out of sight while I checked in again with Emilia, anxious that for the next hour to the rising of the full moon, I would not be able to protect her at all. But there she was, safe in a car about a mile away, humming a song without a care in the world. 'Not long, Emilia, not long. Stay safe!'

16

The River Road

10.45pm, Thursday September 9th, Our time

I T WAS A BEAUTIFUL NIGHT. The river ran fast after recent rains so Emily lowered the windows in the back seat of their Subaru Forester to catch the wet breeze from the weirs on her face while she hummed *The first time ever I saw your face*.

Rhys had turned onto the Bonhay Road after a quick visit to Exeter University. Julia had picked up her underground kit for tomorrow's exploration of the granary.

'how ru?' Jack texted. 'v happy singing away', Emily replied, 'tired just want 2 sleep'. Emily watched her mother checking one item after another from her kit. She feared, as soon as she was through, a deep and meaningful inquisition would begin from her parents. 'When in fear of d&m's, distract'.

"Hey, Mummy dearest, how do you think your godson danced?"

"He was fabulous!" she replied, a Maglite in one hand and a headlamp in the other, "and when he did his inside turning back kick—that 540 degree crescent kick—it took my breath away!"

She shook her head in her amazement. "It should be deemed impossible, but he does it anyway. But when you popped your arms, Em, and rolled your head and rotated your shoulders, it was as if this wave passed through you..."

Without warning, Rhys braked to avoid a man, almost invisible in black, who dashed across the road from the right-hand footpath.

"Who the hell was that?" Rhys cried out. "I almost didn't see that idiot!" It was just where the road squeezed in, to allow parking on one side and a path on the riverside. And it was there that the iron railing was down, replaced by bright orange webbing. Rhys quickly glanced into his rear vision mirror to check if anyone was about to rear-end him, but the road was pitch black. It was eerily quiet, even for ten forty-five on a Thursday night.

Suddenly a man's arm thrust through Emily's window and yanked her door open. He flung himself over her yelling,

"I have a knife at your throat! Keep still!"

Emily cried out, "Merlin!" and went quiet, overwhelmed by a rancid smell.

Rhys responded by swinging the car violently to try to propel the intruder back through the open door. Meanwhile Julia reacted just as instinctively; she turned calmly in her seat and, with cold calculation, smashed his head with her Maglite. The blow glanced off his forehead, leaving a bloody gash. Furious, he lurched forward and yanked her hair to slam her head into the headrest. Meanwhile, Rhys roared the engine only to have to swerve to avoid a black Land Rover trying to pass him on his inside from the parking lane. Gripping the wheel tightly, he crossed for a moment onto the wrong side of the road, overcorrected and the car fishtailed and veered towards the river. Julia screamed as the car dashed through the webbing, plunging down the narrow embankment to instantly smash into a tree. The car's airbags exploded on impact and its descent into the river was stopped in a crunch of metal. The carjacker was flung through the open door and left groaning on the bank.

"Everyone okay?" Rhys asked, breathless and shaken.

"Yes, yes!" Julia cried." I'm fine. Emily… my God, I can't see her behind the bag!"

"Out now everyone! "Rhys ordered. "There could be a fire."

Struggling to free herself from her inflated airbag, Julia finally found her seatbelt clasp and let herself out. Only Emily was silent. She did not move. Rhys pushed open his door, but as he reached towards her door he slid backwards towards the river.

"Are you all right, sir?" a polite voice asked, flashing torchlight in his face and offering a hand to steady him.

"Who the bloody hell are you?"

"I am Gerry Hawkins and that's John Frobisher. We're his lordship's bodyguards. He sent two squads of us to keep an eye on Emily and your family after what happened to his son this afternoon."

"Thank God! Gerry, John, pleased to meet you both! Could you help Julia, my wife, while I get my daughter out of the back seat? She seems to be lost in an airbag."

Clawing his way through the bag he found Emily breathing, but very pale and still. Her eyes were closed. Roget had his long neck out peeping to see what was going on.

"We'd better not move her," Gerry cautioned, grasping Rhys by the arm. "She might have a spinal injury."

Her eyes flew open in alarm.

"No, I can move!" she protested. "I'm just praying to St Christopher and thanking him for keeping me alive. Everything's all right. Where's that creep?"

"I've got him," Frobisher called out.

Hawkins now offered his hand to Julia to hoist her up to the roadway, while Rhys lifted Emily out.

"I'm okay. I can walk. Really, Dad, I'm okay!"

"I've just called an ambulance," Frobisher said.

"Shouldn't we call the police?" Julia asked, knowing that their accident should immediately be notified to the authorities.

"We're taking care of all of that, Mam. Why don't you sit in that BMW over there while we attend to your car? We have a towrope in the Land Rover. After I put flares along the roadway, we'll haul your car back up. It could still be driveable."

When Julia had settled Emily into the back seat, she asked Frobisher:

"Where did this BMW come from?"

It was black like the other car, and she thought anxiously that it was the colour favoured by drug dealers. And there was something else that worried her… their names. Was it just a coincidence that they had the names of two of Devon's most famous seadogs? 'All we need now is Francis Drake…'

"Sorry, Professor, I should have explained, that car is our back-up. You just make yourself comfortable and we'll take care of all the details."

"Two large cars, four armed men…" Rhys laughed nervously, trying to make light of the Duke's generosity for what he thought was an over the top response. "The Duke must have been expecting a terrorist attack!"

"Sir, we did think kidnapping was a possibility," said Hawkins curtly. "This evening when you were in the restaurant, we saw that fellow hanging around and got approval from the Castle for backup to follow you home."

"Glad you did. Where is he now?"

"Over there, handcuffed to the guardrail, moaning his head off."

When Emily settled Roget once more in her bra, she spread her coat over her lap. She tried to tune into the young man who had vowed to protect her, but dismissed it thinking, 'Merlin is a million miles away, and tonight it will be Jack who can help me.'

Underneath her coat she texted him: 'thanx 4 yr help. were car-jakt. yr men saved us. waiting 4 cops. luv Em'. The text was sent at 10.54pm.

Jack texted back almost immediately saying: 'our men went home. not ours. where ru?'

Emily went pale and felt light-headed.

By 10.55pm she had replied: 'bonhay rd. just b4 ftbrdge. HELP HELP EM'.

"Mum, I'm going to be sick!" she announced loudly. "Let's get out of here!"

Her mother climbed out, alarmed. She knew better than anyone that Emily had a weakness in her stomach and could descend into fits of violent vomiting whenever she got stressed. Emily started retching loudly as one of the bodyguards hovered behind her.

"The ambulance will be here in a moment," he said, trying to reassure her.

"Maybe, but I'd like some privacy!" she demanded rather than asking politely, and she waved him away. "Mum," she whispered, "put your coat around me and listen. I am not throwing up so calm down, right? I've just texted Jack, and now I want you to read what he texted back to me." As soon as Julia had read both texts, Emily asked, "What do we do?"

"You text him to call the police, urgently, to the accident. I'll speak to Rhys in Welsh. Could you do some more very loud dry retching to cover me?"

When Emily slipped behind a bush to gag, it was the last time Julia remembered seeing her daughter.

She turned around quickly to grab Rhys' foot just as he was climbing into the BMW.

"I need a hug, come with me!" she said as she threw her arms around him and walked down the river side of the road away from Emily. After she whispered the alarming news, she finished it with: "Keep smiling and tell me what we're going to do."

"We're going to ask Em to call Myrddin again," replied Rhys in Welsh.

"Is he a copper?"

"No, he's a magician."

Julia looked at him in amazement.

"Darling, are you in shock? This is not the time for party tricks."

"No. I've been trying to tell you how Myrddin has been protecting you and Emily."

"Well, he's doing a lousy job!"

"On the contrary, all of us are alive, despite these continual attempts on our lives. Someone wants to stop you digging at the Castle and is trying to hurt Em, to stop you!"

"Which Myrddin do you mean? The Merlin of King Arthur or someone else?"

"The Myrddin of King Arthur's Court."

"Rhys, get real, he's been dead a very long while and he was probably never alive in the first place."

"Listen to me. Yesterday the roof collapsed: a jackdaw saves you. Dog attack this morning: jackdaws save us. Bird strike nearly brings down Jack's plane this afternoon: our Em pulls out of that joy ride on his plane but only at the last minute. Two attempts on her before three pm. Now there is this one and the day's not over yet.

"This afternoon I was debating all of this with Em while you were doing the TV interview. She said Merlin, dressed in a Roman tunic, returned your sunglasses last night. She showed me the glasses and his photo and she says you burst through the roof of the granary of his family's villa. I'm sceptical, until this boy— no… he was a young man… steps out of our pantry speaking Welsh, dressed in Roman clothes and jewellery; looking as exquisite as a museum piece. I test him in both classical Greek and

Latin. He speaks the trading Greek of the fifth century, absolutely the right Greek for the Britain in Myrddin's time. He moved from one language to another with the ease of an educated boy and topped it off with a bravado performance of Homer and Virgil, with rapid changes of languages before he started Caesar's Gallic Wars in Latin. And that was when I held up the white flag of surrender. I do not doubt he knows all one hundred thousand plus words of it by heart. It was then he created an illusion that he was dancing on the ceiling with Emily. And Merlin comes when she calls him. You heard her call out to him in the car!"

"Well, Myrddin, where the bloody hell are you when we need you?" Julia demanded in Welsh.

"I am right here," Merlin replied, softly.

"I can hear you, but I can't see you!" Julia replied.

"I am not showing myself. Emily was in danger so I just helped her into the ambulance. I'll look after Emily if you can look after yourselves."

Julia immediately became anxious. "What ambulance, I didn't see any ambulance!"

There was something about his voice that worried Rhys too. As a man gifted with perfect pitch and a sharp ear for language, Rhys knew there was something wrong about this voice; it was too light compared with the voice he heard this afternoon. He asked Merlin the next question in Greek.

"Merlin, you have not met my wife, Julia, have you? But it's hard being introduced if we can't see you. Why don't you show yourself and we could talk about what to do next?"

"I have put the keys to this car under the front wheel," he said, and Rhys immediately recognised the ancient Greek of the classics, not the trading Greek that Merlin used previously that afternoon. "Take the keys and drive quickly away and I'll meet you at your place with Emily."

"Thanks very much for your help," Rhys replied in Classical

Greek.

Once they were alone, Rhys whispered in Julia's ear,

"Darling, put your arms around me again because that wasn't Merlin. He spoke the wrong Greek, and whoever he was, he says he's got 'Emily' and Merlin doesn't call her Emily—he calls her Emilia; you know if you think in Latin you need a word ending in something like '-a' so that you can decline it easily. So I'm going to call her now."

"I've got our University security on speed dial, I'll call them."

But before she could contact them the night air was full of sirens and a large black Bentley arrived, driven by a man in a dinner suit. Jack, Toby and Casey spilled out of its doors. Two police cars followed, their bright blue lights strobing the night. They parked across the road, completely blocking the access and immediately put up blue and white tapes to set up a crime scene.

"We're here!" Toby announced loudly, just in case no one had noticed. "Are you okay?"

"Where's Emily?" Jack demanded.

"We don't know." Rhys then said quietly to Julia, "I'm not getting any answer from her phone. It goes to voicemail."

Hawkins barked commands to his men, and abandoning the Land Rover, they dived back into their BMW. Discovering the keys had gone, they were out again, in time for the waiting police.

"What are we going to charge them with?" the constable asked his superior.

"That one handcuffed to the railings, he tried to hijack our car and held a knife at Emily's throat," Julia said. "They've got to be criminal offences."

"And the others working with him almost forced me off the road and caused the car accident you can see down there."

"Which one is handcuffed to the railings?" the constable

asked, "Because I can't see anyone."

"He was there a few minutes ago," Julia insisted, "I just saw him!"

"Well, he's gone now!" he replied.

Answering a previous question, Jack said,

"You could charge them with identity theft and acting under false pretences, because they all impersonated the bodyguards of my father, the Duke of Dartmoor. But the most important thing, for my father and myself, is to find out who they really are, who sent them, and why they are masquerading as his staff."

"We'll do that back at the station, Sir."

"Where's Emily?" Jack asked again, urgently this time. "She can't have just disappeared!"

"Supposedly she was taken without our knowledge or permission away in an ambulance," Rhys insisted.

"The last time I saw her was only five or six minutes ago," Julia added, "and she was behind this bush bent double as if she was vomiting."

"Em texted Toby and me at 10.56, saying HELP, HELP," Casey added.

"That's immediately after Emily texted me at 10.55 saying the same thing," Jack said. "So that's the last time we heard from her."

"I suppose she could have been taken away in the ambulance." Rhys was now very worried and blaming himself for taking Merlin at his word when he promised to protect her. "But why didn't we see the ambulance or hear it? They are not exactly stealth bombers, you know! Why didn't she call out goodbye like she always does?"

The police officer-in-charge called the Emergency Department of the Royal Devon and Exeter Hospital and was informed there had been no admissions in the last hour and no call-outs for ambulances.

"We'll turn on our searchlights to check this area," the officer suggested to reassure Rhys. "She might have been dazed and wandered away, or your missing man may have abducted her. In the meantime, we'll put out a general call for any ambulances seen anywhere in this vicinity."

"My God, she is really missing, isn't she?" Julia cried, as if the reality was just dawning on her.

"Maybe not, because she's just texted me," Toby said as his phone pinged.

"And me." It was Jack.

"And me!" It was Casey.

"Well, what does it say?" Rhys demanded.

The identical messages sent to her three friends said: 'dartmmmmmmmmm o'. It was sent at 11:05.

"But what the hell does that mean?" Casey asked.

"Hey, the dart part could stand for Dartmoor or the River Dart, or Dartmouth, or the Duke of Dartmouth pub, or Dartmoor Castle," Jack offered, as the others shook their heads at his every suggestion.

"What about all the 'm's?" Casey persisted. "They have got to be significant."

"What if she held her finger down and the 'm" repeated because she's got concussion and was not thinking clearly," Toby said. "I bet she was trying to say Dartmouth because there's a hospital there."

"Then why did she put the 'o' last and not 'th'?" Casey asked.

"An 'o' means 'love', Casey," Toby explained. "It's her sign-off."

They all looked at one another perplexed. Jack tried a different approach and turned to the police officer.

"Would it be possible, sir, for you to trace where Emily is from the location of the phone towers she used to text us?" And when the policeman looked perplexed, Jack persisted: "You have that technology, don't you?"

The policeman nodded.

"Yes, we have, sir. If you lend me your phone I will get it checked now."

"But what if she wasn't in an ambulance?" Julia asked. "We were only across the road for no more than a few minutes."

Rhys said, "All I saw were shadows and a flickering light and then she wasn't there any more."

The police officer nodded patiently. He had experienced many accident victims who were nursing concussion and claimed to have seen all kinds of amazing things.

Julia turned her face away because she had started to weep.

"I have only one child to hug and kiss and now she's gone!" she whispered to Rhys.

When Toby saw his godmother crying, he was amazed because he had never seen her like this before. Julia had so many sharp edges; he had to be careful not to get cut anytime he was around her. It was now starting to sink in for him how serious this all was.

The police officer stepped forward.

"It's a busy night for us. We've just had a report of a grass and gorse fire in southern Exeter and a three-car pile-up on the A30 at Whiddon Down near Okehampton."

"Were you able to track her phone?" Jack asked excitedly.

"The station has just called," the officer said. "The victim used the Whiddon Down tower to send those texts."

"That's off the A30. So she's heading for Okehampton, or to the Castle, or to Dartmoor," Jack volunteered. "Or even Cornwall…"

"My colleague lives in Whiddon Down," Rhys interrupted him. "And it's at least 15 miles and over twenty minutes away from here. She'd only been missing five or six minutes at the most when she texted all of you at 11.05. How can she have travelled that far in that time?"

"Maybe she's flying!" Toby said, trying to lighten the mood. "But now we know where she's gone, maybe we can work out what the 'm's' mean in her message?"

"I have an idea," Casey said. "How many 'm's' are there?"

"Nine," said Jack, "followed by zero."

"What if it's not zero or an 'o', meaning love, but it stands simply for a circle? Then the message would read… 'Dart', as in Dartmoor; nine 'm's as in the Nine Maidens; the circle as in Stone Circle! Remember, it was where we went yesterday to do the dare and where we heard that baby crying? That must mean the Nine Maidens Stone Circle at Belstone!"

"You've got it! Let's go!" Jack cried. Then speaking to the silent man in the dinner suit, he directed, "Alfred, straight to Dartmoor!"

"We can't drive to the Nine Maidens, Your Lordship, it's on the Moor!"

"I'm sure there'll be a track; try to get as close as you can!" Jack was already in the front seat. "Let's go!"

17

Baal's Stones

11.05pm, Thursday September 9th, Our time

LIFTED BY AN UNSEEN FORCE, Emily had no idea what was happening to her. One moment she was listening to her parent's Welsh, the next she was in the air. Overwhelmed by a putrid smell, her first thought was dramatic… 'I am dead and my flesh has started to rot!' But as soon as she felt a sensation similar to the one from last night, when she flew with Merlin to the Saxon camp, she figured she must be flying again but clearly not with him. It was then that she looked down and saw the four lanes of the A30 buzzing its way to Okehampton and nothing could have reassured her more. 'I haven't gone very far at all; I am still in Devon and still in the twenty-first century.' Never had that beautiful highway looked as good as at that moment.

It was then that one of her father's favourite dictums came to her mind: 'cogito ergo sum; I think, therefore I am.' She reasoned: 'If I can smell and if I can see, and most of all, if I can think, therefore I must be alive, and not dead. But I am scared and dry-mouthed. What is St Christopher doing about this?

Where is Merlin? Help, please, please, please!'

It was when she realised she was sitting on something, something that smelled awful, something that carried her in the sky in an undulating movement, something that was soft, that flapped, and squeaked... she knew it was a... a giant bat. And bats spread diseases like Ebola. Her skin crawled. 'Oh my God!'

Slowly they lost height and landed in a parking lot. Immediately she knew where she was. She was in Whiddon Down, just behind the Post Inn, and she could smell their famous roast lamb dinner. 'So,' she reasoned, 'I must have travelled west and quite fast, and because this village is the highest place on the A30, it could be an energy point where they could refuel their flight. Just like when Merlin stopped, last night, to recharge his staff. Whatever the hell that means! How do you refuel a bat?'

When her pilot climbed down, Emily followed. There was whispering, in a language she couldn't understand, to somebody she couldn't see. There were two words which made sense: Baal, pronounced to rhyme with 'hail', and the word 'stone'. She knew what Baal stone meant because her mother was always telling her the meaning of place names, and it could have been the original meaning of Belstone, a village three miles from the Castle at Okehampton. 'Could that be where we are headed?'

Then two more words made sense: 'fuchs' and 'glofe'. Fox? Glove? Foxglove? A flower? Or, could it be her experience yesterday with foxes and the missing glove? Suddenly she remembered the foul odour that she smelt just before she realised her glove was missing.

'Hey, wait a minute, I smelled it again just when that man forced himself into our car. They were the same nauseating stench drenching my senses now. Could the man who has abducted me also be the man who stole my glove yesterday and gave it to the mastiff? It seems we are going back to the Nine Maidens!' Standing next to a wall, she blindly texted her friends in code. 'And just in case Merlin cares what is happening to me, I will murmur his name as well.'

An older, blonde woman with thick plaits came through the wrought iron gate of the pub and smiled at her.

"Have a sip of water, dear, you look done in!" Emily gulped it down thirstily.

"Thank you so much," she said. "Can you help me? I've been kidnapped!" And when the woman looked puzzled, she phrased it differently: "Look, I've been abducted. Could you get me help?"

"I know, dear..."

"Does that mean that the others have been taken, too?"

"You are not alone." And she faded from Emily's view.

'Where did that woman go? I can't see her any more. I can barely move. I feel thirsty. I've been drugged.' That very thought, and the putrid smell, made her retch and in slow motion she watched some pizza pour from her mouth to the ground between her feet. Then she heard the words 'ex sanguis' and knew it was Latin. It meant something like 'blood loss', but she wasn't injured. Maybe they were talking about the man who attacked her. He bled over her after Mum hit him on the head.

She was feeling a lot better, when a metallic voice like a voice disguised electronically said,

"Come here, my lovely! No point in calling Merlin, he cannot help you now. We are going where you cannot be found. Our transport this evening is my beautiful bat, Mot. She carries rabies so make sure you do not do anything to annoy her or she could bite you. Up we go!"

The moon had just risen and Emily was able to use its light to look for landmarks. They passed over the hill of Belstone, where thatched houses surrounded the village green, before the darkness of Dartmoor. Only seconds to go. At least she had company; her Roget was safely tucked away.

They landed quietly on Belstone Tor where shadowy figures greeted her abductor. Once more on firm ground, Emily realised she could barely move. She slid into a sitting position, her back up against a rock, and vomited again.

'Oh my God, help me, I feel like I'm going to die! I can't remember why I am here. I can't remember where I am. I can't remember who I am!'

A moment later Emily blacked out.

18

The Legend of the Nine Maidens

11.10pm, Thursday September 9th, Our time

A S SOON AS ALFRED REVERSED THE CAR OUT, Jack asked him, "You know the local stories and legends; why do you think anyone would take a girl to a place like this?"

"Well, it's a girls' place, if you know what I mean, sir." Alfred spoke with a Devon burr. "There are lots of legends about Dartmoor and about the Nine Maidens. The main story is that maybe a thousand years ago, maybe more, young girls, all unplucked maidens, used to dance around this circle on a Sunday. It was blasphemy, of course, to dance on a Sunday. Those girls were punished and turned into stone. But that wasn't enough, so there was further punishment and the maidens had to dance every day at midday for all eternity."

This was not quite the story that Jack remembered: "Isn't there something far darker than that to the story?" he persisted.

"Yes. It's very gruesome, my lord, and it's probably why this Christian story was invented to replace the original story to make sure that nobody ever went there. There's a tradition that traders from the Middle East came here for their tin and copper. They found the ancient stone circles, used by the Druids as lunar calendars, back when these circles were complete with twenty-eight stones. They hired the Cornish tin miners to tunnel caves underneath the stones. These caverns were more like dungeons, where if you screamed all day you'd never be heard. There was a stone altar in the centre with a gutter around its edge. There at midnight the traders sacrificed young maidens or newly born babes to their god Baal. They cut their victims' wrists until they bled to death, and you can guess what they did with their blood..."

"They drank it," Toby offered, enthralled by the story.

"You've just made me feel very sick," Casey said. Her sense of foreboding was growing after her own experiences there, and she wanted re-assurance. "Nobody does those dreadful things any more. You can't seriously think that could happen to Emily?"

"What did you just tell me happened yesterday?" Toby asked. "Didn't you say you heard a baby crying in the centre under the stones? Didn't you say it was like there was light behind the stones, as if there was a chamber underneath?"

"Yes, that's right, but..." Casey protested.

"Well, then..." Toby replied as if he'd found the answer. "Do you guys know the human body has six litres of blood in it? That's far more than the sacrificial lamb Christians used, which only has less than half a litre."

"Toby, how is that information useful at this very moment?" Casey asked, amazed at his lack of sensitivity.

"Well, it shows if it's blood you're after, humans offer much better value to sacrifice than lambs," Toby continued, smiling.

Casey punched him, "Will you put a sock in it?"

"I think you're both being histrionic," Jack interrupted. "There have been four so-called attacks on the family in twenty-four hours: the cave-in, the dog attack, the bird strike on my plane and the carjack tonight. We don't know for sure they are linked; and if they are, we don't know who's doing it, and we don't know why they're doing it."

"Jack, how much worse do you think this has to get before you realise someone is trying to kill Emily?" Casey was exasperated with him. "Didn't your father send bodyguards tonight? He clearly thought something's wrong! Given there's now been a fifth attack on Emily since she's been abducted, isn't it safe to conclude that she's in grave danger and that taking her to that site is highly suspicious?"

Jack's phone rang.

"Yes, Dad," he said. "We'll be at the Castle in five minutes. Could you ask Lawson to organise my kit? We'll be heading out again straight away."

19

Moonrise

11.10pm, Thursday September 9th,
Merlin's time

*A*S SOON AS *A*URELIUS AND *U*THER *withdrew with their men into the garrison, I gave my possessions to Doone.*

"Put our birds and mice in some safe place away from all the smoke and embers and send out whatever alarm calls you can to alert other creatures that there is danger coming."

Once again, I had to master the wind and change its direction. But I could not concentrate. All I could hear were the distress calls from Emilia. Her first call of the evening had been playful. The next became pleading; now she was panicky. I saw her captured by Morgana and each time she has called me for my protection, the protection I had promised her father to provide, I have had to bounce her pleas over to Ingraine. Even my mother is feeling overwhelmed.

"Myrddin," she protested, "how much longer are you going to be? Whenever you or your fox go into Emilia's time to look around, Morgana can follow your trail and be there causing trouble too. Now she has followed Dolossus' trail and captured Emilia, who is white with terror. Whatever is her predicament, you must be loyal to the

commands of your father and let me manage her for you."

"Do you not think I know all of that? I am torn because all I want to do is to drop everything and go to her, right now."

"That is not a good idea. Your family must come first, not someone you have just met. Be comforted, I will keep her safe for you."

All I could do was mumble, "You know I do not want to be here, Ingraine. Earlier I sent my fox across, and yes, I knew the risk, but I can use him to watch what is happening to her, and if I see they are going to harm her, you know what I will do. Our last battle was over quickly, and I hope this one will go the same way."

"You must carry out the commands of your father, Myrddin!" Ingraine insisted, raising her voice—something she never did—and added, "For Britannia and for all of us. There is too much at stake!"

Reluctantly, I agreed, not knowing what was supposed to be at stake here. Was this not a minor skirmish? 'Let's get this battle over with, and over quickly.'

I measured my breathing, and once it was regular, I built my energy until, on my command, the easterly wind swirled around again to blow as a gusting westerly. Like an infant having a tantrum, I threw myself on the earth and lay with my ear to the ground; the rumbles told me that the group ascending from the river was no more than five minutes away, while the party from the east would arrive a minute or two after them. My timing had to be precise. Everything had to happen fast: fire, smoke, dust, noise, wind, blur, followed by dizziness and panic. I signalled to everyone above to be ready.

Withdrawing a flint and a fire steel from my pouch, I struck the rust off the iron to ignite a bed of dry moss. It flared quickly. I torched the grass and gorse and watched the wind lift my flames towards the Saxons advancing from the east.

I signalled Doone again, who in turn signalled Aurelius on the ramparts, and his archers drew back, their arrows in readiness. Aurelius walked behind them and patted their shoulders to calm their nerves, murmuring their names. Above the crackle of the flames, I heard Aurelius cry,

"We are Romans and children of God and Britannia. Heavenly Father, protect us! Let us humble these pagan barbarians one more time."

I am sure each of his men straightened, becoming taller as he spoke with them.

"Cry Victoria!" Aurelius called out, and he paused while patting the air to quieten them, continuing in a hushed tone, "Now hold your fire until I give the command."

Once the dry gorse caught, the flames spread rapidly creating clouds of suffocating smoke. It was an angry fire, full of orange and red because that was how I felt and my emotions leapt across into my creation. I was angry. I was angry because I was in an impossible position trying to protect a vile man from two rightfully vengeful brothers, while the girl I had vowed to protect faced death. The fire was not enough for me, and because I wanted this battle over even before it began, I scattered a pungent herb into its flames. I slung my staff, like an animal, across my shoulders and hooked both my arms over it to stabilise it. I turned in a circle, slowly at first until I mastered my footing, then faster and faster, rotating like a shot-putter winding up for the perfect pitch.

At first, my whirlwind only limped into life, but with each turn it gained more uplift until, with a loud whoosh it flared up, and as Vortigern reached the clearing, the fire leapt away towards the moon rise. And whatever that bastard imagined was going to happen when he arrived at the fort of Isca, he could never have imagined this. He did not expect to be assailed by a storm of dust, ash, soot and cinders, and the intoxicating fragrance in the smoke that made his head reel, his eyes run and his throat burn. The archers on the ramparts held their fire until I stopped spinning. I quickly calmed the wind, and when it stut-

tered to a stop, there was only one beat of my heart before the large Saxon party from the east, their weapons drawn, burst into the clearing.

I threw myself on the ground and wriggled out of sight before Aurelius yelled,

"Victoria! Shoot!"

First the arrows, then the spears, rained from the battlements into the coughing and sneezing Saxons. Some fell screaming onto the burning ash while others fell down with arrows in their necks or legs. Then it was my moment! I rose slowly from the smoke as an enormous bear standing over seven feet tall, and when a wail of terror spread through the Saxons I felt a touch of pity for their fate.

"Who's there?" Vortigern demanded. His handsome face was grotesque in the moonlight. He yelled again, "Answer me! Who is doing this shit?"

Using the pause in the fighting for its full dramatic effect, I spread my paws to create a howling enchantment. I created tens of vicious bears that rushed from every direction. As they pounced, the Saxons saw them gnaw and tear at their arms and legs. Their screams pierced the night.

It was time for our second attack. Aurelius and Uther, together with their men, rushed down from the battlements into the confusion. The Saxons were stuck in a firestorm, and while the growling bears terrified them, the new fighters who came at them from above simply bewildered them, and not knowing which way to move, they were easily skewered on our swords.

It was then that I saw something almost hidden in the smoke, something I did not expect to see, and something I am sure no one else expected me to see. I saw Doone jerk his head up ever so slightly to Vortigern; it was just the smallest movement of his head, and I saw Vortigern lift his little finger in a tiny acknowledgement of him. It was a move so slight it was almost not there at all, but the impact of their gestures boomed across the battlefield to me. I saw *that they knew one another! But how could they know one another? What did it mean?*

I, Myrddin the bear, rushed at Vortigern, the betrayer, who was blindly swatting with his sword everything he thought moved, and when I kicked my left foot into his groin it felt like it was armour-plated. Vortigern swore violently and doubled over, clutching himself. Despite my foot being so badly bruised that I could only hobble, I was able to grab his sword with both my hands and wrench it out of his grasp. I backhanded him with the hilt of his own sword before I dragged him out of harm's way, leaving the Saxons without a leader and leaving my comrades to clear up the battlefield. Meanwhile, I did the bidding of my father and saved this wretched man from the wrath of the sons of Constantine. I sent Doone home to prepare our villa for the prisoners, and to keep him well apart from Vortigern until I had understood what their connection was.

When the battle was over, Aurelius prowled the smoking scene and counted aloud each of the Saxon dead until he stopped at twenty-three.

"Victoria!" He called out in jubilation, waving his sword above his head. "Victoria! Deo gratias! Merlino gratias!"

There were eleven wounded, some so severely it was just a matter of time. Then Uther assessed the damage to our own troops: three dead, seven wounded. It was truly a glorious victory! Aurelius directed his able men to take prisoners and pulled aside Christopher, one of his men who spoke the Saxon language. Uther wanted him to question the captives, and to do so very carefully. And, if their answers were not forthcoming, he wanted them to know that he, Uther, would personally cut off an ear, then another ear, and then a nose until all the answers came screaming out of their mouths. He wanted to find out who was in charge of their Isca expedition and how long they had been lying in wait for us. He wanted to know whether his brother and himself were their targets, and if they were, was the purpose to kidnap them for ransom or to kill them? And if they were not the targets, who or what was? Holding Christopher by the wrist, Uther demanded any scrap of gossip that could be extracted from them about Vortigern. On mouthing the name of Vortigern, Uther swivelled around looking for him. It was then that he realised his quarry was missing.

And so was I.

20

What Troubles Merlin

11.30pm, Thursday September 9th, Merlin's time

THERE WERE PLENTY OF THINGS *that troubled me that night. Before I could hunt down Morgana, before I could rescue Emilia, I, too, had to understand the role of Vortigern in tonight's attack and understand as well what role my father played. Once I was sure of what had really happened here, my anger could abate and the calm I needed to confront the Dark could return.*

So I paced the river path, keeping a close eye on the inert Vortigern and churning over the questions of the night. It was only four and a half hours ago that my father surprised me with this special assignment. It was a mission to protect the two sons of his dear friend, and to ensure they did not murder Vortigern, a man Bruto described as a 'crafty little shit'.

I reviewed all intelligence Bruto had given me, about Vortigern's boat, about the men travelling with him, about the time and place of their attack; and his intelligence was indeed accurate, as was my father's information about Aurelius and Uther's boat, and their men and their plan of attack. Yet his intelligence missed two whole troops of men.

Bruto's spies must be better than that. He had framed my assignment as a minor skirmish between the sons of Constantine and their enemy, and I never questioned this. And that led me into errors. Those errors were serious and they could have been fatal because they led me to underestimate the tactics and strength of my enemy. For example, that everyone would agree it was too risky to march forces through a wildwood of wolves and bears, and I had assumed no one would be dumb enough to do it, ever! But that was exactly what Vortigern did. He exposed his troops to extreme danger, and there was no evidence that he lost even one of them. How was that so? Was he crafty or was he getting some unseen protection?

And my father, a seasoned campaigner with over ten years as a general, must have known that the plans of Vortigern were not merely for a stoush. His plans were detailed enough for a major engagement, and they would have had to have been hatched months ago. Bruto, more than anyone else in Britannia, must have known that to move at least forty Saxons, from Brough in the far north on the Humber River to the southwest in Isca, would be at least four hundred miles by land, and maybe more by sea. His men had to be recruited from Saxony; then trained, armed, fed and transported by sea to be fresh to fight. Why had my father downplayed this encounter? Why had he not briefed me properly? Why had I not asked more questions? Why had I deferred to him?

It was only last night when I had engaged and captured a Saxon raiding party and observed their Norse-style keels beached on the Exe, that I knew they were large enough to carry a total of fifty men. But I had not linked those boats with the encounter this evening and nor had my father. But he should have. My father had been fully informed of our success. But why had not I, Myrddin, linked the two? Had love addled my brain? Or was I intimidated by my father? Did I believe he would always be straightforward with me?

But my questions did not end there.

Why did the Saxons raid our land last night? Was it just to sack our farms? Or was it to gather food for forty men just off the boats?

Today at home, I knew someone interrogated our Saxon prisoners. Why had I not been informed of the results?

There was another problem: that of the escalation of Vortigern's troops—first his own boatload plus ten, then another ten, then another twenty. How much force do you need to capture two young men and their retainers? Would not his strength of fifty-two men be at least thirty too many for that purpose? Could you not capture the garrison at Isca with twenty? It was those troop numbers that made me question the very mission of Vortigern.

The question was, what if the sons of Constantine were not really his objective? And if not them, then who or what was? Pacing below the wall, I looked up at the town. Could his goal have been Isca? But what value would a town like Isca in Devon be to a northerner such as Vortigern? None! It was too far upstream from the sea, too far away from his own fort, creating too long supply lines. It had to be something else.

The only other place of significance in Devon was our villa at Okehampton, and it was only significant because in a few hours it would be packed full of kings. What if the purpose of Vortigern was to sabotage the Moot and kill the kings? If so, then would not a troop of fifty-two men make some sense? And if the kings were his real objective, could that explain my mother's strange entreaty: "You must carry out your father's commands. For Britannia, and for all of us. There is too much at stake." That entreaty was out of character for such a mild-mannered and sensible woman. She had sounded like someone from the Roman stage.

But Ingraine's plea made sense if both my mother and father feared there was a much larger plan of attack than I had been told about. It was dawning on me that my father had sent me on a mission to save the sons of Constantine from abduction, but it was a sham. My real mission may have been only to warn those two sea-soned campaigners and lead them to disrupt an attack on my very own home.

And I had no one else to blame because I had allowed myself to be deceived.

Then there was Doone. What was his connection to Vortigern? Was Doone the spy in our own household? If he was, where was the evidence of his betrayal? Because had not Doone reported accurately to me on whatever he saw? Had he not fought fiercely beside me, killing the Saxons over the last two nights? Could it be that Doone was the Cotta spy in the Vortigern camp? Or could he be serving us both, playing a dangerous double game?

Had I allowed myself to be deceived by him too?

I did not know the answers as to what was troubling me because I had only just formed the questions. I would put them aside until I was able to ask them of my father.

11.45pm, Thursday September 9th, Merlin's time

"Report, Doone!" Moloch commanded.

"I think that Merlin saw a connection between Vortigern and me."

"Why do you suspect this? I thought my instructions were clear. There was to be absolutely no contact between you."

"There was absolutely no contact, but Merlin will not look at me. He did not want to fight the Saxons tonight. He is a Druid, and as you know they are exempt from fighting in the land of their birth. And he wanted to be with his ladylove. She is missing. Do you have her?"

"Why do you ask? What business is it of yours?"

"It's not. I am just trying to understand his mood and whether I am at risk."

"I will tell you this much," the Prince of Lies volunteered, "we are using her as bait."

And Doone had no way of knowing whether he was telling him the truth or not.

21

Vortigern Exposed

11.35pm, Thursday September 9th, Merlin's time

P EOPLE SAY VORTIGERN WAS NOT A DUMB MAN, *although I have
never been completely convinced of that! Crafty, yes, with
a brazenness that those who were more learned would never
risk. He might have been my captive, he might have been in a hostile
land and he might have been trussed up like a pheasant in all its
autumn finery, but from the very moment he awoke, he started to
negotiate.*

Wriggling into a sitting position on the riverbank, he began:

*"I am King Vortigern, Lord of Petuaria. I am a rich and powerful
man. Whatever is the price for my freedom, I will pay it. Just name
it. I have slaves, pretty girls and prettier boys, and I have more gold
than you can haul with a team of bullocks. Now, when you untie
me, we will talk some more about this."*

*I said nothing. I had never seen a man who had betrayed his
country and who showed no shame. I had never seen a man who
had ravished his daughter and who made no secret of it. I had
never seen a man who had murdered his parents and who boasted*

about it. Nor had I ever seen a man who worked with Darkness and seemed enthralled with his own cleverness. All I could taste was the sourness from the revulsion in my mouth.

Yet Vortigern was not what I had expected. I had expected him to look like a master of the Dark Arts, like some character from the stories that my nurse, Angharad, whispered to me on winter nights. Her villains were strange and tall and slender with crude scars slashed across their faces. Their floppy black hair made their sharp noses even longer, and their small dark flashing eyes pierced every defence you could offer. They all looked like our enemy, the Picts. Vortigern looked nothing like that. He was a golden dandy, a man handsome beyond belief, who looked like a Greek god. I asked my-self, 'Is it not a wonder of the world that this man, who is so fair on the outside, is not fair on the inside? For within, he is venomous. How can I make any sense of him?'

It was soon after I had stared at my own filthy fingernails on my blackened hands and realised that they looked as if they belonged to someone else, that I leaned forward to examine his beautifully manicured fingers and wonder at the rings bedazzling each finger. They looked good enough to eat! Good idea!

Suddenly I grabbed both of his ringless thumbs and chomped on them as hard as I could right down to his bone. Vortigern, in a starburst of agony, screamed:

"You savage! Do you want to eat me? Well you are not going to do it. I will not allow it!"

He really had no idea what this cannibal would do next. His eyes darted around looking for some advantage.

I leant as close to Vortigern as I could and screeched all my rage at him, mimicking the 'pia-ow' of a peacock. If you had heard me, you would have jumped out of your skin, but you could reassure yourself that Myrddin just imitated one of his birds. But that is not what Vortigern heard because he heard the scream of a devil. Terrified, he wet himself.

"What are you doing?" he shrieked at me. "Who sent you? It must have been Moloch. Tell me, was it him? Do not kill me! I will cover you in gold! I will give you anything you want!"

I said nothing. There was a deathly silence; the very mention of Moloch had sent a cold chill through me. So it was Moloch, the Prince of Lies, who was the engineer of all of this! I stared at the Betrayer; now I understood that Morgana was not alone in these attacks on Emilia; she was the agent of someone else, and to keep Emilia safe I would have to defeat Moloch. 'But, please God, not tonight! Some other time, please! Give me time to prepare myself and to compose my feelings, to dampen my fear and to plan my tactics. I am not ready. Give me time to discuss every move with Lord Michael, the master of combat in the sky.'

Finally, I spoke. I spoke in the language of Cornwall, a clicking mixture of Celt, Phoenician and Carthaginian, and Vortigern did not understand one single word I spoke. Nor did I. Because in my disguised voice I spoke random words and hopped around, trying to ease my throbbing foot.

"Can you not speak Latin or Greek?" Vortigern whined. "One of the languages of civilised people?"

I saw it dawn on him that this uncouth being had not understood one word he had said.

I said nothing. I could hear my father speaking: 'Ambrosius, if you want to gain power from a bully, ridicule them, it is then that you will be able to prick their pride quickly and they will collapse.'

'So, for my father's sake, I will ridicule this piteous pretty boy rather than kill him now.'

With that in mind, his kilt had to be next. I drew out my gladius and leaned over him, pointing its tip to where his pulse throbbed in his neck. Vortigern, convinced this was the end, whimpered,

"Just tell me what you want..."

Moving very slowly and deliberately, as I had seen my father do, I slid my sword down the middle of his chest until I reached the knotted ties at his waist that secured his kilt. I cut them and pulled out his skirt and, balling it up, I threw it down to the river.

Every now and then there is something I see, something I had not foreseen. It does not happen very often, but in that moment I saw something that took my very breath away. There, sheltering between Vortigern's thighs, and attached to him by God knows what, was a giant iron husk that pointed towards the heavens. What on earth was it? It looked like plumbing! And then I knew! This man wore a codpiece, an armour-plated codpiece that was made to protect his manhood in battle! And I had just discovered why I had a throbbing foot!

I said nothing. Although my skin did prickle at this man's folly, it was my bottom lip that gave me away, because it began to tremble and then my eyes began to tear, and try as I might to stifle it, and I must confess I did not try too hard, my mouth quivered and I burst out laughing.

I seized a moment of joy. Pushing his head backwards, I pinched his nose and poured a sleeping draught of mandrake down his throat. A while later he passed out.

With my falcon and my jackdaw on my head and my mice secured in my pouch, I hauled the dead weight of Vortigern over my shoulder and, using my staff to navigate, I took to the sky. Up there I tried to empty my mind by letting the cold air wash over me and clean me of unanswered questions and of the Saxon's blood. But on that journey home, transporting the Great Betrayer like a sack of manure, I upbraided myself:

'Myrddin, you are a Druid. What are you doing killing a man and thinking of killing another?'

As I searched for an answer, I found it when I saw the face of my father.

"I fought without armour tonight to show you my courage, and with my sharp sword I sacrificed that Saxon for you, old man, so you will never think I am a coward. Because when I go to war I will build forts and tunnels; but you will not be able to brag, like other fathers, about your son's fearless slaughter of your enemies. Because of this night you will be proud, but now my sword arm is numb. How will I make restitution to his family?"

Once home, I arranged Vortigern on a couch in a cellar room and left Motius to guard him. Then, remembering the hidden exchange between Doone and Vortigern, I told Motius,

"Do not let anybody, and that means nobody, into this room unless it is my father, the General. At five, when my father awakes, you are to unlock the door and allow him to enjoy this tableau on the couch."

Although I felt filthy, I dismissed the thought of bathing first. The involvement of Moloch created a greater sense of urgency and I moved into the consciousness of my fox, to find Emilia. I scanned the Belstone Tor and the standing stones. Underneath my blackened skin I went pale. She was nowhere to be seen.

22

Three Friends Search

11.35pm, Thursday September 9th, Our time

THE THREE OF THEM, anxious and scared from not knowing what to expect, ran along the gravel path to the Nine Maidens. At least Jack was well prepared. He had everything: rope, torches, water, first aid, his bag of commando gizmos and, in case he met that Hound of the Baskervilles, his Taser gun. Toby, on the other hand, had his Swiss Army knife. When they came down a low rise they saw the standing stones, washed in pale moonlight, looking as though they had seen everything before. All was quiet and calm until a fox squalled. They jumped.

"That's the Belstone fox!" Casey cried. "We danced with him yesterday. He'll help us find her!"

"That doesn't sound like you, KC," Toby protested. "You sound like Em. Next thing, you will be talking to him and asking him where she is."

"Okay, Mister Sarcasm, you got a better idea?"

"Let's leave our stuff here," Jack suggested, attempting to break the tension. He was the only one who had changed and looked ready, with his usual understated elegance, for an invasion. He was in well-pressed army fatigues and well-shined boots, with night goggles perched on his head, and he displayed a commando watch on his wrist. He handed out torches and water bottles, and hooked various ropes around his shoulders, and generally took control. "Casey and I will search this area around the stones. Toby, could you go up the Tor and have a good look round up there? Okay?"

"Okay!" came from Toby as he raced up the slope, about a quarter of a mile away from the stones. It did not take him long to sweep his light across the granite seat of the Tor and discover a discarded meal, the puke of a pizza that could only belong to his favourite serial vomiter: Emily. He looked around the area carefully and there, beside a tall rock, was the familiar long neck of his favourite reptile as well. He waved frantically.

"Hey, look what I've found up here! Come on, come up!"

He reached down to pick up the live evidence of Emily's presence and paused, because even in the faint light he could read the glare in the reptile's eyes. Casey, the sprinter, reached him first.

"She's been up here," he yelled at her very excited, "because I've found the remains of her last meal!" And he displayed it with a bow and an outstretched arm: "Ta-Da! And I have found her tortoise of the half shell, Roget. Ta-Da! This is more than enough forensic evidence to prove conclusively that she has been here!"

"Great! Come on down with it!" Jack yelled.

"Why don't you take it, Casey?" he asked, trying to hide how anxious he was. "I think it likes girls better." And very warily, Toby handed the reptile across.

As soon as they returned downhill there was a sense of relief.

"At least we're on the right track," Casey said as she stroked the tiny animal before handing it over to Jack, who had a pocket for everything.

"Well, where is Em now?" Casey asked. "She'd never let her darling tortoise go. No one, not even me, is ever allowed to touch it! And what do you think it means if Roget is here and she is not?"

Her question hung there and the mood turned bleak again as each of them silently answered it for themselves in their own gloomy way.

"Why don't you two explore this area further?" Casey suggested, and glaring straight at Toby she continued, "And I, without any distraction from you-know-who, will try to get some information from Mister Fox." Then she added sharply, "Okay?" It was more of a challenge to Toby than a request.

Before anyone could disagree, she bounced across the hill to the fox who was sitting near the centre of the stone circle, as if waiting for her.

She approached him very slowly making the soft crooning noises she had heard Emily utter whenever she was near something wild, until she came close enough to whisper:

"We met here yesterday, Mr Fox. Do you know where my dancing friend is? Where's Emily?"

Gingerly the fox slunk around her to a large gorse bush about fifteen feet away from the circle.

"That's funny," Casey thought, "I don't remember that bush being here yesterday."

The fox nosed carefully around the bush until he stopped and flicked his head back to dislodge the bush. It hid a round hollow. It was a perfectly formed hole that suggested it had been dug recently. She shone the light down it and at the bottom there was a round wooden platform.

"She's down there, isn't she Mr Fox?" The fox flicked his brush and sat down.

"Hey you," Casey called up to the others, "Mr Fox came good! Come and see!" As soon as they arrived, she continued:

"Look… it's a bit like a mining shaft. It's about twelve feet deep. There… you can see the bottom."

"I just saw something flash!" Jack cried out, pointing down. "Shine your torches on it. If we take where Casey is standing as twelve o'clock, it's at the edge at four o'clock. It's gold, it could be a ring or something."

"Em's doing a Hansel and Gretel," Toby exclaimed, "leaving a breadcrumb trail of spew and turtles and gold to lead us to her!"

"Hey… it's looking good!" Jack exclaimed. "It could mean she's alive. Let's send a torch down to get a better look."

Jack tied a thin cord tightly around the torch and lowered it down the hole. Holding the light above the glittering object, it looked like an earring. But there was something else; there was a large opening beside it.

"I think there's a tunnel!" Jack was now very excited. "And it goes back under us towards the centre of the circle. I'm trying to manoeuvre the torch into it. Can you two lie down opposite me and see what's there?"

"I can see that your light is going in about six feet along an even surface," Casey said. "There could be a light at the end because I can see a pink glow in the distance."

"I'm worried," Toby said. "Just suppose somebody has taken Emily to a dungeon like Alfred described, and if this is a somebody smart enough to mastermind all these attacks on her, wouldn't they have left a guard to warn them if someone was coming after her? Hey! Wouldn't they even be expecting us?"

"Well, coming down here I was scanning our environment looking for a spotter," Jack answered. "So far, nothing. Only some sheep. If I was setting up an early warning signal for a tunnel, I'd use something silent and lethal like a trip wire. Anyone got phone coverage here?" he asked.

"You can get it a short way down the track towards Belstone," Casey offered.

"Give me your phone, KC, I'm going to key in my Dad's number. He's waiting up and expecting a call. Fill him in on everything. Ask him to contact Emily's parents and tell them that we've found a trail that we think Emily left for us. Toby and I are going to abseil down this shaft and find her."

"We are?" said Toby with a gulp. He looked into the shaft where moonlight and wind swirled around the dust and the darkness. "It doesn't look very safe, Big Red."

"Emily's in there, Tobes!"

"It's not Emily I'm worried about. It's whoever took her in there that I'm worried about, because twice, remember, they've tried to get me too."

"I know this may disappoint you but I think you were only collateral damage. It's Emily they want for some reason. They have no interest in either of us."

"Okay. I will try to believe you. Hey! Let's do it!"

23

What Lies Underneath

11.45pm, Thursday September 9th, Our time

EVERY SO OFTEN, EMILY HAS A DREAM, a dream where she can fly, with her face down towards the earth watching the landscape below. Now she is in that dream again and flying high above Okehampton, when Merlin lets her go. He lets her go like a kite, one that suddenly breaks free of its string. She whirls around searching for him, but he whooshes away up into the silence of the stars.

"Merlin, Merlin, help me!" she calls out to him.

"You and I are made of stardust," he replies. "We belong together in the stars."

What a dumb thing to say, she dreams. How is that of any help? He takes being a bard far too seriously.

She hears the buzz of the Piper Cherokee.

"Jack, please give me a ride, I am falling to earth."

He waves cheerily: "Climb in."

But no matter how many times she tries to get on board, she cannot and she falls to earth softly, like an autumn leaf.

It is then that Emily smells something. It is something decomposing like the stench of rotting flesh. She is swaying, being carried, like a sick patient, head to toe in a sling. A fox squalls. Her ears ache and, with a chilled hand, she tries to take out her earring.

"Stop it, keep still!" and an elbow smashes into her temple, whipping her head to the side. Her teeth puncture her lip and blood dribbles down her chin. Everything is black.

Ingraine screams in pain.

'Who knocked Emilia out? Emilia's dose of mandrake has worn off. Where is Myrddin? Myrddin, can you hear me? Her friends are trying to rescue her and they are walking right into a trap. Where are you?'

The first shaft that ran from above ground to the tunnel entrance was safe. It had walls, either a dry brown or russet and quite smooth, that led down to the wooden platform.

"Stable and recent enough," the tall one said as he jumped on it, "it could easily have supported a ladder, and this platform shows signs of recent use." I thought he sounded older than his years.

As soon as his white-haired friend landed beside him he started warning, "Don't go barging off down that tunnel. Think trip wire, Big Red, booby traps!"

The cross-cut tunnel curved to the left. Its walls were hard-chis-elled and hammered, and near its roof there were iron plugs spread apart at even distances almost at my head height.

"Brackets for lanterns," said the tall one whom I had seen at his castle with Emilia. "I'm going to flash a torch down there. Look for a fine wire, Tobes, probably at knee height."

With a light in each hand, he scanned the tunnel. Slowly, as their eyes adjusted to the darkness, they could see about two thirds in, and just before the tunnel started to decline, there was a glint of copper wire. They moved towards it cautiously.

"There it is," his friend whispered. "What do we do?"

"Unless you want to risk slithering under it, that's what I brought my wire cutters for."

"Let's do it now, Jack, so we don't have to worry about it on the way back."

"Right!" And cautiously the red-haired one, Jack, cut the trip wire and was amazed when nothing happened. "That's funny, Toby. What's the point of a trip wire if there are no consequences?"

"And what were you expecting?" Toby asked as they inched their way further along the tunnel.

"Anything," his friend replied, "...but something... an explosion... a rock fall... even a grill that came down to block our way."

I had to smile. This Jack was good, he thought like a soldier, and his expectations were almost accurate. I had defused the wall of iron spikes that would have impaled them.

"Anyway, what's next?" he asked.

"Stop there, Jack, or you'll fall into it."

It was clear that the second shaft surprised them. I had placed a few rocks there as a barrier so they would not stumble down into the sudden hole. There was a drop of fifteen feet. It was hewn smoothly from the rock and the walls were hung with webs of a vivid green copper. At its base a pink light flickered.

"This should lead down into the chamber," Jack whispered. "If we just wait for a moment and put on our headlamps and listen, I will try and figure out where we'd land if we rappelled down there. I'm sure that's where Emily is, but the challenge is this... it looks like a sink hole, and once you get in it, it can be very hard to get out, and impossible to get out of there fast."

They lay down in the tunnel and his friend Toby moved a light on his head across the roof. He was dressed very peculiarly, like Emilia, so he must be her dancing partner. He moved with the caution of a cat.

"Look at that," he whispered. On the roof directly over the centre of the shaft, there was a knob carved with three hares that chased one another in a circle. The three hares shared only three ears, yet each one of them had two of its own. I love puzzles like that. And it prompted me to do the square root of 333 to calm my mind. Once I had the answer to ten places... 18.2482875909... I gave them my full attention again.

Jack had the other answer. "In these parts, that's what's known as the Tinners Rabbits," he explained, "even though they are actually hares. You can see them carved in our churches around here. Maybe the tin miners built the churches as well as these shafts."

"That they did," I said in a deep voice, one that set up an eerie echo. "These shafts and caverns were sweated from the earth by the tin miners."

"Who said that?" Jack gasped, looking around startled.

"This is an Arch-Druid's cavern. He is buried under that sign."

"Who's talking?" Jack demanded.

"I am Emilia's friend, Merlin, and I have come here to find her too."

"This could be dodgy, Toby, or some kind of sick joke," Jack stuttered whispering to his friend, most unsure of my disembodied voice. "Who's talking? Where are you?"

"I am where you cannot see me. I have been following you and disarming the traps along the way. Now you are here it is safe enough for us talk without risk of injury to yourself or myself."

"You said your name is Merlin and you're a friend of Emily's," Toby declared. "We know all her friends and we have never met you!"

"I come and go in the cracks of time through to other realms."

"And what's that phoney talk supposed to mean?" he demanded.

"It means I do not live in your time, I live some time else."

"I only know of one Merlin," Jack said, "and he was the wizard to King Arthur, the Once and Future King."

"I am only sixteen and not yet a fully accomplished wizard, just a simple weaver of magic, but I am a Master Druid and one day I hope to attend on King Arthur. At this very moment, I am here to help you rescue Emilia." I was pleased with my explanation so I added, "I hope I have reassured you, Tobias."

"How did you know my proper name? Well, Merlin, if that's your proper name, if you are a weaver of magic, you could rescue her all by yourself, or at the very least, with Jack's help, because I am neither a soldier like Jack nor a magician like you, and I'll just go back to Dartmoor and find Casey."

Both Jack and I ignored his offer. Both of us knew, but for different reasons, that Tobias had bottled up all his bravery when his dad died in a tunnel just like this, and he had hidden it in his heart.

"Could you come out here where we can see you?" Jack asked me.

"I prefer the shadows; I am looking quite scary at the moment because I am very dirty. I've just been in a battle and my skin is covered in charcoal and soot."

"We've seen that before," Jack said reassuringly.

"Speak for yourself, Action Man!" Tobias just wanted to get out of there.

"Look up," I asked them.

It was quite a sight, they told me later. There, hanging like a bat from the roof over the shaft was a figure with a darkened face that suddenly dropped down to their eye level. I was smiling at them, upside down. My dark tunic had fallen around my face like a ruff; underneath I was bare except for a loincloth, and my skin was streaked half white and half black. In a playful mood, I squeaked like a bat and they both laughed.

"Merlin, I can see you're just hanging around!" Tobias quipped, and we laughed again.

I was feeling very pleased with myself. It had been years since I did anything with lads my own age and this was fun. When I gracefully re-appeared beside them the right side up, Tobias challenged me:

"Well, Merlin, what's your plan to rescue Emily?"

"That is the question I was going to ask you, Tobias. Do you still have those smoke bombs, Jack? Ropes? I can see you have lamps on your heads but where are your swords?"

"Sadly, Merlin, the fighting game is not played with blades any more. It is now played with guns." Jack pulled out his Taser and waved it in front of me.

"How does it work?" I asked.

"It stuns the victim with bolts of electricity. You know, like stored lightning."

"That could be very dangerous. But what is your plan to use it?"

Tobias interrupted, "My plan, you guys, is just to wing it out of here."

"Well, we were just checking things out," Jack said, and he continued to outline his plan using language that I barely understood. "After we attach our ropes to those iron sconces we will rappel down into the chamber where I will throw a smoke grenade. In the confusion we will grab Emily, who we suspect will be on an altar; and we must assume she won't be in a state to escape easily. Toby will truss her up in his rope while I monkey up mine, and then I'll drop it back down so I can haul her up, and Toby will follow, and we will be out of here as fast as we can."

"Just what I was thinking, Jack," Toby grinned.

"Good plan!" I agreed, very unsure of what exactly I had agreed to.

"Let's do it!" Tobias cried out. "But Merlin, you don't have a rope..."

"I do not need it. I will use other ways," I added with a smile. "I think I will manage."

'They are just boys,' I thought, 'and great to play with.' But the twenty-first century seemed to make babies of boys who should be men. I only hoped they knew what they were doing!

24

Moondance

11.55pm, Thursday September 9th, Our time

T HEY DID NOT. *Toby fumbled his knot, causing his rope to split under his weight. He fell the final six feet and cried out when he landed on his knee, bruising it—but not badly because he knew how to take a fall. Beside him, Jack pulled the pin on his smoke grenade, and when he pitched it into the dim chamber it bounced across the floor and fizzed out. They both landed in a rush and into the arms of hooded men in long robes. Startled, they were lifted by their elbows, kicking and squirming, over to an altar at the centre of the cavern. It reminded Jack, he said, of the bench where he skinned and filleted his deer after a hunt and where he would puzzle how easily a graceful life could turn into red meat on a slab. This was a slab of granite, dimly polished, with a gutter running around its edge.*

Emilia, as I had expected, was nowhere to be seen. I was standing in the shadows clutching my fox and using his mind to see what had happened to her when I had a startling thought. Why not bring her friends with me for the sheer fun of it? But let me offer you a quiet word: I told you I am a trickster, and sometimes I only reveal what I want you to know at the time. Yes, I wanted to have some fun, but there was another reason and soon you will know why.

"Myrddin, are you thinking what I think you are thinking?"

"Yes, Mam. I want to bring them with me to our realm. They are friends of Emilia and they will give her consolation, I am sure, when I find her. I cannot take my eyes off them. They are wondrous in everything they do. They bounce about like balls, and although they are my age they are so much younger and full of surprising ideas and games."

"They are mad-caps. You will expose them to all kind of dangers that they will not know how to deal with."

"They will have me."

"And you will have enough to worry about."

"As you know, I cannot touch Morgana. When she and her servants were carrying Emilia in here, I had the opportunity to rescue her, but I could not without touching Morgana herself. Presumably both of her friends can touch Morgana without hurting themselves and that will help in Emilia's rescue."

Meanwhile Jack, with all the authority of thirty generations of the best of British breeding, dispensed with any pleasantries and demanded of the assembled group,

"Where is Emily?"

"And who, if you please, is Emily?" came the polite response from the person who seemed to be in charge.

"We know she's down here, we found her earring. Who are you anyway?"

"We are Druids and I am the Arch-Druid. We've been expecting *you since you cut our wire. We are here to celebrate the full moon."*

On the note of a flute, the hooded figures formed a circle and I knew immediately what they were doing. They were going to teach the boys a lesson, but like all Druidic teaching it would be a very slow lesson, and we just did not have the time for it.

"We create a circle here below, within the moon's circle above." He gestured below and above as he spoke. "We create a universe within a universe. Here, at midnight, we revere the light of the sun reflected off the surface of the moon. Our round mirrors reflect the moonshine down through slots in the stones. Tonight is a time of balance."

"Okay then," Tobias began. "This is seriously weird, Jack, and I'm sure it's about to get to all new kinds of weird. Okay then," he repeated, "can we keep this real? You wouldn't have seen a young man with a blackened face and dressed in Roman clothes around here by any chance?"

"You mean Merlin?" the Arch-Druid answered with the slightest smile at the corners of his mouth. "Has anyone here seen Merlin? No. Not tonight."

He was really enjoying himself and I expected the mage to wink at me hiding in the shadows at any moment, but I signalled to him that for now his fun with the intruders was over and this was serious. He changed his tone and continued.

"He sometimes joins in to help us with our rituals. He was initiated here in this very cavern when he was only thirteen, and we are teaching him modern English. He's coming back, you know."

"Well that's good, because we need him to help us find Emily."

"No, I mean he's coming back here in a completely new life as a spiritual teacher. We expect him to be born soonish, quite near here in Okehampton. We all hope we will be around to initiate him again."

"Well, we came here looking for our friend, Emily. She was abducted this evening and brought here and we fear she is going to be sacrificed."

"Goodness! Then you do not have a moment to lose because midnight is the critical time for those Baal sacrifices. She may have been brought to this place but her abductors will have slipped her into another time-frame, possibly to a time when those foreigners had commandeered this place."

"How will we ever find what time frame she's in?" Tobias said, quite exasperated.

"We have an ovate here." When they looked puzzled the Arch-Druid added, "We have a seer here and she will take a look for you. Willow, can you tell me what you are seeing about Emily?" he asked one of the hooded women.

"The year is 451. The place is right here!"

"We're really worried about her," Jack said. "If she is in the year 451, I presume she was taken backwards in time by some device or other. Just supposing we could time-travel too, how would we do it?"

"The realms are very close here," Willow answered. "And the doors between our world and theirs open over there at this altar. If you both sit on the altar, we will create a cone of power and I will call on Merlin to guide you through."

The Druids tightened their circle around the altar and Willow began:

"We call on the angels of the North, South, East and West. We call on the winds of all directions."

The Druids sidestepped around Jack and Tobias, going faster and faster, until they felt quite giddy. You know I am a trickster and I cannot resist showing off a few of my tricks, because what is the point of knowing them if you do not have an audience?

So there was a sudden puff of russet smoke, and when it dispersed, I stood in front of the altar with Dolossus on my shoulders, my bird and mice in my pockets and my staff in my hand. When I went over to sit between them it was a minute to midnight.

"With the power vested in us, we call on beings of Light, and no others, to transport our friends to this place when it was a tomb of Darkness. We call on all beings of Light, particularly the Lords Michael and Raphael, to protect them with their electric blue light. We welcome Merlin and we ask him to liberate this sacred space from the Dark to allow the Druids to return. I will hold the focus for you until you can find your way back."

I bowed to the circle of Druids.

"Thank you for your service, my friends. The door between the worlds is now open and I will try to free this place from Darkness," and I put my arms around the shoulders of the anxious friends and pulled them tight. "Let's go!"

While Jack seemed uncomfortable with my fox, Tobias played with his ears.

"Remember, Merlin, that I don't have travel insurance!" It was a quip, I was told, which was a joke and often a play on words, and he continued with another: "So go-go gentle into that good night." More often than not, I had no idea of what Tobias was talking about.

25

The Enchantress Morgana

Midnight, Thursday September 9th, Merlin's time

S LOWLY, AS OUR EYES GREW USED to the dim light, Tobias and *Jack realised we were still in the same place, still in the same cavern, although now we were engulfed by a foul stench. The cave's walls were hung with the rotting carcases of my favourite animals: badgers and bears and hundreds of foxes. Suspended from a metal rod near the roof was a large, winged creature, its mouse-like face hanging close to the floor. In the centre, where we stood, was a granite altar with the gutter around it, only now the gutter had a round plughole in it with a wooden bucket underneath it.*

A woman reclined on a pile of bearskins in front of us. She was dark-haired and voluptuous with pale skin and clothed in a scarlet robe that was slashed with fox fur. Jack could not take his eyes off her because he told me he had never seen anything so beautiful, but Tobias, avoiding my glance, looked down and stared, where I dared not look, at whatever was on the floor.

"Just in time, Merlin," she purred, "the honey trap always works, does it not?" As she spoke she gestured downwards to the

166

place where both Jack and Tobias stared transfixed. As soon as I saw her I flinched and felt my gut seize as if I had been hit by a nailed fist. Lying at my feet was Emilia; her arms above her head, her wrists and ankles bound tight, her eyes closed and one of them looked badly swollen and bruised. There was dried blood around her mouth.

My heart ached. But I kept my face impassive. 'This vile woman, this enchantress, has desecrated this sacred space, this belly of the Mother Earth, and turned it into a charnel house!' I was angry at everything she had done. But still I kept my face emotionless and said nothing. Tobias looked first at Jack and then at me, and when neither of us responded, although for very different reasons, Tobias blurted out at her,

"You had better not have hurt Emily! This place looks like a chamber of horrors, and if you slaughtered all these animals you must be one of the cruellest and most dangerous of women in the world!"

"I have tried hard, so I would hope so!" *she laughed.*

Falling to his knees beside Emilia, Tobias checked her pulse and used his small knife to cut the twine that bound her hands and feet. He passed another desperate look to Jack while he massaged her wrists and ankles. When he looked at me he mouthed.

"Don't just stand there, Merlin, do something." *And I looked right through him as if he was not there.*

The enchantress bent down over Emilia and purred in her most alluring voice,

"There she lies, like a lizard on a rock, alive but looking dead. And you," *she kicked Tobias quite viciously to emphasise who she was talking to,* "and you thought I wanted to open her veins, did you not? You thought I wanted to exsanguinate her? You thought I wanted to drink her blood like the ravening undead? Did you not?" *She threw back her head and laughed, a forced sound from such a beautiful face.* "Wrong! Wrong! Wrong! You are wrong on all counts!"

"I do not share my thoughts with anyone," Tobias flung at her, "let alone a being like you!"

She ignored him. Instead she walked over to Jack, and as she walked she rolled her hips seductively. And then, standing on tiptoe, she gently played with his hair, combing its strands through her long fingers.

"What I really want is you, my pretty boy!" she purred, and, bunching a fist full of his hair she pulled his face closer to hers to make her point, and then abruptly changed her manner again to coo in his ear, "My sweet boy, my russet-haired one." With that she paused and flicked her eyes over to me to gauge my reaction before she went on, "You are so like your forefather Pendragon, and yet you are so much more attractive than that desiccated old bag of bones. And it is with you, my darling boy, that I have a longstanding score to settle."

"Even if Uther Pendragon was my ancestor," retorted Jack, pulling himself free from her hands and trying not to let his voice shake, "which I very much doubt, because that was fifteen hundred years ago, whatever any of my ancestors may have done, it would have absolutely nothing to do with me, now. None of that matters." He began to pace the cave holding his head so high it nearly scraped the roof. "Besides, if you really wanted me, why did you attack my plane this afternoon?" Towering over her he demanded, puzzled, "Who the hell are you anyway?"

"Who, me? In this time I am yet unborn and my real name is a secret. When I do live again I will be known as Morgana, daughter of Ygern and Gorlois. I will be the half-sister of the Pendragon's bastard child, Artorus." Morgana turned her back on him, to stare at me. "And if I attacked your flying machine, Pendragon," she spat out the name with scorn, "you would not be talking to me now. Would he, Merlin?" I ignored her.

As if he had suddenly had a divine revelation, Jack asked:

"Are you the Morgana le Fay?" His tone was quiet and reverent, *a tone one reserved for talking to a saint and not this mad woman full of devils. "Are you the real Morgana le Fay?" And when she said she was, Jack bowed and continued, "My heartfelt apologies for not recognising you!" As he spoke his voice deepened until it became smoother and full of charm.*

"Do you know, my lady, that your portrait hangs outside my bedroom door? Now that I see you in person, I can see our portrait does not do your beauty justice nor does it capture your amber eyes. The Duchess of Dartmoor, my mother, says you are the queen of sorcery and that you possess the most extraordinary powers of healing. It's an honour to meet you!" And, as he spoke, Jack reached out to kiss her hand, but when Morgana refused it, he bowed instead.

Her eyes darted around quickly because she had been taken by surprise; discovering an admirer in Jack pushed her off-balance. There was nothing she enjoyed more than an appreciative audience, especially of her finest features, her amber eyes, so she murmured graciously,

"Your mother, the Duchess, is recognised as an expert in the legends of our time and she is a discerning woman."

"In your opinion, as a renowned healer," Jack said to her, "do you think Emily will be all right?"

"Oh, I am sure she will recover," said Morgana. "She has been roughed up a bit but not by me."

"Good to hear." Then Jack changed his voice so that he scooped up some of his words dramatically, leaving any listener, except hopefully Morgana, in no doubt he was play-acting. "Could you tell me what is it like to be such a beautiful woman?"

"That is a good question, but I do not know the answer," she shrugged, "because I have never been anything else. Tell me, Pendragon, why do you still associate with Aurelius here, or whatever ridiculous name he is using now? He has always been such a pious prig!"

Tobias was sure she was talking about him and he had had enough. The last thing on Earth you could say about him was that he was a pious prig. His friend Emilia was unconscious and barely breathing, and his other friend Jack was flirting with her abductor. He had had enough of Jack and Morgana. Why didn't Merlin just creep up behind and shove her into a sack?

"Listen, you witch," Tobias began. He stood so close to Morgana that she started to inch backwards from him. "Your bloody picture doesn't hang in my hallway at my bedroom door knocking to get in and it never will. I can see into your eyes, Morgana, and they are not amber, they are the colour of a night-time piss. And I don't believe a word you say. Of course it was you who tried to kill me, not once, but twice, and of course it was you who organised the bird strike on Jack's plane. Why you are after me, I don't know. But hear this... You may have bewitched Jack, but I can see you, and see you as who you truly are. You are a woman of intense malice; in fact, you are the harpy from hell. So, why don't you return to your bat cave and file your teeth into points? That's the only feature missing from your vampire face."

I said nothing. I just bit the inside of my cheeks, to stop myself from laughing. Good knight, bad knight, a clever strategy, I thought. I waited, barely breathing, for her explosion of rage.

"You foul-mouthed grub!" she screamed at Tobias. "How dare you even speak to me! I will squash you like a beetle!" and she made the merest gesture with her wrist and Tobias flew backwards through the air towards the rough stonewall of the cavern. Instinctively, as a dancer, whenever he was airborne, he did his inside turning kick and it sent him careening back towards Morgana. He landed on her chest and knocked her to the floor. Furious, she threw up her arms and Tobias spun again in mid-air and sped to smash into the wall. A fraction of a second before he slammed into it, he froze, suspended in mid-air, his face a mask of alarm. I thought about the mechanics of his mid-air kick and marvelled at the control he had acquired over his body and his mind to execute it. And he had wit! This boy had the makings of a magician. I did the square root of eighteen to eleven places because it was easy. Answer: 4.24264068712. It keeps me still.

"To leave him suspended there must be your work, you worm, but at least it shuts him up!"

She laughed wildly at me and I did not as much as blink, I was thinking about what a lovely number eighteen was! It has six primes.

"You are going to have to bargain with me for that girl," and she pointed to Emilia before she dropped her voice to continue, "let us begin with your opening bid. Let's say: your life for hers. How does that sound?"

I said nothing. But I still liked the number eighteen as an opening bid. I actually thought she lacked subtlety, for surely she could bargain better than that. I masked my face again with indifference and assessed the state of the cavern: Tobias was safe, Emilia was safe, and Jack was trying to seduce a seductress. Why should I change my plan?

As Jack moved closer to Morgana, he clouded his face with disappointment and resumed his dramatic emphasis.

"But you said you wanted me, not Emily." He almost cried.

"Well," she retorted in a child-like sing-song voice, "I have changed my mind!"

Jack stared at her in amazement as if she had done a triple somersault.

"How can you do that?" he demanded.

"What is the use of a mind," she asked petulantly, "if you cannot change it?"

"Yes, a woman of your power and beauty can change whatever she wants. I wonder what else you can change. I know you can fly through time and, can you believe this, Merlin," Jack glanced at me wide-eyed as he spoke, "she even brought Emily with her and they time-travelled together!" Ignoring the obvious, that he and Tobias had done the same with me, he turned back to Morgana. "But, I *have heard that only the truly great sorcerers can shape-shift as well? Can you, my lady, change yourself like that?"*

Morgana looked at Jack with scorn.

"I can change into whatever I want!"

"Can you change into a man?"

"Of course! I have been a man many times. I was one earlier tonight."

'Amazing!' and Jack thought for a moment, concluding that she was the one who tried to hijack the Hughes' car. "What about something more difficult and a lot larger, like a horse?"

"Yes, I have often been a mare too."

"That's truly amazing!" Jack gushed. "What about something smaller like a fox? Foxes have amber eyes just like yours."

"Once or twice I have even been a fox."

"How does it work? I've never seen shape-shifting happen. Could you show me?"

Morgana looked around at them and, moving a distance away from Jack, spun with her hands forming the apex of a graceful arch above her head. In a moment, she vanished.

"Where - has - she - gone, Merlin?" Jack exclaimed in mock wonder.

I remained still and silent with my eyes closed. I just knew what was coming next, and coming next after that, and I had to make sure my fox stayed out of her line of sight and did not make a meal of her. She would burn Dolossus to a crisp.

Because in place of Morgana there now stood a red vixen with a magnificent brush crowned with a silvery white tip. The fox moved a few paces, its nostrils quivering, searching for the scent of my predator hidden in the shadows.

"Look, Merlin!" cried Jack. 'Morgana le Fay is now a fox. Have you ever seen anything as graceful as the way she moves?"

I had, because I had seen the angelic grace of Emilia. All I could do was hope that Jack knew that when you flirted with fire, you got scorched. In my mind I asked, "Ingraine, are you watching this? Help me keep my fox silent for his next move, will you? I am sure you know like me what he will ask for next. Are you ready?" She answered all my questions with a single 'Yes'.

As if in slow motion the edges of the fox became blurry and appeared to vibrate, and after the fox gradually disappeared, Morgana resumed her true form.

"That was the most breathtaking thing," Jack gushed, "I've ever seen in my entire life!" He punched the air. I groaned inwardly and shut my eyes tight because I did not want to signal to Morgana his next step.

"You move like a ballerina, Morgana!" I sensed he was pleased. "But, you are far more graceful. Even though I know I should not, I must ask you for one more favour." I sensed he was smiling. "While you would not know that my personal crest has a hare on it, you would know that the hare is like a woman. I personally think that the hare has more grace and speed than a fox." Now I sensed he was beaming. "Do you think you could change into a hare? But a hare with amber eyes?"

"Just this last one then," Morgana replied, and while I sensed Jack was still smiling adoringly at her, she went through her graceful dance before her audience of one.

I had to see what happened next, because the moment when Morgana transformed into a hare I knew Jack would change too, and his seductive Dionysius would vanish and his avenging angel would re-appear. From the back of his waist he pulled out his Taser gun, lunged forward and blasted the hare with all his might. The hare screamed and collapsed.

The cavern was plunged into darkness and not a word was spoken until a nebulous purple haze swayed in the blackness. There, barely illuminated, were cowled Druids, each carrying smoking lanterns and stout wooden staffs. Before them on the uneven stone floor, the hare lay still. 'My God!' I thought to myself, 'I should have intervened. *Jack will pay for this, and he could pay for the rest of his life.' But that was not what I told him!*

"That was a brilliant performance, your Lordship!" I cried. I had genuine admiration for his skill at leading her astray. "And you seduced her with dazzling charm!" I leant towards him so only he could hear and murmured, "Someday you will be a great lover."

Jack went bright red. "Can I take that as a prophecy?" Once he decided he liked the idea, he asked me with a smirk, "Will you give me that in writing? Honestly Merlin," he tried to explain, "all I did was sidle up to her and smile a lot." Tobias would say later that was a typical Jack understatement said by someone who would stop at nothing to save Emilia.

"And all I did was to tether my fox because a juicy hare is his favourite game. Would you help me lift up Emilia so you can carry her out of here?" I lifted her first before I handed her limp form to him, trying to appear disinterested. "I will take care of Tobias. When the Druids have finished their descent you can use their rope ladders to carry her out."

Half expecting Morgana to rear up at any moment, Jack looked at the prostrate animal and asked,

"Have I really killed her then, Merlin?"

"You cannot kill a spirit, Jack, because it is not alive in the first place. It is a different form of being and is immortal. God, the great magician, created that spirit and only he can destroy it," I said solemnly. "But," I added with a twinkle, "you can interfere with her energetic force and stun her for a while, and that is all we will need to get out of here as quickly as possible. Once you are outside you will not know the terrain, because it is all, except for the Tor, now heavily wooded. Wait for me up there and I will send you my nurse, Angharad, to look after her bruised face."

"Do you know what happened to her?"

"Yes. Regretfully, I had to knock her out," I confessed, brushing her hair gently off her face and longing to kiss her lip better. "It was the best way of keeping her safe."

And Jack's face said it all: one moment it shone in victory, the next it collapsed in confusion, only to recover when he realised that an ancient Druid like me tenderly touching his girl could not possibly pose a threat to his closeness to Emilia.

"She is going to be so mad when she comes to, Merlin. I wouldn't be in your place for anything!"

But I sensed that Jack meant the opposite of what he said.

26

At Belstone Tor

0.20am, Friday September 10th, Merlin's time

As SOON AS JACK REACHED THE LADDER, Emily stirred in his arms and opened her eyes. Her voice croaked as she whispered, "I'm scared. Where are we?"

Immediately she began patting her ragged top and pants and, turning her head in alarm, demanded, "Jack, where's Roget? I can't see him anywhere! Do you know where he is?"

"Toby found Roget and he is here in my pocket, safe and sound. We're back in Merlin's time in a cave underneath the Nine Maidens. We've got to get out of here fast for Belstone Tor."

"Put me down, will you? I don't remember you being kidnapped. Why are you here?"

"When Toby and I came looking for you with Merlin, we found out that Morgana le Fey had captured you. And Em, let me tell you what a piece of work she was! She brought you back through time to here."

"Until you rescued me."

"Well," he said, "not exactly."

"Thanks, Action Man!" She lifted up on her toes and kissed him quickly on the cheek, which she just as quickly regretted. "Ouch!" she cried, putting her hand over her mouth. "I forgot about my fat lip!" But she still managed to laugh.

"Later, when the swelling's gone down," said Jack, smiling at her, "I'll expect another one of those!" And across his face he sketched a line to his lips. "Only it will be a little further down and to the right. Can you crawl your way up this ladder, Em? Don't worry; I'll be right behind you."

Once they were sitting on the granite seat of the Tor, Jack explained what had happened to them since the accident on the Bonhay Road. He concluded with,

"This is where Toby found Roget. And here," he added, fishing in his pocket, "is your turtle, and the earring that you left as part of the breadcrumb trail for us to follow."

"I'd never leave Roget, and I didn't drop my earring, either!" She was indignant.

"Well, someone did," Jack declared, "because we found them both and they are clearly yours!"

For a moment Emily searched for an answer, and reflected on who could have created the trail, and the only person she could think of was Merlin. She blushed and asked,

"Now you've met an Arthurian legend, what do you think of Merlin?"

It took Jack only an instant to realise the danger in this question because he recalled Emily saying she preferred Merlin to Sir Galahad. He began his reply very cautiously, carefully picking each word.

"Well, first of all I will have to get to know Merlin a little better because I only met him an hour ago. But he described himself as a weaver of magic, and from what I've seen he can do some awesome tricks. He can fade in and out like the Cheshire Cat, and hang upside down by his feet like a bat. But his best trick was time travelling from our time back into his time. It's amazing! I only hope he knows how to do it in reverse to get us out of here. Being around him, I kept seeing things I know to be impossible, and they happen right in front of me. How did you find him?"

"I've only known him for a short time too, just a day or so. Honestly, I keep thinking I'll wake up soon, because what I see is not my idea of how the universe works. You and I have moved from our living present to his living past, and by all our reasoning his time should be done and dusted. I find it hard to get my head round all that's happening. Anyway, Merlin appeared in my bedroom last night to return some sunglasses that his jackdaw stole…"

Jack felt her brow and interrupted her, smiling.

"You must have concussion because it couldn't possibly be true. No one, but nobody has ever got past your dragon mother and into your bedroom, and God knows I've tried! So you must be hallucinating…"

"No, I'm not, but I do have a terrible headache. But it's like you say; something impossible happens whenever Merlin's around. When I was attacked he saved me, but tonight he let me down. I called him over and over…"

"He said he's been fighting the Saxons, and his face was blackened commando style…"

"Jack, he promised me that he'd protect me and he didn't. I had a man with a knife at my throat… We had a car accident, I think our car is totalled… Next thing, I was captured, lifted into the sky on a giant bat and then I vomited and passed out." Emily was close to tears.

"You know, Merlin could've been protecting you in ways you

don't know about." Jack was trying to console her and put his arm around her. He, too, was puzzled at Merlin and why he just sat there in the cavern saying and doing nothing and leaving him to do all the work.

"Anyway, you're safe now from Morgana."

"Who the hell is this Morgana?"

"She's of Merlin's time, not ours. She's a spirit who's not born yet. You remember the painting we have of Morgana le Fay? That name is her future name. When she's born she'll have the same mother as King Arthur. She's unbelievably weird. She's very sexy and very beautiful, but she's totally manipulative. One moment she's quite warm and human and the next minute she's like the Bride of Dracula, ready to walk over you in spiky, black boots."

Emily giggled and her mood lifted. Jack continued,

"I suspect that disguised as a man, she was the one who kidnapped you."

"You're making her up, Big Red, or she fronts one of those death metal bands you adore. Merlin told me someone wanted to kill me to stop Mum's archaeological excavations. But given what happened with attacks on you and Toby too, I'm sure there's something much more to this than he has told me so far."

"You know I was doubtful—well, I'm not any more. All I can conclude is that Morgana has got it in for me because of some misguided belief that I am Uther Pendragon, the man who seduced her mother and cuckolded her father. She's quite delusional."

"Let's assume you are right and she loathes Pendragon, then why doesn't she invade his time and kill him before he can seduce her mother?"

"To that I can only conclude: she would if she could. Something or someone must be preventing her from doing that."

"And why does she attack Toby?"

"She doesn't like anything about him. She claims he was the older brother of Pendragon."

"I remember hearing you talking to her at some stage in the cave. What happened?"

"I was playing a game with her based on a fairy tale I remembered. I was trying to get her to shape-shift into something small enough that I could kill with my Taser. Once I had convinced her to be a hare, I zapped her and thought I had killed her, but from what Merlin says it seems I only stunned her. But at least it gave us a chance to get you out of there."

"Yes, it did. But I think you're right to fear. She would be really mad with you now!"

"Maybe she is," Jack shrugged. "I know it would be a mistake to underestimate her, but because she loves being the centre of attention I was able to flatter her by appealing to her vanity and trick her quite easily. So easily, that I think someone else must the brains behind these attacks, but I don't know who."

"Nor do I. It doesn't make much sense... Where's Toby, by the way?"

"Merlin's bringing him. Toby made Morgana so angry that she flung him across the cavern. But just before he smashed into the wall, Merlin saved him."

Suddenly they heard a strange snorting sound coming up the hill.

"What's that?" cried Emily, jumping to her feet in alarm. "Who's there?"

A short, round woman with breasts like cabbages and her blonde hair in long, neat plaits, huffed and puffed noisily towards them. There was a rush basket hanging from the crook of one arm, a staff in the crook of the other. Emily thought she looked vaguely familiar.

"Greetings!" the apple-shaped woman piped. "I am Angharad, Myrddin's nurse. I have come to attend to the young woman." She bowed her head towards Emily. "Myrddin said he had given you a knockout blow."

"He what?" Emily cried, alarmed by what she heard. "Are you saying he hit me?" She glowered at the nurse.

"Calm down, now!"

But Emily was not in any mood to calm down. Her head ached and her disappointment at Merlin welled up so much that she burst into tears instead. This was the man who was supposed to protect her, not assault her.

"Come on, Em." Jack took her hand. "Big girls don't cry. If you keep crying, do you know what I'll do?" And Jack did not wait for her answer before he threatened, "I'll start telling you all of my Camelot jokes again until you beg for relief!"

Looking at her, puzzled, Angharad sucked the end of her plait, as if trying to understand her tears. Finally, she said sharply,

"The best protection for you at the time, my young lady, was to render you senseless."

"Knocked unconscious, you mean?"

"I don't know the meaning of that word, unconscious, mistress. I had given you a dose of mandrake—only a knock-out drop—in the water at Whiddon Down, and you reacted quite violently to it by vomiting and seeing things. Because I could not risk using it again, Merlin elbowed your temple and his blow caused you to bite into your lip. Now let me see how you are. He has asked me to put some salve on it."

Pushing her away grumpily, Emily persisted,

"The best protection for me was not to be abducted in the first place!"

"If Morgana had not taken you tonight then she would have grabbed you sometime soon. She was determined to kill you, and it is not open to me to explain why."

"But Morgana said," Jack protested, with a smile on his face and trying to lighten things up, "that she wanted me, not Emily."

"And you believed her? Tosh! She stinks with lies! But you can be sure she wants you now. So, your lordship, you had better be careful. But as soon as Myrddin comes home to us, the gate will close and she will not be able to touch any of you because she cannot get through. Tonight, our Myrddin was ordered by his father to fight the Saxons and he had to do his filial duty. It was a difficult conflict for him because Druids do not fight, and because he had promised to protect you. But his fox allowed him to check your movements, and his mother was with you every moment in his place until he could reach you."

"I didn't see her!"

"Maybe not, but you felt her. She took your little tortoise and left it as a sign for your friends. She squeezed your ear until you took out your earring, and she used it to show them where you had gone into the tunnel."

"But why did he have to hit me?" Emily asked with almost a whine in her voice.

Angharad began quietly, "I am telling you this reluctantly, Emilia, because it seems I have to spell it out. Morgana loves struggle, she loves teasing her victims with great cruelty while she gets excited by feeding on their terror. If you were quiet, your blood was not pumping and she loves it to spurt. Lying there lifeless, you were absolutely no fun for her and you were safe." Angharad moved with deft but gentle strokes to bathe Emily's face and apply a salve over her lips. And then, as if she read Jack's mind and saw he had misgivings about Merlin too, she continued her explanation.

"Kind sir, you will notice how Myrddin protected himself when he sat in silence in the presence of Morgana. Silence is the language of the Light, and silence is the language of the soul. In silence, Myrddin can steady the power of his reason, those immense mental powers he has, and not give anything away. When he is in silence, he will not engage her darkness. That way he could keep your physical bodies safe and your spirits would not be corrupted by her… which is what she really wants. Now," Angharad continued briskly, "Myrddin's mother, Ingraine, asked me to give you this, Emilia."

From her basket, Angharad pulled out a very long rectangular piece of finely spun wool, dyed in the colours of heather.

"It pins around your shoulder like this… There. That looks good! It's very fine and the wool thread, though light, is as strong as spider's silk."

"Will you thank her for me?"

"You can do that yourself…"

Angharad suddenly broke off. Moving quickly, she opened her hands, and with her palms she ran them over an imaginary wall. Her eyes blazed as if she recognised something that made her face collapse in disgust.

"Sit down!" she whispered urgently. "I need to protect you both again!"

It was then Emily flinched, and fearing another blow, she instinctively grabbed Jack's hand.

"Do not worry, Emilia, there is no hitting. This protection is different. Once you left the cavern of the Druids you became invisible to the Dark's eyes, but they can still sense you are here. I have built a shield around you, a haven of safety about ten feet around this Tor. Watch around you, be vigilant, and if you know how, pray. You are safe here, but Moloch, one of the Princes of Darkness, is close. He is a vile spirit who demands his followers sacrifice their first-born babies to him.

"Now because Myrddin has enjoyed too many victories over Morgana and Vortigern, Moloch is here to knock him back into his place. Morgana has recovered and I can sense her plotting something close by here. She will come after you, Pendragon, because you have mightily embarrassed her, and Moloch will come after Myrddin to settle old scores. Myrddin will deal with him. They will engage in a battle of their powers.

"Watch, and be watchful. You will see a great contest. The Druids and all the country folk will be waiting and watching. I did not think this would happen until Myrddin was older, until he came back to us from Gaul. So I can only hope that he has matured his powers sufficiently. I know he has the wit. Ingraine may need my will to send power to Myrddin."

She pulled everything into her basket and, using her staff like a broom-handle, she climbed onto it and took off into the night.

27

How to Prepare a Feast for Bats

0.30am Friday September 10th, Merlin's time

TOBY CAME BACK TO LIFE WITH A JOLT. Then he stretched and slowly warmed his body while keeping his mind at rest. For someone who believed every day was a good day, his last twenty-four hours had been such a problem that he did not even want to think about them. That was until Merlin, who watched his routine intently, grabbed his arm and changed his life.

"Tobias, how are you feeling?" he asked before he added appreciatively of Toby's quick recovery, "You look in good colour!"

"I'm okay, Merlin, but it's strange being slammed through the air; it was like falling, only upwards not downwards. Was it you who saved me from smashing into that rock wall?" When Merlin gave a slight smile, Toby gave him an admiring glance and added quickly, "Thank you! You saved me from a life in a wheelchair!"

Druids in flowing robes pushed past them murmuring, "If you please, make way, make way." They unwound twine from their shoulders or from their waists to lash the carcasses together ready for their removal. While they worked, another group reinforced the roof of the cave because others, working from above, were lifting up the stones to create an opening big enough to haul the animals through. Taking his elbow, Merlin guided Toby to a safe haven behind the altar, away from their traffic. In hushed tones, as if it was a secret, he asked,

"I was interested, Tobias, in how you learned to fly through the air and kick at the same time."

"It isn't any mystery, it's very simple really. I practise a martial art called taekwondo and my dojo, or master, teaches me that my legs are the longest and strongest defence that I have ready, always ready, to use in any fight. I have a special way of breathing to build my chi, or spirit, until I'm ready to leap and twist and kick. But, Merlin, I observed you too, when I was up there on the roof, because although I was immobile I could follow everything, and you appeared disinterested in that strange game between Jack and Morgana. I think you feigned your disinterest."

"Not feigned exactly, Tobias, but I took deliberate control of my emotions to prevent any engagement with the darkness of Morgana."

"If only I could be a magician like you and learn your toughness and how to fight in your way."

As soon as Toby expressed his wish, a look full of hidden meanings passed between them. It made Toby feel so exhilarated that he changed the subject quickly.

"So, I'm okay. But how's Jack? You mentioned he's taken Emily somewhere safe?"

Merlin nodded politely that he had.

"All is good."

While Merlin agreed, he was not prepared to let the subject drop.

"...Your mid-air kick was..." he began, and then paused before deciding whether to speak his new word here, "...awesome! You leapt like a speckled salmon when it rises through the air. Because it was so clever I realised I could use your help."

But Tobias, who was only half-listening, missed the impact of Merlin's compliment. He was studying the stunned hare that was being thrust into a linen sack by a Druid, who then secured it tightly before throwing it over his shoulder. When he spoke it was full of dread

"That Morgana will return, won't she?"

"Any moment she will revive and be as mad as hell, therefore we have to act quickly. I have been thinking about your request to train as a magician… could you fly her giant bat out of here?"

Toby looked horrified.

"Look, Merlin, Jack is training to be a pilot—that would be an excellent job for him."

"You would be right if this bat needed a pilot, but she does not. Instead, she needs someone who is very agile and quick-witted like you. She really needs an acrobat; someone who will respect her while at the same time not taking any nonsense from her. In a minute I will enchant her for you," and when Toby looked perplexed, Merlin explained: "Emilia calls it hyp-notising… and the bat, at least to begin with, will believe you are Morgana, and no matter what happens you will be safe. The Druids have almost opened this cavern to the sky…"

"…Hello down there, where are you?" a Druid interrupted them, poking his head through the hole in the roof, and once he found Merlin in the gloom asked, "Myrddin, where do you want us to put these sacks of moths and buzzing things?"

"Tobias here will pick up three of them and hook them to his saddle. Have someone ready to hand them to him as he comes through the roof on Mot. And Blaise, will you look after my fox until I return?"

Pointing anxiously to the sacks, Toby asked, "And what are those for?"

"I am expecting a companion of Morgana, because wherever she is, he is not far behind. He is the Prince of Lies called Moloch, and he will arrive here soon from across the heavens and will herald his arrival with his army of bats. And I have a plan—"

"I'll bet," Toby interrupted, now delighted with the prospect of a night flight, "that you will release those insects into the sky and drive his bats ape shit with desire!"

"Well, yes, and the bats will divert to feast on them. Ready?"

"Hey! Let's have some fun and pee on his parade. I'm ready to give it a go. I love bats!" he cried, trying to convince himself that he really did. He added, "And this has got to be cool!"

Merlin doubted it, but liked his attitude.

"But, Merlin, really I'd love to learn to be a magician. Would you teach me?"

"It is a lifetime study and it is only open to men and women of honour. You need a Master magician to teach you and I am far from being that yet. I started learning when I was six."

"But I am a fast learner."

"Provided you acknowledge I am not fully trained for the task, I will teach you fast and push you hard and see how you go."

Merlin paused, and looking closely at Toby, said, "We begin with three precepts followed by three lessons. They took me six years to accomplish and I will give them to you within less than a minute, and because you have already been trained in another discipline, they should come much easier to you. The overall philosophy can be summarised in these precepts." Merlin's teaching had attracted an audience of Druids who stood around him listening. He ignored them and spoke to Toby as if he were the only person in the cavern.

"Learn these by heart:

"Within you is the universe. Therefore, all knowledge must lie within. Unlock your deep knowledge and trust your inner knowing.

"All magic is created from commanding with a clear and pure intent. It is created from the breath and by the heart. It is a humble path.

"Take risks and try things, because it is only through the failures that you will learn anything.

"Working with Light can be very exciting. Now, repeat back to me, word for word, what I have just said from 'Within you…'."

It took Toby six attempts before he had it word perfect and Merlin was satisfied.

"Now, we begin by applying these precepts immediately. So your first lesson will be to learn to conquer your fear and self-doubt, and I will teach you that lesson together with the second, which is to obey your Master without argument and never reveal his or her name to anyone else. And there is a third lesson, and it is about self-restraint by giving modest commands and living a modest life."

Feeling pleased with himself, Toby ventured: "You know that your philosophy stuff is not too different to what taekwondo teaches me: courtesy, perseverance, integrity and self-control."

"Yes. There is definitely overlap there. Now, watch me."

As a weaver of magic spells, Merlin usually cloaked his work in shadow, but this time he would treat Toby like an apprentice and demonstrate his art of enchantment before him and to the swelling audience of Druids. But first he needed to clear the air, because Toby had doubts about himself and about Merlin's ability, and they were strong enough to get in the way. When Toby approached Mot, he doubted he could tame an animal as big as a draught horse. He also had qualms about Merlin who had admitted he was not fully-fledged as a magician. Toby knew Merlin could fly but he was disappointed he did not look anything like a wizard, nor did he act how Toby thought a wizard should act. And Merlin knew that when a student as educated as Toby had doubts about his master, it would be impossible for him to obey without question.

"Obviously, before we can conquer your self-doubt," Merlin said, "we will have to conquer your misgivings about me. I think there is a question you want to ask. So, ask it now."

"You know, Merlin," Toby blurted out, "this is going to sound really dumb, but you look like a regular Roman and not like a wizard. Why don't you wear a magic garment like a cloak or a wizard's hat and why don't you carry a wand!"

Merlin laughed.

"And why don't I have a clean face? Seriously, Tobias, would you fight a Prince of Darkness in a cloak and pointed hat? For all the time that I am a soldier I will dress like a soldier and carry a sword." And waving his staff in the air, Merlin said, "My staff is my wand," and he pointed it towards Toby before lifting it above his head, releasing a shower of stars from its tip that circled Toby's head and left him bedazzled. "Besides, Tobias, a wand is just a cut-down staff!" And before his eyes Merlin broke his staff across his knee into three pieces and waved a wand-sized piece in front of Toby's eyes before restoring the piece to a full length staff.

"When I am discharged from the Legion I may change my garments, but dressing as a soldier, as you see, does not diminish any of my powers. Nevertheless, you have given me a brilliant idea for tonight because tonight I do need to look astonishing. Therefore I will wear a robe so grand and so long that even Emilia and Jack sitting down at the Tor, and all the other country folk, will be excited to see me in the sky. Now, stand beside Mot while I enchant her."

"You know, Merlin, I still doubt I am going to be brave enough to fly a giant bat..."

"Tobias, you cannot breathe until you inhale, you cannot walk until you stand on your own two feet, and you cannot know unless you try and begin to scale this mountain of your self-doubt." Merlin spoke while smiling and waving his hand at the bat. "Behind every veil of fear lies a prize. Be excited, or be fearful, or be both, but do it!"

Waving his hands again, and this time before the upside down face of the bat, Merlin spoke in the Cornish language unknown to Toby. Of course, he hypnotised Toby as well, and Toby told Jack later that deep down he knew that; but at that moment he was so fizzed with excitement, he did not care to look too closely at what was happening. He just loved being centre stage, ready to star in his own adventure and in the hands of a Master. But it was going to be hard for him to learn to give modest commands because he was not in the mood for modesty. Perhaps he could fake it.

Taking a deep breath, and in his most theatrical voice, Toby boomed his first command:

"Get down from there, you odious creature, and kneel before me, for I am your new master!"

The giant bat slid from its roost and, turning her mouse face away from him, dropped the contents of her bowels on the cavern's floor.

With effort Merlin managed to keep his face composed around his twitching nose, and in an even tone said:

"Given the message that she has left on the ground for you, I am wondering whether Mot considered what you said was a modest enough command." Merlin turned to the bat and touching its head gently he ordered: "No licking, no drool, Mot," but deliberately did not explain to Toby why.

Crawling onto her back, Toby grasped the reins and whistled.

"Giddy up, sweetheart… now it is show-time!"

And when Mot did not move, Merlin suggested,

"If you try less exuberance and less spirit, it could be a more modest command!"

Perhaps Toby was incapable of understanding modesty because he dug his heels in and yelled,

"Give me uplift, Rat-face, uplift!" And when he found that even that method of command was just as ineffective, all Merlin could do was smile his I told you so smile and sigh.

"Why do you not treat your beautiful bat with some respect, saying something like: 'If it pleases you, Mot, can we go now?'"

When Toby finally took Merlin's hint, Mot took off smoothly.

But Toby was in a hurry to prove to the world he was fearless and could do everything. He raced through the cavity in the roof and Merlin thought it prudent to let him go first. When the Druids handed them three bulging sacks apiece, Merlin fumbled his to allow Toby to keep his head start.

"It's hard to believe that I'm flying a giant bat through a moonlit sky to God knows where," he called out to Merlin, "beside the greatest wizard on earth who flies like he's pole-vaulting with his staff and defying gravity. Is this better than being a rock star?" Toby waved his hand at his imaginary audience: "Yep! Sure is!"

With that, they looked up and saw them: thousands and thousands of them. The sky was filled with bats, they rose and dipped on wings no wider than the span of a hand and, manoeuvring very quickly, like a school of fish, they changed their direction as soon as Toby approached. Merlin drifted away to join their flight, and only to return quite suddenly to catch hold of Mot's reins to stop her flying home.

"Are they not beautiful, Tobias?" Merlin asked, lost in a glow of admiration. "Are they not exactly like flying mice? I just flew as one with them to warn them about what we are going to do.

I am angry that Moloch could use these dear creatures as evil omens to create a sense of foreboding to herald his presence."

"Who is this Moloch? How come, Merlin, he has squadrons of bats at his command?"

"Well, I will tell you what Lord Michael told me about him," and Merlin climbed behind Tobias onto Mot's back and tied his sacks to the back of Mot's saddle. Then silently and with utmost care so as not to alert Toby, he surrounded them both with a silver chord of protection from the vileness of Moloch, because Merlin knew that whenever he or anyone else of the Light spoke about a being of the Dark, they drew that spirit towards them. Merlin's Light always attracted Moloch's Dark.

"But Merlin, before you begin, who is Lord Michael?"

"He is an archangel."

Toby's irony was just short of sarcasm when he exclaimed,

"Of course, he is!" and Merlin let Toby continue with, "How silly of me! And you generally discuss the meaning of life with archangels?"

Merlin sighed and practised patience before he replied evenly,

"I have found that archangels announce and pronounce, and I listen and there is very little discussion in it."

Once Merlin had crossed himself again for his own protection, he began:

"Now to Moloch. He is one of the lords of the underworld who govern the legions of the Dark in the Roman Empire. We, and by that I mean we Romans, defeated Hannibal, who was the leader of Carthage in the Punic Wars, and that was hundreds of years ago. We burned Carthage, which is the city of Moloch, and once we'd burned it right down to the ground we destroyed all of his vile temples. Ever since, Moloch has stalked the Roman people wherever we have colonised in this world.

"Under Emperor Constantine the Great we became Christians, and that is when the trouble with Moloch increased, because he engaged the barbarians to destroy all the God-fearing people. Moloch is a malignant spirit. In his beguiling voice, he offers anyone who will listen whatever they desire, and once they are intoxicated by it, he exacts his price. These poor bats are creatures of the dark places he inhabits, and he has made them his slaves."

"It crossed my mind to ask you," Tobias interjected, "whether Morgana was working alone or whether she had some help."

"Morgana is well and truly in the clutches of Moloch. Morgana once desired to be the ruler of Carthage and, the throne being Moloch's to bequeath, he sold it to her for an extraordinarily high price."

"What was that?"

"His price was the sacrifice of her first-born son by slitting his throat and tossing him into his fires. But that was not the end of it, because once she climbed onto the throne of Carthage she wanted to stay there; so he exacted a further higher price from her. Moloch explained it to her this way:

"'Your first-born was the price of gaining this throne, but now because you want to remain there and repel all usurpers, there will be a further price. But it is a postponed price, my dear one, which you do not have to give a second thought to now. However, in a thousand years from now, you are to hand the kingdom of Britannia to my chosen servant.'

"In other words, Tobias, she has to deliver our Britannia to the Dark. My purpose is to stop her, and becoming a magician entails that you work for the Light, you act with valour with your sword of Light and you take a pledge to fight against the Dark. Tonight Moloch and I will enter into a contest; a battle for the mastery of the elements in this part of Britannia. This is a battle I have been preparing for all my life, and recently I have been tutored by Lord Michael on how to increase my proficiency, because I fought Moloch once before and lost. This time I intend to defeat him and chain him back in his under-world."

"Then Merlin, why in God's name," a quite bewildered Toby asked, "are we chasing around after his bats?"

"Because, my friend, I want to win this battle on my own terms, not on his, and I will strip away his pretences and stop his abuse of God's creatures. Are you ready? As soon as you see me release my moths—that's the blue string—let go of yours as well. After a little while, when the moths have spread out across the sky, release the yellow string, and last of all let the green string go."

And Merlin left him so he could attend to his own feeding of these beauteous bats.

As soon as Toby pulled the blue string, a cloud of moths flut-tered around his head and dissolved silently into the night. Mot, who feared that this fine feast was escaping her, bolted after them, and Toby, lost in the beauty of moths backlit by moon-light, almost fell off. He vowed to be far more careful before he untied the yellow string.

"But the night is stunning," he called out to Merlin, who was too far away to hear him, "and watching these bats is like being in an air-show of antique planes. God, life is good!" And he swal-lowed his fear before he released cautiously the contents of the next jumping-sack. From it came a swarm of angry bees that took off, leaving only a small rear-guard to buzz around him. Toby jammed his heels into Mot.

"Let's go, Rat-face, let's get out of here before they make a pincushion out of both of us!"

Merlin, anxious about his apprentice's welfare, returned to see how he was faring.

"Well, Tobias, that went well… those dumbledores buzzed beautifully. We have scattered all the bats and they are distracted while they catch their supper. Now it's time to let the wasps go."

Toby went pale.

"Wasps? Shit, Merlin, you're mad! The bees were bad enough. Can't you get us some more moths?"

How could Merlin reassure him? If Toby wanted him as his Master, it was not his role to reassure him. His role was instead to instruct and command him.

"It is autumn, Tobias, we are fortunate that this is just the right time of year for wasps, and we have thousands of them. And it is not for you to determine what these bats want. They eat, as we do, whatever is in season," Merlin said with a straight face. "If you tie the reins around your ankles and lean well over the side, you can release them underneath Mot, and then if you jam your heels into her ribs and climb into the sky as fast as you can, you should be free of stings."

Well that worked, Merlin thought, because Tobias changed the subject, asking:

"How do you fly, Merlin? How do you defy gravity?"

"What do you mean, gravity? I heard you mention it before. What is it?"

"Well, we're not really sure. But we think gravity is a force that causes all matter to be attracted to other matter. There's a law of this Earth that says whatever goes up must come down, so that whenever I let go of something, it falls down to the ground, it does not fall back up into the sky! Gravity is the force from the Earth that brings us down. Birds, wasps and bats fly, Emily and I should not. So how come you are the exception? How do you fly?"

"I use this staff. I point it at a source of magnetic power on the ground and my staff, with the crystals and minerals I have embedded in its tip, countermands its power. Perhaps that power is what you call gravity. I can then use my staff like a rudder to steer across the sky or to lift something very heavy like a giant tor. Later I will give you a go, but for now..."

"Okay," Toby said, but it wasn't okay. If Merlin with a few rocks could countermand gravity, why wasn't our science doing it too?

"What's next?"

"Next, I will create some rain to bring the remaining bats to land, and onto this land, the land of my father, and into his caves where they will be safe from the madness of Moloch."

"Now listen to me, Merlin. Surely it's easier just to exterminate the bats—kill all the buggers, or do anything rather than this all complicated snack-time served in mid-air?"

"Never, Tobias."

Sometimes your best students will disappoint you, Merlin remembered his tutor of Greek saying, '...they disappoint because they do not have enough respect.' He spoke to Toby sternly again, as you would to an impudent child, and pointing to himself said,

"I, Myrddin, am a bat." And pointing to Toby, "You, Tobias, are a bat. Remember, inside you is the universe. Bats are our brothers, and they have been bewitched by the darker magic of Moloch. And we will free them, not kill them. I will show Moloch that whenever he subjugates any living creatures in Britannia, I will free them.

"Now we will move onto stage three and free the wasps."

Toby, with his heart in his mouth, tied the reins as Merlin directed and delicately hoisted the bag over the side of the giant bat. As soon as he let the wasps go free, he yelled,

"You said you needed an acrobat, which was fine; but if this is what you meant, if this acrobat falls off the bat, where is my safety net?"

Satisfied he could reassure him this time, Merlin yelled back,

"I am your safety net!"

As Emily and Jack observe the vast aerial display, they are enthralled by the bats diving and swooping, and Toby's pluck in handling them. Jack thinks, 'Wow he's become fearless and free!' and he really admires his guts.

As thousands of bats swooped on the buzzing wasps, they created a wonderful spectacle, a frenzy of feeding. Lying down across Mot, Toby watched some of them head for local caves with their food tucked into their wing pockets. Eventually there were only a hundred or so left swooping around him, holding out for more treats. Breathing a deep sigh of relief, Toby murmured to himself, 'Thank God that's over!'

But it wasn't. Toby, the student who wanted to learn, did not know his lessons were just beginning.

28

The Battle of the Elements

1.30 am, Friday September 10th, Merlin's time

FAR ABOVE TOBIAS, AND FAR ENOUGH *above Dartmoor that it looks like a blur, the crimson mask of Moloch stretches across the night sky.*

"What is that?" Emilia cries, and I hear her with my inner ear. And when Moloch roars, "I will make the sky crackle, Merlin!" she jumps and remarks to Jack, "Whatever this is, it can't be good!"

And straightaway, Moloch does what he says he will do! And I, Myrddin, watch him in awe because I have never seen such artistry in the sky! Here is a true Master at work. From the thunder-heads that he forms in the clouds, he forks thousands of horns of lightning that embroider the heavens with their delicate tracery. And as his lightning flicks around the sky, Dartmoor turns silver in its light.

"I will match your challenge," I boom back, "because I will make my rain wild and my wind roar!"

From below him, I tell myself I am as good as he is, and then bite my tongue. Where is the modesty in that, Myrddin? I spin inside my massive cape. My helpers slashed its fabric into ribbons of purple and green, and by enchanting every single strand it pulses with colour. Now the cloak falls a hundred feet under me and swirls wildly in the wind. Can Emilia see me now? I twirl my cloak again to be sure. She waves; I smile at her and empty my mind.

When Emily realizes that Merlin has changed into his cloak of many colours, she gasps. For a moment she feels like a girl in an Austen novel who is dazzled by her soldier when he parades for the first time before her in his full dress uniform.

"My God, he is hot!"

On the other hand, when Emily looks at the spectacle, she is full of awe and wonder. From her safe and remote distance on the ground she finds it is like admiring a far-off fireworks display.

Once our challenges roar again across the sky, the remaining bats vanish and the heavens become safe enough for me to begin my alchemy. It is easy for me to imagine what effects I want because I have practised them for over five years in desolate places; and rain and wind, as you know, are my weather of choice. I appreciate their every nuance and I love their power. With my staff balanced across my shoulders, I spin around so that the skeins of colour in my cloak haze, and the faster I rotate, the faster I can shift the direction of the wind.

But to do even more I will need help. The moor below me will not give me any, because it is impassive and will not take sides. But it does react when it feels the impact of our contest. It flares suddenly whenever the lightning of Moloch strikes a giant tor, or when the lightning twists hundreds of the pin-oaks surrounding the tor by setting them ablaze. Then the moor sighs back down again into its quiet indifference.

As Jack views the battle in the heavens, he becomes impatient because he wants to watch it like he watches a Rugby game; this is a match between Merlin and that angry red face in the clouds, and he longs for the brawl. He wonders aloud to Emily, 'When are Moloch and Merlin going to stop screaming at each other and truly engage? When am I going to see a bit of biff?'

Although Ingraine and Angharad send me in pulses of rose light their own power, it is not enough. I know I will need even more. I call for my spirit helpers and my sprites to take form. Ariel, a blaze of emerald fire, Pook, a flash of purple, and Wisp, a crimson streak, swoop before me shooting their colours across the sky like the Northern Lights. They appear as one in a column of blue flame.
I sing to them:

> *"This is the hour, my friends,*
> *To enchant the winds*
> *Make them rattle and whistle*
> *Through the hollows of the Dark.*
>
> *Oh, wild spirits,*
> *Bend the trees to the earth,*
> *Shake loose their apples*
> *And spill their yellowed leaves*
> *And shatter all the precious glass*
> *In the castles of greedy kings*
>
> *I pray that you*
> *Empty the raging rivers of heaven,*
> *Suck up the sap from the ocean,*
> *Wring all the tears from the moon*
> *And dump all their ooze over*
> *The phantom of Moloch*
>
> *And deliver him from his evil.*
>
> *So be it."*

Ariel flies up to join Crook sitting on my head, and Pook and Wisp perch beside my mice on each shoulder. There they will work with me until we can create a storm of wind and rain, the like of which Dartmoor has never experienced.

When the first heavy drops of rain hit the head of Tobias, he tries to protect his gelled hair with the only thing he has to grab: his sack for his wasps. He disturbs the few remaining insects and tries to shush and shoo them away. But as the water streams down his face, his stiff peaks melt and his fair hair becomes plastered across his forehead. His unease grows because he knows better than anyone what happens to bats in the rain. Tobias has studied how rain disrupts their sense of where they are, and once they lose that sense, they quickly return home to the safety of their caves. This is when he realises that he, too, is riding on a bat, and therefore his bat in the rain should return home to the Druid's cave under the Nine Maidens… But does my enchantment countermand Mot's instincts? Because he does not know the answer he calls out to me.

"Hey, Merlin… I've got these questions: Will Mot's sense of direction become disrupted in this rain? Will she crash-land or will she fly off with me to her bat-cave? Or did your enchantment waterproof her?"

I ignore him. Tobias has to be tested to find his own well of courage, and I have other things on my mind.

KABOOM! The crack comes out of nowhere. It is a clap of thunder that makes the heavens rattle and the earth tremble. I have to admit it is one of Moloch's best.

Mot drops suddenly, and as she falls from the sky Tobias instinctively tightens the reins and tries to level her off to what he believes is parallel to the ground.

"You will be fine!" I yell out to him.

"Wherever I go, Merlin, I look up and there you are, stretched across the sky; and wow, you look fantastic!"

As the sky dances, it billows with the curtains of colour from my sprites, and Tobias shakes with fright. To calm himself, he tries to whistle, but when only a squeak escapes from out his mouth, he forces a song out instead:

> *"I see a bad moon rising*
> *I see trouble on the way*
> *I see earthquakes and lightnin'*
> *I see bad times today."*

"You'll be okay, Rat-face," he consoles Mot. "There is this storm that is muscling its way across Dartmoor. It is only a Category One, and you'll be okay with me because I love to chase storms. Come on, you'll be fine if you just enjoy the glorious terror of it all."

It would be days later before Tobias realised that he had built a clever way to cope whenever he was under threat—he deceived himself; and his self-deception worked so brilliantly that he was able to convince himself that he loved chasing storms. And because he could not question me, he assumed my enchantment was perfect for all weather conditions and he and his bat were safe. But he would soon come to realise they were not.

My rain batters everyone. It falls in heavy sheets from a sky that keeps on changing. Gone are the beautiful lights of only fifteen minutes ago, and now even the darkness is bruised by the same colours of purple and green that shine in my cape; and it is slashed by the lightning that comes so close to us that almost instantly the thunder replies. Tobias sings to Mot:

> *"Don't go round tonight*
> *It's bound to take your life*
> *There's a bad moon on the rise."*

"This is awesome, Merlin!" Tobias cries out. He counts aloud the seconds from the flash to the boom. It is exactly three seconds. "It's close, very close. So despite the thrill, I think we will edge away a bit, Rat-face."

But the giant bat has other ideas. Mot has caught a storm fever, and this is a delirium that turns her into a bucking and swivelling mule with only one purpose, and that is to toss Tobias off her back and return to the shadowy safety of her cave. For what seems like a forever, Tobias loses control. The bat dives and rises and dives again, then levels before it rises only to dive again.

"Merlin," he yells out, "how long will this go on for?" I know that he is becoming really anxious when he sings:

> *"I hear hurricanes a-blowin'*
> *I know the end is coming soon*
> *I fear rivers over-flowin'*
> *I hear the voice of rage and ruin."*

The pleas of Tobias shriek out into the sky.

"Why don't you do something, Merlin, and give us a break?" His face is pale, and when he is breathing more rain than air, he realises he is in an unmanageable fall and only by constantly changing his position can he hope to regain some control. But in so doing, he loses all sense of location and time; and he may have been in this state for five minutes or fifty. And in truth, for all he knows, he may also have been riding upside down and never have known the difference. Because for him the sky has become moor and the moor sky and everywhere, everything is water, boiling water. A twitch of panic makes him look over the side, and when *he realizes he does not recognise anything, he screams out in my direction,*

"Merlin, I should have written a will!

> *Hope you got your things together*
> *Hope you are quite prepared to die*
> *Looks like we're in for nasty weather*
> *One eye is taken for an eye."*

I ignore him. He has to do this himself.

"Please listen to me, God. Merlin is simply wondrous," Emily is praying, "and I thank you for creating him, but his immense power surprises me. Flying is one thing… it is even within the realms of possibility. But what he is doing now… this is different… this is completely different. How can an ordinary person do that? It is like watching giants play chess with the stars!"

Then, becoming really anxious, her questions flood in again.

"Why, God, does Merlin have to contest with this strange creature? Can this really be what you created him for? Can't you find someone else? There must be someone who can fight this evil? What about Saint Michael, the Dragon Slayer? What's he doing tonight? Isn't it his job to take on evil? Michael, where are you? Can't you help him? Please?"

Emily goes cold inside as the combat continues.

"Who was it who said," she demands of God, "that you can't conjure something from thin air? Well, God, I am watching Merlin do it. I thought it was something that only you could do. Or do you delegate certain powers?

"And God, who is this Moloch? He has no form or substance but demonstrates these extraordinary powers. Is he pure mind?

Did you delegate these powers to him, too? Does he think he is normal? Does he know he is evil? Does it worry him? Maybe he is as delighted with his powers as Merlin is with his. Did you hear what Angharad implied? She implied Moloch was a malignant force… What were you doing creating something like that? And if she is right, what happens if Moloch wins? Will all hell break loose and will that be the end of us?"

The spectacle above made her feel insignificant and completely out of her depth. Only nine hours ago she was dancing with Merlin on the ceiling, knowing she had been hypnotised, and thinking how wonderful it would be to kiss him. Now she is watching him conjure wind and rain in an epic contest like a master of the universe. What kind of a man is this? How will he get out of this alive?

"Dear God, I am terrified because I am completely and absolutely out of my depth. Help me!"

'This is easy,' I tell myself. 'My Emilia has no need to worry. While it is not child's play, it is not really a mortal combat. He moves, I counter-move. It is like a game. It is a display of power, and we each source our power from different beings. As soon as Moloch cries out again and makes the lightning crackle and the thunder explode, I will answer him with my roar of wild water. I will whip up my wind until I turn the rain itself on its side so it will sting the whole world like a million wasps.'

When the branches and leaves fly past in such wild abandon I wonder for a moment if I should slow my assault, but fearing that it would be seen as weakness, I increase it instead. The howl of it, which begins faintly, grows and grows until it screeches with terrifying shrieks and the trees roar and the branches crack. It even rat-

tles the stones that Jack sits on. He wants biff! Well, Jack, here is some biff… the brawl is on!

"Why don't you sing us all another one of your lullabies, Merlin," Moloch sneers at me, "and send us all to sleep?"

I say nothing. This is a battle of powers, not of minds. I am absorbed in changing the rain to hail and building a spark of lightning so powerful it will shatter all the scorn of Moloch across the heavens.

Tobias is really worried; his swagger seems to have deserted him. With hail lashing his face, he falls forward across Mot's neck in an attempt to calm her again. At first she is merely trembling, but as the noise and the lightning increase she starts to convulse, and they both shake uncontrollably. It is then that Tobias starts to pray in earnest. And that is good.

I strengthen my breathing and draw on all the blue energy available from the sprites and from another surprising source that seems to be angelic… Has someone been praying to Lord Michael? And I mix them together with the stream of rose light from my nurse and mother, and at the moment when I am close to exploding, I release it in a purple rush of power. My bolt of lightning splits the sky and catches Moloch by surprise. It pierces his crimson light and shatters him into a million flicks of flame. As he disintegrates, he screeches,

"I will get you, Merlin!"

I shrug and smile.

"Moloch has not even touched Merlin," Jack calls out. "First of all, Merlin won by reclaiming all those bats, and even though Moloch kept challenging him he never really put up a fight. In their battle of powers, Merlin turns the lightning back on Moloch and smashes the bugger to smithereens. So round two goes to Merlin... and Merlin wins. Good on you, Merlin!"

"Awesome, Merlin!" Emily cries out. "Come on back, please!" She prays silently to Michael the Archangel again, "Thank you. Please help him come back alive."

"Merlin, where are you?" Toby yells. "I need you!"

I race across the sky, I am so puffed up with my own importance that I challenge the Prince of Darkness again. Taunting him, I boom, "Now Moloch, I will make your darkness light! I will bring in light to God's earth and make the sun shine!"

"Leave it alone, Merlin," Jack screams a warning. "We saw you smash Moloch to smithereens. You have won! Now come back to us."

With the tempest howling around me, I disregard Jack's warning and listen instead to Moloch, who answers me with calm calculation,

"I will turn your autumn, Merlin, into my very own winter!"

I call on my sprites again and sing jubilantly into the violet night:

> *"It is the hour, my friends*
> *To enchant the sky and*
> *Charm her to kiss the night goodbye*
> *And release our world from*
> *Its shadow's grip.*

Tell the moon it is time
To pull her cape over her face
And go to sleep.

Tell the sun that night's eclipse is over
And the moon gives him free reign
To light the sky.

Oh my wild spirits, banish the stars and
Pinch all the cockerel's feathers until they crow.
Can you not see?
Now it is dawn!"

I wait and I wait. The spirits of air and light are silent beside me. I wait to see the effects of my enchantment, but nothing happens. The moon stays behind a cloud and the dark night reigns over the sky. I wait, and no matter how hard I use my will to demand that the sun return, absolutely no light returns!

"Do you think he's still winning?" I hear Emilia asking in the ear of my mind. "Why won't Merlin come back here and just let it be?"

She is anxiously watching my challenge, and after hearing Moloch's reply she can see that it is his command, and not mine, that rules. The moon disappears, taking her light with her, and a bleak north wind whips across the moor. The bitterness of winter descends on Dartmoor! Both Emilia and Jack know in that one act that Moloch had won, and somehow, someway, I had slipped from winning to losing.

But I have not given up.

I sing another appeal to the heavens.

"Still the sun does not rise!
Will you tell him?

He is lazy and
While he sleeps in
Our teeth chatter.

The sprites ask you
To warm this world
With your beams of fire.

So be it!"

The sky roars with the laughter of Moloch.
Over-reaching yourself, you pup?
The sun is not yours to command.
It belongs with the stars,
Not here with the earth.
The Dark is my domain, not yours.

Watch my white veil spread
And wither your father's fruit.

It will suck
With each wheeze of its icy breath.
Like a spectre
All life from the living

You lose, Merlin.
Now rush home to your mam.
This Dartmoor is mine.
What will be next?

The rain still blusters but the wind eases in fits and starts, until eventually it lets up. It is only when the thunder becomes a distant echo that an eerie silence wraps around Tobias as if someone has just slammed the shutters on the storm.

Bit by bit, Mot calms too. Tobias keeps his eyes closed because he is utterly exhausted. But in this sudden quiet, he feels very cold and his hands, still gripping the reins, shake as if grasped by a wintry claw. Sensing a gentle touch on his face, his eyes fly open and he sits up, and as he surges to life he cries,

"Who is it? Is that you Merlin?"

"No. It is not me."

Since the moon left, it is pitch black and he was merely touched by the snow and dusted by its powder.

As if I had not noticed he calls out to me grimly,

"Moloch's winning, Merlin!"

My face frozen, I land beside him. Now it is washed clean, and gleams with droplets of rain. There is ice in my hair. Tobias is so cold he is almost speechless, but he still manages a wisecrack:

"Merlin, old man, you lost your war paint, because I can see a very white face. But, you know, we will have a talk about this weather. It's very nasty. In fact, it's bloody awful! You keep this up and I'll be so fit and so thin, I'll be able to give up my gym membership."

When I look at him, perplexed, he changes his approach. Full of that sudden euphoria you experience when you know you have survived something awful, he cries out to me,

"Hey, that was one wild ride, and you did a great job with the special effects, Merlin! Now, what's happening?"

"As you saw, I was able to coax the wind and rain to life but the sun has not returned. There is no light; and instead we have Moloch's dark. He was one step ahead of me, Tobias. Each time I

countermanded his moves, he counteracted mine. Now the snow is falling heavily over my father's land, and ice storms will come in September and they will freeze our animals and destroy our crops. I will have to source some hot African wind. This will be a long night because he blocked the light of the moon and the stars as well. I know you are able to tell me the time, what time is it?"

"We've been up here one and a half hours. So it's about two in the morning."

"Inside my clothing my poor animals are nearly frozen. Could you take my mice and my jackdaw? Once you lose height, set my jackdaw free and follow him to Belstone Tor where you will find Jack and Emilia. When you are there, can you call him back to you and put him under your clothes to thaw him out?"

"What about you?"

"I cannot let Moloch ruin our grain and leave our people to starve this winter. I have to outwit him. But then I will be back."

"Good luck!" Tobias waves to me.

But I know he is not optimistic that I will regain the lead. And nor am I.

"Ingraine, why did I fail? Why could I not make the dark, light?"

"Be humble, Myrddin, and learn. I instructed you, just as you instructed Tobias, that our enchantments only work from humble commands. The results of this contest are equal... he made thunder and lightning, but they faded under your wind and rain. You failed to make it light because he countermanded it... One each... you are in balance. In your first challenge you worked with the spirits of the air and water to create wind and rain. You did not instruct them how to do their work. Instead you described the intensity of the wind and rain you wanted. You were prayerful and you were successful.

"*In your second challenge, you took on a very difficult task. And you know as I know how heady you were with success. To turn dark into light is the work of an accomplished master. And how did you do it? You commanded the spirits to extinguish the moon. Why? Does not the moon get its light from the sun? You commanded the spirits to trick the sun into wakefulness. Why? Is the sun our only source of light?*"

When I did not answer because I was thinking through my errors, she insisted,

"*Well, is it? Is the sun our only source of light?*"

"*No, of course not. There are others. There are fires and burning oils and elements that blaze and lightning and swamp gas…*"

"*And light that comes from fireballs, and fox fire and glow worms, and volcanoes that spurt and from lava that flows. All these are sources of light and each of them are of our earth. You chose and commanded only one source and the sun is not yours to command, Myrddin. The sun is the flame of heaven; it is not from or of this earth, like wind and rain. Did you not break the first rule of manifestation?*" *Ingraine demanded.*

I nodded my agreement, miserable.

Ingraine pressed me in an even tone, "*And what does the rule say?*"

"*Do not prescribe the manner, nor the way to achieve what it is you desire. The magician's magician, God, is The Way, and not you; and The Way is always the choice of God who knows and sees all.*"

"*So when you prescribed that the sun and only the sun must shine, you cut out every other kind of light from blazing, and any one of them or all of them could have been available to serve you. So, on reflection, what is the proper command?*"

"*It is, 'Let there be light'.*"

"*And the prayer? You forgot the prayer.*"

"*'God willing'. And the command: 'So be it'.*"

"Learn the lesson! And, by the way my dearest son, for heaven's sake stop showing off in front of Emilia. Tonight you will meet Moloch again and in this contest it will be a truer match of the Light and the Dark. As ever, I am here to help."

"There is one last thing, Mam… I heard Emilia say I was 'hot'. Do you know what she meant?"

Of course my mother knew exactly what she meant but she suggested something else.

"Perhaps, Myrddin, she thought you had a fever or you had become over-heated from all that exertion. Go with my love."

29

Snowstorm

2.00 am, Friday September 10th, Merlin's time

"I THINK HELL IS EMPTY," Jack declared, shivering, "and every devil on earth is here with us to cheer Moloch. This is a bone-slicing cold."

The moor around them was deserted, the Druids had melted away after the rain and snow had extinguished their attempts to burn the remains of the animals. All that was left was a smoking hump.

"Moloch has won, you know!" Jack insisted.

"You could be right, and if you are, we are not safe," Emily too insisted. "We should get out of here!"

"Where are we to go? Could you find your way in the dark through these woods to Merlin's house? Even if we followed the Okement, listen to it, it is now flooded and bursting its banks. It's at least a half-hour walk back to the castle, and once we go, we leave the protection that Angharad set in place and expose ourselves to who knows what out there."

"You are saturated, Jack," she said, feeling his clothes. "At least I have this shawl. Everything around us seems to be snap-freezing." With the snow swirling around her she stood up, strained on her tiptoes, because something in the distance had caught her eye. "Jack, what do you think that is out there, barely moving in the snow? It looks like an animal of some kind. You know, it looks like a Brittany spaniel."

An orange and white dog limped up the slope and collapsed some fifteen feet away from them. It whimpered pitifully.

"I think that's Kelso, Jack, and he's hurt! I must go to him." She could not explain why she thought it was him, all she could say was: "It sounds very like him."

"Wait a minute!" Jack was straining to see him through a squall of snow. "That can't be Kelso; he's fifteen hundred years away, safe at the Okehampton Vet. It's got to be a trick!"

"Maybe Merlin brought him through."

"Get real, Em. You saw Merlin with Toby feeding those flocks of bats. He loves animals. I don't believe he would torture your injured dog bringing him through time to leave him out in this biting snow!"

"Well, who owns that dog if it isn't mine?" she persisted.

"Hey, maybe it isn't a dog at all. Maybe it is Morgana herself trying to cause trouble by shape-shifting into an image of your dog!" and Jack immediately ran through with Emilia his arsenal of ways to terminate Morgana if she pretended to be a suffering animal. Inevitably, he decided on the Taser.

Once again he hauled it out of his belt and, rushing to the edge of the ring of protection, he stood about five feet from the whining dog and took aim.

"Jack, stop! Please stop!" Emily grabbed his arm and pushed the gun down. "I think that dog is really Kelso! Really, he is!"

"It's not Kelso, Em, it's Morgana, and this is what she does to make you think it's him. She wants to get even with you for escaping from her clutches."

"But, what if she brought Kelso through a wrinkle in time

because she wants to get even with you, Jack, not with me? What if she wants you to think it is Morgana herself so you will Taser it like you did her in the cavern?"

Emilia paused here because, on seeing Jack redden, she knew she was onto something.

"Listen to me," she said, pulling him around so that he looked at her. "Morgana wants you to kill Kelso so that in my anger and distress I will blame you and that will hurt both of us."

"You could be right..." He lowered the Taser and shook his head saying, "You know, I just don't think like that, but I suppose she could think like that."

"Hey, I will take it as a compliment that you believe I can think as deviously as Morgana but you cannot," Emilia observed drily. "But you're right," she added, smiling at him. "You are too straight and decent to think like Morgana!"

"Why don't you call Merlin and ask for his help?" Jack asked, putting the Taser back in his belt.

"Merlin's sharp elbows knocked me unconscious..."

"Get over it, Em... Angharad already explained to you why..."

"He hasn't explained a thing. Merlin hasn't been anywhere near me!"

"Tell me you noticed that he was busy trying to rid the world of Darkness."

But Emilia, in her distress about her dog, had also forgotten that saying Merlin's name would bring him close to her. And there he was, in the shadows, cloaked by his invisibility and weighed down by a feeling of miserable failure. He longed to hold her at last.

"Well, this is exasperating," Jack went on. "Here's this dog whimpering away in pain and freezing to death... maybe it is Kelso and maybe it's not; maybe he's real and maybe he's a spirit, a dark spirit. So, if it's really Kelso, we have to worry whether he's going to die from exposure because I'm sure as hell not going to Taser him. Now, what do you suggest we do?" And Emily had an idea. She had seen how her mother revealed her plan to her father by pulling him close and asking him…

"Hug me," she asked, imitating her.

"Hug you? Are you cold, Em? You must be freezing!"

Jack took Emilia into his arms and lifted her onto a nearby granite boulder until she was level with his eyes, then he pulled her close; close enough for his gaze to drift across her face. Merlin's eyes followed his. Moloch's art had bathed her in milk and was turning her lips as blue as sapphires. She shivered.

"Kiss me…" she whispered.

He kissed her lips, then her eyelashes, then her lips again.

"Come on, once is enough," she protested and broke the spell between them. "I need you close enough so we can whisper to one another without Morgana hearing what we're saying. I'm going out towards Kelso. Can you pick up that stick and pretend to hit me over the head? Kelso is ferociously loyal and will attack anyone who attacks me, no matter what. Okay?"

Jack stammered, "Okay…" I knew his head was spinning because mine was too. He had just kissed Emilia, something he must have dreamed of doing for years, and he could not think straight. And it was in this state that this poor man volunteered to be attacked by a dog!

"Here Kelso! Kelso!" Emilia cried while walking towards the spaniel. As Jack drew back the stick to hit Emily she yelled, "Where's my boy? Where's my darling dog?"

As I stood there watching Emilia and Jack trying to outfox Morgana, I did not expect jealousy to burn a hole in my heart, but it did, and I was utterly perplexed by them both. One moment Jack

was kissing her, the next he was hitting her and that dog... What is Kelso doing here? That dog is growling and trying to attack him! There is only one answer to all this craziness and it has to be Morgana.

I scan the energy in the surrounding area, and while Angharad's wall of protection is well built around the Tor, at this moment both of them have drifted outside it, and there, behind Jack, is Morgana watching the scene with puzzlement equal with mine. Below me, near the Standing Stones, there is an eddy of darkness and once my gaze falls on it, it takes on the more solid form of a huge grey wolf, which emits its menace through its blazing vermillion eyes... Moloch!

30

Moloch Pounces

2.15am, Friday September 10th, Merlin's time

ORGANA MOVED FIRST. *Unaware of me, she screeched in her wild rage.*

"*Moloch, I want him, I want that prick Pendragon!*"

Somehow, and she does not know how, Emilia and Jack have uncovered her ruse and Jack has failed to Taser Emilia's dog. She is defeated at her own game. On hearing her, Jack pushes Emilia to the ground beside Kelso as he reaches again for his stun gun. It is clear he has no idea where her attack will come from... he just knows it will come.

It is now up to me to choose whether I will act, and reveal my presence again to the agents of the Dark. But if I do not act, and leave them to defend themselves, can I be sure Jack can outwit Morgana for a second time? And after Emilia's trials tonight, will she have enough strength to deal with them at all? And if I do act, who will I save first? While I asked myself these inane questions about what I should do, Morgana threw an immobilising spell that captured Emilia, crouched on the ground, and also caught Jack as he scanned his surrounds.

'Why didn't I protect her first?' I demand of myself. It was as if I no longer understood anything about myself. What was I doing even contemplating whether I would save anyone from Moloch, let alone whether to save Emilia? Had I left my head in bed?

It was then that I took a calming breath, and closing my eyes for a few moments, pictured what I could do next. Yet the heart-burn of my envy of Jack still pierces my control and robs me of my calm. I feel dejected when I need to be quick-witted, and I know I have to clear out my head and lock away my heart until I have time to repair its damage. 'Vincit qui se vincit—he conquers who conquers himself,' I told myself sternly. I needed a diversion.

"Where is Tobias?" I asked Ingraine and she answered,

"The bat and the boy are drawing very near to you, Myrddin."

"Warn him, will you? Tobias is a daredevil. He must land in the safe haven, no matter what else is going on."

Here I was giving Tobias a command, but I knew I could not yet trust him to follow a command of his Master. My misgivings were well placed. I heard Toby first, singing exhilarated at the top of his voice:

"I can see clearly now, the rain is gone
It's going to be a bright and snowy day."

Swooping close to the Tor, Tobias saw a frightened Jack frozen in action with his Taser drawn and Emilia crouching as if in the middle of something. He knew immediately it was the work of Morgana and, knowing what it felt like to be immobilised by her, he resolved neither of his friends should go through what he did. But he could only grab one of them to pull them onto Mot's back.

Tying the reins carefully around his ankles, Tobias rechecked my animals and yelled to them,

"Hang on, creepy crawlies, and hang on for grim death!"

He urged Mot to bank sharply into the snowstorm before diving suddenly to swoop onto his two friends. But which one? Jack was *closest and he was standing up. He grabbed Jack, who toppled like a statue onto Mot's back.*

"Let's go, Rat-face!" Toby was instantly air-borne and, in less than a few seconds, was over the Tor and back in Angharad's circle of light.

"I can see clearly now, the rain has gone," Toby sang.

What could I do but smile?

What could Morgana do but shriek?

And what could Moloch do but snap the terrified Emilia in his jaws and leap skyward?

And what could I do but feel an absolute failure?

I now had to countermand all of Morgana's spells. I had endangered Emilia and would have to rescue her; I would have to confront Moloch again, and on top of these problems I had to banish an ice storm. And I had nobody to blame but myself.

I dealt with the easiest problem first. The counter-spell for Jack was a simple charm. It worked and slowly brought him back to movement. I spun around first to counteract my invisibility and reappeared beside the Tor. Everyone jumped.

"Merlin, mate, you scared me, appearing out of nowhere like that! I thought you'd gone." Crook struggled out of Tobias' shirt and landed on my shoulder and welcomed me, chewing my ear. Packed with self-pity I said to the bird,

"At least someone loves me!"

My mother had had enough and gave me an earful.

"Snap out of it, Myrddin. Look at those young men, Tobias and Jack, whom you dismissed as boys, they have shown valour and strength! And look at Emilia, abducted again by the Dark, and this time because you stood there doing nothing but commiserating yourself on your own misfortune. Emilia is the one who has experienced very little but misfortune ever since you came into her life."

"Well, what's your plan, Merlin?" Tobias interrupted. "Or, what's your new plan?"

A new plan was finally taking shape in my mind.

"Have you got feeling back throughout your body, Jack?" I asked. "Can you move everything? Some gentle exercises. Tobias knows what to do."

All Jack could ask was, "What about Emily?"

"For the moment she is all right," I said, firmly intent on disguising the fear I felt for her safety. "I used a slow release spell on her and it will take about the length of her journey for her to recover. I can see where Moloch is taking her. It is to the west of here to a tunnel complex above the Camel River in Cornwall. Morgana is still close by us, eavesdropping. I am, therefore, not going to discuss my plans in front of her. But I can change the atmosphere in this haven and warm it up a bit. I will re-enchant Mot and I will call Angharad back here to ferry you all to our villa. I will be home within the hour, and I promise you I will have Emilia with me!"

Well, that was my dream, anyway.

31

Morgana's Nursery

2.30am, Friday September 10th, Our time

MOLOCH LEAPT INTO THE SKY in the unlikely guise of a wolf. It was an odd choice, because if there ever was a being who was solely a backroom operator and not a pack animal, it was Moloch. He liked dungeons, dank caverns, cellars and tombs. When he was pushed and could not find any of them, he would reluctantly use a tunnel. Cornwall was perfect for him thanks to the tinners. It had a maze of underground opportunities. In a few years, depending on the prowess of Gorlois, the war lord of Cornwall, Morgana would be conceived and delivered as the daughter of his virtuous wife Ygern, and Moloch planned to surprise the child with a nursery, in a tunnel below the Rumps Castle where she would be born.

In the meantime he would store Emilia there and leave a trail so obvious that even Merlin could find her.

Moloch was unused to light; and even the dim moonlight of the snowstorm made him queasy. He could not understand people who swam in sunlight or danced around maypoles. He was photophobic.

And he had another problem. He had selected the animal form of a wolf because it had powerful haunches and sharp fangs, but most of all because it struck fear in the hearts of humans. Unfortunately, it gave him two distinct drawbacks. It gave him an acute sense of smell and, being unable to chatter, he could not enjoy the beauty of his own voice.

'Which is more repulsive?' he asked himself. 'Can it be the fresh, fruit fragrance of her lips, or that floral bouquet that she has doused the rest of herself in?' She smelled revolting. He'd have to abandon his animal disguise as soon as he landed because the waves of nausea interfered with his wolf persona.

It was at that moment that Emily revived and, looking in astonishment at the wolf, a wolf that was soaring through the night sky, she wondered who it was. Morgana? Perhaps, but this putrid smell was different from Morgana's putrid smell; this one smelled sweeter and more like the smell of death. The growl seemed to her to confirm the wolf's identity. It was Moloch! Emily sighed, a deep fatigue passing through her body, and her empty stomach growled back to him as if in reply. She was sore, she was tired, and she was hungry; but most of all, down in the marrow of her bones, she was angry. How dare Moloch even touch her! How vile!

"What are you doing, Moloch, got up as a big bad wolf?" she spat out. "Are you trying to scare little children?" She paused to gulp air and recharge. "Well, I am not a child and you don't scare me. In fact, I've just turned sixteen."

Unable to reply, Moloch ignored her.

"Where are you taking me? Wherever it is, Merlin will just come and rescue me. So why don't you put me down now and save us all a lot of trouble?" She glared fiercely into the wolf's face and thought about the macho self-image Moloch must have to choose to disguise himself as a wolf. "You suck!" she concluded, and stuck a finger in each of his blazing red eyes.

'Bloody hell!' Moloch thought. 'She is hard work. Even though she has her dog back, she's the real bitch who is doing all the barking and snarling. Why don't I just open my jaws and drop her?'

With bleary eyes, as he surveyed the countryside below looking for a spot to dispose of her, he realised he was already over the fishing village of Polzeath, near the mouth of the Camel River, and only a few seconds from the tunnel entrance. To his north, the Atlantic Ocean rumbled at the base of the cliffs. It was time to land. Here he could shed this stupid disguise and set his Emilia-trap for Merlin.

He executed a perfect crash landing and its impact jolted Emily from his jaws. She rolled down an almost perpendicular hill, stopping only when she reached a small, earthen platform. There she lay breathless, gulping salty air, listening to the screech of gulls whose sleep she had disturbed. She tried to gain her bearings. A large rock stuck out of the earth of the hillside to her left, and high above her was a primitive castle built right on a cliff's edge.

At first she had no idea exactly where on earth she was, but she slowly pieced it together. She knew she hadn't left England, and she could always recognise her mother's speciality, and that primitive castle had to be an Iron Age Fort. It looked similar to the mock-up of The Rumps on the kitchen table, which was to be her mother's next project. And when she heard the crash of waves on rocks she guessed she was right. She was on the western coast of Cornwall.

But when the rock beside her wobbled and suddenly sprang backwards to reveal a dark space, she was scared stiff. This was a new magic and it was something much darker than what she had seen so far. She patted her chest to reach the comfort of Roget and she could not find him. Her stomach sank... because the last thing she remembered before being lifted skywards was squeezing him. He must have fallen out. But where?

"In we go," a metallic voice with no form announced, followed by a blast of frigid air that pushed her into an underground tunnel.

When another strong gust of cold air shoved her forward and a metallic command shouted, "Move!" she put her palms on each wall and refused to budge until her eyes adjusted. She turned to yell 'Leave me alone!' but her words choked in her throat because the wolf had gone, and there above her floated the menacing head of a bull with large fierce horns that curved back on themselves.

The head drifted in space, and from its hollow eye sockets there sparked jets of red flames. Moloch had no form, no edge; he was just a swirl of foul odour who spoke. Emily was shocked by his change from that of the big bad wolf of fairy tales to some form of primeval spirit with the head of a bull. 'This is,' she thought, 'seriously scary, but there is no way I am going to show it. How can I protect myself?'

The only thing she could think of was a cross; it came from the belief that a cross protected people from vampires and evil. Under Ingraine's shawl she arranged her fingers into a cross and she prayed: 'Please God, ward this evil away and protect my turtle. Help me, Michael. Please do not expect me to do this all by myself. Come here and be with me to fight this beast. Today is my birthday and I have lost both my animals and I am feeling very alone.'

Again, the echo-chamber voice commanded, "Move!"

"Quit bellowing!" she barked back. "It's pitch black in here and I will move when my eyes are used to the dark and I can see where I'm going. This floor's uneven and it drops away. And I'm sure I will be of little use to you with a broken neck!"

"Stop." His voice was a little quieter this time. Directly in front of her was a flight of steep narrow steps carved from the rock and woven into a tight, downward spiral. "Go down, one step at a time. I'll give you some dim light." And it was then that Emily deduced something about Moloch. If she swallowed her fear and pushed back against him, he gave ground. So this was going to be a battle of wits.

Immediately, with a sparkle of hope, Emily changed. Merlin would come. This flight of steps was a passage down under the earth into a place of death and it would be, with each tread, a journey into herself too. But once she started counting each step she felt she had more control of the situation. She stopped at forty-seven.

"Move!" he hissed. She turned around and smiled at him and stopped again at seventy-four.

"I need to catch my breath," she lied, smiling still. Rather, she needed a chance to look around at the dripping walls, slimy to her touch, and the steps that twisted down towards the sea to remember how she was going to get out of there.

"How much further?" she demanded.

"You are the one counting, not me. But it is almost another fifty steps," Moloch replied. "We're more than halfway down."

'That means there are about one hundred and thirty to run up to get out of here,' she thought. 'I'll need four minutes.'

"And what's down there?" she demanded.

"It is Morgana's nursery and her maze."

In the same instant he mentioned the word 'maze', Emily received a very clear picture. It was not the vague flash you get when you think of something, but a highly detailed and well-lit picture of a marble statue, like a museum exhibit, of a woman holding a spindle of wool with her name carved underneath: Ariadne. She had a jackdaw on her shoulder. Emily smiled and she knew it was a message from Merlin, and now she understood the gift from his mother of the shawl. At some stage, like Ariadne, she would have to unravel it to find her way back through a maze, and by clutching it and holding it close she felt protected by both him and his mother.

Reassured by her unseen support, she thanked God and Michael and resumed counting her steps. At one hundred and twenty-five the stairs grew wider until, at one hundred and thirty, they opened into a cramped space, hung with heavy cobwebs that was fitted out like an ancient science laboratory. It was lit by an unknown source. 'This must be the nursery,' she concluded, and her blood chilled as the rats climbed over the table and fought over something lying on it. It was awful! The whole place had the whiff of death.

"You can rest here before we go into the maze," Moloch said quietly.

A cloak flew through the dank air and swirled around the dark wraiths of his energy and settled below his mask. It defined his vapour as a space, although not one proportioned like a human shape. Instead it was conical, the shape of a sorcerer's hat, with the bull mask floating eerily above its apex. Now she could see the menacing shadow of his outline on the wall of the cave.

Immediately wary of his change, Emily sat on one of the child-sized stools and hooked her shoes around its rungs to keep them from touching the rats. She pulled the woollen shawl tightly around her and again formed the cross with her fingers while she composed a vacant stare on a sullen face. Meanwhile, Moloch fussed around the space, rearranging bottles and flasks, shaking the fluids and checking the labels, oblivious to the squeaking of the rats.

32

What Merlin Desires

2.30am, Friday September 10th, Merlin's time

O N A SMALL ISLAND, *where the waves lash the rocks and the mist clings to me like the cape of a bard, I look across to the Rumps, to Gorlois' seat of power, where Moloch has Emilia imprisoned. The local folk call this place Puffin Island after the birds that breed here in thousands of burrows, but I call it Merlin Island. Not after myself, of course, but after the falcons that hunt above here. Emilia calls the island the Mouls. What does that mean, the Mouls? Maybe they thought the burrows of the puffins belonged to moles.*

"It is time!" I declare to the curious puffins. "It is time once and for all to enchain this Darkness. But how can I do it? If I touch him I will fry to a crisp. How can I capture him and remain free?"

Usually, whenever I confront an adversary, I move into their skin and look at the world through their eyes. You will remember what I did when the Saxons were moving through the woods of the wolves and the bears. It allowed me to predict what they will do next. But I cannot do that with Moloch. Moloch is like a worm, a worm that bores into your skull and lives on in your brain. Given any opportunity, he invades the mind of a thinker. Just like he did with Vortigern—turning his brain to mush and suborning his will to his own. I cannot risk giving Moloch the opportunity to capture my thinking and turn my mind into an instrument of his control.

But that is not all because his tactics do not just stop there. Moloch is even more devious than that.

Like Morgana, Moloch eavesdrops. He amasses titbits of information about whatever his targets long for, about whatever they secretly crave. Once he uncovers what they want, what they want so hard they can taste it, he offers it to them, just as he did with Vortigern. There was a man who wanted one thing more than anything else. He wanted fat land. He wanted rich, safe, southern land. And Moloch gave it to him.

Then, of course, Vortigern wanted more.

When I turn my mind to Morgana, please understand that I know her secret name. I know the name she used as the malignant queen of Carthage, but I dare not say it or even think it because that could be another way for her to worm into my mind.

I know Moloch has studied me since I was a child. He has probed our servants and slaves for gossip, and gathered any scandal about the young boy with the powers of a magician. He paid spies to discover what I desired because what I desire will form the man I become. And what did he find?

Not much! Anyone can guess what I want. It is easy. I desire my mother's love and my father's approval. What son of Britannia does not?

I want to rid Britannia of the Saxons, Jutes, Danes and Angles, and I need a war chest to do it. Moloch does not need spies to tell him that. And there is more: I also desire what Moloch desires. I long to master all the elements and bend them to my will, and I am almost a match for him. But is there anything else?

I pause and struggle to find the words because these feelings are new to me.

"How do I put it?" I ask the puffin pecking my toe. Eventually my words come.

"I want Emilia to feel about me the way I felt about her from the moment when my soul changed colour."

I blush when I remember the heat of it. I think I have kept my forbidden desire for her regard and affection well hidden from others. My mother knows, but my father does not. My nurse guessed, and Doone knows because he saw me showing off in front of Emilia. Yet tonight, when she was bound and bloodied on the floor of the cavern, I was in control of my emotions and I showed Morgana nothing but indifference to her victim. Tobias does not know how I feel, and if Jack guessed when I gently touched Emilia's face, he did not let on. Only Doone knows. Could Doone explain why Moloch changed his plans?

Because up until midnight, Morgana and Moloch wanted to sacrifice Emilia on the altar of Baal because they knew her future and the risks she posed for them. But some time just before midnight they changed and let Emilia live. What changed their mind?

The answer I reach, again and again, is Doone, our household slave, who has been my teacher, my guide and my dear friend.

I am certain only Doone knows. But a short time ago, unaware of the presence of Morgana and Moloch, I turned green-eyed with jealousy. Nobody could have seen me, and it may have been just coincidence, but seconds later, Moloch grabbed Emilia. I can only blame myself if Moloch saw how I reacted. Now he will know what I want and know, too, that I cannot have her; but he will conclude that this will not stop my desire, only fan it. Thus he will release Emilia for the highest fee because he now knows I will pay it.

But emboldened by his recent victory, Moloch may be cocky. And if he is cocky, he may make a mistake.

"Of course, my lady, Merlin will come to rescue you." Each of his words echoed and the result was unnerving. "That is the main reason I took you. You are my bait. But he knows you will have a maiden fee and all you have to worry about is whether he will pay it or not."

"I have no idea what you're going on about!" she snapped. "I'm not up for sale! What fee are you talking about?"

"You do not come cheap. I make it my business to offer powerful people their heart's desire, and whether you realise it or not, I suspect you are what Merlin wants, what his heart desires."

"Do you only come out at night, Moloch? Because you—have—not—got—a—clue! Merlin is not the least bit interested in me."

"Well, I do agree with you that it is hard to believe! You humans are a great mystery to me. I found it hard to believe when I was first told that a bitch like you, of all creatures, was his ladylove. But then I got proof. I watched him flood with jealousy when you kissed Pendragon and I knew I had him. And did you not just tell me he would rescue you?"

"Yes, I did, because that is what he does." She spoke to him in a condescending tone as if he were a moron, someone who did not know the bleeding obvious. "Merlin rescues people, Moloch; he even rescued your bloody bats!"

She paused and tried not to think about Merlin being jealous of her with Jack. Instead, she stared at the rats tumbling over one another so she wouldn't smile and reveal to Moloch how inside of her, at this very moment, there was a graceful butterfly spreading its iridescent wings and fluttering around. 'How could someone like Merlin, who can spread himself across the sky like a sunrise, be interested in someone like me? I am a nobody person. I can't race across the sky. How could he be jealous of me?'

But eventually her curiosity got the better of her and she asked,

"Anyway, what's the maiden fee?"

"It is a price and it is not much. It is that Merlin works for me."

"Doing what?"

"Whatever I want."

"Merlin's not going to be at your beck and call. That's slavery! Look, I do not know him that well, but from what I've seen, he is a clever man who is playful and decent and fearless!" And Emily drew a deep breath, and speaking as loudly as she could without her voice quavering, continued: "I hope you heard that, Moloch! He is fearless and he would never do your bidding. So, what happens when he refuses to pay your price?"

This was the question Moloch had been waiting for and he wanted to relish every moment of her reaction. So he moved right in front of her, and stooping he laughed in her face.

"First, I will make him watch me as I break each of your knees with my stone mallet…"

"Oh dear, Moloch, I know what you mean." She interrupted him to parody his approach to torture. "But you've got to be kidding, it is not a very effective method. Where I come from it has become commonplace. It is a paramilitary technique we call knee-capping. You need to know it is painful, but not fatal, and one in five can walk with a limp afterwards, and four out of five recover…"

"…And that is before I release the trapdoor and push you into the sea where, my dearest Emilia, you will drown…"

She did not even blink. She just shut out whatever else he was saying, just as if he were her maths teacher who droned on through a double period on a Friday afternoon boring her spitless. She replied in a cold, calm voice,

"You and who else, old man? You haven't got it in you, Moloch! I watched you and Merlin battle over Dartmoor. He is only sixteen, and how old are you? I'll bet you are thousands of years old! And he beat you twice and nearly beat you a third time. You have to admit it, Moloch; you are someone who is well and truly past it!"

"I am outside time!" Moloch huffed and moved away from her as if he was stung. "I am as young or as old as I was the moment I was created."

"And, may I enquire, what scumbag created you? I'll bet it wasn't God!"

Moloch's behaviour did not make sense to Emily. Why was he so focussed on Merlin? Had Merlin crossed him in some way or challenged him too often? Was this not the first time Merlin had won? Or did these two have a history that she did not know about.

"And so, Moloch, what has Merlin ever done to you?" she demanded.

"Nothing. Well, nothing recently. This time it is not what he has done, it is what he will do. It is about his potential. Do you think all this is happening by accident? It is not. He and I are locked in a struggle, and as we fight, it is mirrored in other realms; above in the heavens and below in the underworlds."

'What is it Merlin was supposed to do in his life?' Emily asked herself. She tried to recall what the legends described Merlin doing. She knew they said Merlin would bring Uther Pendragon to Cornwall in disguise as Ygern's husband, and their passion would create Arthur. She also knew he would become Arthur's foster father to teach him the ways of the wood, and later, when Arthur became the king, Merlin would invent the round table so all his squabbling knights and kings would sit together, allowing each and every one of them to think he sat at the head of the table. But that's about all she knew.

Wait! She knew one more thing: that if you Googled his name you got thirty-nine million hits, more than three times what you got for King Arthur, and thirty million more than for Julius Caesar! She felt overwhelmed by his celebrity. It was clear to her, though, that Moloch must know far more about Merlin's future than she did if their conflict engaged all the realms.

"Look, Moloch," she spoke in a more conciliatory voice, "I didn't choose to get caught up in this. I met Merlin less than two days ago because my mum broke into his storage shed. I barely know him and he barely knows me. He does not know what music I like or what my favourite food is, or who my friends are or what football team I follow. He doesn't even know what school I go to. Whew! Actually, he doesn't know anything about me, really. So, what you are claiming is simply not possible. We only met by chance…"

"…There's no such thing as chance, my lady. You chose your life and, as with Merlin, so with you. You have known him for thousands and thousands of years. It's not what you have done. It's what you have the potential to do that is important."

'Perhaps,' Emily thought, 'this is the key to Morgana's attempts to scare or hurt me. And this could be the real reason why Merlin came to my aid. But what on earth am I going to do in my future? I was not planning to take on the powers of Darkness. I am a nobody. All I ever want to be is a social worker and help protect kids. How absolutely uncool is that! It is hardly a career that could upset Moloch.'

Eventually she replied tartly,

"I don't have a crystal ball so I can't see the future. I don't know what you mean."

"Let Merlin tell you, he knows." Moloch said it in a way, a knowing way, as if Merlin telling her would place him in a trap of some kind.

"I can tell you this, Moloch. I am a very ordinary girl. Nobody has ever heard of me! I am very uninteresting; I am quite boring, in fact."

She paused for a moment thinking, 'I have to keep him engaged until I can see the way out of here.' So she droned on, saying,

"I want to get on with my life; I want to go back to school next week, and I will go swimming and surfing with Casey and laugh with her until I am breathless. I will go riding with my dad and finish my painting with Jack and keep on dancing with Toby."

She decided to stop there because, despite being boring, she was beginning to feel homesick because she might never see them all again.

"Seriously, Moloch, how could someone like him like someone like me? I am not any object of Merlin's desire any more than he is the object of mine." But as she listened to what she was saying and as she reviewed all that she said to Moloch, her words seemed very peculiar, even alien, as they tumbled out of her mouth. It was as if they were spoken by someone older, someone much tougher than she really was. In fact, they really did not sound like her at all.

With that she had a flash of insight, and she realised she'd grown harder by her experiences of the last two days. She'd changed, she'd grown up even. And if she pushed her tiredness and homesickness and anger below the surface, she was left with the growing realisation that Merlin was the most glorious being on Earth, and that if she was his heart's desire, he was her heart's desire, too. God, he was hot! And if this foul-smelling fart in the hat tried to hurt him in any way, she'd take him on! And if that meant she had to jump into the bloody sea, she would not be pushed, she'd jump into the bloody sea by herself. It is only 17 degrees, for God's sake, and she could survive for twelve hours in that! She felt as if she were capable of anything. It was then that Moloch broke into her train of thought…

"You are an unusual girl, Emilia. You have just realised you have been hiding the truth from yourself, have you not? I know more about lies and truth than anyone else on Earth, so do not think you can lie to me. Lying is my speciality and I have made it an art-form. The girls around here at your age dream and swoon, and although you look fragile and delicate, just like a little bird, you haven't shown any fear even when I described your death. You are much tougher than I thought you would be and you haven't begged for your life. You don't seem very frightened."

"That's because you don't seem very frightening. The fault is with you, old man, because you are losing your touch. I know you are the Prince of Lies, but your forked tongue and rickety old lies just don't scare a girl from the twenty-first century because we're so tired of villains. I've watched thousands of them on TV and at the movies!" And Emily glared at him, trying to mask her fear. "And you sound like a very bad movie from the fifties!"

"But, Emilia, you do seem to have a fear of rats, do you not? So let me introduce you to some of my favourites."

Moloch whistled and a very large grey rat, about four to five pounds, rushed to him. "Razza, bring your family over here to meet my new friend, Emilia!"

There was a growl and a hiss as if of agreement before he disappeared into the darkness and rats teemed from every hole and crevice, hundreds of them, squealing. Emily, her heart pounding, jumped up onto the small stool where she had been sitting and yelled,

"Moloch, get them out of here! Get rid of them!" He ignored her, watching his handiwork and hissing them towards Emily. When one of them ran up her leg she screamed, and jumping down, grabbed her stool as a shield and raced to the stairway. Moloch, a sheet of fire, blocked her escape.

"And you, Emilia," he roared, "did not believe I could scare a girl from the twenty-first century! You're all huff and puff, young lady, because those rats are merely my artifice. Look, pouf—and they are gone!"

"The one that ran up my leg was real because he smelt musty and sweet and acrid all at the same time, just like a rat!"

Moloch ignored her, changing the subject.

"Why don't you sit back down and we will talk about something else."

"What about?" Emily took her stool and sat back down, shaking. "We don't have much in common."

"Yes, we do. We have Merlin. We could talk about him for hours. Do you know he killed a man tonight? Did you know he is now a murderer?"

"If what you are saying is true… because how do I know when a liar is telling the truth? But let's suppose it is true, then taking a life can be a very serious act. But he could have done it in self-defence or as an act in a just war. In either of those cases, the taking of a life could be a reasonable and permissible course of action."

"Morgana told me you go to a Jesuit school where you learn to debate the devil…"

"Did she really? Then she should have told you the rest of our motto—at Exeter Academy we learn to debate the devil and win. But debate, Moloch, is a discourse only possible between people who are free, and although I am not fettered by chains, I am clearly not free to run out of here. Even though I am not free to escape you, I am free to contradict you when you are wrong."

Moloch must have decided the subject had reached a dead end because he asked her,

"Well, do you like Morgana's playground?"

'Why ask me?' Emily asked herself. It was hard to imagine a worse place for a child. Quarrelling rats, dripping walls infested with spiders, and flasks of God knows what poisons lying around in bottles, and something unspeakable that was dead and desiccated on the table. It was the last place on earth she would want her daughter to play in. It was more like a purgatory than a playground.

"Well, do you like it?" Moloch insisted, seemingly because he was waiting for her compliments.

"No, I don't like it. It's ghastly! It's completely unsafe for a child. You will be lucky if Morgana survives to five if she plays in a place like this, let alone ever grows up into an adult."

"It seems I have got it just right then. She will love it!"

"By the way, where is Morgana?" Despite everything, there were moments when Emily enjoyed twisting this devil's tail. "I am almost missing her. Where is she? Morgana seems far more intelligent than you, because her forward-planning for my kidnapping showed some cleverness. It was not just a snatch and grab, like yours, Moloch..."

"She is not allowed in her nursery until she is in a human life. She has to wait, and you will learn, young lady, I am not easily provoked. I have time on my side. And you will have some company soon. Any moment Merlin will arrive upstairs to visit that luscious woman he should have married, a woman who is far prettier than you. Morgana and I pushed his mother out of the way from the marriage negotiations and we selected a father that Morgana deserves, a warlord with a fierce temper, a man full of anger.

"Now this is going to be my best night ever!"

'You wish!' Emily thought. 'You even lie to yourself!'

33

This Ungodly Hour

3.00am, Friday September 10th, Merlin's time

THERE ARE ONLY TWO ENTRANCES *to that tunnel and I wanted to use the one that Moloch did not use.*

In the early hours of Friday morning, I rapped my sword on the oak door of the fort belonging to Gorlois, the war lord of Devon and Cornwall. It is perched on one of the twin heads of the promontory that juts into the sea, where he built extensive wooden palisades to ensure his home is safe. Everyone agreed he had good reason, because inside under lock and key he kept one of the most beautiful brides in Britannia. Married at fourteen, and now only a year older than Emilia, Ygern is carrying their first child. She decided she was not going to accompany her husband to the Moot in Devon. And Gorlois has sealed her safely in his castle, behind his fortifications and surrounded on the other three sides by a dramatic drop to a forbidding sea.

A sleepy servant answered on my third rap and demanded to know my business at this ungodly hour, and on hearing it, she slammed the door in my face. She then sought advice from her mistress as to whether she should let in this scruffy caller with a bird on one shoulder and a bow wound around the other. "And," *she continued,* "Would you believe, Mistress, this stranger claimed to be the son of Marcus Octavius Cotta!"

"Myrddin," *she murmured.* "Yes, yes. Let him in. Get me my cloak."

Ygern and I were childhood friends and she, the girl of my daydreams, had often whispered to me she wished her father had offered her hand to the Cotta household for marriage instead of to a man twenty-six years older than herself.

A few moments later, the statuesque Ygern with her long, unbraided hair spreading over her shoulders like a cascade of melting snow and her large, shining eyes invited me inside.

"Ambrosius, you are most welcome! I am surprised you'd call at this hour when you know my husband is away staying with your father. I do not want any scandal, and it will be hard to avoid one if you stay here another minute."

This beautiful woman lived with the threat of the clenched fist of her husband, and I pitied her.

"Please invite your servants to be present for the short time that I am here. My mother sends her blessings and she offers to stay with you when your child is ready to come."

"Thank her for me, will you? I will write to her, it is most kind. Why are you here?"

"Let us speak the Welsh of our childhood, because spies may be about. As you know, there is an escape tunnel that runs from your castle under the fortifications at the narrow neck and goes to the north. In there, tonight, a malignant energy has nested. He has abducted a girl, and I need to clear him out of there and purify the space to protect you and to set her free. This is urgent, and I must do it now because, like your husband, I must be with my father just after dawn. I will offer Gorlois a full explanation when I see him, I assure you. Can I gain entry through your cellar?"

"Of course, I will show you myself where to go."

"There is one more thing. Could you make sure that all your maids sleep around your bed tonight? Lock the door and keep the key with you. It is just for your extra protection."

I knew it would protect her, but it would also ensure that the Moloch's spy among her servants would not be free to get up to mischief.

Ygern held up an oil lamp and I followed her down a few steps into the cellar. In the corner of the room was a large and empty oil jar which I rolled to where she pointed.

"The entrance is here, under this chest," she said, touching a heavy, carved box with a hinged lid.

"Keep well, Ygern. I have never seen you as beautiful as you are tonight!" I kissed her hand. "And thank you!"

"Goodbye, Ambrosius." And then, after I pushed aside the chest, she added in the faintest whisper, "Wish this baby was yours!" I took her hand and kissed it, whispering back,

"If you only knew, dear one, the blessings that will pour over you for having this child with him."

Disappearing down the stairs, I held the lamp high with one hand and hauled the terracotta jar with the other, thinking that I too would have liked my life to be different.

I almost ran down the tunnel, only slowing down when it became a steep, slippery ramp. At a recess in the side wall I paused and, still speaking Welsh, I whispered,

"Are you there, Arianrhod? My Lady Silver Wheel, are you there?"

"Of course I'm bloody here, because I have been pestered almost to extinction by your bloody mother!" Her voice sounded like Welsh cream.

"Thank you for coming, my lady. Where are you?"

"Where do you think I am? I'm hanging from the roof, where else! Tonight I am a raft spider from the marshes of Wales and I do not like all this salty air. I am going to start coughing before you know it, so let's make this quick. Very quick! What do you want?"

"Do you know the plans of Moloch?"

"They go something like this: "If you don't pay his maiden fee, he will break her legs and push her through a trapdoor that opens down into the sea. If you want my advice—and I can see you do not—I would let her go. It is not at all worth the fuss. I can fix you up with one of my daughters. I even have some with two legs…"

I stared at her coldly.

"That was a joke, Myrddin. Smile!"

Really I did not have time for her banter, I was becoming exasperated.

"Could you spin a web across the chute that is under the trapdoor? A web sticky with your silk where Emilia would be caught like a butterfly until you wind the skeins of it back up?"

"Oh, I see. You plan to save her, not sacrifice her. You will never get on in this world, Myrddin, with that Christian attitude of always trying to do good. Not worth it! All right, I can see you are determined. How heavy is she?"

"About the same as a half sack of apples."

"Not much heft there. I will have to leave the raft spider behind and change into an orb weaver… the golden one… Yes that will be perfect. Five minute's work, how is that? Seeing I am here, I would not mind ridding the world of Moloch. If you need any help with dramatic changes of light, or with love potions, or poisonous bites, false walls, or even collapsing floors… anything of that sort of thing…?"

"No, thank you so very much. I think I have that all under control. But there is one other thing. Can you move this jar into the centre of the maze—and remember, I need a strong cradle across the chute, one that rocks."

"As always, Merlin, there is a price to pay."

I raised an eyebrow. "And what is that?"

"One kiss, because you never know, I may turn into a fairy queen."

"That you already are, and it is my pleasure," and I reached my hand up so that the goddess of the moon and the great weaver of dreams could cling onto my wrist.

"I want it right here, on my cheek, just above my fang. Ahhh! The most handsome man in Britannia has just kissed me! If only I were a thousand years younger... Good luck, Myrddin!"

"You will keep her safe, will you not, Arianrhod?"

"Listen, maggot pie, I promise I will not eat her, because any man who is such a fool in love that he will kiss a spider woman deserves the best of my charms!"

In the nursery, Emily sat on her stool thinking her life through. She had no idea what Merlin would do. Maybe he would be able to outwit Moloch, but she had just watched their contest over Dartmoor, where Moloch eventually showed powers far greater than Merlin's, so she had more than a niggling doubt. Having made up her mind what she would do, she stuck out her chin defiantly and she was just not going to think about it. She was not going to think about her mum and dad, she wasn't going to think about Roget and Kelso or Casey, Toby or Jack, she was just going to do it, and do it before Moloch had a chance to knee-cap her. She resolved to make Moloch realise that: 'twenty-first century girls don't wait to be rescued; we look after our-selves; and I am going to leap and pray and hope that I won't leave this world on the same day that I came into it.'

Moloch hovered around her, expectantly, waiting for Merlin to appear. He was very quiet, and all she could hear were the rats scurrying on their creepy feet until they too went quiet. There was only the slightest rustle, too faint to be a warning, but Moloch spun to face the noise just as Merlin burst through the door. Instantly, Merlin fired two arrows in rapid succession into the most quarrelsome of the rats and they exploded into a blinding, white flare of magnesium. Screaming in pain as the bright, searing light burnt into his sensitive sight, Moloch threw his cloak over his mask.

Firing a third and a fourth arrow, Merlin lifted up Emily saying,

"Unpick your shawl! You may have to find your own way out of here in the dark, alone. I'm going to duck through the maze then push you down into a sling below the trapdoor. That is only if you will not jump."

"Why should I jump if I don't have to?"

"Trust me, Emilia, please trust me! We don't have a moment to discuss this. Unpick the shawl and leave a trail to follow so you can get out of here fast when you have to!"

Ducking and weaving, Merlin raced through the maze at breakneck speed when it should have taken him a plodding thirty minutes to complete.

He put Emily down quickly, opened the trapdoor and peered down into the night to check on Arianrhod's work.

"Can you take Crook?" he asked as he gave her his jackdaw and cried, "Jump! There's a strong safety net at the end of the chute. You'll be hauled up as soon as it's safe!"

But Emily clung to him, her courage weakened by the closeness of him.

"Now it's come to the moment to look over the edge of this precipice, I'm terrified! I want to stay with you."

He pulled her to him and held her tightly and whispered,

"Have I ever told you, Emilia, that you are the most desirable and courageous girl I have ever met? You are not just a nobody, you are a somebody who asked God for his help, and he sent Lord Michael to aid me right now against Moloch. Now it is my turn to save you from Moloch." And he kissed her hair saying, "Now shut those wondrous green eyes and jump!"

So she jumped, resolving that as soon as she got home she was going to learn to shoot arrows like Merlin and begin a course in ocean swimming, just in case. And once she jumped, Merlin slammed the trapdoor shut and rolled the large, terracotta jar into the centre of the floor just beside the trapdoor.

I calculated I only had seconds left before Moloch would regain his sight and begin his search for me. Staring at the trapdoor, I imagined that Emilia had just jumped to her death and I, overcome with grief, shed tears that ran down my face.

When the grim darkness of Moloch burst into the space he barked,

"Where is she?"

"Emilia jumped." A sob caught in my throat as my tears streamed. "She has gone, Moloch!"

"I do not believe you!"

"You are the Prince of Lies, not me. I am speaking the bare-boned truth. She jumped."

Turning around abruptly he searched the cave, but not only was he unable to find his bait but he missed the very large spider hiding in plain sight above him.

"Show me what happened!" he demanded.

As slowly as I could, I raised the trapdoor, and presented to him the waves crashing below.

"The night closed over her like a shroud," I murmured, and squeezed out another tear.

"This is a trick! It is absolutely typical of you, Merlin!" And Moloch desperately tried to figure out what my trick was. I watched him reason and persuade himself that because he was not

made of a physical substance, I would not be able to enchant him. But was he right? He had never asked himself that question before. He assumed that because I could not enchant him, therefore, I must have enchanted the girl. But as he twisted around searching, he could not figure out what had happened to her or where she had gone. And because he was still seeing blinding after-flashes, he was unaware, completely unaware, of what I was doing.

"What the bloody hell are you doing?" Arianrhod demanded in my ear, unheard by Moloch. "Oh my God, you cannot be thinking what I fear you are thinking! If you touch his dark material, Myrddin, it will consume you!"

I ignored her.

"Stop it, stop it!" she hissed. There were only seconds left.

"I call on Lord Michael and all the powers of Light to be with me!" I silently commanded. "Now!"

And while the Goddess of the Moon called on the mightiest powers, I cast the shrinking spell over Moloch.

Slowly, quietly and discreetly, almost imperceptibly, Moloch shrunk. He did not suspect that his very essence of envy and malice was being drained away into the terracotta jar; that is, not until his mask clanged to the floor.

"No!" he shrieked. "No, no!"

It was too late. In a blaze of blue light, a gift from Michael, I fell over the jar and covered its narrow opening with a shower of stars. The inhuman wail of Moloch was silenced as I plugged the jar to bar his escape.

"Merlin, are you mad?" the spider woman cried. "You are mad!" she concluded. "Stand still a moment so I can spin a cocoon of Light to protect you!"

Opening the trapdoor once again, I grasped the jar to my chest and wound my belt around it. And knowing it would be a quick flight, I jumped. The sky flashed blue with the swords of the legions of Michael.

The Merlin Island, that small rocky place, is less than a quarter of a mile off the Rumps; and held, at the level of the sea, is a wave-eaten cave. There, in the sand, I planned to bury the terracotta jar and cover it with a pillow rock.

Ablaze with the gifts of light, I flew as fast as I dared, very anxious about whether the tide had dragged the sea out from the floor of the cave. I need not have worried. The floor was almost dry, and it was sandy and deep enough to cover the jar. I struck my bow on a rock to mark his grave and used my staff to chisel a dire warning of a plague burial.

"I call on the Guardians of this place," I sang, "and the master spirit of the birds that nest here. Be present, now!"

There was a brief flap and flutter that revealed a large and quizzical puffin who, in a deep squeak, proclaimed, "Greetings!"

"Thank you for agreeing to hold this Dark One," I replied with a bow. "When I return from Gaul, if you do not want to continue this service, I will move him to another place."

"We are pleased to be of service," the Master Puffin squawked, "as long as our nesting sites are safe from your merlins."

"They will be," I agreed.

"Leave him here then. I will let you know if there is any change."

Before I left the cave I threw up my arms, and with my staff pointing to the heavens I called down my own Guardians.

*"I summon the peregrines and the merlins and the
falcons of the updraft.
I command you always to hunt over the suck of this sea.
Do not hunt the nestlings of the puffins;
Summon me if there is any trouble here.
Emilia must see you in her realm
And know she is safe from Darkness.*

So be it."

The Master Falcon, the king of his species, swooped into the cave and perched on my outstretched staff. Once he agreed to my requests on behalf of all his progeny, I lowered my staff and the raptor rose in a slow circle over the island. You, too, should go there to admire them.

Looking down to where the jar lay buried beneath my feet, I cried out.

"Farewell, Moloch. Use your time to ponder love, the most powerful force in the world; it is that which inspires shining courage in us all."

'Stay a while, Myrddin, my son and hear me sing!

> Are you not a poet of brilliant speech?
> Are you not a master of the wind?
> Are you not an enchanter, a creator of wonders?
> Are you not the chief of the sky and the stars?
> Are you not a hero who fights without a sword?
> Are you not your father's son,
> A defender of our realm?
> Are you not my son who
> Buries Darkness under the unharvestable sea?
> Are you not called Myrddin?
> In praise of whom my tongue sings!'

34

Stop Everything and Freeze Time
4.00am, Friday September 10th, Merlin's time

"ARIANRHOD, MY LADY SILVER WHEEL. *Where is she? Where is my Emilia?*"

I hovered under the trapdoor below Morgana's maze, the spider's silk gusting in ribbons around my head. I felt in a panic. How was it possible that at the very time when I had no time I was sick with love?

"Emilia has gone, Merlin. She has got pluck, though. I promised to help her again if she needed the wiles of an old arachnid. I am very good with scorpions... My, aren't we shining tonight!"

"And you, my dear lady, know why! Thank you, and thank Lord Michael for me. Where's Emilia?"

"Following the thread, I took her back through the maze and left her on the saddle of land near the battlements. She had your blooming nuisance of a kak-kaking bird with her, too!"

There was no need to recall my jackdaw because Crook flew out of nowhere onto my shoulder.

"Take me to her!" I demanded. "And thank you again, my dear lady, for your service!"

As Emily, who lay stretched out near the cliff-path, heard the scrunch of the pebbles and the cackle of the jackdaw, her heart leapt into her mouth. She knew it was him. He was safe! When Merlin knelt down quietly beside her, he did not know what to expect. He may have been all that his master, Ingraine, sang about him, but now he was just as anxious as any other boy who managed to get everything wrong with his girl.

"Are you all right, Emilia? Moloch did not hurt you, did he?"

She came up fighting. Getting up onto her knees so she could face him, Emily blazed,

"Never, ever do that again! You ignore my pleas and distress all night, you leave me high and dry, and you even hit me! Look at my bloodied face! You go ahead and save the whole bloody wide world from Darkness rather than help me, and if that doesn't show where your priorities lie, I don't know what does! So isn't it just as well I can look after myself!"

And then, drawing a deep breath, she went on,

"You command me, Merlin, to jump from a great height into the sea to drown—on my birthday! But if that's not enough, you send me a giant tarantula bigger than a horse's hoof to console me! If this is how you treat your heart's desire, how do you treat your mortal enemies?"

Merlin's face collapsed, and on seeing his fallen face, Emily burst out laughing, a loud, tinkling laugh of absolute joy.

"It's so good to see that you're safe, Merlin! You won!" and she grabbed his arms and threw them above his head in victory before she threw her own arms around his neck.

"I cannot understand you, Emilia! Are you angry with me or not?" he said in her ear.

"I just had to get all that off my chest! I had to tell you how

I felt. Now I have done that I am fine—really! Where's Moloch? What happened?"

Still kneeling, Merlin wrapped his arms around her.

"Moloch can wait. All I want to do is kiss you better." And kissing one eyelid he murmured, "This kiss is for ignoring you all night when you were in trouble... and this kiss," he gently brushed the other eyelid, "this one is for deserting you and for seeming to prefer any fight rather than the one to save you. And because, just like you said, I did everything wrong, I guess I will have to keep kissing you until you feel better. And of course, there is your swollen lip from my stiff elbow; I will kiss that better, too."

He paused to draw his breath and let his eyes move slowly over her face.

"This kiss, however, is for all my other transgressions." And he pressed his lips tenderly on her lips.

"Ouch, ouch!" Emily cried out. Then seeing the hurt on his face, she added quickly, "Oh, no! No, Merlin, I didn't mean it that way! I'll put up with the pain. But before you start all over again from the beginning, please reassure me we are safe... Where is that Moloch?"

"He is safely tucked away in a terracotta jar under the sea on that island over there."

"How did you do that?"

"I had Arianrhod's help..."

"Arianrhod is a spider, Merlin!"

"Arianrhod is the Goddess of the Moon and of the Silver Wheel; she is the weaver of dreams."

"I don't know whether you've noticed, but she's got eight legs and eight eyes and she talks. And although she talks a lot, she is still a spider!"

"She is a goddess, Emilia, who shape-shifts into spiders. One moment she is a ravishing beauty who commands the Northern

Lights, in another moment she will be some spider I have never heard of, and next she will turn into an interfering busy-body. Now, I left her below, but if you keep talking about her, she will sense it and will join us in a flash. A few moments alone just with you would be so good!"

"Sorry. You were kissing me..."

"I was about to kiss you..." And then he pushed her gently to the ground. "I want to kiss you like a hungry merlin, soaring over that sea, searching for your soul..."

And all Emily knows, for the first time in her life, lying there and seeing the stars whirling around his head, she is melting into a blissful place and from this point her life begins again. Maybe their kiss took a moment or maybe it took an hour, she could not be sure, but when she had enough breath again she cried out,

"I feel alive, Merlin!" and she whispered in Latin, *"Sentio vivere."* Then, just to be sure he understood: "Merlin, look at the stars. They are so close, there are millions of them; they're watching us and blinking out."

"They are bastards, those stars! They are unmoved to pity that we, in this newly-made morrow, have only a few minutes together. Very soon our world here will crack open. When the lantern of the sky is lit, it will send all the spirits back to their abodes. Sunrise is a moment of danger because it is when the veil is thin between what we can see and what we cannot see, and the cronies of Moloch will be out searching for him."

Emily was puzzled.

"Merlin, what on earth are you talking about? Do you actually believe the sun is lit like a lantern every day or are you speaking poetically?"

"I am a bard who loves a colourful way with words... And," he continued with an innocent look spread across his face, "how else can I explain the heat of the day and the cool of the night?" And then, laughing at her amazed face, he murmured,

"I am only joking, Emilia. But because I have never discussed astrology with a woman before this, it does feel very peculiar. The heat of day and cool of night are caused when our round Earth spins every twenty-four hours, and any place on Earth will be heated by the sun as it moves overhead. I have read Aristorclus, and while it is hard to believe that the earth is spinning, because I do not feel it except when I kiss you, mathematically his theory explains what I have observed in the sky."

Although Emily knew that Copernicus, who placed the sun at the centre of the solar system, is yet to be born, she is puzzled by Merlin's knowledge of the heavens. So she asks him,

"And what sits at the centre of this system? Is it the sun or the earth?"

"As Aristotle and Ptolemy wrote, it is our Earth that is at the centre of the heavens."

'Oh dear,' she thought, 'his genius does have its limits. I will have to be tactful and move to safer ground.'

"As for astrology, Merlin, when were you born? What star sign are you?"

"I am Scorpio, early November, my ascendant sign is Virgo. My moon is in Sagittarius, that's where my athletic ability comes from, but it also means I am a mystic and capable of great conspiratorial activity. I am good with secrets and I want to know the why of everything and uncover all the answers."

"Then you will enjoy it when we discuss the solar system. I am a Virgo and today is my birthday. I am sixteen."

"Then I will compose your astrological chart and find out who you really are... But we must be back at the villa before the true dawn breaks. Today is our last day and we will not have a chance to debate one another because... most of this day I will be scribing for my father in the big debate at the Moot, and then

I have planned a spectacle for them after their feast. It will be midnight before I can take the three of you home…"

"So this could be the last time we will ever see one another alone. I want to stop everything, Merlin, and freeze time—I want you to know I would have jumped into the sea rather than have Moloch own you…" and Merlin stopped her with a finger on her lips.

"No, Merlin, don't stop me. I want you to know something, and even if you know it already through your magical listening abilities, I want to tell you myself. Down in that tunnel, I felt like an attack dog… If Moloch had… I would have jumped into the sea to save you."

"When you think of me, I do know, and when you resolved to risk your own life, I was so scared having failed once with Moloch tonight, that I too begged for help. Your father said you were brave but I never expected you would commit to giving up your life for me. It was an honour that I did not expect and I have not deserved. Before I die, Emilia, I will earn that honour. I seal that now with this kiss."

It, too, was a tender kiss, and Merlin's eyes filled with big, round tears that he didn't bother to brush away. Then he rose, and lifting her to her feet said,

"Can you see over there above that little island where Moloch is entombed, can you see the merlin above it? As long as this land and sea meet there, you will be able to see the merlins and you will know Moloch is imprisoned there and that you helped to enchain his Darkness. And when you see a merlin showing off in the wind draughts above that island, I want it to make you laugh, because you will know another Merlin who is also a show-off, and perhaps then you will remember our brief time together."

But it was the next moment that Emily would remember whenever she had a birthday. It was when Merlin climbed onto a rock, and standing over low bushes, he opened his mouth and from his throat came a melodic rippling of bird song. Chiff-chaff, blackcap, warbler, song-thrush, robin, blackbird and white-throat, and all around them his song encouraged the other early morning risers to sing out a reply, and Emily heard in autumn a dawn chorus that was only ever heard in spring:

"Happy birthday, Emilia!"

Emily burst out laughing, a merry ripple of happiness that made Merlin laugh too.

"That made me feel, just for a few moments, that this is our spring and not our autumn. It's just our beginning. That was cool, Merlin, awesome!" And she moved closer to him and studied his face as if she had never seen it before, and for the first time she kissed him. She kissed the magician hard and urgently as if he were a miracle, as if it were for the last time, and as if the feeling of his lips would have to last her a lifetime.

Later Merlin, writing in his first letter to Emily, recalled that moment:

'Emilia, do you remember when you asked me about Moloch? I was churning with bile when I tethered his Darkness under the is-land but, in truth, I barely thought of what I was doing because I was so worried about whether Arianrhod had caught you safely in her web. I flew to you over the headlands that lay in that pink dawn light like sleek seals, fat from their summer feasting, but they, like the stars and the planets that were blinking out, were oblivious of everything we had done to entrap the Darkness. Our first kiss tasted of sweet berries, but when you kissed me farewell I too felt alive and washed clean of all his vileness. In my heart I called you Vivian be-cause you revived me and brought me back to life, and I felt blessed by the Mother.'

35

Merlin's Chamber

5.00 am, Friday September 10th,
Merlin's time

THE WIND TURNED TO THE SOUTH-EAST: a warm, dry wind, a wind that was gritty with sand. It was a wind that gusted from the desert over Carthage. It tossed Morgana's hair about, and all the frost and snow that covered the fields and the woods melted, and the grasp that winter had on Dartmoor loosened. Even as the sun rose, the leaves dripped and sighed with relief.

And Morgana fumed. In a matter of hours she had lost so much. She had lost Pendragon, the one who had defiled her mother, and Emilia, the one who had been chosen to lie with him. But, most of all, she had lost Moloch. When she searched his usual haunts and called on great Baal for help, Moloch was silent and there was only the faintest trace of his scent scattered in the hot breeze.

Morgana knew Merlin had won. But Merlin should know it would only be allowed for the moment. His triumph would not last long because he belittled her learning and he had disparaged her powers. He was proud, he was such a know-it-all, and a man of his arrogance would soon make mistakes.

When I landed in the courtyard of my home, it was already stirring to life. I walked Emilia through to my sleeping chamber but it was already full. Tobias and Jack, their feet meeting in the middle, were sprawled either end of my bed. My two dogs, my fox, my mice and my merlin were all at the door to welcome me. Mot hung from a rafter in the roof, and when I moved my hands around her, like a blessing, to thank her for keeping Tobias safe, the bat looked at me strangely before settling into sleep. She had never been thanked for anything before in her life.

"What is that?" Emilia whispered. On the wall beside my bed there was a charcoal drawing of a girl leaping, her knee drawn to her waist, her body twisted to fire an arrow behind her, her turtle clinging to her chest. "That looks like me!" She was shocked.

Morgana, outside Merlin's window, smirked,

"Oh, I am going to have fun with that! But, by the great God Baal, she is not a real woman, Merlin! She looks like a cow suckling a tortoise. I would have drowned her at birth!"

"Of course, Emilia, my drawing is of you," I claimed with some pride. "I sketched you the other night after the skirmish with the Saxons when you wanted to fight them. You can just see the outline of Kelso leaping at your feet and Roget at your breast."

"I'm mortified. Oh, my God!" she groaned as she ran her hands over her eyes. "Merlin, I want the earth to open and swallow me whole. I don't have many clothes on, Merlin. You've drawn me almost naked."

"Goddesses usually are, Emilia." I was still perplexed. "Did you not see the sculpture of the huntress at the door of the villa? I drew you as her, the goddess Diana."

"But the boys are going to wake up and see me looking like that!"

"And now you are just like Diana, angry at someone seeing her at her bath."

"Yes, and do you know what Diana did to the man who saw her?" Then, with a weak smile, "She turned him into a stag and his own hunting dogs ripped him apart!" And shaking her head for emphasis with her eyebrows raised and her head to one side, "That's what happens to mere mortals like you who embarrass a goddess."

"If you can forgive me, I will get the wall draped now and they will not see you. It is a pity, because I thought you look very beautiful. And I will find you somewhere else to sleep. Let us go to my mother's quarters," and I steered her to the next room. "I will call her maid and she will bring you water and some bread and fresh clothes. Remember, the maid will not see you but she can sense you. I have to bathe and attend to family business. You will meet my mother and she will be able to see you." And kissing her lightly on her forehead, I said, "I will return later."

But Emilia grabbed my hand and I could feel that she was as tightly strung as my bow.

"Please understand, Merlin, I am not angry with you about that drawing. But my head is full of horrid thoughts. I can hear Jack and Toby waking at dawn and making crass comments about me. But worse than that, I can see my mother excavating this villa and having to explain to her colleagues why her daughter, with an Australian turtle on her chest, is displayed on the fifteen hundred year-old wall of a Romano British villa."

And I left, whistling for my animals, and smiling about the complexities of her life. The mural would stay once she was gone, and I congratulated myself on drawing what I had only imagined, but I now suspected… was true to life.

Almost immediately, Ingraine arrived to supervise. Emilia told me that when she first saw my mother she remembered how she had imagined her, this woman who eavesdropped on some of her most intimate thoughts; but she had never anticipated she would be this tall, raven-haired beauty in her early thirties who looked like my twin sister.

"Welcome, Emilia. Yes, I can see you. Welcome to our home. I honour you with this circlet of laurel, the victor's crown, because you are worthy of it. I knew you were headstrong and I suspected you were brave, but you surprised me with the strength of your courage and your willingness to die for my son. How could a mother choose anyone better? Thank you!"

And she hugged Emily warmly.

"Thank you, my lady. I know you are a princess, but I don't know what to call you?"

"Ingraine will do."

"Thank you, Ingraine, for the countless times you saved me," Emily said with a little laugh because it seemed to her such a silly thing to say. "I was ill-prepared for what happened to me, and without your watchfulness I would not be here now."

"I have another gift for you." Ingraine clapped her hands and the door opened and in bounced Kelso, still battered, but not the broken dog she had seen a few hours earlier. She sat on the bed and he leapt up to lick her.

"Oh, I'm sorry—he always sleeps on the bed with me. Kelso, you'd better get down!"

"He can stay. My hounds sleep with me too, and your turtle fell out as Moloch grabbed you. I will get it for you from the washstand," and she strode back to her with Roget on her neck. She clapped her hands again to summon her twin wolfhounds who bounded through the door.

"Do they really sleep on your bed?" Emilia asked as Roget crawled up her arm. "Where's the room?"

"*In the winter, yes, they keep me warm, but there's not much room for me!*"

Ingraine walked around her bed and pointed at the walls.

"*If you look at my frescoes you will see the childhood of Myrddin. Look at that little angel over there! That is Cupid, my Myrddin at two years; and this one is of him as the young Apollo when he is ten. He will not stand still long enough now for the artists to paint this wall, but from one of my sketches we had this mosaic done for my floor. Apollo again. Do you like it?*"

Poor Emilia, what could she say?

"*It is simply splendid!*" *she said.* "*My mother loves the mosaics in the villas she studies and she has pictures of them on her walls. I am puzzled, though, why you call Merlin 'Myrddin'. Why does he have so many names—Ambrosius, Myrddin and Merlin?*"

"*Can you speak Latin? Yes. Well, what is the Latin word for excrement… for shit?*"

"*Merda. At my school we learned all the swear words first.*"

"*Exactly. When the Roman veterans around here heard me call him in Welsh 'Myrddin', which I say as 'Merthin', they heard it as 'Merdin', and they split their sides thinking I was calling him the 'Little Shit'. So I changed his name for them to 'Merlin' after the falcon he loves so much. But my husband always calls him Ambrosius. As soon as Myrddin lands in Gaul, he will change his name yet again to Ambrosius Merlinus. Do you know why? He does not want the immediate promotion to Tribune and the preferential treatment that comes with his noble name of Cotta—it's a family name of Senatorial rank. He just wants to learn how to build camps, and siege weapons, and—*"

"*– Sewers?*"

"*Yes! And drains and bridges, wharves and tunnels… all the work of the architectura.*"

"*Why is he so interested?*"

"*The army is our school where you can learn such practical things, and what Myrddin wants to do more than anything else is to drive the Saxons out of Britain. He knows that to do that he will have to rebuild forts and camps around Britain and quarter the soldiers there, just like the Romans did. So for a young man so engrossed with planning a counter-attack, it has been a surprise to see him engaging his heart with you. He has never been much interested in girls and said he never, ever wanted to marry. So I was as surprised as you to see the frieze in his room. I am pleased he met you."*

"And he only met me because I was under attack. Ingraine, do you know why Moloch and Morgana are so driven to kill me?"

Ingraine paused and carefully considered what she would say.

"Yes, I do know the answer to your question, and so does Merlin. If we give you the full answer, the knowledge we will tell you, without doubt, will interfere with your free will and disrupt the choices you make about your life. And we would be penalised for telling you that secret by immediately losing our gift to see the future and the power to prophesize that goes with it. But there is always the possibility that you will work it out for yourself, of course, without penalties for any of us.

"But Merlin has already told you all he can and I cannot tell you any more than that. Just know that you are much loved by those that know you and by those who, unseen to you, answer your prayers. Now, give me a hug and I will leave you to sleep."

36

A Roman Bath

5.30am, Friday September 10th, Merlin's time

"HOW ARE YOU SWEATING?"

The Roman greeting echoed in the marble room. My eyes flew open at the sound of my father's growl. Sitting on the cool step in clouds of steam, I knew I should be grateful for the thirty minutes of peace I had already enjoyed because I had never known my father to wait so long. Protocol between father and son demanded that immediately I leap up and greet him; instead I immersed myself in my bath and spoke to him from there.

"I am fine, father. And you? How are you sweating?"

"He is a chicken hawk, Ambrosius," Bruto spluttered. "A chicken hawk that cannot fly, a chicken hawk that cannot get it up..."

I smiled. "I presume you have seen Vortigern displayed..." The howls of Bruto's laughter cut me short.

"His pee-pee," he wiggled his little finger, "must be wee-wee, and because he would never find it in the dark, he had to dress it up in glory," and he roared again, "so he could find it again!"

"I will bet you checked!" I said, laughing too.

"Of course I did! I insisted Aurelius and Uther search for it as

well, because I told them, with my old eyes I could not see a thing!"
And he howled again.

"Mother told me there was a disturbance here last night."

"A couple of those Saxons broke free and one of them tried to break into her room. I do not understand how she is able to protect herself, but by the time she called me, he was flat out on the floor and she was standing over him. We caught the other bastard too."

"Where was Doone in all this?"

"I have seen Doone and he reported, in hushed tones, on your victories of last night. It seems our intelligence was flawed, but you recovered and managed the skirmish well!"

It was now or never. It was time to challenge the purpose of my mission in Isca and save my concerns about Doone until later. I drew a deep breath.

"Do you know, father, at Isca, instead of ten enemy men, there were five times that number: fifty-two! Instead of an enemy marching down Fosse Way, most of them came from the opposite direction, and by sea! Vortigern had enough well-trained Saxons to capture the whole of Isca and most of the surrounding countryside. So I doubt his mission was merely to capture Uther and Aurelius. So what was his mission, I wonder?"

I tried without success to keep any sarcasm out of my voice, and ducked under the water for a second or two, to allow my father time to compose his reply.

"I suspected Vortigern was planning to attack here during the Moot, but I was not sure..."

"And...?" I prompted him with my newly-found courage.

"And... I wanted my son to be toughened by surprise and bloodied from his first kill before, as a Cotta, he went to Gaul. Wars are not won by sweet people like your mother, Ambrosius. They are won by tough bastards, who get their hands bloodied, like me."

"And...?"

"*And by all accounts, because of your success, we should have a peaceful meeting today.*"

"*And who is managing our security to ensure it is peaceful?*"

Although Marcus Cotta may have wanted me to honour the Cotta name, he was not used to his sixteen-year-old son quizzing him like a lawyer. The insolence! As my mother was always telling him, you have to be careful what you ask for. He sent his son to a blooding, unprepared, and into multiple ambushes, and I returned a man, a man who could take command and demand answers.

"*Security is being managed by Primo with twenty armed men,*" *he replied tersely.*

"*Do we have the results from the interrogation of my prisoners?*" *I dared my father by calling the prisoners correctly as 'my' and not 'ours'. Bruto was about to growl, but instead he answered calmly,*

"*The interrogations gave us some shocking news. One prisoner, a commander you captured at Isca, told us after considerable persuasion that Vortigern secretly poisoned Constantine's eldest son, Constans, the monk. His family thought he died naturally.*"

"*I believe they already suspected his role in Constans' death, because something other than the greed of Vortigern for their land drove Aurelius' and Uther's passion to see Vortigern dead.*"

"*I do not believe Constantine suspected his son was murdered or he would have said so and mauled Vortigern slowly with his bare teeth, biting off what he could, and with his two hands tearing the rest apart.*"

"*Perhaps his sons had different intelligence… Is not Constantine fighting the Pict rebellion in the north, the one no doubt instigated by Vortigern? If this information is correct, then how safe is he?*"

"*As safe as he ever was. He is a powerful soldier. On second thoughts, if Vortigern planned to kill Constantine, now would be a perfect time. As long as he is held in my custody, he will have the perfect excuse to point the finger elsewhere.*"

"Perhaps we have not yet discovered the real reason for his heavily armed excursion," I said slowly, thinking aloud, because the ambush last night could finally make sense. "If Vortigern's real purpose was to create as much noise and strife in the south-west as far away from his home as possible, and kill Constantine's two sons while he arranged the murder of their father, he could wipe out the whole family and take all their land. He could not have timed it better. Is there anything you can do to warn Constantine?"

"There is only one thing I can do. I can go to old Gaius, the pigeon keeper, and ask him to use one of his birds to send Constantine a coded message and warn him to triple the guards around him and have all his food tasted."

"And you will tell him about the murder of his son?"

"I will hint at it," my father replied. "When Olwen the Bard comes here later in the day, we will all adjourn to the courtyard to watch his antics. Could you slip away with both of them to reinterview the prisoner? He used to be in the Auxiliary Army and his name is Albanius. It is better if they hear the full story from him. They, too, could use the pigeon service to contact their father to reassure him again they are safe."

"On a different matter," I said, and Bruto looked at me quizzically, because here I was initiating a new topic of conversation, another first: "Remember last night when you warned me about spies? I need to talk to you about Doone. Could he be Vortigern's spy?"

"I have always found him an excellent source of information," my father said ambiguously, choosing his words carefully.

"Could it be that others do, too?"

"Why are you asking?"

"Someone freed those Saxons last night, and while I thought I had ensured Doone could not get to Vortigern, he could have released those two Saxons."

"Leave it with me," my father said quickly.

"One more thing. Given Vortigern's skill with poison, who is the taster of the food today?"

"Your mother is already taking care of it, I can assure you."

"I will ask her to have antidotes ready just in case. When are you expecting the kings?"

"Within the hour. In the hall I want you sitting behind me on my left hand to scribe for me." A perfect place, I thought, to scrutinise them all and build the case for the most able one to command the British forces against the invaders.

My father continued, "Murmur to me any advice and observations. Now, let me give you a hand."

And Bruto unhooked my linen, pulled me out of the water and wrapped the long white cloth around me. Then he looked me in the eye and jerked his head back in a salute and patted my back. I knew the Dux of the Third Legion was well pleased with the son he would send off to war tomorrow against the barbarians.

37

The Groans of the British

8.30 am, Friday September 10th, Merlin's time

WHEN ONE OF MY MOTHER'S WOLFHOUNDS *threw back his head and howled, to be answered by the sweet baying of a pack, we knew the kings had arrived. The cacophony of barking and growling and snapping that accompanied their arrival told me I must stop gazing at my sleeping goddess and kiss her goodbye and run for it.*

The main hall looked splendid. The mosaic floor showing the exploits of Mars, the god of war, was strewn with thyme, rosemary and laurel, and the frescoed walls coloured with ox blood and sky blue woad were hung with ivy and berries. The board was not centred in the room; Bruto had ordered it to be placed to the left so that the central octagon of Mars, sparkling in tiny squares of glass, could be admired and hopefully the god would inspire the kings to martial action.

The kings jostled to find their allocated places along the length pf the trestle table, where each place had been marked with the painted head of their particular animal: bear, boar, stallion, hare, wolf, stag, lion, eagle, fox and falcon, and because most of them could not read, their animal pictures saved them from em-barrassment.

When Marcus Cotta raised his hand for silence, they ignored him, but when he smashed his fist on the board, the slaves jumped up from the floor to remove the dogs. A hush descended. Father's slave carried wreaths of laurel along his arm like bangles, and stood at attention until his master was ready to crown each king as a guest in our home. He paused, however, when the slaves returned with steaming pewter bowls of water to offer each king his choice of washing his hands or his feet. They all chose the comfort of both. Meanwhile, the man who held all titles of dux, legatus, dominus and pater began:

"Dear friends and kin, you have travelled long and arduous jour-neys to reach here, and thanks be to God you have all reached here safely." Standing in a white toga with the purple stripe of nobility, Cotta paused for their loud applause.

"You are most welcome, here. Will you please welcome Caradoc, the Wolf of the Silures, my brother-in-law," and Bruto crowned him with the laurel wreath; "Ermin, the Boar of Cornwall; and Audren, the Fox of Lesser Britannia in Gaul; welcome if you please, Ectorious Coel, the Hound of Chester; and Lot, the Stag of Lothian and the Orkneys; and Ambrosius Aurelianus, the Lion, known to us as Aurelius; and Eusebius, the Eagle, known to us as Uther, both sons of the Dux of the Northern Legion; the great Constantinius Maximinius, who you may know by his British name, Custennin Macsen Wledigs. His sons are also the grandnephews of Audren of Lesser Britain. And lastly, Gorlois, the Falcon, the War Lord to the Kings of Cornwall and Devon.

"Borholt, the king of Devon sends his apologies and his vote. He welcomes you to his land and hopes you will understand that his baby son has just died and his wife is gravely ill and he, in his grief, will stay with her.

"We are gathered in a Romano-British Council for a Moot; a de-

bate to discuss the invasion of the Saxons and the coming of other refugees to our shores and to decide what we are going to do about it. We will also debate Constantine's draft of *The Groans of the British*, a petition for military help to the Commander-in-Chief of the Roman Legions in Gaul.

"We begin by asking for the blessing of God; and Father Geraint, the chief abbot of the monastery at Avalon, will bless our work.

"All on one knee!" my father commanded before he called forward: "Pater Geraintus!"

A small, nervous monk, the front of his head shaved like a Druid in the shape of a half moon, lifted his shaking hands in blessing:

"Et benedicto Dei omnipotentis, Patris et Filii et Spiritus Sancti, Amen," he sang.

"Deo Gratias. You can stay, Father, or leave, whatever is your wish."

Relieved, the priest scurried out as Bruto resumed standing at the head of the board.

He waited for absolute silence before he began his introduction. Any *dux* of any legion can address five thousand men and be heard in a howling gale. His voice boomed and no one even dared to whisper as he spoke.

"We are all besieged by starving peoples, driven from their homes by bitter winters and sodden springs. By Picts from across the northern border, some of whom loot by sea, and by the invaders, Irish, Frisians, Saxons, Angles, Jutes and Danes, who come across the sea to pillage the riches of our lands.

"Vortigern, the Great Betrayer, whose land abuts that of Constantine in the north, invited the Saxons and the Jutes to Britannia as his mercenaries. Before that a few of them, mainly Jutes, had come as auxiliaries in Roman Legions. But Vortigern gave his newcomers monthly rations and corn in return for protecting his east and north borders until five years ago, when he gave some of them land. Soon their families followed.

"*These people are not farmers; they had previously fished the northern seas and raided remote islands. They had no understanding of our landscape so their crops failed, and now they are in revolt and raiding the countryside. And what do you think Vortigern did next? Do you think he quelled their rebellion or crushed their revolt? No. He brought in even more of them here, supposedly to protect us from the Picts. Only last year he gave two brothers, Hengest and Horsa from Jutland, the tip of Kent in which to settle their large clan, and he commenced negotiations to marry their sister.*

"*Now this very man, Vortigern, is a prisoner in the cellars beneath this very hall…*" Marcus Cotta paused for the loud applause. Gorlois, who had the taunting look of a practised bully, bellowed,

"*If only I could get my hands on his face, I would rip his eyes out!*"

"*Let us hang the bastard by his iron cock and his painted fingernails!*" Uther yelled out.

It took a while before every king except Lot had expressed his outrage, and Bruto waited until they finished their rant before he continued.

"*Vortigern was captured in the early hours of this morning by my son Ambrosius, who sits behind me on my left.*"

I rose in the noble toga of the Cotta family and bowed to the applause of the assembled kings.

"*But he was not alone in this victory. Aurelius and Uther fought bravely beside him.*" They too stood up and bowed.

Immediately pewter tankards were banged on the table and Bruto clapped for a slave to replenish their watered wine. While he did not want a rowdy rabble, he did believe that a toast was in order for his and Constantine's sons.

"*Ambrosius!*" The tankards were raised to me. Then to "*Aurelius!*" and finally, with loud cat-calls of "*Oota, Oota!*" they were raised to Uther. Gorlois called out to him.

"*Uther, why did you not slaughter that shit-stirrer when you had the chance?*"

"Why, indeed?" Uther murmured, looking straight at me.

With a grim smile and a command to return to their seats, Bruto resumed:

"Constantine has drafted this plea to Flavius Aetius, who is Magister Militum, the Commander-in-Chief of the Roman army. Constantine sends his apologies for his absence; he is fighting an uprising in the north and begs for all your signatures so we can present a united force to the Roman command. This plea asks for new Roman troops to stem this pagan tide of barbarians. Whatever changes you wish to make he will accommodate.

"My son, Ambrosius, who is our scribe today, will begin to describe our current situation before I ask you all to join in."

I scrambled to rise and wipe any ink from my hands before I bowed to the group. It was the first time I had ever spoken in public and I was nervous.

"Besides the Emperor's Wall, which separates us from the Picts, and the forts along the Saxon shore that overlook the channel, there yet is a third way by which we keep ourselves safe. And the third way is the sea that surrounds us and keeps invaders away. But that sea is also the road the Saxons use to raid us. The seas to our south and west coasts are treacherous and tempest-strewn and only Irish pirates and some Danish raiders have dared to sail them. Until now.

"Two years ago the first Saxons crossed those bitter seas to raid us down here in the south-west. We know they were helped. In these last two nights alone, we have destroyed four of their raiding parties—and now we know who was helping them and giving them the local knowledge of tides and safe havens and copies of traders' maps of our ports, rivers and estuaries. We have the proof that these attacks were aided and abetted by the Betrayer, Vortigern.

"Under interrogation, Vortigern claimed that his presence in the battle last night leading an army of Saxon mercenaries could only be explained by the invitation he received from my father to attend this Moot. He must think we are dim-witted, because we captured him as he led the Saxon ambush at Isca..."

At this point, Bruto interrupted in a voice dripping with sarcasm:

"And what do you think was the real objective of Vortigern? Do you think it was to capture Isca with his fifty-strong Saxon troops? Or do you think it was to wait until you were seated around this board, softened by our hospitality, and then to mount a surprise attack and butcher you all?"

There were gasps and cries and, as one, the kings reached for their swords.

"He is without Christ!" Aurelius cried out. "He is heathen, like his pagan allies, the Saxons!"

"And he would do anything to prevent more Roman troops returning to Britain," Uther added. "He sees every one of us as Romans and he exploits the weakness of the kings of the Saxon Shore."

"W-w-well, I w-w-will sign our Groans right n-n-now," stuttered Ermin of Cornwall.

"So will I!" added Caradoc of Gwent, my uncle.

As Lot rose to speak, I watched him closely. He had failed to condemn Vortigern. I was trying to gauge whether he was our friend or foe.

"Let's find out what The Groans say first," Lot smirked, and he continued dripping his voice in sarcasm, looking straight at the only Roman in the room. "After all, these Romans invaded us first." But my father just shrugged. Lothian was barely eighteen, yet he had the haughtiness of a man born to the throne and the self-satisfied smile of a stag that had met and defeated all his challenges.

"He is no friend of ours," I whispered to my father in Greek, satisfied that only Aurelius and Uther could understand me. "Doone says he already has two concubines but no wife."

Reading from a parchment, Bruto began, making it clear that Lot's contribution had passed him by:

"'To Aetius, thrice consul, the Groans of the Britons, hear us… the barbarians drive us to the sea, the sea drives us to the barbarians. Between those two means of death we are either killed or drowned.' Could you endorse this so far?" Bruto asked.

"So far, yes." Caradoc spoke on behalf of the others, with his wolfish caution and cleverness. "But we have to make the case for why we are worth saving; we have to include our strengths other than our wretchedness." My uncle with his strong attachment to his clan and his wolfish ferocity in fighting made me wonder whether all the kings embodied the traits of their animals as clearly as Caradoc and Lot did.

"There are twenty thousand Roman veterans retired here, and at least thirty thousand other Roman citizens. That's fifty thousand strengths," Bruto said. "And that should appeal to Aetius. Among them are men and youth ready to be trained to help us."

"We have other riches," Aurelius the honey-tongued interposed, and my father whispered to me,

"This one is not to be underestimated. He is so clever with his tongue he can talk flies away from shit."

I listened closely to Aurelius' oratory and tried not to be distracted by his wall left eye that today seemed to wander all over his forehead.

"Our dense woods give us sturdy timbers and our mines are rich in coal, tin, silver, copper and lead. And, of course, there is our gold. We smelt our own iron ore. Our land is fertile and gives grain for bread; our seas are silver with fish. This is a beautiful place, rich in God's gifts."

"Let us include all our gifts that you have mentioned in our plea, Aurelius," Bruto continued. "Your father Constantine then writes: 'We are beset with plagues and the Roman cities of the east are deserted.'"

"Don't blame the plagues or the dung in the water for people clearing out of the cities," Coel of Chester spoke. "Aetius will think it is our fault." He paused and laughed. "Blame everything on the barbarians!"

"Hear, hear!" There were calls and whistles.

"And what you cannot blame on the barbarians, blame on Vortigern," Aurelius added, also laughing. "Let us keep this very black and white."

Above the disruption, the two shadows of Jack and Tobias slipped into the minstrels' gallery directly above Gorlois at the end of our long board. Only I could see them and I smiled faintly to them in recognition. This morning, returning from my bath, I saw Jack, through my window, lift the cloth I had draped over the mural of Emilia and then rush off to Ingraine's chamber. I am sure he feared he would see me sharing a bed with Emilia, and when he did not, I saw his relief as he tiptoed over to her and kissed her brow. In a few short hours, she would be his for life.

"What military support does Constantine ask for?" Gorlois demanded gruffly, bringing me back to the present.

"A goodly bunch. Three thousand men, made up of two thousand foot soldiers and five hundred cavalry to be garrisoned at Eboracum (York) and spread down along the Saxon shore," Bruto replied.

"I think we can ask all we want," offered Audren of Lesser Britain. Here was a man everyone listened to. The uncle of Constantine, he was always the voice of reason, yet crafty as a fox. 'Count your fingers,' Bruto had told me, 'after you shake hands with him because you will never know which one he has nicked!'

"I do not think he will give us one single soldier," Audren continued. "And why should he? Look at it from his point of view. Caesar began his Gallic Wars saying Gaul was in three parts. That is no longer true. About fifty years ago the great river of Germania froze and thousands of Vandals, Suebi and the grey-eyed Alans came rushing across the river into Gaul. It is only forty years ago

when the Visigoths sacked Rome and the Emperor told us we must from then on defend ourselves.

"Now there are only two parts of Gaul: theirs and the Romans. And separate from all of that is our small part in Lesser Britannia. Just before I left for Greater Britannia I met Aetius, whom I consider my ally, and I agreed that he could settle some Alans on our land to help him pacify them. The Legions hold the line at our rear in the Loire Valley, but only just. So I do not think he will send one single soldier here. And be very clear about this: it is not in my interests for him to send you even that. Therefore, do you think I want to sign the Groans of the Britons? No! But will I? Yes! My nephew, Constantine, and my grandnephews, here, are in peril and I will sign it for them."

"Thank you, Audren," Bruto said. "Perhaps you are right. However, Constantine and I know Aetius as well as you do and we know him as a fair man. He is a brilliant soldier and he holds our best interests at heart."

Aurelius rose to speak again.

"Those long hairs, the Saxons, slay our monks, they burn our monasteries, they murder our children, they spoil our crops, and they plunder and rob us. Our silver and coins sleep, and instead of creating more wealth they lay idle, buried underground or shipped to Lesser Britain for safekeeping or used by the Romans to fight the barbarians in Gaul. But we are a stiff-necked and haughty people, we Britons. We are the same blood as the people of Lesser Britain. But Britannia is not as easy a country to defend as Gaul. It is heavily wooded. It cannot be easily crossed. Some of our forests are impenetrable. Yet those forests mean the Saxons can be stopped at our shores. Their attack will always come from the sea and all our oceans will foam to the beat of their hostile oars.

"I realise that what is happening here is happening elsewhere. My question is, what are we going to do about it? We need a plan

that uses the men and the gifts of our land to fight back, regardless of whether we get Roman help or not."

Next, Coel of Chester spoke.

"I agree with Aurelius. You will notice there is no one here from London or from Lincoln or from anywhere in the south-east. They have climbed into bed with the daughters of the Saxons and Jutes, whereas we, here, have the beginnings of an alliance. We Roman Britons can raise an army and fight them for control."

"Are you suggesting a civil war, Ectorious?" Bruto asked.

"It is murkier than that. We must raise an army and fight back. We have a way of life to protect. We still have some good trade in tin, apples, woad and wool; we have straight Roman roads and fair Roman laws; we have, as you said, thousands of Roman veterans who are itching to swing a sword to protect their way of life; we have sound ways of teaching our children right from wrong; and most of all we have the Christian faith brought to us by the uncle of Jesus Christ, Joseph of Arimathea. Are we going to let this sacred soil, this holy land, where the Lord himself walked be pissed on by heathens and infidels? We have to protect it, and our Christian way of life. Both Aurelius and Uther, here, served with the Legions in Gaul, and now Ambrosius is going there, and under the wise military direction of their fathers, Roman Generals both, we can build up our strength and expertise. It may take a while, but we can do it."

When Coel sat down he was satisfied he had taken the discussion in a new direction and avoided acknowledging that it would, of course, be a civil war cloaked in the rhetoric of fighting a barbarian invasion. He was a man who thought differently. Coel knew that the Saxons were gaining entry to this country because most Britons did not even know they were cuckoos in the nest. Bruto always recognised the wisdom of Coel's argument. I saw something different, I saw a friend. He was only a few years older than me, but unlike Lot his wisdom and virtue were already well known.

"Coel," Bruto addressed him, "we are all agreed we need a military response, and your opinion that we fight with or without Roman help has merit. We are going to stay our proceedings here for the arrival of Olwen the Bard and his high jinks. He will also entertain us after dinner. When we resume in one hour, Vortigern will be brought in here for your inquisition."

In the minstrels' gallery, Toby murmured to Jack,

"What do you think of Merlin's father?"

"He's a big fellow, isn't he? You know, I have been looking everywhere at his astounding wealth," Jack said very quietly. "He has all this land, the village and this enormous villa decorated like a palace, and all these servants and slaves. And look at the mosaics and the treasures he has put on display... it's like a Roman version of Buckingham Palace."

Toby had to smile. Jack was the only person he knew, or was ever likely to know, who had not only dined at the Palace with the Queen but who had breakfasted there as well and who could speak with authority about whether any wealth was truly 'astounding'. As the kings rose and milled around below, Jack continued,

"This display is no doubt to dazzle the kings, but I am reminded of something a tradesman whispered to his mate when he came to our back door. Because I was very little they probably thought I would not be offended. Anyway, this man looked around at all our luxury and biting his lip and shaking his head said, 'Behind every great fortune there is a great crime.' I did not know what he meant then..."

"...And at that age you did not know that you were listening to a plumber who was a philosopher and had just quoted you bloody Balzac!"

"Nope, but I sure knew he wasn't quoting Michael Jackson!" Jack retorted with a smile. "I just filed it away with all those other episodes from childhood you don't understand. But now, looking at all this grandeur, it makes me wonder about Bruto. How could he possibly have acquired it? Look at the gold and silver on that one table. In our money, that alone has got to be worth millions!"

"It must be the spoils of war," Toby replied. Toby came from Struggle Street with a widowed Mum on welfare until she was able to retrain as a nurse. He would not know whether all the glittering bowls and goblets were real or fakes, but he was an amateur archaeologist. He swept his hand mid-air towards the table, asking, "Are you surprised about how Roman all this is? Whenever I think of King Arthur I think about it being a very British time, with medieval castles and knights in shining armour who jousted one another and went on quests."

"Same, same," Jack agreed. "I thought the Romans had well and truly left by now. But down there is Uther, who will father Arthur... and both he and his brother are dressed in Roman military uniforms, and their father is a Roman commander as well. And over there stands Merlin, and who could be more British than him? But next to him is his father who was the Dux of a legion, and that lineage makes Merlin and Arthur half-Roman at least and definitely Roman citizens. This house is Roman; they speak some kind of Latin—well, I think that's what it is. They all seem to be Christian and they all want Rome's help, and Merlin..." Jack broke off as if distracted by another thought and looked away dreamily.

"Do you remember whether they get it or not?" Toby prompted him.

"Get what?"

"Rome's help?"

"They can't have got any help," Jack began slowly, leaning on his elbows and speaking as if he was distracted by something else, "or we would not have needed Uther and Arthur… to fight the Saxons… because the Romans… would have got rid of them already."

His friend wanted to ask him what was wrong with him, about why he was drifting away, but he reasonably concluded that whenever Jack had his goofy look on his face, he was thinking of Emily and not of Roman Britain. The best way to snap him out of it would be to bring her up here.

So as if he had suddenly had this brilliant thought, Toby suggested:

"Hey, let's wake up Emily for the entertainment. She's had at least six hours sleep by now."

Jack was instantly present again and covered in smiles.

"You know she asked me to kiss her last night just before she was snatched by Moloch. And I know the kiss was just a ruse to trick Morgana, but finally I did it!"

"And did the earth move?" Toby asked, and when Jack looked at him sheepishly as if he had swallowed heaven, all Toby could think to say was, "Awesome!" and smile warily in return. One friend, one master and one girl, which made three… it could only mean tears. It was time to move to safer ground. Back to music. Toby announced:

"Hey, I'm dying to hear a bard sing. They are all supposed to sing in C minor, like the Beatles in Eleanor Rigby."

"Rigby's in E minor," retorted Jack, fully present. "Remember, I play the cello bit whenever we cover it." Then he added, "But it was originally in C minor before the Beatles changed it."

"I knew that!" Toby bluffed. "I wonder what instruments they will play."

"I think it's too early in our history for fiddles. There could be some harps and lutes and drums. But," Jack added with a moan, "it's probably just boring bagpipes."

38

Olwen the Bard

10.30am, Friday September 10th, Merlin's time

WHAT A SOUND! It was merely a drone but it was a delicious, long, mournful squeeze of an elbow on a pig's bladder.

"God, that was good. That's got to be a Northumberland pipe!"

Toby smiled in delight at Emily and Jack as they all leaned excitedly from an attic window to watch the grand entrance of Olwen the Bard. In front of them, the oak doors in the palisades were drawn back by two dwarf men dressed in scarlet tunics. They bowed to the applause and rushed forward to leap and somersault among the farmers and villagers. The audience stood in knots of drab clothing, draped with skins and bunched close together so they could elbow one another in awe whenever the bard did a trick. Everyone knew that Olwen was a magician with a prodigious memory and a powerful tenor voice—and did not he, himself, claim to be the best in Britannia? Did not he conjure tricks that left you speechless in wonder?

When the horns blew, Olwen entered slowly, and with all eyes on him he savoured each step. Even from a distance it seemed his magnificent cape of quills could stand up by itself without being draped over his shoulders. Emily guessed at least thirty swans had to be plucked bare to provide the glistening white feathers for such a garment. There were gasps of 'Can you believe it?' and cries of 'Have you ever seen such a wonder?' and everyone agreed they had never, ever seen anything like it.

The Bard raised his arms to shush the crowd. He twirled dramatically to show off his cloak before he began a sweet ballad which everyone, except the three friends, seemed to know. Toby dug Jack in the ribs.

"C minor!"

"You got it!" Jack replied.

After the audience clapped and twirled and stamped their clogged feet on the paved stone, the dancing began.

But, when the Bard brought his staff down for silence, he was granted it instantly, and all you could hear were the blackbirds singing and the unceasing chorus of insects. Everyone stood, breathless, just waiting to be amazed. And after twirling his cloak again dramatically, Olwen pointed his staff in every direction at eye level and almost imperceptibly moved around them in a full circle. Of course, he was mesmerising his onlookers, and once he had enchanted them, he tossed his staff up in the air like the leader of a marching band, grabbed it on its descent and flung it into the ground—there it stiffened into a black snake and slithered across the cleared space.

The shrieks of the villagers pierced the silence and they parted in the serpent's path as it slid one way and then another. When Olwen had retrieved his snake he called for calm.

"Look you, look you, you are completely safe because I am going to kill this serpent." Olwen approached a man whose face was speckled with mud and asked: "How should I kill it?"

"Cut off its head!" he replied, using his finger like a scythe to his own neck. "A snake is a sign of the devil himself." But his neighbour had another suggestion:

"Stamp on its head!" But no one seemed to like his plan either.

"No, that won't do it at all," Caballus, the blacksmith declared. "I will slice it with my whip!"

"Thank you, one and all!" Olwen cut off any more offers with, "I have another idea! Watch this!" And opening his mouth wide, he sucked the serpent through his lips. There was a hubbub of gasps and groans as he slurped its passage down his throat until he loudly burped his enjoyment. He rubbed his tummy with delight when the tip of its tail disappeared down his gullet.

A farmer started whistling sharply through his fingers, and others joined him while the rest clapped. What could be next?

The Bard squatted elegantly on the ground to allow a dwarf to climb on either knee. They scrambled quickly from his knee to his shoulders, and for a few moments he paraded around the space with them taking turns to stand on his head. Suddenly, one man dropped into his hands and the bard alternated tossing one then the other into the air, catching one while the other was airborne, until he was rhythmically juggling them.

The crowd was aghast, fearful as they knew that, at any moment, either could be dropped on the stone and injured dreadfully. But there was nothing to worry about because Olwen threw them neatly, head first, into a water butt—where they would have drowned if a sturdy soldier hadn't pulled them out, gasping.

"Did you know," Toby asked, "that it is statistically accurate to say that eight out of nine dwarfs are not Happy?"

Emily laughed, and Jack smiling said,

"And you, Tobes, have had to wait a lifetime to find the right moment to inform us of that!"

But Olwen hadn't finished. He moved to a woman from whose breast he pulled a frog, and he found mice behind a farrier's ears, and then catching the eye of a very disinterested youth he walked over to him and pulled two maggots, one after the other, from the boy's nose.

Undoubtedly, Olwen was building to his big moment. He spun around, his cloak billowing until he reached a point where he was a blur of white feathers, and it was then that he slowly lifted off the ground like a saint ascending into heaven, and hovered above the heads of the crowd. Even the kings gasped at this. Even those who had grown weary of the wonders performed by their own bards had never seen one of them ascend before. Slowly, Olwen descended, and once he was steady on his feet, he opened his cloak and out flew a flock of white doves.

The excitement was too much for two of the older women, who clutched their breasts and swooned. Immediately, the clapping began, and looking directly beneath her, Emily could make out Ingraine, a slash of scarlet on her lips, and standing beside her was a commanding figure who she assumed was the father of Merlin. They were dressed in white togas, much like her own, but they wore the purple stripe of nobility down their left side. Beside them stood a blend of Roman and British kings, who wore circlets of laurel leaves around their heads and soft cloaks over their shoulders that billowed in the breeze. Greeting the Bard first, Bruto grasped his elbow before he introduced him to Ingraine who offered her hand up to be kissed. She inclined her head ever so slightly as she looked up at them in the attic before she whispered something to her husband, who gave the command, seemingly at her insistence, to clear the courtyard.

"Does Olwen look familiar to you?" Jack asked of no one in particular.

"Yes, definitely! With all those feathers he looks like Big Bird," Toby quipped, although he thought he saw below the stairs, from the corner of his eye, the giant sleeping bat stir.

But it was Emily who caught the rancid odour when the Bard passed just below her. It was a foul yet familiar smell that lingered, and almost in unison the three friends realised what Ingraine and Bruto already knew, that the Bard had amber eyes.

Morgana had just entered their villa.

39

"Who saw that coming?"

11.00am, Friday September 10th, Merlin's time

Inside, on the staircase, Jack asked his friends,
"Well, hands up who saw that coming? What the hell is Morgana up to now?"

"She misses you, Jack. Madly!" Toby smirked, and tousling Jack's hair continued, "She just can't keep away from you, lover boy. She's come back again to ravish you, this time big time."

"Seriously, Tobes!" Emily gave him a shove. "Get real! She's an evil woman. I think it is payback time! She wants revenge on Merlin for capturing her mate, Moloch. If she can make a fool of Merlin and embarrass him in front of all the kings, he will be less effective in the future." As she spoke Jack watched her closely and saw that whenever she mentioned Merlin's name she blushed. And Jack knew what that meant.

"What if," Toby said, oblivious to their interplay, "instead of kidnapping you, Jack, Morgana is here to kidnap Merlin's prize prisoner?"

"...Or to set it up so that a prize prisoner can escape?" Jack offered, building on their ideas.

"If she did that she would make a fool of everyone and disrupt everything," Emily concluded.

"While I agree that is possible, Em," Jack said, "my question would be, why bother? Why go to all the trouble of creating such an impersonation as complex as Olwen and infiltrating this household to free Vortigern, when all she had to do was open his door and set him free? I think she must be up to something else."

"If she's here to rescue Vortigern, how would she get him out of here?" Toby asked.

"She could fly him on her bat..." Emily offered, thinking aloud.

"Even an enchanted Mot can't fly in daylight," Toby said. "But Morgana herself can fly; why wouldn't she just carry him out of here herself?"

"If she did that she would have completely blown her cover as Olwen and whatever else she had planned for the day, and they would never allow her to return here again," Emily said.

"All we need is a plan," Toby announced, "to recapture Vortigern if he escapes."

"What if she had a horse saddled for Vortigern?" Jack suggested.

"What if we had a horse saddled for us?" Toby asked. "And we, invisible to Vortigern's eyes, were already mounted and just waiting until he escaped and then we could..." and here Toby paused for dramatic effect and bowed to the others, "...heroically, of course, recapture him and return him to the prison. Ta-Da!!"

They all grinned at one another and gave instant 'high fives'.

"Shouldn't we tell Merlin what we're doing?" Jack cautioned.

"You two recapture Vortigern, and I will tell Merlin," Emily offered as Jack's mouth tightened. "I know the cellar room where Vortigern is a prisoner. I walked past it a little while ago.

I can stand in the shadows there and watch what happens. You prepare the horses ready to give chase if and when he escapes."

"This way, sir, in here." The cook shepherded Olwen the Bard into the large kitchen. All around him knives darted in clouds of steam. There was plucking and dicing and boiling and roasting, while a delicious aroma of spit-roasted boar filled the air. Everyone's eyes followed Olwen, and every move he made was closely studied in case a new piece of magic should escape their notice. But Olwen's eyes searched the room for something else: the presence of a thin, nervous girl.

"Greetings, Anya," Olwen cried cheerfully, and grabbing her grubby hand, he kissed it. "I'm Olwen the Bard, here to entertain, and I am an old friend of your father."

She flinched and looked up at him from under her nest of dishevelled hair.

"That out there, kind sir," said a round-bellied servant who approached Olwen, "would have been thirsty work. What can we offer you, Sir?"

"I will have four tankards of your strongest cider, one for me and one for the lass here, and two for my dwarfs, and Anya will take the cider out to them."

The girl looked up at the Bard fearfully and fifteen pairs of eyes watched them, carefully.

"How wonderful to see you again," Olwen gushed, performing for his audience. "Last time, Anya, you were just a wee bairn." Leaning over her, he whispered, "Take these ciders to the guards on your father's room. It's just along that passageway," and he pointed to the servant's corridor. "Then go down the stairs. He is in the small cellar under the main hall. Tell them they are from Bruto's son, Ambrosius. The cider will knock them out, and once they are asleep, take the key from the belt of the big one, enter the room of your father's prison and use this knife to cut him free. A Pict, with blue tattoos on his face, will take over from there. Do you understand me?"

Anya nodded and managed a tight, small smile, because if there was only one person on earth she loathed more than any Pict, it was the man who was already in the cellar room. She lifted up the drinks, one in each shaking hand, and set off.

A moment later, the spy of Bruto slipped out to report every word to him.

The gloomy corridor through to the cellar was quiet and dim, and two men dressed as Roman soldiers stood guard on either side of a heavy oak door. Emily watched as a skinny girl, she may have been twelve or thirteen, shuffled towards her carrying pottery tankards. At the cellar door she stopped and spoke to the soldiers,

"This cider is from Ambrosius Cotta." She spoke in a dull monotone, "Something to wet your whistle while you do your duty."

This is very strange, Emily thought, why would Merlin send alcoholic drinks by such an odd girl to the very men who are guarding Vortigern? But the soldiers were delighted. They lifted the jars in a toast, saying, "Bibamus," and poured the drink straight down their open throats.

Almost immediately they buckled at the knees and clawed the walls for support. The girl stood by watching them with a vacant smile until they slid down into crumpled heaps. It was easy for her to unhook the keys from the guard's waist and enter the dark room. As Emily followed, she dismissed the thought of calling Merlin. 'I can handle this myself,' she thought.

On the bed was a small man, blinking with jewels and spread out in a star jump, tethered by his wrists and ankles to the bed frame. He was gagged and naked from the waist with a cloth covering his private parts. But when Emily saw the thin blade in the girl's hand, and the sheer terror in Vortigern's eyes, she knew she needed help and put her arm over her mouth and breathed,

"Merlin, come quickly to the cellar, it's Vortigern!"

The girl raised the dagger, but paused to search with her finger for the right spot before she stabbed him, almost surgically, below his rib. There was a spurt of blood and a gurgling sound from his throat. At that moment Anya smiled and drew back the dagger again, and Vortigern moaned through the gag,

"Doone help me!" as the Pict burst into the room.

Anya spun around at Doone angrily and caught him off-guard with his eyes blinked shut, but his all-seeing eyes wide open. She kneed him in the groin and thrust her dagger up through his tattooed eyelid. Perhaps Anya hated tattooed eyelids or thought his eyes were open and staring at her, Emily would never know. Doone collapsed forward onto the girl, screaming in pain, and immediately began convulsing and vomiting.

Emily, the unseen presence, watched the girl wriggle free of him and remove her bloodied knife from Doone's eye socket. Turning away from him with disinterest, she knelt down beside her father. She fingered his navel to steady her aim, and with quiet and calculating malice, drew back her knife for a fresh attack. But Emily caught the girl's wrist before she could stab Vortigern again, and in that moment Merlin was somehow there between them. He grabbed the girl by the throat and threw her against the wall where she cracked her head and slid down to the stone floor, unconscious.

"Bryten, piss on my eye, for pity's sake!" Doone implored him. He wanted Merlin to treat him like any Pictish warrior and spray his antiseptic urine on his wound.

Before Merlin, numb with his own pain and horror, could agree, he brought his head down to Emily's and in a hoarse whisper said,

"This is terrible! Fetch Ingraine and Angharad. They are in the hospital, that small hut near the river. Tell them to bring medicines. Get Caballus so he can take this poor unfortunate girl out of here. Hurry!"

Emily went running.

40

He is dying, Myrddin

12pm, Friday September 10th, Merlin's time

I T ONLY TOOK INGRAINE A MOMENT to assess the bloody scene. Her distraught son was cradling the dying shaman whom he adored, and the pitiful daughter, her face contorted with hatred, sat motionless glaring at her wounded father. Ingraine spoke quickly in Welsh to Angharad.

"Take out the gag from Vortigern's mouth and cut him free. I think it is only a shallow cut, just a flesh wound, because those hard muscles of his stomach stopped it going any deeper." Then in a whisper, she said, "I must protect this space from Morgana's eavesdropping!" And while it would only have taken her a few moments, she became distracted by the horror of Doone's injuries, and that pathetic wretch with all her dirty secrets sitting on the floor, so instead of immobilising Vortigern as she intended, she never gave it another thought. The smell of Vortigern's sweat and blood and Doone's vomit stung all their nostrils, and it was hard for her to focus on what to do next. Whichever way Ingraine turned, the scene looked ghastly.

"How's Doone?" she asked quietly of her son. "It looks to me like he is dying, Myrddin."

"He is settled for the moment, but every now and then he will have a violent spasm, jerking his arms and legs and head."

Even as Merlin spoke, Doone moaned and began shaking again, so Merlin wrapped him tightly in his arms to stop him throwing his head backwards onto the stone floor. Angharad hovered over them both, tenderly washing Doone's blood-stained face. His voice, a mere whisper, said to her,

"Tell her I love her."

She lifted his hand to her kiss, "I will, I will! She's just outside here, with Emilia."

"I have seen arrows go through a man's eye and pierce the grey matter behind it," Ingraine explained to Merlin who was barely listening. He felt like he was viewing this gruesome scene from the ceiling. "They twitch rapidly and soil themselves," Ingraine continued.

Meanwhile, the smith knocked on the open door and came up to Merlin for his instructions.

"Take Anya here up to the convent at Avalon and ask the nuns to care for her until they hear from my mother, and—just wait a minute, give them this." And Merlin took off his gold torc. "Ingraine will visit them soon to make arrangements."

"Thank God she's gone, Myrddin," Ingraine said. "She gave me the creeps and never said a word, poor thing! Now, give Doone this tincture of willow bark and opium to relieve his pain." Merlin gently pushed Doone's head back and poured it down his throat.

Lifting him upright again, Merlin spoke directly into his ear.

"You taught me the tongue of the wildwood, Doone, so thank you. You taught me to read the movements of the otter and deer, to stalk and trap my food, and to fly like a swallow over the mire. You are like my family. But tonight Emilia and I could have died. Why did you betray us to the shadows of Darkness? Why did you do it? "

There was absolute silence in the small room, because everyone else had drawn in their breath and held it tightly in shock. What was Myrddin talking about? Had he taken leave of his senses? Ingraine shook her head vehemently from side to side as Angharad plastered her hand over her mouth to stop her scream from splitting the cellar in two.

Struggling to form the words, Doone answered,

"I did not, Bryten, I did not betray you. Master Bruto promised to free me and make me his gamekeeper if I convinced them I worked for them. Every secret I heard from them I told your mother and your father, all their evil plans, everything I could do to keep you safe."

"He speaks the truth, Myrddin," Angharad cried. "Surely you suspected? Doesn't every slave try to buy his freedom? Why would I lie in the sweet grass and mother the child of a traitor?"

"His child? Is this right?" The blood drained from Merlin's face. "I did not know who the father of your child was. Honestly!" He looked desperately at his mother. "Was Doone spying for both us and them?"

"Of course he was," Ingraine replied. And as she continued, Merlin's faculties went numb, "In its arrogance the Darkness never suspected. And you, in your innocence of the complexities of how we love and protect one another, you never suspected it either."

"How could I not have seen this?"

As Merlin looked down to apologise, he saw the spirit of Doone leave.

Emily stood in the shadows outside the door. The guards lay still, and the small child who came with Angharad pulled knuckle bones from her pocket and marched them like soldiers across the floor.

"What's your name?" Emily asked, and the child stared at her, not understanding. But when she repeated herself in Welsh, the child answered.

Emily could hear snatches of conversation from the cellar room and it was just enough for her to understand the depth of Merlin's distress as he nursed his dying teacher. There was little about the crude man she liked, but she would not have wished his gruesome end on anyone.

No one in the cellar was watching Vortigern. So no one saw him take advantage of their distress and quietly slip out the door, a cloth around his waist like a towel. He could not believe his luck, because he saw two sleeping guards and a two-year-old playing on the floor.

"Thank you, Morgana!" He raised his eyes to the heavens and said it like a prayer. With one arm he grabbed the child as hostage and with the other he pulled a sword away from a soldier.

Realising immediately that while she may not have the strength to disarm Vortigern, Emily did have the advantage of her invisibility, and that meant she could at least trip him up. She acted quickly and plucked the toddler from the unsuspecting man and, with a stiff leg, brought Vortigern crashing down. In a moment, a stunned moment, there was a whiff of a familiar pungent smell and Vortigern was lifted into the air and disappeared. Just as she cried out, "Merlin!" Ingraine appeared.

"Where is Vortigern?" she demanded.

"It was Morgana." Emily replied. "One moment Vortigern was here, then poof! he was gone. He tried to kidnap this child."

"Oh, no, what a mess!" Ingraine moaned, shaking her head. "Give me the little one so she can kiss her father goodbye. Can you come in too, because Myrddin needs you? Please try to help him, he's gone into a deep shock. Even if all you do is hold his hand and listen to him when he is able to talk." Then she added with a knowing look, "Please keep him engaged as long as you can, in his bed if possible. I will speak to his father and cover his duties for him."

"I will try, Ingraine," Emily said over her shoulder as she pushed into the crowded cellar and wondered what engaged actually meant. "Don't worry about Vortigern. He won't get away because Toby and Jack anticipated Morgana's plans. They're ready to give chase and recapture him."

41

Vortigern Escapes

1pm, Friday September 10th, Merlin's time

IT WAS TOBY WHO SAW HIM FIRST. A well-muscled, small man with a bloodstained loincloth tied between his legs and a large breastplate over his upper body. He hobbled towards a brown moor pony.

"Where did he come from?" Toby whispered. "He just appeared. Can this be the great and feared Vortigern? He looks like a pimp!"

But Jack was absorbed with something else. They were hiding in the stables with their two saddled ponies close by them and watching through a crack in the timber wall. Jack was worried.

"Can't you smell her, Tobes?" His voice quavered. "Everything tells me Morgana's around us, somewhere."

"I can't smell her. But can you reassure me she can't see us?" Toby asked.

"According to Merlin, Morgana can't, but she would see our ponies if we were riding them now, and to her they would be riderless. How could they have let Vortigern escape? I hope Em is okay."

"She'll be fine, Jack. If she can outwit Moloch, the Prince of Darkness, then that poncing pig over there should be easy-peasy. But why aren't the gatehouse guards stopping him? What's wrong with them?"

They watched as Vortigern clumsily mounted the pony and fled unchallenged through the gate. All Jack could say was:

"This has got that bitch stamped all over it. She's somewhere out of sight gloating at this. I can still get a whiff of her."

"Then let's change our plans, let's allow her to think he's got away. If you could follow him out of here at a safe distance, I will go back and get the rat-face, Mot, and catch up with you in ten minutes. But where?"

"If we were in our time I'd know this land very well, and even though over the last fifteen hundred years it's probably changed a lot, I think the rivers would have to be still where we left them. If I were Vortigern, I'd go right out the gate, follow the river path down to the ford and pick up the East Okement at the next ford. Then I'd head up back to Belstone, and although it's not easy riding as you've seen, there's plenty of cover."

"Okay. I'll be above you at the ford in fifteen. Good luck! It's a nasty job flying a bat, but somebody's got to do it!"

"Yoo hoo!!" Toby's feet barely touched the ground. Life was good. "Yoo hoo!!" He was moving again. And if the chance of chasing Morgana on her very own bat came up, he was the man. Ever since he realised the true identity of Olwen, he'd been tossing around a theory about how he would like to test her. There was a trickster gnome in the fairy tale that spun straw into gold for a beautiful girl in return for her promise to gift him her first-born child. When the time came for her to deliver on her promise, the gnome said he would forgive her debt—if she could discover his name. When she revealed his name, the trickster disintegrated. Toby was sure that Morgana was hiding her real name for some very important reason, and he believed she would not reveal it because she feared that once spoken aloud it would diminish her powers. And Toby's magic weapon was: he knew Morgana's real name!

But first he had other business to attend to. He wanted to examine the outer building that he nearly fell into yesterday, because tomorrow in the real world he would have to abseil into it.

Across from the stable, there was a granary with typical Roman-style buttressing at its sides. Through the creaking door, he saw terracotta jugs held up by their necks in the lower racks and grain stored in sacks on the upper shelves. Above all, there was a yawning hole in the roof. He pulled out his phone and took pictures of it from every angle. That should save time tomorrow! The Professor will love it!

He skirted around the rabbit hutches to find the back door of the villa and stopped in his tracks. There, shadow-fencing, was Aurelius, who spun around and said loudly,

"I know you're there, you shithead!" He quickly drew his sword and advanced to where Toby was standing. "Show yourself, Vortigern!"

"Hey, I'm not Vortigern. Cool it!" Toby cried out as he dodged his blade. "I am Toby, Tobias really, Merlin's friend. You can't see me and maybe you can't hear me either, but you must be able to sense me. Can't you?" It seemed he couldn't. If this bloke is me, Toby thought, he's a half-wit and I don't want anything to do with him because he will kill me if I don't get away fast!

Suddenly Uther appeared bellowing,

"For God's sake, brother, stop thrusting at shadows. We've got news! Three pigeons came in and it's not good."

"Quick, what news?"

"Constans' death first. Vortigern's been boasting about it, and claiming credit. He did not die of an illness. It was poison."

"That confirms what the Saxon prisoner revealed." Aurelius went white and crossed himself. "It was murder as we feared. Is Father safe?"

"Let's hope all the warnings we sent to him this morning got through to him in time. There's no news from him yet." As if itching for immediate revenge, Uther started pacing and Toby leapt out of his way.

"But what else?" Aurelius insisted.

"Our spies are all in agreement. They have seen him. Vortigern is up north in Brough. There is not a whisper of him being anywhere here in the south-west."

"Then who the hell is here? Surely this is Vortigern and not someone else!"

"Maybe he is doing what they do in Gaul and using a double."

"Bloody hell—two of them! But which one is here?"

"Was here—he just escaped," Uther said.

"Who's given chase?"

"Not Merlin, that's for sure. He's locked in grief. Merlin's teacher, Doone—you know, the fierce fighter covered in blue pictures—he was killed by Vortigern's daughter as he tried to stop her murdering her father. In the utter chaos Vortigern just breezed out the gate. It was a planned escape. Seven guards were drugged."

"Uther, we've got to get him. Let's round up our men and bring him back. We can sort out later whether he's the imposter or not."

Toby tiptoed away to find Mot in Merlin's room.

When Toby opened the door, nothing had changed. The servants had missed cleaning it, and because it was deserted he took the opportunity to look around. After tickling Mot 'Hello' he wandered over to peep behind the draped wall-cloth.

"Holy shit!" he said to no one in particular. "That's Emily! There's Roget in his roost and those headlights are her boobles.

Now I know what you're after Merlin, and this drawing proved what I always told Jack: Roget gets the best view.

After he patted Kelso, he led the reluctant Mot out into the declining light.

"Look, dearest rat-face, it will be dark enough in just a few moments. Come on!" and he tickled her under her chin again. "Give me uplift, Rat-face—oops, sorry, very sorry," and he made a kissing sound through his lips, "my very honourable bat.... let's go!" And he took off to the north over the roof towards the rushing river.

42

Let Me Love You

1pm, Friday September 10th, Merlin's time

EMILY BEGAN CAUTIOUSLY.

"I'm so sorry, Merlin, for your loss; and Angharad, for yours, too." Merlin had not moved. He was still cradling Doone on his lap, just sitting there numb and mute. She gently touched his cheek.

"It's time for us, Merlin, to leave Doone with his family. Let me help you lift him onto the bed."

After she pulled the blood-stained cover from the paillasse, Emily managed Doone's legs while Merlin laid him down carefully and shut his good eye. It was the first time that he realised that even an eye as lifeless as Doone's could still hold a look of cold fear. Now with his Druidic eye open and his other one a yawning bloody hole, Merlin feared Doone was winking at him.

"Come on, Merlin, you are to come with me," and taking his hand Emily led the dazed magician up the narrow stairs through the back passages to his chamber. There she shooed away his seething knot of animals—except for the fox, who after smelling Merlin cautiously, refused to move.

"Okay, Mr Fox, if you want to stay with him and me, you are most welcome," and once she had locked Merlin's door, she hoped his room was well protected from the dark arts of Morgana. She did not know that Ingraine, Angharad and Merlin had all become distracted from their usual protective rituals and as a result the shade of Morgana could settle comfortably outside the open window of Merlin's room, resting at the breeziest spot, where her tell-tale odour could not drift into the villa.

Emily led him to an ornate Roman couch where she sat him down, very aware that the sickly sweet smell of Doone's blood hung all over him. His room was so hot from his African wind that she stood behind him for a while and fanned him with a small metal shield. He stared straight in front of him, motionless, and Emily, fearing he could stay locked in that state for hours, sat beside him and took him in her arms. She imagined herself soaking up his pain, absorbing it into her heart to help restore him to the Merlin he was this morning when he sang with the birds to wish her a happy birthday. Emily held him tightly until her arms were numb, and when his tears eventually came it was with moans and sobs. At times he howled like a wounded animal. He wept long enough for the autumn sun to dim and leave his room, and once he had quietened, she kissed away his tears. It was only then, and perhaps it was after an hour or even much longer, that Merlin could speak.

"Doone died in my arms," he said and paused, holding his arms out as if Doone were still in them; he rocked them, and only after he had examined his blood-drenched toga and raised it to his lips to kiss, did he continue: "And I, who can change the direction of the wind, was powerless to stop any of this." There he paused and shook his head before whispering to her, "I felt helpless and I falsely accused him of treachery."

Emily stroked his cheek with the tip of her fingers. "Shush, shush, Merlin!"

"Do you know my father gave me clues about Doone, yet I did not hear them? I did not read his signs. I never asked my mother how she knew all about the comings and goings of the Dark. I just assumed she had second sight and saw it all by herself." Rocking back and forth Merlin repeated loudly, "I never asked!" He paused again, and staring into space he continued:

"My nurse and my slave had a child together. Although I was with them every single day, I did not even know how close they were to one another. I can tell you, Emilia, all about the motions of the planets, all about the circulation of the west wind, all about the geometry of the mosaics on this floor, or about the engineering of Fosse Way, and I can calculate the square root of any number you name to over the tenth decimal point, but I cannot tell you the name of the baby of my beloved nurse or the name of the father of her baby. I never asked."

For the first time, Emily spoke to him using Welsh.

"Myrddin, the little one told me she had two names, and she is called Carys Angharad, which, as you know, means 'love' and 'much loved'. It sounds very much that her mother and father were making a point about their love of each other and their love of her."

Merlin stared at her grimly.

"I do not think I know much about love, it was all around me and I did not see it."

Emily took his hands and replied softly, "You cannot analyse love, Merlin, or study it to know it. You have to experience it, to feel it. Let me show you what love could be." And she gently disentangled herself and went over to where his clothes were hanging. "Are you watching me?" she asked, confident he was. She selected a clean toga and threw it over her shoulder, and then she poured from a jug some fresh water into a basin with a sponge in it and carried it to a table near him.

"I cannot feel anything, Emilia," he said through a tightly clenched jaw, his eyes puffy. "I just feel numb."

"I couldn't feel anything for a week after my dad's mum died. But I knew she was going to die because she had cancer."

She took his hands, one by one, and soaked them in water, and when they were clean she dried them on her own toga. She carried the bloodied water over to his window and unknowingly tossed it over a startled Morgana. Then she rinsed and refilled the basin. Dolossus followed her every move until he finally settled beside the window and delicately sniffed the breeze. It was only when the fox quietened down that she could continue.

"Everyone would agree that Doone's death was horrible: it was a dreadful shock and, unlike what happened to me with my Nannie, you weren't prepared for it at all. You thought Doone would be with you all your life. Now you are in shock."

She wondered if he heard her because he started talking again straight away, continuing where he left off as if he had merely been interrupted.

"You know, I never even asked myself what was Doone's heart's desire."

Gently she bathed his eyes before lifting his toga over his head and balling it onto the floor. She began sponging his chest and noticed his skin was smooth without body hair. She shut her eyes as she realised he had already been through the ritual depilation of his skin in preparation for joining the Legion. The heat dried him instantly and his skin shone.

"I did not really know Doone, and because he was my slave, I never thought he would have a special desire. I was too immersed in myself. It is my fault."

Again tears formed in his eyes, but this time they did not fall and he looked wretched, and when he finally drew in his breath, it stuttered like a breaking sob. Emily sponged his face and whispered gently straight into his ear,

"You are doing a very good job of beating up yourself, Merlin. I am going to put my hand on your heart when I say this to you so you can feel where in you I am speaking to, because I have not been able to get through to you any other way."

She pulled his chin so that his face looked directly at her.

"Now, look into my eyes while I ask you these questions: Who saved my mum and Toby from falling into a sink hole? You did!" And whenever she said: "You did!" she would touch his heart. "Who saved me from that menacing hound on the moor? You did. Who saved Jack and Toby when their plane stalled? You did. Who fought the Saxons and captured Vortigern? You did. You did all this in the very brief time I have known you, Merlin. And only a few hours ago, who imprisoned the vilest form of Darkness in our country? You did!" And she added with a smile and the merest brush of her lips on his, "And you even freed his bats.

"I do not need to continue, but I am going to because who was it who outwitted Morgana at every turn, and who showed all the creatures of Dartmoor his mastery of the elements? You did, Merlin. Now you have been humbled, you have been brought back down to the earth to realise again you are a mere human being, like the rest of us. Even my miracle boy, Merlin, can make a mistake."

And when the corners of his mouth turned up ever so slightly to smile weakly, she brushed her lips again on the edge of his.

He allowed her to raise him to his feet to remove the rest of his bloodstained undergarments and his pouch, leaving him standing there in his loincloth.

"Please Merlin," she asked smiling, "could you put all your grief in this little pouch with your field mice for a while and only allow it out once I have gone?" And she began to wash him gently again. "We have so little time together, you and me," her face beamed up at him because she could feel he was starting to come back, "and we have so much to discover about each other."

Then suddenly he sprang back to life, and in that moment everything changed. He felt better and he wanted to go. Emily stared at him shocked.

"First," Merlin cried as he abruptly turned towards the door, "I have to find Morgana!"

"Turn around," and she pulled him back, "I am not finished yet. Let Morgana find you because you do not have to do everything."

Emily paused to think how she could divert him and decided that talking about Morgana could keep him engaged like his mother wanted.

"Jack questioned why Morgana designed such an elaborate masquerade as Olwen just to free Vortigern, when she could have done it simply by other means. What do you think she was up to?"

"The Dark's first objective never varies. It is always to cause chaos, to make you anxious about what is coming next, to waste your energy anticipating their next move..."

Emily interrupted him, sponging his face, "That's what we call 'terrorists'."

"That is merely a new name for a very old game. One advantage we have over them is that they are predictable, and Morgana prefers poison to eliminate her enemies. And this is what Jack did not know. As Olwen, Morgana will head for the kitchen and use her arts to enchant the staff and lace our food with her vileness."

"If you know all this, you can anticipate her and stop her."

"Yes," Merlin nodded. "And that is what we have done. One of the stirrers of the food had his eyes bandaged so that he could not be enchanted—or hypnotised, as you say—by Olwen. He was to listen to Olwen's voice, and when it changed in cadence to become like a song, he was to turn away slowly from the voice, and just as slowly turn back, and through a peep-hole in his eye-compress observe what Olwen was doing. Did he poison the food? Yes! The stirrer saw him do it and reported everything to Ingraine, who fed samples of all the food to some piglets. She was able to diagnose what was poisonous. She had other piglets to test the rest of the food, and it was safe."

The eavesdropper at the window smiled gratefully at this news.

Emily, however, was reassured. "Thank God for that!" she said as she wrung out the sponge. Then carrying the bowl over to the open window she tossed the bloody water out again. Returning with fresh water from the ewer, she wet his hair and tousled it with her fingers into curls and twists, like black ice cream. Then she knelt on the mosaic floor to wash his feet.

"My Lady, thank you so much for washing away Doone's blood," he managed a wan smile as he raised her to her feet, "but I really must be going. If it pleases you, will you pass me the clean toga?" He kissed her forehead, and while she held him tightly with one arm she hid his toga behind her back with the other. "I have to go now and tell my father that Vortigern has escaped."

"No, you do not, Merlin." She kept her tone light and playful. "Because your mother would have told him over an hour ago."

"But now Olwen has gone, I will have to plan the music for the evening."

"No, you do not," she laughed. "I will do that. It's already taken shape in my head, and Toby and I have lots of set pieces in our repertoire and I am sure I can get loads of help."

He tried to pull away again, saying, "But I have to find Vortigern!"

"No, you do not!" and she held him tighter still. "You don't, you know, because Morgana by herself cannot carry Vortigern away that far, and Toby and Jack will find him if he is to be found. You can see Mot has gone and that will be Toby's work."

Morgana, now knowing all she needed to know, spun away into the treetops.

"All right, Emilia." There was the slightest smile on his lips. "I think you are playing a game with me!"

Emily shrugged her shoulders and said to herself, 'Finally, he's got it!' She glanced up at him from under her eyelashes.

"You must know my heart stops when you look at me like that. But I do have to scribe for the final session of the Moot."

"Yes, you do, but they are on a break for a while. Can't you hear them? Later I will send a messenger to you with the words of a song for you to learn for our final piece. Can you still hypnotise?" and she waved her fingers playfully in front of his face.

"Well, I am not aware of how I could have forgotten."

"Of course you remember, but do you still have that special energy that enables you to enchant?"

"I am afraid it is very low, it is much depleted."

"How do you recharge it?"

"Well, I have seldom felt as low as this, but when I have, I leave with my animals for the wildwood across the river. There in the cave in darkness they guard me while I sit like a monk lost in a holy silence until my strength returns and I am refreshed."

"There are other ways, Merlin, to feel refreshed." And glancing at him again from under her eyelashes, "You are already undressed, what if I put you in your bed, right now..." She smiled her sweetest smile and gestured towards his large, dishevelled bed.

"I am not tired, Emilia..." And then Merlin paused and a look of amazement spread over his face as he finally understood. "Or do you mean... both of us... in bed... together?"

"Yes, I do." It suddenly struck Emily that he too had not done this before.

He held her face in his hands and asked, "Are you a maid?"

"Do you mean have I done this before? No, I have not!" she replied firmly.

"I thought when you called me to Jack's castle, when was it—yesterday?—you were flirting with him..."

"Yes, I was. Or I was trying to. But he's very straight, you know."

"But then, last night, when you kissed Jack, I thought you two were... well, you might be, together."

"I am silly sometimes but I am not that kind of girl!" Emily said indignantly.

"I did not mean, My Lady, to imply that you are not chaste..."

"Look, Merlin, I was only playing, trying to confuse Morgana by whispering my plans in Jack's ear while he kissed me as a cover. Jack and I are just friends. We are really, truly good friends. If... you know..." and she was embarrassed, unable to complete what she wanted to say. He was staring at her, puzzled, and feeling a need to reassure him, she murmured, "As soon as I saw you in daylight, I wanted it to be you. You would be the first ever."

She could not believe what she was asking, and Merlin looked at her intently, saying nothing. He stayed silent for a long time as if he was weighing up her worth.

'Say something, please say something.' Emily pleaded to herself. At last Merlin shook his head slowly and murmured, "Then, no."

Emily, who never expected to be refused, asked him, hurt and bewildered, "What do you mean 'no'?"

"Although I asked your father for his permission to court you, I have not had a chance to do it. I was foolish and should not have raised your hopes in that way."

"Don't be so old-fashioned, Merlin! You and I, we do not have time to 'court'... "

"…As much as I want to, and I have desired you ever since I first saw you dancing with my fox… but we…we are not meant to be together… You and I cannot marry, you and I cannot have children, we will not even see one another after tonight."

Grabbing his hand, Emily insisted,

"Hey, aren't those the perfectly good reasons why you should lie down with me now? Right, now! And if I can add one more reason… tomorrow when you go to war in Gaul you could be wounded or killed. But what's going on with you, Merlin? I don't understand you. You want me but you won't. Are you still protecting me? Protecting me from whom? Moloch's gone and Morgana, as you say, is very predictable. So what is your worry?"

All he could do was mumble: "Jack."

With a sudden flash of insight, she repeated scornfully: "Jack! Oh no, now you are saving me? You are saving me for Jack?" She waited for him to reply and when he did not, she continued, "I think it's time you and I talked about my future. I know yours and I know you know mine. I know there is not a role in your future for a woman called Emilia, but I suspect you are saying that there is a role in mine for a man who used to be called Uther Pendragon. Am I right?"

"You could be…"

"…Oh no! I think, you think you are saving me for Jack? How dare you!" Now she was so angry she flung his hand aside and spoke with quiet intensity. "How dare you! I decide who I will love and who I will make love to, Merlin. It seems to me there is a plan of my destiny that all you people and the Dark Ones appear to know all about, and I think it goes something like this…You push me aside now, because what I want does not matter, and I will match up with Jack… and if that is right, I know now why they want to kill him… And then what? Wait for it… he and I will have a baby. And guess what it will be? It will be a baby boy! And, wait for it, I know what he will be called... he will be called Arthur!"

Thoroughly distraught, Merlin again shook his head. "No! He won't be called Arthur this time. But, my lady, the rest is true, that could be your destiny."

"Hey, that is a dangerous destiny. Because now I know why they want to kill me too!" she said bitterly. "Because they do not want King Arthur to return to Britain. Well, Merlin, I am changing my destiny. I do not want that destiny and I do not want it because it is very dangerous to you and to me and to Jack, and it seems it is dangerous to my mother as well. Besides, I've got free will, and there is only one man in the whole world I want. And I want you, Merlin, even if I can only have you for an hour."

And Emily jerked down the covering from the mural, and standing right in front of it beside the bed she looked at him up through her eyelashes, loosening her hair... daring him, and loving him to bits. And very slowly, with faltering fingers, she unpinned her toga until it, too, fell to the floor.

"Well Merlin," she asked him very quietly, amazed at her own boldness, "did you get a true likeness?"

He was dumbstruck. For what seemed like minutes, his eyes moved over her and later, when he wrote to her of that moment, he said: "I looked at you, Emilia, through the squinting eyes of an artist and I saw the pure lines of your body, your pallid skin veined like marble, and the tumble of your hair and your robe cast on the floor, and I caught my breath. If you could offer me such purity and grace and beauty, what could I possibly offer you in return?"

But when at last Merlin could speak to her, he was so hoarse she could barely hear what he said.

"My words will infect my meaning, yet I must speak." And he spoke as if his tongue were coated with clay. "Looking at you, Emilia, I feel alive again, and my blood boils. You are a work of art, and whoever was the Merlin who drew you should crush his charcoal underfoot, because he has failed your beauty. There is something more I must tell you..."

"Please stop it, Merlin," Emily pleaded as gently as she could. "Please, no more words, no more analysis and no more regrets. You are a kind, good man. Come lie with me... and let me love you."

43

Jack at the Ford of the River

1pm, Friday September 10th, Our time

A FIERY BREATH—IT WAS MERLIN'S WIND—blew through the woodlands and chewed the leaves of the beech and the oak and the ash into small shreds.

Jack was cranky. Somewhere, somehow, something in his world had shifted and he sensed he had lost his lovely Emily and he could not see how he would ever win her back. Somehow, too, his friend Toby had made a leap he had not been able to, and Toby had adjusted to this magical world. Any minute he'd be here, flying, riding a bloody bat like a B-52 bomber.

Then there was Oota. 'How could *I* be him?' Jack asked himself, annoyed. 'And if I am Uther and Toby is my older brother, then who is Emily? Here, I have to suspend reality all the time, and remember that I am invisible to most peo-ple. It is very annoying. Hey, it is futile! Like whenever I try to imagine myself King Uther. Me as a ferocious warrior? Me as the father of King Arthur? I don't think so!

'Though, both of us are tough and tall with red gold hair and we will end up soldiers, but so will Henry the Eighth and

George Washington. It does not prove a thing. Unless Merlin is going to do a great reveal and say "Yep, believe it or not, King Henry and Washington are both Uther Pendragon too". Shit, what a burden that would be.'

He sighed and shook the thoughts away.

'I want to fast-forward Uther's life to the exciting bits rather than waiting around here while his future slowly unfolds. What I find most puzzling is why anyone, including Uther, wants to keep this Vortigern alive. Why don't they rid themselves of this sick pervert? Doesn't Uther know he killed his very own brother, Constans? Doesn't Uther know Vortigern killed his own father, Constantine? I know the Arthurian story like the Book of Common Prayer, but what I don't know is what has happened already and what is still yet to happen.'

Then a new thought came to him. 'Why is it only Morgana who uses the name Pendragon? No one else does. Does that mean Uther has not been given that name yet? So exactly where am I up to in this saga?'

Jack paused and looked around and thought even the trees looked different.

'Flying here with Merlin I passed through a mirror, like going through the looking glass where everything is the same but really completely different. Here, my present is in Britain's past, yet I am like a prophet because I know their futures. And that leads to another question. If I know their futures, can I alert them? Could I go up to Uther and say "Listen, mate, you don't know me but..." And if I could arm him with what is coming, would he alter his future or, like Julius Caesar in Shakespeare's play, ignore the warning and end up dead before his time? God, it is hot and it is only September. Can't Merlin turn that bloody thermostat down?"

Above Jack, thousands of black birds were gathering, birds that should have found their roost by now. Eerie voices and insects louder than he had ever heard before masked the senses he normally relied on. This land had been his family's domain for hundreds of years, yet he felt like a stranger here. He had lost his compass.

Trying to see familiar landmarks, he looked around him. If he were in his own time there would be a rise on his right, a shortcut, a quick up and over and down to the bridle path at the ford. His heart leapt—there it was! Something, at last, was in the right place. He could cut Vortigern off.

'Let's do it,' he breathed, and then yelled, "Go, go, go!" to encourage his pony up the rise.

The jackdaws—of course they had to be jackdaws, not blackbirds—weren't they Merlin's birds? Maybe something disturbed them because they rose as a shrieking chorus and settled overlooking the ford, each one arguing for the best view while they waited for... what? Their master's instructions?

It was when Vortigern saw the riderless horse racing towards him that he froze. It never crossed his mind that it had a rider, a rider he could not see. The next thing he knew he was winded and spread on the ground with a heavy weight on his chest. An invisible pair of hands wrenched him up and tied him to a tree. His face turned as dark as the night sky, full of rage.

Using his torch, Jack flashed the tops of the trees to signal his position. Any moment someone would appear and he would be ready. Finally, he felt a sense of purpose.

He heard Toby flying above the buzz of the woodland long before he saw him.

"Don't go 'round tonight," Toby sang,
"Well it's bound to take your life,
There's a bad moon on the rise."

Toby landed Mot on the path, and when Jack positioned his torch under Vortigern's chin to create a monster face, Toby yelled in delight.

"Nothing I love more than a captive audience!" Toby declared as he snapped at Vortigern's restraints and pinched the captive's cheek before singing him another chorus of Bad Moon Rising.

"Do I sense some of your wit there, Tobes? He cannot see or hear you... you know."

"I know, I know, but because a captive audience is such a good line, I had to sing to him to make it work. What a sad sack of shit he looks. I'm getting a whiff of rotting flesh. Where's your stench-on-a-stick, Jack?"

"I can hear you and I am already here, my lovelies," and the voluptuous Morgana descended from the trees like a rock star in a concert.

Jack had expected her, but not this tickle of surprise from her ravishing beauty. Green silk, loose black hair, bright red lips and those large amber eyes: her loveliness took his breath away, and although he knew she was dangerous to look at, he could not drag his gaze away.

"And what's your game this time, Morgana?" he asked her. "Because the last endearing words I heard from you were, 'I want that prick, Pendragon'."

Interrupting Jack's gaze, Vortigern cried out,

"Come here, Morgana, and cut me down at once!"

"What, so you can get yourself captured again? Shut up, you pea-brain. You can stay where you are. I am going to have some fun first."

And she scooped up a startled Jack and deposited him gently in the upper branches of a very old oak. It was called by the local folk 'the Mother Tree' and was sacred to the Druids.

"How are you, dearest Jack? You have more talent in your little finger than that mongrel has in his whole body." And she ran her fingers through his hair and kissed his eyes.

Jack answered her honestly: "I've been better, Morgana."

"I can see that. I have been watching you since you left the Villa."

"I didn't think you could see us, Morgana."

"Of course I can see you!" she insisted.

Jack asked himself, 'Is she lying? Merlin definitely told me that she could only see me in that cave below Dartmoor.'

"And I can hear you as well or we could not be having this conversation, could we? Nothing gets by you, dearest Jack, does it?" She laughed and added, "You are the clever one trying to catch me out like that!"

He knew he needed a moment to puzzle this through. 'Because,' he thought, 'it's as if our deadly game only hours earlier, when I tried to kill her with my Taser, had never happened and we are meeting again like old friends. She must want something. But what is it? I have nothing to give her.'

Morgana paused too. It was just the faintest pause to listen before she continued, and patting him over his heart she said feigning sympathy,

"Yet how your heart aches, big boy! You and I share secrets, do we not, Jack?" And speaking in a soft voice right into his ear, she whispered, "Let me tell you my secret: I am in love with Merlin. He is the only man on earth whose power matches mine. And I know your secret too; you are in love with Emily. You blush. I can see I am right. And I can use my guile so that you can get me Merlin and I can get you Emily. Are you interested? Oh, oh... I can feel that you are!"

'Did she read my thoughts that I had lost her to Merlin?' Jack asked himself. 'Or am I so transparent that whatever is going on in my head is stamped on my forehead for everyone down here to read?' He decided then and there that he would play along with her until it became clear what path she was trying to lead him down. It was a decision he later regretted. What was that old-fashioned saying his father used? 'He who sups with the devil had better use a long spoon'? If he transferred his father's wisdom to his present predicament it would surely mean 'keep your distance', and he knew Toby would fly up on that bat in a matter of minutes.

It was then that Jack heard what the keen hearing of Morgana had caught before him. From below there came the clatter of mounted troops approaching, followed by loud protests, and above him the birds wheeled and swooped again. Was that Vortigern being taken away? Had Toby left with them? Was he alone with this treacherous woman?

She swung the branch Jack was standing on to get his attention again. Jack replied cautiously,

"Just give me a minute…Morgana." And when he finally spoke it was as if he had considered her proposition very seriously. "Morgana, I can't see how we could help one another. How could I ever get Merlin for you, or how could you ever get Emily for me? You will have to enlighten me, because didn't Moloch try to use Emily as his bait to get Merlin and didn't he fail? I think any messing with Merlin could be very dangerous."

"But my approach is far more subtle than Moloch's, because the way I work, Merlin would never know he was being messed with. All he would see is my disguise—and did you not see Olwen today and how well I disguised myself as him?… Who will I be disguised as this time? Not Olwen! I will be disguised as Merlin's heart's desire: Emily! I will be Emily and you will not be able to tell the difference!"

Jack felt sick. Any chance of him being again the most important person in Emily's affection, something he had enjoyed since he first saw her, was tempting. But he knew the legends of King Arthur as well as anyone else, and therefore he knew that this woman would, sometime in her future, have the guile to seduce the King himself. He also knew, though, that any agreement with Morgana was a pact with the devil. But he was tempted and weighed up the possibilities and, sure he was safe, he continued and declared:

"It wouldn't work."

"And why not?"

"Well, this is hard for me to say, Morgana, because it is most impolite..."

"Try me."

"Perhaps I can put it this way. We all knew you were Olwen because you could not hide it."

"Hide what?"

Picking his words carefully, Jack continued, not knowing how she would react. He wanted to avoid, as he wobbled on the tree tops, an outburst of her violent rage.

"You have an unusual odour and unfortunately its aroma is very strong."

"You think I do not know it! All the perfumes of your world and mine, all my spells and all my enchantments have not been able to cleanse me of this stench. Whatever my disguise, everyone eventually recognises who I am. I have asked sages, witches and wizards for advice and they say there are only two ways I can be free of it. One way is for me to be born again. As soon as I am the daughter of Ygern and Gorlois I will have a perfume as sweet as any other baby. The other way is for me to make love. And that requires a man willingly to make love to me, and then my perfume will change."

"Into what, may I ask?"

"Into his! In this instance it would be yours, because your signature would be written all over me."

Jack laughed. "You cannot be serious, Morgana. What you are saying is: you will go to bed with Merlin, looking like Emily, and smelling like me." Then Jack repeated slowly, "You cannot be serious!"

It was time to pause here, Jack thought, feeling a chill run through him, and ask himself whether he had fallen through another rabbit-hole, and this time drunk from Alice's magic bottle. He felt anger mounting in him. 'How is everything so screwed up here? Why am I even talking to her? Why would I ever be interested in making love to Emily under the rules dictated by Morgana?'

The moment Morgana realised that Jack lacked an equal enthusiasm for her tryst, she tried to make her proposition more enticing. She moistened her lips with the tip of her tongue and manoeuvred her face into her sexiest pout.

"Jack, you would not be making love to me because I would always appear to you as if I were Emily, not as myself," she purred.

"Don't you understand that you are offering me heaven as deceit, Morgana?" Jack continued to speak very quietly, masking the anger inside him. "You say you see me, but I know you do not. I look into your yellow eyes and I see only lies. What makes you think I would ever want Emily like that?"

Was it clever to wind Morgana up, he asked himself? But it did not seem to matter to her. Whatever he was saying appeared to be of no interest to her because she did not know what deceit was, and had no interest in finding out. Nor had she any interest in why someone like Jack would cherish the truth. She could only hear one voice, and that was her own. Yet still Jack continued by asking her, "And what do you think Emily would feel about this?"

"It is not my concern. She does not come into it. She will not know now and will never know—unless, of course, you are foolish enough to tell her. I assume you can make this work."

"I am puzzled how this plan of yours delivers me what you think I want."

It was then that he became aware that he had an audience. Hundreds of jackdaws had settled in the trees around him, and perched along the limbs were quietly listening to what he said. 'What are they sitting around waiting for?' he asked himself. 'Is Merlin watching me? Listening to this? Oh God no!'

"Let me put this in plain speech to you," Morgana went on. "As soon as I have Merlin, I can severely limit his power to travel across time. On my word of honour, I will make sure they will never be together again, and that gives you a lifetime to woo her. And there is more. I have proven love potions that you can give her. Here is one. You can take it now or keep it for later because you never know when it will come in handy. And that should settle this issue." She tossed her head back and ran her fingers through her hair, pouting her lips again and adding in her deep sultry voice, "When will we begin?"

He squirmed and thought, "I feel like I am live prey!' and a slow panic rose inside him because he had a powerful urge to squeeze her throat until there was no life left in her. But as he watched her pull out an arrow from her belt and break it over her head, he knew she was quite mad, but probably not dangerous.

And Morgana flashed her finest smile at him, well satisfied that she had plucked him like a harp.

44

Morgana, the Goddess of Death

2pm, Friday September 10th, Merlin's time

"WHAT ARE YOU TWO DOING DOWN THERE?" Toby yelled, hovering on Mot above the treetops, and staring down as he descended near his white-faced friend. Immediately Morgana jumped up and flew away from Jack. Flocks of screeching birds rose quickly and wheeled around the oak tree, only to settle again. Jack knew that Toby must have heard some of his conversation with Morgana, but he did not know how much.

It was then that something from somewhere hit him and he felt his head spin and nausea rise in his throat as his fingers and toes became numb. It took him all his strength to whisper,

"Code Red, Tobes, I can't feel my feet." He did not know if Toby heard his alarm or if Morgana knew what he was talking about. If she did, she did not let on, because smiling she flew back across the branches toward him.

"Toby, can you believe this?" Morgana purred, lifting Jack's hand and stroking his palm. "This beautiful man has just declared his love. His love for me! And do you know, despite the absurdity of his declaration, I wholeheartedly return his affection. Merlin, eager though he is for my love must wait, because only Jack and I can feast tonight."

Realising this comedy was serious, Toby climbed off Mot and tethering her to a branch he kept a straight face, saying,

"Awesome, Jack, awesome! Lucky you!" He felt dizzy.

Meanwhile Jack, sitting precariously on the swaying branch, could only say weakly, "Morgana…", as if beginning to say something about her.

"Now Jack, do not protest your love for me any more. Toby, you can see he is quite overcome! So I am borrowing him for a while and I will need Mot." And half pushing, half carrying Jack, she stumbled towards the upside-down bat.

"What have you done to him, Morgana?"

"Nothing. Not a thing. He just swooned with love."

'Action Man doesn't swoon,' Toby thought, 'he swoops. Something here is very rotten.'

In Toby's view a Code Red was a desperate situation and it demanded a desperate response. But how could he rescue Jack and outwit Morgana? 'If I hit her with my aerial turning kick, will she throw me and freeze me as she did in the cave? If I fly at her on Mot, will she enchant the bat and send me flying into eternity? What is there I could try…?'

His mind returned again to stories of powerful and manipulative gnomes who, when their real name was spoken, lost their power.

'Nope,' he thought, 'this reality is not a fairy story… But yes, it has to be a fairy story because I just flew through one thousand five hundred years and I met Merlin who is training me to be a magician and I just flew above a forest on a bat and this only makes sense if it is a fairy story…' And why would Merlin, his master, who could see the future, have told him the story of Morgana if he did not think it would be useful to his student? 'That is it, then!'

Full of bravado, Toby assured himself: 'Merlin rid this world of Moloch; now is the time to rid this world of Morgana.' Then he stopped, because he suddenly remembered how Merlin handled Morgana. Suspended near the roof of the cave, Toby had watched Merlin keep to himself, remain aloof, almost impassive. He had left Toby below the roof where he was—safe; and he had left Emily on the floor where she was—safe, when he could have resuscitated both of them. Instead Merlin gave the impression he was disinterested in everything. He allowed Jack to handle Morgana. So Toby asked for help and prayed,

'Dear God, let me learn from my master and make this work for both our sakes.' He took a deep breath and, against his better instincts to joke or sing or yell, he began to engage Morgana with the same careful indifference he thought Merlin would use. Sounding pleasant and truly, truly puzzled he asked:

"Jack and I have been wondering, Morgana, why you do not use your real name." Moving as close to her as he dared he continued with a shy smile, "Why do you call yourself something you are not? Morgana may be the goddess of the sea, but she is also the goddess of death. Why would Jack want to make love with a woman called Death? It's not a good impression. Can't you call yourself something with more life in it?"

"What are you talking about?" she stormed. "Morgana is the Welsh name my mother will choose when I am born because the sea will crash around me! It will be night time and I will be able to see phantoms invisible to babes born during the day. Night is when the dead walk and tales of the other world are told. It also happens that night is death time. I am the goddess of the sea and the goddess of the night, but I am not the goddess of death!"

"You know the sea has dangerous undercurrents, Morgana; it has rips that pull men to their death. My question is: why don't you use your true name now, instead of your future name? Surely it would be more powerful!"

"Well, I could tell you my true name, Toby!"

"No, don't," he giggled at her playfully, "I would prefer it if you didn't. Please lie to me instead, because I suspect your lies will be the truth!" and he laughed as if he was telling his very best joke. Then taking another deep breath, he looked at the terrible colour on the face of Jack and decided to challenge her with a gentle voice without any hint of menace.

"Because I know what your true name is, Morgana; and it is not Morgana, and you know it is not. You also know that when I say your true name, you will lose all your power."

She continued to smile at him, although Toby saw from the slightest flicker in her eyes that his threat had registered with her. Did that mean he was right? But whether he was or not, Toby realised he had to draw her away from his bewitched friend to ensure that whatever he caused to happen would not further endanger him.

"If you come closer to me, I will whisper it to you," he teased her gently. "If you are close to me you will lose less power than if I have to scream it." But Morgana was not convinced and did not move. "Come on." Toby stretched out his hand to her, smiling broadly as if it was a children's game. "It's a whisper or a scream!" She ignored him.

"Okay," he said reluctantly, "I'm going to have to scream it." She rushed to him.

"I am here!" she smiled, a little breathless. "I like this game!"

'Not as much as I do,' Toby said under his breath.

"Why don't you come a tiny bit closer still?" She was still not close enough. "I want you to hear it when I whisper it, because if you do not, you could disappear at the sound of your own name. Now, come closer until I am simply overwhelmed by your fragrance."

Morgana's nose was almost touching his and he was gazing into her yellow eyes—eyes the colour of rotting fruit,

"DIDO! Your name is DIDO!" Toby roared with all his might. Morgana's reaction was instant. She collapsed backwards as if hit by an iron fist, and once she recovered her footing she flew at Toby's neck and clawed his windpipe.

"Shut up, you prig, shut up!" She tore at his throat. Until, losing what little control she possessed, she kicked him wildly and heaved out of her mouth a putrid mass of dead lizards and frogs all over him.

"You are DIDO!" Toby yelled, and sidestepping her he gasped for air; and using his hands to guard his throat, he kept on, "You are the Queen of Carthage, and I know what you did. You sacrificed your baby son to the fires of Moloch so he would give you the throne, and now you want Britain's throne, too. You are DIDO!"

Her skin wrinkled.

"Yes, my name is Dido!" Morgana cried. "And remember when I say this… I have already ruined your Pendragon because I am the most powerful sorceress in this realm!" Her skin puckered into folds and her lips shrivelled into a grotesque smile. "I have done a thousand venomous things and I cannot wait to do a thousand more. Do not think you have got rid of me!" Her mouth fell open and her beautiful face shrunk into a death mask. "Who told you?" she hissed with her last breath, and her body deflated like a leaking balloon.

It was then that Toby gave her an almighty kick to force her to fall through the branches, and he watched as she whizzed away into the darkness.

But he had no time to celebrate the usefulness of reading fairy tales because with one look at his friend's face, Toby could see it was flushed by a rash and frozen in an expression of alarm.

"I have to get you out of here, mate!" were his first words. But as Toby summoned Mot to load Jack on to him, a screeching jackdaw flew in his face. Startled, he windmilled his arms to regain his balance and, once securing it, he left his arms extended to steady himself while he gasped again for air. Onto his outstretched arm flew a jackdaw with a crooked foot and immediately hopped up to inspect his throat.

"Oh Crook, that's just where she grabbed me! It is so sore. Are you kissing it better? Or does Merlin want a better look?" Toby panted trying to regain his breath. "Hello to you, too!" He lifted Crook up in front of him and saw a scroll of parchment wrapped around his leg, held on there by a brass ring. He reached for Jack's torch in his belt and read the message. It was ominous.

'Do not move, Jack. Poison. Wait for me. Coming now. Merlin.'

While he shone the torch on his friend's face, Toby felt for a pulse. It was rapid and Jack appeared to be unconscious. Carefully, Toby lifted him onto his lap and turned him on his side in case he threw up, and then he wrapped his arms around him to stop him falling through the branches.

"Merlin's coming, Jack, he is on his way and he will help. Morgana's gone, poof, poof, like a fart on fire. Merlin's coming. Hey there, stay with me, Jack. You'll be okay!"

But he wasn't okay, Jack looked very bad and Toby felt he was losing him. What could he do? Yes he had done a First Aid course. It taught him that if the patient was as unresponsive as Jack was, and if poison could be involved, 'call an ambulance'! At this moment it was as useful as saying call Paw Patrol or Michael Jackson. But what if he could sing to him like his favourite singer?

"Hey Jack, me mate, how about a song? You will not believe who I have here... Here is MJ himself... the King of Pop!"

As Toby became Michael Jackson, his fear drove him into one of his best impersonations yet. Imitating MJ's slow, high pitched drawl, Toby announced,

"Hey, Jack, it's me, Michael. You do great music and I'd love to work with you because I like your chords and your beats are infectious. But heaven is not that great, buddy. Stay where you are, while you can. Do you seriously want what I've got here… an eternity of Maria von Trapp dressed in cut-up curtains singing, 'Doe, a deer, a female deer'? Heaven can wait, Jack. This is what it sounds like: 'Ray, a drop of golden sun. Mi, a name I call myself…' It's all 'kittens and mittens', 'strudels and noodles' and 'girls in white dresses with blue satin sashes'. And it's not technically advanced at all, everything's unplugged. Can't you wait until we can get them away from harps and C major? Heaven can wait!"

Returning to his regular voice, he whispered in Jack's ear,

"Everything is okay, Merlin is here."

As one the jackdaws rose to welcome Merlin, only to wheel away from the strange creature he rode. He called out, "Thank you, my friends," and as they scattered into the night, he added, "See you all soon!"

Toby was dazzled by Merlin who rode on an animal of golden light with eagle's wings and lion's haunches. He circled gradually until he could land his strange creature smoothly on the crown of the oak.

"Stay!" he commanded it.

"Nice set of wings, Merlin!" Toby laughed, full of wonder. "Can I have a go?"

"It is far steadier than Mot. It's a gryphon, a gift. It flies between realms. So maybe later you can fly it home. I feared we might have to fly Jack back home to his castle to get him to a doctor, so I brought it." He looked at the distant spot where Morgana disappeared. "Thanks for deflating Morgana. It was a triumph, Tobias—truly a triumph! And despite your instincts to scream and yell and kick you were a modest hero. Here, let me clean you up." And Merlin sent the remains of Morgana's vomit flying into the night.

"How is our Jack?"

"Not good. His breathing is very choppy and his hands are dry and they smell bad. He groans as he drifts in and out. Do you know what Morgana did to him? Has she poisoned him?"

"I have been watching, through the jackdaws. She tried to seduce him but I did not see him ingest anything."

"You're right, there was no food. So I have to ask you, could she have poisoned him in some other way?"

"Like what?"

"When I landed up here, there was something around him like a mist or a vapour that he had obviously breathed in. It smelled a bit like incense. He told me 'Code Red'. And in our language that means 'Emergency! Help!'"

"Let me see him. Keep holding him steady."

Carefully Merlin began examining Jack. When he saw the broken arrow stuffed into Jack's belt, he was sure it was a message for Jack from Morgana, but he did not know what it meant. Not wanting to alarm Toby further, he slipped it into his own robes and resolved to unravel its riddle later. He recommenced his examination by pulling back Jack's eyelids to discover whether his pupils were dilated. They were. He then held his wrist to gauge his pulse before pushing his mouth open to smell his breath and study his tongue.

"I've brought three antidotes," Merlin announced, holding up a wicker basket, "and an emetic of ground mustard to get him to throw up. And other aids like smelling salts to help revive him afterwards."

"That's fine, but you cannot give any liquids to someone who is unconscious. Do you know what the poison is?"

"Not yet, and he may not be unconscious, he may be in a deep sleep, a drugged sleep. His heart is jumpy and fast and his

pupils are very large. I have some questions first. Has he vomited? Have his bowels fluxed?"

"No, not at all."

"Have his limbs jerked?"

"Yes, they have. And you're right, as I think about it, it is as if
he has been sent to sleep. See that stupid look on his face now?
Well it changes to one of terror every so often. It's a bit like he's
delirious."

"Morgana uses three poisons that Ingraine, Angharad and I
know of: she uses wolf bane, sometimes mandrake, and rarely
belladonna. I brought antidotes for all three of them. He is
showing some symptoms of belladonna. But I think there is
something else too. I thought at first Morgana wanted to kill
him out of revenge or to interfere with his destiny, but maybe
not. She could have given him an aphrodisiac—you know, to get
him in a romantic mood, and he has reacted badly to it. Did she
touch his hands at all?"

"Yes, she was stroking his palms."

"Let me smell them." Toby lifted Jack's hands to Merlin's face,
and once he had smelt them, he held them to Toby's nose.
"Here, smell that!"

"Phew, what is it?"

"Belemuntia or Baalenutia, the herb of Baal. It is called by
witches 'the flying ointment'. It is also called henbane. Here she
has mixed it in some pig's fat with belladonna."

"So first there was that mist, then this ointment."

"Do you know that only last night I used the smoke of henbane against the Saxons when I threw that herb onto the fire? It
made them imagine things, and it distorted their thinking. It
gave them a dry mouth, a red skin and a jumpy heart."

"If he has been given this herb, this henbane, how do we get
him back?"

"I am going to make him vomit now, then I will soothe him

with some nettle tea and follow it up with some ground char-coal. Can you wash his hands? Here is a pitcher; can you get some water from the river? I only want enough to wash his face and clean his hands, while I give him the mustard tea." Merlin continued to hold Jack and stare into his face, puzzled.

"We do not have much time. But just one thing. How did you know her name?"

"How did you know her name, Merlin?"

"I read about Dido of Carthage in Virgil's poetry, in The Aeneid."

"Same, same. Not as dumb as I look. I'm off. Zoom, zoom, Rat-face!" And when his master glared at him, he exclaimed, "Oh sorry, Merlin, change is hard when you've got as much talent as I have, and modesty is even harder!"

And Merlin, still cradling Jack, waved him away, smiling. He took a moment to cut small sprigs from the Mother Oak and sprays of mistletoe to adorn the grave clothes of Doone.

"Would this not be a beautiful place to lay you to rest, old friend?" he asked the spirit of Doone, and he resolved to discuss it with Ingraine and Angharad on his return. But first, he must turn his attention to pouring his emetic down Jack's throat.

45

This Country is Glas Myrddin

4pm, Friday September 10th, Merlin's time

THE LIGHT WAS FADING when Emily stirred and reached across anxiously for Merlin. But the bed was empty. Immediately Kelso jumped up to lick her toes and Roget, on her pillow, extended his long neck to glare at him. She reached down to hug Kelso because she did not want, like gossamer, simply to float away.

"Would you look at this?" A Welsh voice, smooth as silk, made her jump and pull the sheets up under her chin. "I am told, Emilia, that beauty and brains are not natural bedfellows, but you two are the exceptions."

"Arian-an-hood…" Emily stuttered, and after sweeping her eyes around the room and finding no one there, she called out, "Where are you?"

"Up on the ceiling."

"Have you been peeking?" Emily demanded. "Have you been spying on us?" But as she patted her head she found she had been crowned with flowers and she smiled at the absent Merlin and murmured to him: 'Thanks!'

And drawing breath she turned on the spider.

"You know you should stop peeking, Arian-ana-hod, where you should not!"

"If you have trouble saying my name, Em-il-ia," Arianrhod said huffily, "try 'Lady Silver Wheel'."

"Okay, Lady Silver Wheel. I'm sorry I stuttered your name in my shock and embarrassment. Have you been watching us?"

"Listen, Sweet Pea, nothing goes on in this house that I do not see and hear," and she lowered herself on a silken strand and swung close to Emily's face. "I am more than long legs and luscious lips, you know... I spy with every eye and I have many allies... Now, Ingraine will want a full report because she asked you to..."; she paused before she sang the word: "...'engage' him!" But seeing the distress in Emily's face she added quickly, "...No, no, I am just kidding!" She gave a dramatic sigh. "Please understand, we have been trying to match Myrddin up for years. We despaired of him, and I think you just saved us from a national disgrace!" and she swung back and forth until she came in so close she was looking Emily in the eye. "How do you feel?"

"What do you mean, how do I feel?"

"Well, as I see it—well actually I didn't see it, Sweet Pea, but I just know it—you've just had a once in a lifetime experience. We all remember our first time."

"What business is this of yours, Arianrhod? Do you see this? This is Roget, he is my turtle and he eats spiders for dinner. Say hello to the yummy spider, Roget!"

The spider woman ignored her threat and went on:

"So you do not want to talk about it?" Arianrhod continued in a mocking voice: "You moved Merlin out of his grief, out of his head and into his heart. Good work! And I loved your dramatic revelation of his art piece and then... Ta-Dah... the dramatic revelation of the real you. Nice touch! Somewhat impetuous, but then you're still young, very young. However, I have never seen that done before and I think it worked!..."

"Oh, will you shut up?" Emily pulled the pillow over her face. "You're embarrassing me." She had just touched the stars and now this! In a muffled voice she protested, "This is our private business..."

"Well it's not, Sweet Pea. Your Merlin is ours. What he does is everybody's business. He is the guardian of the whole of Britannia. Emilia, this country is Glas Myrddin, the enclosure of Merlin... All the lands enclosed here by the barrier of our seas belong to him. Everything he does affects all of us. And from this day forth whatever you do, wherever you go, you can be sure there will be thousands of eyes watching you. Every animal, every tree, every bird, every rock, every stream, every breeze is Merlin's to watch over, and it in turn watches over him, and now you. No one foresaw he would fall in love with you or you with him, because it was not your destiny. And, fortunately, you have some strong points...

"But all you can think about is why he was so reluctant to sleep with you. Am I right?" And as Emily emerged from under the pillow, finally interested in what the spider was saying, Arianrhod batted her eighteen imaginary eyelashes in Emily's face.

"Well, am I right? Oh yes, Sweet Pea, I can see I am. The reasons he put forward were true, but they were, at the same time, a little bit untrue, and you saw through them. You thought he was gallantly saving you for someone else. Well, yes, that is true. But the real reason for his caution is that no one, I repeat, no one, who has ever joined across the abyss..."

"What on earth are you talking about? What is the abyss?"

"It is the unknown space between one realm and another, the realms that God deliberately kept separate and hidden from one another. We think it was created so people would know where they were in time and space and not go mad from seeing the past and the future mingled with what was happening now in their lives. The abyss is the space you cross when you come to or go from here. It is when Merlin holds you very tight."

"It is spooky. Once there were strange animals there, some cousins of dragons that Merlin shooed away."

"The abyss is guarded by gryphons; they are beings who are half eagle and half lion, a blend of two of the greatest predators on earth. They leap at anyone who tries to cross over. You and Merlin have blended the realms and no one knows all the consequences of what you have done, except for one thing. Each of you will now have a devoted gryphon that shines red-gold and lives only to do your bidding."

"You asked me how I feel. I could have answered you at first saying I felt light and bodiless as if I was just a blush and a smile. That was how I felt; now I feel terrified!"

"There's no harm in that, Sweet Pea. It will keep you chary and on your toes. Whatever you have done will have consequences, and these must be significant or at any old time all the other magicians would be seeking out lovers from the Otherworld.

"Now, you were going to call me about tonight's entertainment?"

"How do you know?"

"Am I not the weaver of all dreams? It is my business to know most things because I am present in most dreams and I create the cleverness in the rest of them. Here's what I suggest..."

And once she had described her ideas and agreed to Emily's suggestions, Arianrhod simply disappeared.

46

Emily and Ingraine

5pm, Friday September 10th, Merlin's time

"CAN I COME IN, EMILIA?" It was Ingraine knocking. Emily took off Merlin's gift from her head and lifted her arms to pull on her toga and tie it up quickly. After her encounter with Arianrhod, she felt uneasy and did not know what to expect from Ingraine.

"Yes, please come in!" she called out.

Seeing anxiety spread all over Emily's face, Ingraine smiled.

"Greetings, I am sorry to disturb you!" and she reassured her, saying, "My news is good—well mostly." And as she spoke there was a low rumble like thunder, followed by shouts and bangs and barking dogs.

"What's going on?" Emily asked, now feeling alarmed.

"It's just the Moot. Your friend, Jack, recaptured Vortigern, but it was Aurelius and Uther who brought him back here and now they are parading him before all the kings. Uther is strutting up and down as if it was all his own work, and claiming that Vortigern murdered his brother, Constans. The brothers and their uncle want to execute Vortigern now, but Bruto wants a proper Roman trial, and Myrddin, who is not back yet, will want the Arch-Druid to arbitrate. Most of the Briton kings will agree with Myrddin."

"Where is Merlin?"

"Myrddin is in the forest near the ford in the river. He went there to rescue Jack who is very ill."

Emily suddenly felt sick and reached for Kelso.

"What's happened to him?" she asked anxiously.

"It was after Jack captured Vortigern," Ingraine began, and she went on to describe the events in the Oak. "Myrddin and I watched all this through his jackdaws. I was sure Morgana had poisoned him. So Myrddin rushed over there to help with different antidotes to different poisons. Tobias, in trying to save Jack, provoked Morgana with her secret name. It caused her to shrink away. Thank God, she has gone! Soon they will be back here, and with so many kings in the villa we will need to put Jack somewhere safe," and she gestured towards the bed, "where he can sleep it off."

"Of course, I will move out right away. Do you think he will he be all right?"

"The next hour is the most important. He should really be back in your realm at his home. Your antidotes for drugs would be far better than mine after fifteen hundred years of work. I have done all I can. Yet I am still worried. No one is as skilful as Morgana in blending poisons, and neither Merlin nor I can predict what may happen when so many of her potions are working together within Jack..." She paused at a knock on the door... "I hear the slave is ready to fix this room. I wondered if you would allow me to accompany you to the bathhouse and take in some night air. I am really feeling the heat and the strain of a day when so much has happened. And you need to change. I have sent fresh clothes for you. They have been enchanted, of course, so they will match your invisibility, and no one from this realm will be able to see them."

As Ingraine led the way through an outside door, the flickering lights fell on a stone path. In the darkness where both their faces were masked, Emily dared to ask,

"And Myrddin… how is he?"

"Thank you for looking after him so tenderly in his grief. He has long promised me a special event tonight, a farewell gift, and if it were not for you, we would have had to cancel it." Ingraine lifted Emily's hand to her lips and kissed it. "At the moment, he is working to cool us down with a nor 'easterly wind." And pointing to the circle of flowers around Emily's head she asked, "Wear that chaplet tonight, will you? Those sweet peas and rosebuds are summer flowers. He had to go far away to find them. Look, he has even sent Dolossus so he can keep an eye on me. And there is something I would like to broach with you. Why do we not stay here a moment where I can lean against this wall."

The darkness created a sense of intimacy between the two women, and Emily realised that Ingraine knew exactly what had happened between her son and herself, and that she not only approved, she seemed to be thankful. Emily could only wonder what could come next.

"I know how much you care for my son. Coming as you do from another realm, you know a story about his future. Love him for the man you have discovered him to be, not who you think he is from your legends. If you ever reveal to him even part of his future you will interfere with his destiny and you will find that you will no longer be able to see him or be with him. He must struggle, like all of us, to overcome his imperfections and to grasp whatever his nature has blinded him to. You must not interfere; if you do, you pay the price. Do you understand?"

"Yes. Putting it simply, Ingraine, whatever I know about him that is yet to happen, I cannot reveal to him or anyone in this realm and the penalty could be never seeing him again." She thought for a moment and realised that what Ingraine said did offer hope of a future with Merlin, if only she played by the rules. It gave Emily the courage to ask other questions that had been troubling her.

"Arianrhod just explained to me that there were unknown consequences for two people joining from either side of the abyss. Do you have any idea what they may be?"

"Well, while you were sleeping we have been talking about it, and each of us thought it was something quite different. In Myrddin's view the reason you both were given the gifts of the ferocious gryphons means that whoever arranged that gift believed you could become more open to attack from the Darkness. But in my view it could mean that if children came from your union they may become something unnatural like changelings or giants or ogres. But Arianrhod thinks it will be something different again, she thinks you both will be blessed with gifts unimaginable, and that you could gain some of the powers of Myrddin while he gains some of yours. More than likely we are all wrong and it will be something completely different. We have a few hours to see if anything changes, do we not?"

"Yes. But all this is very scary. And there is Moloch and Morgana… and, like Merlin, I am worried about them. Ingraine, do you think Moloch will stay enchanted forever? Has he gone for good?"

"I would love to reassure you, as Myrddin did, and say in triumph, yes, but my answer is regrettably, no. There are thousands of Dark Ones. He is merely our One, and I am sure they will, sooner or later, find some way to set him free. Myrddin has given us a breathing space, a chance for our future king to be born safely."

"But why does his sister Morgana have to be reborn? Why can't she be stopped in some way from coming back? You know her mother… can't you warn her about what Morgana plans to do?"

"No. We have just talked about this with Merlin. Morgana must be born with free will to choose the Light. Ygern will give birth to both a child of the Dark and of the Light, and one is the price of the other. There is balance, do you not see?"

Emily didn't see. She didn't see at all. "Why must we have someone as manipulative and awful as Morgana so we can have someone as innocent and courageous as Arthur?" she asked passionately. "And why do we have to have balance? And, while I am at it, why is there any evil in the world? What's it here for?"

"It, too, is there for balance. If we have the Light, we also have the Dark. But let me answer your question by asking you a question. You spent time with the Prince of Lies, and what happened to you then?"

"Well, first of all I did not become evil. Honestly, I was enraged by what Moloch wanted to do to Merlin and all I wanted to do was protect him. And I realised I would do anything to save him."

"And what did Moloch allow you to see about yourself?"

"That I loved Merlin and I was stronger, older and more ferocious than I thought."

"So what is evil here for? It is here to tempt us to take an easy path and to test us with a difficult path. It is through these tests that we discover what is important and true about ourselves. Morgana will tempt and test Arthur and make him a far greater being, just like she is doing to Myrddin now."

"Do you think Morgana tested Jack?"

"Yes, I am afraid so. And the results of that are still unknown." And Emily watched as Ingraine pushed herself from the wall and continued their walk. She seemed revived and threw her head back and laughed. "Did Moloch tell you that God created him before anything else?"

Emily shook her head to signal "No."

"It is a wonder. He is always boasting and saying he was the first Divine Act. After the Dark, he will say, God said 'Let there be Light,' and I tell him that God did not create the slime and the scum and the ooze first, He created a starburst of Light from where there was nothing, and the Light is the source of love, courage, surprise and joy. Do not you and Myrddin find surprise and joy in one another?"

"Yes, I find it in him all the time," Emily agreed, remembering the awe she felt when he filled the heavens with his challenge to Moloch, or later her surprise and joy when she heard his imitation of the Dawn Chorus. But there was, too, his act of mercy for Vortigern's deranged daughter who had just killed his friend, Doone.

"That's love, and I am sure he finds it in you, especially in your intelligence and courage. And nothing surprised him more, he told me, than your knowledge of astronomy… and if you heed my words of warning you will have to be very careful discussing this subject with him. It is up to God, not you, to release knowledge about His firmament at the time God sees fit.

"And talking about surprises, my Bruto still surprises me every day; like when he insisted Myrddin go to Isca last night to blood him before he went to Gaul, and again just a few moments ago when he said he would consider allowing an Arch-Druid into his house to judge Vortigern. He calls the Arch-Druid the scumbag!" And Ingraine laughed heartily at her husband's description of Hu Powyll, before she added, "And Bruto is right, of course, for he is a shrewd judge of character."

"Ingraine, there's another completely different thing I wanted to ask you. Why, after tonight, can't Myrddin return to my time? What is stopping him?"

"I am. If I am not available to hold his anwen and keep him safe and bring him back here again, if I am not steadfastly holding his light, he could end up in any other time, past or future, and in any other place or country anywhere in the world."

"You have been wonderful with your patience, but why can't you help him in the future?"

"You see,—" Another great roar interrupted them.

Spooked by the noise, Dolossus came bounding back to Ingraine and looked as if he was about to strike up a conversation with her about her health. Emily wondered why Merlin had Mr Fox guarding his mother and not her, and she was soon to get the answer.

Pushing open the door to the bathhouse, the heat hit Emily like a blast from a furnace and stopped her first step inside while she cautiously held the door open for Ingraine. As soon as she closed the door behind them both, Ingraine crumbled to the floor. Emily had to juggle the door open again and drag Ingraine under her arms out into the cooler air.

Ingraine stirred.

"Are you okay? How are you feeling?" Emily asked.

"The heat overwhelmed me," she murmured as she sat on the path and her hands fluttered below her waist. "I'm with child, Emilia. It is coming in the early spring. I am not showing yet, but Myrddin will have a sister and I will not be able to go into a trance for the long periods like I used to."

"Congratulations! You must be very pleased! I'll get you help."

"No, Dolossus has already gone for Angharad. Could you please get me some water from that rain butt over there?"

When Emily returned, Angharad was already wiping Ingraine's face. She smiled, and taking the water Emily offered, she held it in a metal cup to Ingraine's lips. Another woman stood by wringing her hands.

"I'll be fine, Emilia. You go on. You have your bath and Gwyneth here, my maid, will help you and dress your hair. I want you to take this gift that I made up for you. It's a tincture of pennyroyal. We women use it when we think fit. It stops a little surprise coming in the spring," and Ingraine patted her belly, "like this one."

"Thank you!" Emily said.

"A few drops in water, that is all you need. After your bath you will meet Lady Silver Wheel in the courtyard. Because it is so hot tonight we have decided to have everything outside. She has already stretched the wire and nailed the wood and placed the ladders and rolled the cobwebs up into the right places. Our jugglers and acrobats, musicians and singers are all practising with the still unseen, but now definitely heard, Tobias. But first the Druids will take Doone away for burial, and Myrddin is ensuring it will be a glorious event. He is already composing the death song in his head." Ingraine squeezed Angharad's hand. "The show will also give Doone a happy farewell, will it not?"

"It will indeed. Myrddin and you have made sure of that," Angharad said, patting Mr Fox. Emily joined her. "He is one of the most beautiful animals I have ever seen."

"Myrddin is going to sing first, and later on you, I believe, my lady, you are going to dance, wrapped in something or other so everyone can see you."

"Yes. My condolences again, Angharad, on Doone's passing. The show will be awesome; I hope Doone, from wherever he is, will enjoy it too. I'll see you all later."

As Emily slipped into the hot water she submerged herself until her hair floated along the surface. All she could think of, despite everything else, was Jack, and she silently prayed for him to recover.

'Please God,' she asked, 'will you somehow, someway, make Jack all right?'

47

The Trial

5pm, Friday September 10th, Merlin's time

"B E SILENT!" A VOICE BOOMED.

When the Arch-Druid, the great Hu Powyll, swept into the Moot I followed him, soundlessly, holding up high the cleansing fire to light the candelabra along the board. Hu Powyll, in flowing white robes, wore a golden breastplate studded with jewels and his long brown hair was shaved back from his forehead into a tonsure of the half-moon, while his head bore a pewter crown engraved in runic symbols.

Studying him I was reminded of Vortigern, because everything about Powyll too was slick and groomed to perfection. He carried his oak staff straight above his head and turned it in the air more like a ship's rudder than a wand, and as he navigated every eye followed him.

My father greeted his arrival with a curt bow. Bruto claimed that Powyll would glance at his reflection in a cesspool rather than pass by the opportunity of admiring himself. But then, my father did not begin to understand the Druids and preferred his Roman justice based on the evidence of witnesses with clever lawyers to cross-examine *their claims. But all his guests, the kings, had insisted: a Druid, they said, and it must be the Arch-Druid, the best in Britannia.*

If my Christian father seemed puzzled by the British kings, he was even more puzzled when these men went down on one knee and reverently bowed their heads to the Arch-Druid. What did they really believe in, he asked me later. Could they be the same men who spent the last hour howling insults and hawking spit at Vortigern? Bruto believed there was a higher power, one higher than Rome who was a fitting judge of all kings, but he was very sceptical whether Hu Powyll was what God had in mind. I knew Powyll's reputation for cruelty and his thin lips and his sneering face seemed to reinforce all the common gossip. I smiled at my father to reassure him and to try to get him to wipe the scowl off his face.

The great Druid pointed at each king then raised his staff straight above his head, directing the kings to rise as one until he commanded them to sit down quieter than mice. Powyll bent over dramatically to observe the miserable Vortigern who, with his hands bound behind him, knelt on the floor, stripped to the waist. His wound was open, oozing blood, and his face and hair were hung with globules of spit.

"Rise!" the Arch-Druid commanded as he reached behind Vortigern to untie his restraints and assist him to stand. Flamboyantly he took off his own cloak and threw it around Vortigern's shoulders, and I smiled again, remembering his Druidic teaching: 'Be just to every man because each one is the equal of an angel.' But where, in God's name, did the angel rest in these two vain posers?

"I will ask," Hu Powyll began, "each of the kings to use 'yea' or 'nay' in answer to my proposals. I have been told that Vortigern, this king from the North, is accused of murdering his own kin and the kin of men here present. His case has been turned over to me by Marcus Cotta, the Roman legate, for decision. Do the kings here present agree that I arbitrate? Say 'yea' or 'nay'."

There were loud 'yeas'.

"Do you agree that the basis of our law is compensation or making good the damage done?" And casting a sly look at my father, he added, "And it is not revenge?"

The 'yeas' responded, but there were fewer than before.

"Do you agree that there are heinous crimes that can only be atoned by the laying down of life?"

The 'yeas' burst forth loud and strong. There was no doubt, here, of the kings' position, and Powyll already knew how they wanted this trial to end.

"Do you agree that any king has to be righteous to all his people in the manner he governs them, and that he does not use falsehood or force? That a king can only be removed from power by his own injustice, extorting high taxes from his people, or by murdering his kin?"

"Yea, yea, yea, yea!" the kings responded, impatient to get on with the trial. They had heard all this blather about governance before from their own Druids. Hearing their impatience Powyll hurried.

"I will listen to testimony from three men. First, from a man who claims to have had a relative murdered by Vortigern. Second, from a king who is impartial and not personally affected by any misdeeds of this man; and finally I will hear from the accused. All men here present must swear an oath of truthfulness. Do you so swear?"

Everyone, including Vortigern, answered, 'Yea'.

"Will the eldest son of Constantine rise?" Aurelius walked slowly to the head of the table, and after bowing to the Arch-Druid and to my father and me, he began.

"What is justice?" he asked, and I was distracted by Tobias coming into the gallery to hear him speak. He would hear a man expertly trained in Roman rhetoric. When I nodded to Tobias, the Arch-Druid looked at me sternly and followed the direction of my gaze. Because his eyes flickered ever so slightly, I knew he could see Tobias and he scowled at my mischief.

"In our old ways," Aurelius continued, "justice is to act in accordance with truth." He paused until he was sure he had each of the king's undivided attention. "But, in this case, what is the truth? Did this man poison his own mother and father? From his own mouth, I have been told, so Vortigern boasted in front of my father's paid servant. Why would any man commit such a heinous crime? I can presume it was because he wanted his father's crown and he wanted his father's land.

"Did this man poison our eldest brother, Constans, a man who was devoted to God?" He held up a small scroll that had been wrapped around a pigeon's leg.

"We are informed by this message from the North that a man claiming to be Vortigern has so boasted, and we have had this verified by one of Vortigern's own men, a man called Albanius. He was captured last night in Isca and my brother and I interrogated him only an hour ago. Albanius himself heard Vortigern brag about this poisoning and laugh callously at how easy it was to fool the monks that Constans' death was indeed natural.

"Yet that man, standing over there, denies it. He claims to know nothing of poisons. He claims not even to know our family.

"Furthermore, this man claims that… and this is the most difficult of his claims to believe… he claims not to be Vortigern, and we are informed by another message," and he held up another scroll, "that Vortigern could still be up north."

There was a flash of a white gown in the gallery and Emilia entered like a bride with my chaplet of flowers across her forehead and her long hair dressed up on her crown in the Roman way. Joy spread across her face when she saw me and she blew me a kiss. Uther turned around and looked up at the gallery to see whatever so delighted my eye that it distracted me from his brother's speech. I immediately dragged my eyes away from her back to Aurelius, catching the Arch-Druid's fixed look of disapproval as I did. No matter how hard I tried to stop, all I could do was dream of taking Emilia to Avalon and living with her there for ever and ever.

Somewhere in the distance I heard Aurelius ask, "Are we certain that this man is Vortigern? His daughter was certain. She stabbed him this morning, and she would have killed him if she were not stopped by the Pict. He lost his own life saving Vortigern's. God rest his soul."

'Merlin,' Emilia's thought interrupted, 'can you hear me? Brush your nose if you can.' As soon as I did, she continued, 'Vortigern knew who the Pict was because I heard him gasp Doone's name through his gagged mouth as soon as he saw him. They definitely knew one another.' I smiled at her to acknowledge what she told me and replied,

'Now we know that one of the consequences of our joining across the realms is this gift of being able to pass on thought messages. I am finding it very hard to concentrate…' And I stopped there because Emilia put a finger on her lips. She wanted to hear what came next.

"What drove the daughter to kill her father?" Aurelius asked, shining with a fervent zeal. "We are told he forced himself on her, and from that incest she gave birth to an imbecile son. He is dead now. God rest his soul!

"Are we certain that this man is Vortigern? My brother and I last night observed him command a force of over fifty men, mostly Saxon, intent on ambushing us and killing us. It seems he knew who we were, then. We were saved by the bravery of Ambrosius Cotta. How would an imposter have the wealth to recruit and train, to transport and arm such a large troupe of men? Why would a king delegate such responsibility to another?"

It was here that Aurelius paused for full dramatic effect, as if he were about to reveal Vortigern's ultimate secret.

"Long has it been rumoured that Vortigern, a vain and rapacious man, wore a cod-piece like an iron flute, and I ask you not why he *should wear one, but rather why would an imposter wear such an absurd and painful artefact. And this morning we observed such adornment on this man!"*

It was too much for the kings who, despite the iron rule of Powyll, broke into a titter that grew on itself as one king after another slowly pictured for himself what Aurelius had described; and gales of laughter spread as quickly as a grass fire throughout the Moot. With a straight face and complete composure Aurelius waited until there was quiet before he drew his conclusion.

"It is our view that this man is Vortigern. His daughter believes he is, and she should know. His commander, Antonius, believes he is, and he should know. This is the man who killed our kin and his own mother and father, and who now hides behind this confusion about his identity in order to escape our retribution.

"The Arch-Druid has available to him three remedies: he can compensate those who have suffered at his hand, he can banish the wrong-doer, or he can give the grace of vengeance to those who have been harmed by him.

"Oh Sage of the Forest, this king has shown himself not fit to be a king. My brother and I beg for the grace of vengeance against him."

"Thank you, Ambrosius Aurelianus," and Aurelius returned to his seat.

"Would the remaining kings agree to be represented by King Ectorious Coel of Chester?"

There were sighs of relief and smiles of assent from all as they turned to the most popular king in Britannia; a king who, Emilia informs me, still lives on in your time in a rhyme as Ole King Cole. Here he is, a young man, who although he is only twenty-one years, has already ruled for five years and in that time become the ruler all the good kings aspire to be.

"Yea, yea, yea!" they all applauded. Coel, the Hound of Chester, walked to the head of the board. He, too, bowed to my father, to me

and to the Arch-Druid, and then he crossed himself with a small crucifix and kissed it before replacing it in his robe.

"My fellow kings, who amongst you does not use a double in battle? Who does not employ a man dressed in his own mirror image to trick his enemies and draw them away from his royal presence? When choosing a double, are you not careful to ensure the man has no ambition other than to serve you? Is not this the approach prudent?"

Coel paused and waited until the kings finally owned up to this stratagem.

"But what if this double steals your name? What if he pretends to be you in order to usurp your kingship while you are attending the Moot here? This is one way we could explain present events.

A good king, like a good carpenter, is truthful about who he is. He is honest in the way he acts. He does not pretend to be someone he is not. You can trust that he is who he says he is. He does not tolerate fraud; he does not tolerate anyone who lies about who he is. That is severely punished. So in my view, to the list of Vortigern's transgressions we should add fraudulence. This man is Vortigern, I believe, who is fraudulently pretending to be someone else as a ruse to escape our retribution. But we are not fooled, are we?"

Clearly they were not because even young Lot was agreeing with him.

"There is only one more point I would like to make. This man calls himself Vortigern—a name which means the 'High King'. Who says he is the High King? Well, who? Did we cede our power to him? No. Did we use a ballot to elect him? No. Did God declare to any one of you, I want this Vortigern to rule over you and all other British kings? No. He is self-appointed and he inflates the role of his petty kingdom, a mere fly speck in the north. Not only is he untruthful about the way he acts, he is untruthful about his own name."

And once Coel had said what he wanted to say, he sat down to cheers from his fellow kings.

A servant opened the large door of the great hall and announced,
"Ingraine, princess of Davydd, sister of King Caradoc, and wife
of Marcus Cotta."

Some of the kings ambled to their feet before the Arch-Druid com-
manded, sharply drumming with his staff, that they should all rise
up immediately. My mother was an Arch-Druidess, an equal to him-
self. In her hands she clutched a pigeon speckled with sapphire and
grey. Addressing my father, she said:

"My Lord, here is the latest message," and bending towards him
she whispered: "This is for your eyes only."

And Bruto turned away from the others to read silently and went
bone white. He crossed over to the Arch-Druid to whisper to him
the contents and he, in turn, signalled to Aurelius and Uther and
their uncle to come forward to hear from him the message. Immedi-
ately they left the room while Bruto jerked his head towards me,
signalling for me to join them, and Ingraine as well. I looked to the
balcony and slid my eyes towards the door. Tobias and Emilia un-
derstood my meaning and left quickly. The Arch-Druid raised his
staff for silence.

"Your Excellences," he began, "this news is not good. Sometime
yesterday, Custennin Macsen Wledigs, the Great Constantine Max-
iminius, the author of our Groans of the British, the Dux of the
Legion of the North and brother of King Audren of Lesser Britannia
was poisoned, and he died in great distress."

There was uproar.

"Silence, where is your respect? Custennin's dying words were
to revenge his death, and that also of his eldest son, Constans. On
his death his lands were occupied by the forces of Vortigern." It was
here Hu Powyll paused and glared at the smirking Vortigern.
"Custennin said he was poisoned at the command of Vortigern."

The kings erupted again and there were cries of, "What are we
waiting for? Let's finish him off now!" Calmly the Arch-Druid con-
tinued,

"We Druids celebrate every death as the opportunity to be reborn. Could you raise your cups to honour Constantine's passage?" He paused until the cups were all filled and then said, "To Constantine. To Custennin Macsen Wledigs."

48

Passing Judgement

6pm, Friday September 10th, Merlin's time

TEN MINUTES LATER WE RETURNED. *I followed Bruto, Audren and his grim-faced nephews and we all bowed to the Arch-Druid. My father reached one arm around Aurelius and another around Uther as their uncle began speaking quietly.*

"We have all agreed to the arbitration of the Arch-Druid. I want my brother's poisoning added to the list of crimes against Vortigern, and having lost both my brother and my nephew to his darker magic, I ask your leave on behalf of my grief-stricken nephews for them to have a right of reply when the accused finishes his defence."

"Do the kings here present agree?" Hu Powyll asked the Moot, to which there were loud yells of 'Yea!'

"So I grant your request. Vortigern, mount your defence now."

This was not a cowed man who spoke. It was one who stood straight and addressed the kings, not as their equal, but as their condescending superior, as their High King.

"My name is Titus Draco," he said. "Yesterday I came by sea for the first time to Isca. I do not know the people here nor do I know this country. Nor did I kill Constantine, if he is indeed dead; we

only have a despatch carried by a bird that could have flown from that stable yonder. Remember, I was a prisoner here when he supposedly died. And I know nothing of poisons. I do not recognise their smell in food nor do I know their names in the woods nor do I know any of their powers. Nor did I kill the son of Constantine. When he died I was away from my home in Saxony recruiting soldiers to protect our people from the invasion by land and plundering by sea of the barbaric Picts. I have been trained by King Vortigern as his double. I had to study his speech and mannerisms, wear his clothes and command his troops. I am innocent!"

And with that he sat down abruptly.

A surprised Arch-Druid asked,

"Are you finished?"

"Yea."

"Stand up when I speak to you. You have not answered all the claims."

Vortigern lumbered to his feet. "I have," he replied.

"What of the claim you poisoned both your parents and boasted of it?"

"As I said, I know nothing of poisons."

"Let me put it to you this way. Did you murder your parents; or ask any person to murder your parents on your behalf?"

"My parents died naturally in their beds."

"So you deny poisoning them?"

"Yea."

"Do you deny ordering the poisoning of Constantine and his son?"

"Yea."

"Do you deny you are Vortigern?"

"Yea, my name is Titus Draco."

"I think the kings present, who often have to face the threat of the poisoning of their food, will agree that if there is a man who is so totally ignorant of poisoning, as this man claims to be, then he

is the best man to taste all their dishes... because in his ignorance he will not know which food to avoid eating? Am I right?" The kings stamped their feet and banged any wood near them in agreement. Turning to a slave the Arch-Druid ordered: "Bring tastings of the food for tonight's feast for him to test. Uther, it is now the time for your right of reply."

"Your Majesties," Uther began, bowing to his colleagues. He prowled the room, and with his towering height and commanding presence he totally dominated it. And when he spoke he laced his tongue with acid. With a knowing smile spread across his face, he raised his eyebrow and began.

"Perhaps you are wondering why this man, who answers to the name of Vortigern, who looks like Vortigern and who acts like Vortigern, came yesterday to Isca with up to seventy armed men? Would you not agree that seventy troops are a few too many to capture and kill my brother and myself, imposing and ferocious though we undoubtedly are? And you, as fighting men, would you not agree that seventy troops are too many to capture the armed guard of ten soldiers at Isca? We must conclude, therefore, that the seventy troops were merely for an impressive royal escort to the Moot. But what would you think if a guest turned up at your fort with seventy troops? Would you not ask yourself, what is this bastard up to?" His eyebrow raised, he soothed the kings with, "Yea, yea... You know you would."

"I would see it as an unprovoked attack," shouted Caradoc of Davydd, "and I would use force to turn him away!"

Uther scratched his head in mock puzzlement, "So what, do you think, was he doing? Who do you think could be the target for such a large troop of soldiers?"

"We were!" the kings responded.

"Could all of you be his targets, my Lords?"

"Yea!"

"But why? Let me answer this question for you: because he wants

your land as well as ours and he wants to be the king of all the Britons! King Coel, what did you say his name means? Did I hear you say it means 'High King'?"

The kings rose again in uproar and the Arch-Druid raised his staff to regain order. A slave entered the room with small dishes and bowls and placed them on the table before Vortigern.

"Vortigern, taste each dish," Hu Powyll ordered, "and while you savour them, Uther will continue."

But Uther, his arms crossed, his foot tapping and his eyebrow at full mast, watched and waited while Vortigern sampled most of the dishes. Then beginning in a voice so faint that all the kings had to lean forward to catch what he was saying, asked:

"How now, my High King, have you lost your appetite? Goodness me, my dear Lord Whatshisname? Did you just intend to slaughter the kings with your army? No, you did not. You had another plan in reserve. You worked with Olwen, the Bard... him of the swan-feathered cloak who is yet another imposter and a skilled poisoner." And facing the kings, bit by bit Uther raised his voice: "Olwen poisoned some of those dishes, the ones now laid before this man, but which ones? Oh dear, I am afraid I do not know. Maybe Lord Whatshisname..." and he thrust his thumb over his shoulder, "maybe this man who says he is not Vortigern... maybe he does know the answer. We will have to watch him closely to be sure that he, who knows nothing of poisons, does not inadvertently poison himself."

As Uther laughed, everyone else except Vortigern joined him. This was great fun. The smile on Uther was so contagious you wanted to reach up and tickle his tummy. He stretched down for my tankard of wine, put his foot on the bench where I was sitting and began again:

"Let me tell you this. While we were meeting this morning, Olwen gave Vortigern's daughter a knife to cut him free, but Anya had other ideas because his depravity had bred in her a treachery.

But Vortigern did not die, did he? No, Vortigern was saved from death by the intervention of Doone, Ambrosius' slave. He was a man who worked undercover to spy on the enemies of this household, and on one such mission he secretly met Vortigern. The true Vortigern. And as soon as Lord Whatshisname saw this man this morning, he murmured his name, 'Doone'. Now, there is no way this popinjay could know a mere slave's name unless he had met him before. But, did he not just say, in his own defence, 'I do not know the people of this area?' Well let me tell you, he knew at least one of them, and that was the man who saved his despicable life."

Uther paused to allow some of the kings to catch up with his argument before continuing in a voice that became more insistent and louder with each word.

"Into Vortigern's sewer of falsehoods we must add his plan to claim his absence from the North as his alibi for the murder of our father. His absence, he says. It is the same excuse he claimed for not being the poisoner of my brother. And how is that an excuse? Has he not heard that commands carry across oceans? Has he not heard that is how our Emperor in Rome governs his Empire? His orders carry across mountains, across countries and even across seas."

Uther, drawing his sword, pointed it at Vortigern shouting, "This man is a liar. This man is a fraud. This man betrayed his country. This man lusts after your land. This man is a murderer. This man planned to kill all of you using either his sword or his poison!" And Uther marched the length of the table to his seat. "It does not matter which Vortigern is which. This man," he cried out, pointing at Vortigern, "deserves to die!"

There was a roar of agreement from the kings.

"One death is too good for him!" Gorlois cried out. "He deserves the three-fold death: let him be stabbed, let him be drowned and then let him be garrotted!"

The Arch-Druid smiled at Gorlois—now there was a man of his own thinking. He stood beside Vortigern.

"I ask both sons of Constantine to approach me again." Once Aurelius and Uther had joined him, he asked them, "Can you count the number of dishes and bowls here on the table?"

"There are thirteen," Aurelius replied quietly.

"Can you identify if there are any dishes that are left untouched?"

"He has not tasted the lamb broth," Uther said loudly, "and he has not tasted the white beans dressed in coriander and cumin that are well known to be my brother's favourite dish."

"And Vortigern, if you please," Hu Powyll asked with the slightest smile, "why did you not taste those dishes?"

"…Because I am no longer hungry."

There were howls of derision from the kings and calls of, "Coward, coward!"

"Myrddin," the Arch-Druid asked, "you know, do you not, which dishes were poisoned by Olwen?"

"Yes. We fed a sample of each dish to one of thirteen piglets. Two of them died. We discovered the white beans had been poisoned with aconite, the same poison that killed the parents of Vortigern, and the lamb broth was poisoned with belladonna. Both were in doses potent enough to kill the piglets immediately."

Now with a wide smile across his mouth but not across his eyes, Uther cried out,

"Got you, you bastard!"

"Now, just in case any of you get ideas," Aurelius declared, "I announce that my favourite dish is one that I will no longer favour," and he grabbed a fist full of Vortigern's hair and, yanking his head backwards until his mouth was a gaping hole, he came as close as he ever did in his whole life to cursing when he spat into the orifice, hissing: "Your toes will be pointing up soon, you devil, if I have anything to do with it!"

Rising to his feet, the Arch-Druid thumped his staff demanding:

"If you please, my lords, will you both remain with me here while I summarise my judgement."

And because it would be impossible for Hu Powyll to follow the performances of Uther and Aurelius and hold the attention of those gathered, he resorted to enchantment. Suddenly, all lights except two were extinguished, leaving only him and Vortigern to stand proud of the darkness. There was silence as he began:

"Our law is about truthfulness. The arguments I heard today are about falsehoods; I heard about incest, poison, fraud, murder and depravity. I am satisfied Vortigern spoke shameful falsehoods to me throughout these inquiries. He has shown no remorse." And Hu Powyll slammed his staff on the tiled floor three times and the candles sputtered back to life. "I order Vortigern to drink the lamb broth and eat the white beans."

Everyone looked at Vortigern and he looked directly into the Druid's eyes; and there he saw two flares of vermillion and in his head he could hear Moloch's voice saying, 'Let me warn you, I am the Prince of Lies, and if I lie, you won't know it. When I steal, you won't miss it. When I strike, you'll regret it.'

Terrified, Vortigern looked from the Druid towards me, and when he saw the slightest smile around my lips he suspected I was the one who was throwing a voice to torment him. I was not. Vortigern drew himself up to his full height, and looking straight at the Arch-Druid snapped,

"I refuse your order!"

"You speak like a true king and one used to power, and you condemn yourself by your own mouth. I order that you, Vortigern, spend the night manacled in the cellar. Tomorrow at dawn, the sons of Constantine have the right to fight you to your death. You will be allowed to defend yourself with an athane, your ceremonial dagger. They, on the other hand, can use whatever weapons they choose to deliver you a three-fold death. Nor will you, after death, be buried

in the Christian way on sanctified ground. Your body will be stored in the granary as a feast for the rats. Your lands will be forfeited to the sons of Constantine as rightful restitution for the deaths of their brother and their father.

"So be it!" the Arch-Druid declared and swept out.

49

A Druid's Funeral

6.30pm, Friday September 10th, Merlin's time

NOW THERE WAS A BEAUTIFUL BANQUET spread across the meeting table. At either end there were swans stuffed with fragrant herbs that floated on ponds of highly polished tin. In the middle, a large silver candelabrum, imported from Rome, blazed with wax candles. Arranged under its light were roasted lamb and goose, venison and boar encircled with bowls of olives, dill and spinach. For the Roman palates among the guests there were baskets of oysters lying open on seaweed, and gleaming trays of Carthaginian dates.

Some of the kings picked cautiously at the oysters, but most had lost their appetites during the testing for poison in the trial of Vortigern or from their shock at the murder of Constantine. Despite the assurances of Ingraine that the banquet had been fully tasted and was perfectly safe, they reached instead for Kentish wine or mead or Bruto's ale and drifted outside with pewter tankards to enjoy the cooler air. The servants rolled their eyes in disbelief and licked their lips in anticipation of a feast to celebrate the crossing over of Doone.

Following Merlin's advice, Emily and Toby stood unseen at a window on the top floor looking down at the burning torches moving around the courtyard. They jumped when Crook crash-landed on the sill.

"What are you up to, old man?" Toby asked the bird, now perched on his head and pulling at his hair.

"It's Merlin who is up to something," Emily answered as she watched Crook fly skywards to a noisy flock of jackdaws. "He will have called all those jackdaws together for a purpose."

"You know, Em, I'm going to really miss Merlin. He gave me the most amazing experience of my life when he allowed me to fly Mot and to feed those bloody bats, and helped me survive that storm because I was sure I was cactus. And although he was the one who gave me the idea that Morgana was Queen Dido, he allowed me to get rid of her all by myself. He wasn't interested in any grandstanding or taking credit, not a bit, he just hailed me like a hero and thanked me for what I did! It's the first time I've ever known someone who was truly noble. Well, that is beside Jack, who was born that way. Noble I mean…"

When Emily smiled in agreement, Toby asked,

"Do you love him, Em?"

"Who? Jack?'

"No, Merlin…?"

"I love him to bits!"

'Oh shit! Poor Jack,' he murmured under his breath so that she supposedly wouldn't hear, and added, 'What a mess this will be!'

But Emily was fortunately absorbed elsewhere. She was watching Merlin emerge down the front steps, his hands reaching behind him to hold the stretcher that carried Doone as Callabus held up the other end. Merlin was dressed in the flowing regalia of a Druid and, once again, he actually looked like what she believed a wizard should look like: tall and powerful in swishing robes and absolutely in command. For a second he looked up at her, and her heart flipped.

It was Angharad who followed them, bent over with grief and clutching her tiny daughter to her; and Bruto followed her, his arm around a pale Ingraine, who was also clad in her Druidic robes.

The pall-bearers moved slowly towards the gatehouse, walking through a guard-of-honour of servants, soldiers and village folk. At the gate the Arch-Druid faced them and stood ready to give Doone his last rites. When Emily looked down on the burning torches of the guard of honour they blurred in two bright streaks of light like a landing strip. She wondered why Merlin had insisted on that detail. Perhaps it was a guide for some of his birds that are not used to flying at night.

The kings, their heavy gold jewellery glinting in the torch-light, jostled for the best places on the steps to observe the ceremony.

"Just look at this turn-out for Doone's funeral: kings, queens, servants, children and farmers, labourers and woodsmen," Emily said. "You know, Tobes, I didn't even like the chap. I thought he was rough and crude and absolutely brutal. Yet Merlin loved Doone like you would love a brother. But do you know that Merlin's father owned Doone as his slave? I cannot understand that bit at all."

"If you think about where Doone came from—from the wilds of primitive Scotland, anyone from there would have to be rough and crude and brutal to survive."

"Yeah, I suppose so. What a life! He died hours before Merlin was going to leave him anyway. I wonder if he chose it that way."

"If I had my choice of exit, why would I pick the agony of a knife poked through my eye into my brain..." and Toby stopped as the music started.

The drums beat a slow march with a mournful melody carried by long curved horns and underarm bagpipes. It sounded to Toby like music he'd heard from Morocco using a five note scale. Everyone clapped in time with the drum beat.

"If this was a movie," he said, "we'd be watching this funeral to something Celtic, like Enya. I suppose this is Roman music. Hey, I wish Jack could hear it. With his ear we'd be able to play it back for your Mum, me on guitar or flute; or I could even get out my bagpipes and he'd bang on his skins."

"Maybe you can do it anyway. You've got a good ear too, you know." Emily paused, wondering about Jack and the dismay over Toby's face when she admitted her love for Merlin. "How do you think Jack is going?" she asked.

"I checked on him when Merlin was changing and he's sleeping like a baby near that sketch of you. I told Merlin he'd drawn you a little top-heavy and he glared at me. It's the only time I've ever seen him cross, and he hastily covered the whole thing up."

Suddenly Crook was back. He distracted Emily from her embarrassment by hopping onto her shoulder and gently nuzzling her ear. She knew that Merlin—he had told her often enough, 'think of me and I know'—had just comforted her. 'Thank you, Merlin,' she thought. 'Sooner or later I'm going to have to encourage Toby to stop his crudeness.'

When Crook flew off, her eyes followed him as he spiralled skyward to join a flock gathering above the river. The jackdaws, flying as a vast grey cloud, swooped down on the procession. Everyone, except Merlin and Caballus, ducked as bird after bird paid their last respects by flying inches above their heads to Doone's body. In a few minutes they re-formed as a flock and swept away over the river to settle for the night. Only one bird remained, sitting like a sentinel on Doone's shoulder.

But the flypast was not over. A colony of rooks took to the air, followed by dozens of white-faced barn owls. 'These are not

Merlin's birds,' Emily thought, puzzled; until she saw the slight gestures of the Arch-Druid. 'This is his gift!' The owls landed around the bier and on the shoulders of Angharad and her child and everyone clapped. They too melted softly, one by one, into the night. As they disappeared Merlin and Caballus carefully lowered the stretcher and Merlin lifted a small ram's horn to his lips to blow it. Through the gatehouse, and nudging aside the Arch-Druid, came a herd of red deer, all hinds, the animals of the shaman's totem. A murmur went through the country folk.

"What are they doing here? It's September, not October," one said. "Their rutting is still a moon away."

"He's never let his girls out without him, but will he come?" another asked. It began as a whisper... 'The Emperor might come,' until slowly it became a shout: "The Emperor will come! He will obey Myrddin, he will honour Doone!"

"Who is the Emperor?" one king asked another.

"It's the old stag," Bruto replied. And when the magnificent figure of the monarch of the woods entered, there was only silence and wonder. With his red shaggy mane and sheer muscle, the Emperor dwarfed everyone, standing ten feet tall and weighing well over three hundred pounds. And when he raised up his massive rack and bellowed, he sent a shudder through the crowd. All the woodsmen pulled their families close, expecting that he was going to charge. Instead, the Emperor ambled over to Doone and lowered his eighteen-point rack of horns in a royal salute before he gracefully turned and headed back the way he came, his hinds obediently following. It was then that Merlin and Caballus lifted the stretcher and placed it at the feet of the glaring Arch-Druid. His hundred pairs of barn owls were no match for the monarch of the woods!

Toby, who prided himself on the way he announced his presence when entering a room, pronounced: "Hey, that stag made the best entrance I have ever seen!" and Emily laughed.

"But, you are a hard act to beat, Tobes!"

Having watched the interplay between Merlin and the Arch-Druid, she whispered to Toby,

"We have seen Merlin challenge the leader of the Druids with his mastery of the natural world and we have seen him win. So it is just as well he's leaving in a few hours. That big boss isn't happy."

Nor was Merlin happy. He had a growing sense of unease about the safety of Emilia and ordered his jackdaw to follow her every time she was out of his sight.

Nor was Bruto happy. During his many years of commanding the northern front of the Empire he had developed a nose for sniffing danger, and although his awe of his son had simply increased, Bruto was still his father and still the master of this household. Therefore he called over his guards and gave them whispered instructions to watch that arsehole, the Arch-Druid.

But there were other men who were happy and impressed with what they saw.

"You know, I did not think it was possible," Uther said breathlessly, "that Ambrosius could improve on the act with the bear we saw last night, but tonight he has done it!"

"Let's engage him now," Aurelius said. "With him at our side anything could be possible… We could drive the Saxons out and unite Britain. I am going to extract a promise from him now to join us the moment he returns from Gaul."

When the Arch-Druid finished his blessing, the drum and a bagpipe began softly, and he invited Merlin to sing the farewell. As the rhythmic clapping of the crowd joined in, Merlin bowed to the body of Doone. But before he sang he spoke:

"Above the Emperor's wall there is a land of dark-haired people who raid our borders and are thorns in our sides. Doone's family driven, he told me, by starvation, slipped across the border where he was captured by the Legion and given as a gift by

Constantine to my father. Doone was like the thistles that grow in his homeland: he was a nest of thorns that surrounded a glorious purple heart."

Then Merlin sang:

There is a tree at the door of heaven
More splendid than any other
A tree of lemon, a tree of green
A tree of crimson hue
A tree that glows like gold
Where the bards of the wood
Sing in perpetual song.

And there he paused for his blackbird, the bard of the wood, to sing to Doone as Merlin strewed oak leaves, green and lemon and crimson, all over his friend. He continued:

Not for Doone
Our hollow hills
Not for Doone
Our peaty bogs
Not for Doone
Our fiery furnace
Not for Doone
A cairn of stones

He will rest

Above the raging waters
Where salmon flash
Where deer snuffle and
Where sun dances on his face

And Merlin paused again while his blackbird sang, and he tossed the mistletoe, the sacred plant which lives on the oak, over Doone. He gave a twig each to Angharad and her daughter and to his own father and mother.

> *For he will lie*
> *In the Mother's Oak*
> *And birds will feast*
> *On his flesh*
> *And in some spring*
> *When the Mother*
> *Unfolds her lemon buds*
> *Doone will know*
>
> *It is time*
> *To return to us,*
> *Refreshed*
> *And ready for battle*

Above them, Emily said,

"We must go. It's time to get dressed." She noticed Merlin's jackdaw was back and following her every move and she felt uneasy about it. She felt she was being spied on.

"And what are we wearing?" Toby asked, and when Emily, distracted by her own thoughts did not reply, he repeated his question.

"Oh, um, Spider crafts... Arianrhod's making cobwebs and spider silk."

Toby was incredulous.

"Hey, that won't leave much to the imagination, will it?"

"I've asked for a modesty panel across my front, but I'm sure Lady Silver Wheel will show off whatever curves you want to offer, Tobes!"

"It was your curves I was thinking of! I don't think the locals will be used to such display," and as he spoke he carved a busty woman in the air.

"Hey, don't you ever get tired commenting on my curves?" Emily asked him firmly behind her smile, and she feared he might be right about the locals. Every woman she had seen was covered from head to toe. "I am more than curves, Tobes, I am more than boobs and a bum. Most of me, you know, lies north of my neck and my best curves are in my brain. Sometimes I feel I want to slap you, because you can be such a silly twit! Grow up, will you? Now come on, we've gotta dance!"

"Morgana, where are you?" The Arch-Druid stood in the granary, straining his eyes in the gloom. "I cannot see you. Where are you hiding?"

"There is no need for you to see me, Powyll. What is wrong?"

"Myrddin is what is wrong. He just humiliated me. Why are you allowing me to be treated this way? Why are you not helping me?"

"So asks the man who just condemned our Vortigern to death!"

"I have to do what I have to do, Morgana. If I do not, I will have no following, and without a following I am of no use to you… I need more help. Beside his mother and the nurse, he has that meddler in everyone's business, Arianrhod, and some girl and boy from the Otherworld. Where is Moloch?"

"He is not available. I will give you some Angry Ones to boost your power. Just do not get in the way of my plans."

"Which are what?"

"Revenge. I will deliver the sweetest revenge a wronged lover can ever inflict on her rival."

50

The Sugar Plum Fairy

7.00pm, Friday September 10th, Merlin's time

"H ow do I look, Merlin?" Emilia twirled in front of me. *"Do you think everyone will be able to see me now?"*

"You look like a sprite, a sprite with pink wings. You sparkle!"

It had taken Arianrhod fifteen minutes while Emilia stood absolutely still, for her to spin and weave her silk into a close-fitting, head-to-toe silver garment, and then to hold Emilia's chin for the goddess to blow crushed stars over her face.

"You look lustrous, Emilia, and Lady Silver Wheel has made you very shiny."

"Fairy stuff is supposed to be shiny and pink. It's kind of a rule we fairies have."

"I do not think any man here will be able to take his eyes off you," and I paused and added very quietly so only she could hear, "I cannot. Will it come off if I touch you?"

"No, and you can touch me if you want. I am going to dance for you tonight... in a tutu... wait until you see that!"

She spun in a circle...

"I just pirouetted."

As I reached to touch her, the space between my hand and her skin heated until Tobias burst between us, an emerald streak.

"The dress code tonight is green elf!" he declared. "I'm pumped, gotta move, gotta dance!" he cried over his shoulder, running up the stairs to reach the ladder on the villa's roof. "Let's climb up, Em." When she turned to follow, I grasped her hand and pulled her to me. She felt very warm.

"Just wait one moment, Emilia. Please be careful up there. Everything is not as it seems."

"It never is in this place. Is that why Crook is following me? It's creepy, Merlin. What's wrong? Is it that Arch-Druid? When I watched him I thought he looked very sour and jealous of your powers."

"He is, but it is more than that. Prior to the trial and thinking of the future, I asked him, without telling him why, whether he could help me travel across the abyss and return here. He smirked as if he knew why I was asking and said he could help but only if I met certain conditions. He wants my subservience and he wants me to take off the cross of Christ," and fingering the cross at my neck I said, "and I cannot do it."

"Hey, he sounds like Moloch when he wanted to enslave you. How is what Powyll's demanding any different?"

"It is not any different, and he claims he was astonished by the Emperor's visit. 'Provocative', he said, and that I made his gift of rooks and owls seem paltry by comparison and that I embarrassed him in front of all Britannia's kings. He cannot understand where my increased powers have come from. He does not know they come from you," and I pulled her close again. "Do you know, it is the first time ever that my blackbird agreed to sing with me? But as soon as Powyll sees the gryphons and you riding one, he will work it out immediately and he could come after you. That is why I am worried and that is why Crook is following you."

"Merlin, let's cut out the aerial race between Mot and our gryphons, we don't really need it," she said breezily, trying to lighten my anxiety, "and there's no point in aggravating the Arch-Druid any further, is there?" When I still looked worried she prodded me. "But there's something more, isn't there, something you're not telling me. Come on—please trust me and tell."

"At the end of the trial and just before Powyll's verdict, I heard Moloch's voice and I could swear it came from Powyll. Vortigern heard it too, because he looked truly terrified. I smiled at Powyll to let him know I heard it, too, but I felt chilled."

"But what does that mean?"

"I do not know yet. I know it cannot have been Moloch speaking because he is safe and secure, and my Guardians promised to warn me if it ever became otherwise. It cannot have been Morgana because she too is out of the way. So I do not know what is going on."

"Maybe it was the Arch-Druid himself. Maybe he is working for Moloch. He gives me the creeps, you know. I'll bet he is working with darker magic, like Vortigern," Emilia said.

"Maybe you are right. I have called my sprites and all the help I can muster. I have an uneasy premonition about tonight, a sense of foreboding, and I am not letting you out of my sight. If anything does happen I want you to know..."

"Come on, Sweet Pea, we are all waiting. Come on. The crowd is restless."

"Bloody Arianrhod," Emily whispered to me.

Yet we both stood there enjoying the warmth between us and studying each other's faces. I was struck again by her grace and beauty and intelligence. And when Emilia broke away from me, her face lit with one of her loveliest of smiles and she blew me a kiss and mouthed, "I love you," and because she was saying it to me for the first time, she blushed pinker than any fairy should, then ran off after Tobias.

The drums always come first: sharp, deep raps; and next the cymbals crash; and the crowd hushes but my head spins—she loves me! A makeshift searchlight jerks around the rooftops until it finds Tobias, standing on a trapeze of cobweb and spider's silk. With another deep breath, Emilia leans back on her silken rope to test its strength and build its momentum, and as soon as the light finds her, she laughs and waves and jumps. The crowd gasps. Never have they seen a woman dressed in a tight cocoon with fairy wings, and never have they seen a woman perform before in public. There is a hubbub of shocked talk until Bruto demands quiet.

She flies above the courtyard to a grinning Tobias, who catches her and pulls her onto his trapeze. Slowly, as more lights sputter on, a vast crystalline web is illuminated, spread across the night sky. It is strung with bejewelled spiders that crawl and swing and jump far above everyone's heads. Tobias counts, and on the count of three his trapeze swings into the centre, fifteen feet above the crowd, and together they jump from it onto a trampoline of rope and spider's silk, flexible enough to hold them both when they bounce.

The crowd claps as they both bow, but I clap the loudest because I am the most surprised; surprised not so much at her graceful physicality and strength but at her perfect sense of balance, the kind of balance that is the gift of the world's best swordsmen. 'Perhaps Emilia could wield a sword and fight the Saxons,' I admit to myself.

And when Emilia gives me her over-the-shoulder head toss, my heart jumps. She just mouthed to me: 'I Love you'—or have I told you that already?

It is time for her to play with Tobias, and with her most dazzling smile she seeks out the Arch-Druid and flashes her teeth just for him, as if she wants him to know she could bite. I think she does love me because her eyes change when she sees me and her lips part, but not enough to show her teeth. Tobias raises his arms and struts about like a gladiator until she sneaks behind him and kicks him hard in the backside. In mock alarm, he lurches forward into a somersault; she cackles and does a back-flip away from him. He spins and points his finger accusingly at the source of all his trouble while she shrugs and gestures, 'Who, me?'

The audience loves their clowning and tumbling, and answers with whistles and claps. And so begins their long chase of leapfrogs and somersaults and back-flips where sometimes she wins and sometimes she does not. And finally he catches her, but as soon as Emilia tries to escape from a triumphant Tobias, he trips her, and grabbing her ankles, he falls forward until she can grab his ankles too, and around they go in a human wheel until they spring apart and bow as one.

As the applause grows the light leaves them and catches a thick rope descending. It is for Tobias, who once he has recovered his breath, climbs up the rope to a platform where he sits down, cross-legged, and picks up a makeshift flute.

Out of nowhere, a crimson spider as big as a tomcat springs on to Emilia's head. She collapses like a rag doll in mock horror. Everyone screams in delighted terror, until Arianrhod pulls out from her back legs a starched skirt made of thistledown and spider silk and ties it around Emily's waist. That must be the tutu.

"Thank you, Arianrhod," Emily mouths.

"You make a beautiful fairy. And you are not alone, Sweet Pea, remember that!"

"How could I ever forget it?" Emilia stands on her toes in her pink tutu and I gasp as she hovers almost on tiptoe. How can she do that? Her long arms and legs, graceful and sinuous, create the illusion she is as light as the breeze around her. The cobwebs pulse with tiny coloured lights, like fireflies, and when they catch the crystals in her tutu, it appears that she is on fire. It is her turn to count and signal Toby.

One, two, three; and once the strains of Tobias's roughly carved flute begin they are underscored with the sounds of the curled horns, and Emilia pirouettes into the spinning dance of the Sugar Plum Fairy, and to my amazement she does not stagger with giddiness. As she dances, I throw starbursts of flowers and butterflies along the web and sketch with my finger in golden light, so that moths and dragonflies flutter around her. It lasts only three or four minutes, but when she curtsies she crosses her hands over her heart and almost blows me a kiss, hinting at what may come. And I ask myself, 'How can I live without her?'

Then the sky went dark and the scene shifted to the ground.

Our local singers, dancers and acrobats all rushed into the cleared space below the outer wall to entertain everyone with haunting pipes and dancing reels and verses of love and loss.

Ingraine had been watching my father carefully. He was full of sadness, close to crying. He did not share our consoling belief that death was a gateway to new life, and in a matter of hours he had lost not only Doone, a man he trusted with his only son, but his closest friend, Constantine; and yet he had been able to laugh and roar at the antics of Tobias and Emilia.

"What do you think of her?" Ingraine pointed discretely to Emilia thinking I would not see. "She is the one I have been telling you about."

"She is very lovely. She is rhywial—sexy. I have never seen anyone dance like that; it seemed she might blow away. But I am shocked because I never thought Ambrosius would become involved with a circus performer. I hoped he would fall for someone like you, like I did." He squeezed her hand. "Let's hope this is just a stage he is going through. She is not following him to Gaul, is she?"

"I think not. I have met her and she is not like that. She knows writing and reading and speaks Latin and Welsh and some Greek, and she has read Tacitus, Suetonius and Virgil." Ingraine was building the case for Emilia by picking out my father's favourite writers. "But her most favoured is Caesar's Gallic Wars," she added innocently, as if she did not know that Caesar's plain and simple prose made it Bruto's favourite too. She concluded by saying, "So maybe Emilia is more like Ambrosius' father than Ambrosius' mother." When my father smiled and looked again at Emilia, she continued, "She is learned in philosophy, and when I last spoke with her, we discussed the nature of evil."

"She is the mural in his chamber, is she not?" and glancing sideways at his wife with mischief in his smile, he added, "Nice pair of teats. Has he bedded her yet?"

"Myrddin is more interested in calculating the stresses and strains on a span of a bridge than bedding girls."

"Oh, come on, Princess! That is not what that mural reveals when a man admires it because there are some really significant stresses and strains there. This morning Ambrosius took his bath like a soldier, a warrior even, but tonight, look at him, he is all dewy-eyed and panting like a puppy!" I stood in the shadows smiling. I wanted to tell them that she had just told me she loves me!

"Sh, sh, here she comes. Do you want to meet her?"

Bruto moved his eyes up and down in a leer and whispered, "Why not! Does she come with high rank and great fortune like you did, my love?"

"Emilia, this is my husband, Marcus Octavius Cotta." He leapt to his feet and bowed.

Remembering how impressed her father was with my language abilities, Emily greeted him in Latin, "Ave, Dux!" and flashed her brightest smile. In his rapid response in formal Latin he said,

"I am very pleased to meet you, Emilia. The princess, my wife, tells me you are very accomplished and much more than a clown and a dancer. How did you ever meet my son?"

"I usually live in Isca," she replied in Latin. "I've been staying close by for the summer and I met him over there," and she pointed over the river in the direction of where their twenty-first century house would stand. 'This is getting very tricky,' she said in my mind. Nevertheless she persevered.

"Ambrosius told me you fought in Iberia and Germania. Are those barbarians from the north as ferocious as Caesar described?"

"Every bit of it," and he lifted his toga to show her the white scars on his legs. "You can see I have the battle wounds to prove it." He paused and said admiringly, "Bona lingua Latina," and then, to her surprise, big fat tears sprang from his eyes which he brushed away quickly with the back of his hands.

"I am sorry," he continued in Latin, "I owe you an explanation. I have not spoken in my native tongue to any woman since farewelling my own mother over thirty years ago. You speak it very well!"

Ingraine rose, and speaking to the assembled kings, she took my father's arm and with that resumed control.

"If you will excuse us, we will take this opportunity to assure ourselves everything is ready for you when you retire. Please enjoy the performance and we will return shortly."

As soon as they were a safe distance, Ingraine asked him in Welsh,

"Are you all right, my love?"

"Yes. Emilia is very like my mother, Octavia, and I realised how much I missed her, and that, like my two friends who died today, I will never see her again either. I am embarrassed by my crass comments about Emilia earlier. Undoubtedly she is from a noble Patrician family. It is a wonder we do not know them already. Is there something, dearest wife, you are not telling me about this girl?"

"All in good time, my love," and suddenly she looked down in alarm at a very frightened maid-servant who fell to her knees at their feet, pulling at her robes.

"Mistress, I hear noises in Master Myrddin's chamber, and when I looked in the bed linen flew through the air. There is a ghost in there, my lady!"

"It is that bloody Arch-Druid," Bruto growled. "I am going to kick him out of here!"

"It is going to be fine, Bruto. Elaine, go to the dancer, Tobias—he is over there surrounded by his admirers—and tell him to run immediately to Master Myrddin's chamber.

"Emilia!" She called Emily to her and held out both her hands for hers. "That was a beautiful dance," she whispered, "but I think your friend is awake. Take care, he may be quite disturbed. Take Tobias with you."

As Emily took off, Ingraine pulled her back and said urgently in her ear, "Wait for him, Emilia. It is not wise for you to go alone."

Yet Emily could not wait. She undid her tutu and shed it as she ran so she could move even faster and weave through the crowd to avoid all those who wanted to praise her. Of course, I did not take my eyes off my fairy, but I thought I should give her a few moments alone.

I whistled my jackdaw to my shoulder.

"Crook, do not let her out of your sight!"

51

Dishonour

7.45pm, Friday September 10th, Merlin's time

AS SOON AS EMILY OPENED THE DOOR to Merlin's chamber Kelso jumped all over her, slobbering and licking her face. She pushed him gently away, not wanting to hurt her dog who, despite his exuberance, was still wincing from his injuries. She also did not want him to tear her fragile costume or ruin her makeup because very soon she had to sing and look perfect.

"Jack, how are you?"

He was sitting on the bed rocking back and forth dressed in a khaki tee shirt and underpants; the remnants of his other combat clothes were scattered around the floor. The heat was oppressive. He was glaring at the mural of Emily beside Merlin's bed and muttering to himself. That was supposed to be covered up! She felt uneasy. There was something wrong. 'Should I call for help?' she asked herself. 'No, this is Jack, for God's sake!'

"How come...?" Jack began in a slurred voice, pointing to the mural. "You wouldn't pose like that for me, Em! But here you are posing for Merlin, whom you'd only known two minutes!"

This was not the welcome Emily had expected and she answered him sharply.

"I didn't pose for Merlin, Jack. That drawing came from his imagination and his imagination alone, and I am very unhappy about it. I asked him to cover it up." She went over and covered the mural again. Taking a deep breath, she put a smile on her face before she turned around. "There you go, it's gone!" He was sitting on the bed tilting his head from side to side as if he had water in his ears.

"Are you feeling okay?" she asked again and very tentatively patted his face to calm him. She sat down on the edge of the bed keeping her distance from him. "You know, you sound like you're drunk," she said softly, still smiling. "We've been so worried about you because you've been right out of it. Morgana poisoned you, you know!"

At the mention of Morgana, Jack suddenly looked at her irritably and his eyes blazed and his face turned red. Perspiration formed in beads along his upper lip.

"What's wrong, Jack? Look, I'm going to leave you now and I'll come back later when you're feeling better. You really need to lie down because I think you have a fever." And when Emily reached to feel his forehead he caught hold of her wrist tightly and twisted her down on the bed, and as he pinned the other hand down, he hissed at her,

"Morgana!"

Filled with a cold fear she could hear inside her head Ingraine's warning not to come here alone..

"Oh my God; I don't like this at all! What the hell are you doing?" she cried as he exhaled loudly. "Jack, you're scaring me. Let me go! Morgana's gone!" She flexed her arms to break his grip, but he was stronger than her.

"Morgana," he hissed again.

Recoiling in surprise, she pulled back from him.

"I am not Morgana, I'm Emily! What are you thinking, Jack? Stop it, you're hurting me! Let go of me!"

But he did not let her go, he fell on her and tore at her spider's silk top.

Crook screeched. Kelso leapt with foaming jaws.

From miles deep inside her came a long, pitiful wail.

"Get off her!" It was Toby who rushed through the open door into the chamber. He grabbed Jack's tee shirt by the neck and pulled him off Emily and flung Kelso onto the floor.

"Man, this is terrible!" All he could see was her blood and all he could hear were the shrill cries of birds because Merlin, looking tall and terrible with a shrieking bird on each shoulder, stood behind him consumed in the fire of his jealousy.

'It's happening again,' Merlin thought, furious at himself. 'My Emilia. Why is this man mauling her?'

Toby shoved Jack over onto the floor.

"What have you been doing? That is your lovely Emily, not some scraggy whore! I'm ashamed of you! Get up and get your pants on, right now. What can you have been thinking?"

Toby turned, and taking the distraught Emily into his arms he tried to reassure her.

"It must be Morgana, Em." But Emily shrugged herself free, she did not want to be touched. Instead she lay face down across the bed dazed.

"It's Morgana's magic, Em, can't you see? It's sent him mad because his brain is full of her chemicals. Are you okay? Here, let me cover you up." And he lifted a rag rug off the floor and draped it over her. And trying to say the right thing by his friend mumbled, "You know this can't be our Jack because he loves you too much!"

"Toby! Look at me!" She turned over to show him her blood-smeared chest. "Tell me is this how you show your love? Isn't it how you show your hate?" And she added bitterly, "He's scum!"

Her words enraged Jack who sprung off the floor and rushed at Emily again; Toby yanked him back by the hair and restrained him.

"You've got to cool it, man. You've gone crazy!"

When Merlin, the silent witness, finished calculating the square root of 46, he finally found his tongue and announced, "I'd better take Jack home."

There Emily lay, plucking at the shreds of her costume and trying to cover herself, and when that proved pointless, she drew the rag rug around her again and sobbed. It was her tears that sprang Merlin into action. He commanded Kelso to heel as he lifted Emily up in his arms and carried her to his mother's bed.

"Lie still, Jack." Toby put his hand on Jack's shoulder to steady him. He was stretched face down on Merlin's bed. "Angharad's got to stitch you up, man. Kelso took a chunk out of you." Toby was breathing in a measured way, as his Dojo had taught him, watching Jack writhe in agony. "Have you got anything to help him with his pain, Angharad?"

She nodded. "Here, chew on this willow bark. I cannot give him anything stronger because there are too many peculiar potions inside him already."

Taking the dried brown strip gratefully, Jack started to gnaw at it.

"Can you tell me what happened, Tobes?" Pointing behind himself to where Angharad was sewing his skin, Jack asked in slurred speech, "How did I get this?"

His friend bit his lip and said quietly, "Hey, this could be the most unpleasant conversation we've ever had, and I don't think you're ready for it, man."

"Hey, come on, what happened? The last thing I remember

was passing out in the branches of a bloody big tree and telling you 'Code Red' because I thought Morgana had poisoned me."

"Okay then." Toby sighed and thought, 'Shit, oh shit a brick!' and he started at the beginning. It took him a while to tell Jack the story of what happened after he cried Code Red. He spoke plainly without any of his usual jokes. Jack would tell him later that he sounded as dry as a police report, and when it got to the part where Toby didn't want to talk about it, he announced, "That's as far as I'm prepared to go, because I wasn't here when whatever happened, happened." And he looked blankly at Angharad.

"Well, hedgehog hair, are you going to tell him?" Angharad asked, and paused dramatically before asking threateningly, "Or am I?"

"Be my guest," Toby said bitterly. "But on second thoughts, I do owe it to him... Jack, look up at me, look me in the eyes because this will be difficult.

"A little while ago, maybe fifteen minutes ago, you woke up and moved the sheets. The servant who was tending Merlin's animals who, of course, couldn't see you, thought you were a ghost in the bed. She became alarmed and rushed out to tell Ingraine. When Emily heard about it she hurried in here to welcome you back to the land of the living, and about four maybe five minutes later I followed her."

"Why is a simple story, Tobes, of dog-bites-man taking so long? I'm getting very nervous. You'd better spill it out."

"Well, Em sat beside you on the bed and you attacked her..."

Jack's stomach lurched. "Bollocks! I don't believe it, and you more than anyone else in the world know how much I care for her!"

"I do. But... anyway, you attacked her and tore off her top and gouged her chest from here to here..." Toby demonstrated on himself. "Her blood is everywhere."

Sickened with what he was learning, Jack could only whisper, "You know I'd never do that. Bollocks!"

"You tried to do more... You fell on her. You tried to..." But Toby couldn't say it.

"No, I wouldn't do that!"

"Well, you sure as hell did, your bloody lordship, because I saw it all!" Arianrhod had rappelled down from the ceiling in the terrifying form of a giant Amazonian spider, and pulled up close to his nose. Alarmed, Jack jumped, and thinking he was hallucinating yelled out,

"I'm seeing an enormous spider!"

And then the spider spoke very quietly: "While Emilia cried out in anguish, pleading with you to stop, you kept at her until I bit her dog and he bit you. There you have it. She is a brave girl, not inclined to hysterics, but she is in great distress. If I had bitten your backside, I would have... Well, I will leave that to your imagination." She paused, and after a very large sigh she announced, "Now, my lord, think about what you have done and how you are going to make restitution to my Sweet Pea. Tobias, you and I must leave now because I have to stitch up your costume for the next song."

"I must see Emily," Jack croaked, trying to get up.

"She's very distressed and hurt," Toby said in a soothing voice. "She's with Merlin, Jack. Come on now and lie down. I'd leave her be and let them try to deal with it."

"I wish Morgana had finished me when she had the chance! How am I going to live with myself?"

"As a man, Your Lordship, not a mewling boy!" Arianrhod snapped. "It is my experience from closely observing the kings and queens over thousands of years, that from great dishonour great honour can come. I will send a slave here to wash you. Come Tobias."

52

Where Were You, Merlin?

8pm, Friday September 10th, Merlin's time

"WHAT DID HE DO TO YOU, MY LADY?" *I asked as I laid her tenderly on Ingraine's bed and tucked the linen in around her before sitting down beside her. "You are wounded, are you not?"*

"It was awful, Merlin!" and her eyes looked scared and hurt as Kelso comforted her, licking her hand. "Let me show you," and she lowered the sheets to reveal the wounds of his attack. While the only light came from a candle on a pedestal beside the bed, I could count at least thirty red weals from Jack's nails that ran from her throat to her blood-smeared breasts. I was shocked! She had warned me that her friends might react to my mural of her, but this?

I leant over to kiss her better, but she pushed me away.

"Don't touch me. I just feel ashamed and dirty." As she covered herself again she turned her head away from me and started babbling, distraught. "Jack kept saying, 'Morgana, Morgana!' like he was possessed," and then she put her hands to her face and cried again. "Jack's not like this, Merlin. He was so full of rage, and he turned it on me as if I was Morgana." Emilia drew in her breath,

and turning towards me on her elbow, she raised her voice: "What have I done? You tell me. I didn't pose for that bloody picture! I didn't pump him full of drugs! Your mother warned me not to be alone with him but I ignored her!"

"Ingraine is a physician and would have suspected the aphrodisiac had not worn off. That mural has been nothing but trouble…" I knew I should not have interrupted her because Emilia only heard one single word I said and cut me off blaring loudly:

"That was not an aphrodisiac! That was an assault weapon! It filled him full of hatred and anger. And you told me that Morgana was so predictable." She drew a sob, and pulling down the linen again to display herself, she flung at me. "Tell me, did you predict this?"

I was squirming as if I had just banged my elbow. "No, I did not. I am so sorry!" And rather than leaving it at that, I headed off in the wrong direction again saying: "But Morgana manipulated him. She poisoned him. She is pure evil."

"Your defence is like saying the devil made him do it. I will not accept that. Jack is still responsible for what he did, and he attacked me. Next you'll be telling me she enchanted him."

And can you believe what I said next?

"I am sure Jack stood up to her, and yes, I think she enchanted him in a way to make him do what she desired."

"Whose side are you on, Merlin?" she asked me bitterly. "Has Morgana manipulated you too? You keep defending Jack when I'm the one who was attacked. And I have been attacked by my best friend! Who is standing up for me? Why bother taking him home—he can stay right here for all I care. Take me home instead!" And when I shook my head thinking how I must take her to Avalon, she became more distressed and continued, "Or better still, show me how to drive that bloody gryphon and I'll take Kelso." Then she backhanded me with: "The best protector I've got." And pulling Kelso to her she hugged him and rubbed her nose against his. "I hope *you took a good chunk out of his backside, you wonderful dog! You and I, Kelso, will go home together."*

While we scrapped, Ingraine silently entered the room.

"Neither of you are going anywhere," she said firmly. She came over, and sitting on the bed with us, she took Emilia's hand in hers. "I am so sorry you have been humiliated and ravaged in my home, Emilia, but you are now in shock and hitting out at whoever offers help. But you are not fit to go anywhere, let alone to try to cross the abyss by yourself."

"I will take Jack back then," I offered, but as soon as I'd said it I heard it through the ears of Emilia and realised I sounded as if I wanted to escape this emotional turmoil, leaving it to someone else to sort out.

"Not before I give him an antidote for Morgana's handiwork, and Arianrhod gets the slaves to pour him into the bath. I have brought you this, Emilia, to help settle your nerves, and I am going to stand here while you take it."

She handed Emilia a small vial of what must have been bitter herbs, because as soon as she had swallowed them she gave her a spoon of honey.

"Good! Gwyneth is here. Every tear in your skin must be cleansed because under his nails he might have some baleneutia. It will not take long. Will it please you to excuse us both for a moment? Myrddin and I need to reorganise the remaining events of the night."

Outside the door, Ingraine paced up and down, quietly furious. Pointing to the door of my chamber she asked,

"What do you think happened in there? In there, Myrddin, on your bed, the very bed whose linen I had just washed?"

"Well, putting it as bluntly as I can, Jack tried to ravish Emilia."

"And where were you? What did I ask you to do? What did you promise to do? Did you not promise to protect her, Myrddin? You were given three days to protect her and you were supposed to be her watchman."

"Well, I was watching her, but I let her dash away to be with Jack alone. I thought she would be safe with him."

"And after you finally…" and she poked her finger in my chest and paused before she said, "arrived… her dog and Tobias had taken action while you stood there and contemplated the meaning of the universe."

"I could not move."

"And why not?"

"I was full of rage at him, at her, at Morgana and at myself."

"Know thyself! We are here on this earth to be disappointed with ourselves! Are you sure that was rage you felt? Name it properly! What was it?"

I said nothing because I was full of self-loathing and shame.

"That emotion is called jealousy, Myrddin! Get back in control; you nearly lost her last time through it. Years back, when we discussed all the difficulties you and I might encounter if you chose your mother to be your master, I never envisioned a conflict such as this! As your master I say this to you: the young woman I commanded you to protect and with whom you fell in love was attacked and almost raped in your very own bed, and on discovering this you stood there and did nothing! You should be shrivelled with shame!"

In that moment I was drenched in sweat and flushed with disgrace. As my face buckled, Ingraine's anger collapsed too.

"Please, help me mother, as my mother and not my master. I am genuinely shocked!" And grabbing her hand I almost pleaded, "What is it that fans this fire in my mind and in my heart so much that it consumes me when I see her with Jack?"

"You will have to share her. You know, Myrddin, you will always have to share her. You can never demand fidelity from her because she lives in a different realm from you and the realities of both your lives will always force you apart. Yours will be a lonely life."

"I do not think I will be able to bear it..." I was facing the walls of the corridor, shaking my head. "I think this will send me mad! I will spend my life alone, imagining what she is doing with him and what she is doing without me."

"It will be very hard living without the one you love. But when you were given your gifts at birth you were also given your imperfections, your defects. Your gifts, Myrddin, are immense; and such gifts carry their cost and your burdens will be heavy. You have met one defect; it is your jealousy. Conquer it or it will burn your love to ash. Now, let us return to the problem of the moment... Can you not see what Morgana has done?"

"She made Jack so angry, he attacked Emilia."

"How did she make Jack angry?" Ingraine asked. "You watched, as I did, through your bird's eyes and heard them in the Oak. What happened?"

"Because she wanted Jack to make love to her, Morgana promised to come to him disguised as Emilia. So Jack, in anger, and under the influence of God knows what, believed he was really attacking Morgana, who was only pretending to be Emilia."

"What was Morgana trying to do?"

"To pay Jack back for tricking her into becoming a hare and then trying to kill her in the cavern. And, of course, she is generally trying to cause chaos—which she has done," I said dismissively.

"Your analysis is bleeding obvious. You have overlooked that Morgana has manipulated you, too, by shining a light on your jealousy. But if you look at it from Morgana's point of view, she sees no difference between Jack and Uther because she is outside time, and outside time there is not any difference. Does she want revenge on Uther? Yes. So does she care whether it is Uther or Jack? No. And does she want to stop Arthur being re-born? Yes. Does she want to side-swipe you for good measure? Yes. So how has she done it?"

"*She has caused a deep rift between Jack and Emilia which makes their successful union now highly unlikely.*"

"*Yes, true. But what if Emilia could, in the fullness of time, forgive him and thereby defeat the intent of Morgana?*"

"*Morgana would have thought of that too. She could have worked out a way to prevent him permanently from fathering Arthur—*" *And I stopped because I had a sudden thought: the broken arrow I found with Jack—it was a love shaft that could no longer reach its target!* "*Morgana could poison Jack so that he was barren and not able to have any progeny...*"

"*And we must assume that is exactly what she has tried to do. And Jack was jealous, too, because after one look at that mural of yours, he knew you would be the lover of Emilia. The rage of Jack at his powerlessness, whichever way he turned, drove his attack. Should we pity this poor man? Yes, with all our hearts; but stop trying to defend him. Shut up and defend her. Do not hand triumph to Morgana. Emilia is the innocent one here.*"

"*But can you help him? He is an innocent victim too!*"

"*Have you not heard me, Myrddin? What are you trying to do?*"

"*I am trying to play peacemaker.*"

"*Leave that to others. Emilia is your purpose. Not Jack. He is mine, and I will discuss his problem with Angharad and we will see what we can do. And I will give you a concoction for him before you leave. Emilia has done nothing but help you; now it is your turn to help her, and I will give both of you time alone together. I will invite the guests inside for some wine and meat and it will do the kings good to share their feast with the commoners. Later there was to be your song with Tobias and Emilia before you did the finale alone. I do not think Emilia will want to sing, and besides that, we will not have time to dress her again to make her visible. I will delay everything as long as I can.*

"*And remember, Myrddin, this is about her, this is about Emilia, and it is not about you; nor is it about Jack or Morgana either.*"

And she kissed him on both cheeks. "You caught a falling star, Myrddin. For the sake of God, look after her and let her shine.

"And promise me you will clear and cleanse and protect our chambers before you re-enter them. Whether Morgana has been in them or not, she has managed to defile them."

But what I did next meant I forgot my promise.

Completely.

53

Bring Me My Chariot of Fire

8.15pm, Friday September 10th, Merlin's time

HER EYES WERE CLOSED *in a face that glinted with tears. Lying there covered up to her chin, with her chaplet drooping around her forehead and hugging Kelso under her arm, I wondered whether she was asleep or just resting. And I did not know what to do. I wanted her hurt to go away. I knew that at every opportunity in the last twenty hours when I should have thrown a protective cloak around her, I had failed. Anxiety from all my failures now burned inside of me. From now on I would watch her as my falcon watches me; but I could sense someone was eying me very closely.*

"Goddess of the Moon, my dearest lady, would you offer me your counsel on how I could shield her?"

Her response was cutting.

"I disagree with Ingraine. My Sweet Pea does not need your protection, Myrddin, and your jealousy makes you a pretty hopeless protector anyway. She is resourceful and courageous and she can look after herself... with my help, of course. If she had only called me earlier..." and she paused to sigh deeply in exasperation. "Well

you know how we, from my realm, cannot help unless we are asked. Anyway what is done is done. Just remember this: any other woman would be so awestruck by you, she would swoon at your powers and your beauty and dissolve into a puddle of tears. What Emilia needs from you most, at this very moment, is your tender heart and your gentleness. She thinks that because she played some girlish game wherein she pretended to flirt with Jack, and because later in a ruse she kissed him, she provoked his attack in some way. That she brought this on herself. This is utter nonsense!

"But because you asked for my general counsel, I will offer you this: You are now both rulers of the realms of Britannia. So what does my Sweet Pea need most of all? She needs your love and reassurance, Myrddin. And I certainly hope you know what that means, do you not?"

And she paused there to give me time to make sure I had understood what I was supposed to do and supposed not to do without her saying it openly.

"And, and, and," she continued, "Emilia, given these circumstances, needs something to wear. Something fit for a queen! Just leave that to the greatest weaver in the world. But from the view where I sit in Caer Siddi I ask you, what does Britannia need? And my answer is, we need our magician serving us all. I will shield Emilia; and you shield Glas Myrddin."

Now as I crept closer towards Emilia's candle, shuffling through the tatters of her costume, I could not tell what state she was in. Her animals stirred. Kelso thumped his tail in welcome while Roget extended his long neck and examined me very cautiously because, I was sure, he too found me wanting.

The coverlet lifted and Emilia patted the bed and beckoned me in.

"I feel so very cold. Could you hold me?" she asked me softly. "Please?"

"If I do, I will never want to let you go."

She looked away. "It is only for a few minutes, Merlin, until your next act. Please?"

"I am the next act and the one after that," I replied as I stepped out of my Druidic robes down to my Roman tunic and slipped under the covers. There I took her in my arms and I said a silent prayer asking for God's help.

You will have observed that I do not have her art with love. What should I do? Should I wash her too, as she did me? She is rigid but shivering. 'Shock,' I thought; I did not even know what shock was until she said that it described my state earlier on. She was still in shock. I held her tightly to calm her shaking and to warm her up.

It was then I looked up for a moment at the large web in the corner of the room. Arianrhod was just finishing weaving a word, a word in Welsh… it said: A R A F U… which means 'slow' or 'take your time'. I nodded my head to her in thanks, and then waved her out of the room. When she did not move I flicked my wrist furiously saying in Welsh: "If you please, my dearest lady, get the hell out of here!" I was puzzled though, that on praying to God, He would choose to send me Arianrhod! Some other time I would have to discover how that works.

"I am worried, Merlin, I may have led Jack on when I flirted with him and kissed him." Emilia smelt different. Was it my crushed roses or her broken dreams?

"Remember, my sweet, I was there in Jack's castle, and I saw you looking up at him through your eyelashes, and while I may have been jealous," I said sheepishly, "he hardly even noticed what you were doing and merely thought you had something in your eye."

Did I tell her the truth? You already know I am first and foremost a trickster but, with Emilia, I always told her the truth because she said to me, "I love you." So I followed the instruction of Arianrhod, and kissed her neck and chin very slowly, and when she did not wince, I kissed her lips warmly until they parted.

"I am going to slowly kiss you better!" I whispered to her. I moved her head from one side to the other to loosen her hair, and as I kissed her she gradually came back to life and she smiled at me. We lay there, side by side, just smiling, completely lost in one another. We were so quiet that my mice crawled out to see if we had gone to sleep. Emilia giggled at them.

"Never, ever let me go, Myrddin!" And I replied, "Dwi'n d yarn di, Carys. I love you, my sweet!"

"I love you too, Merlin. Sometimes, lying here in your arms, it is easy to forget how famous you are..." she said.

"Sometimes, lying in your arms, it is easy to forget how fearlessly you poked the Prince of Darkness in his eyes and how cleverly you argued with him... or with me, for that matter!"

"But it is you who spread yourself like a giant warlock across the sky, who out-magicked Moloch! Do you know I am in awe of you...?"

"Arianrhod just told me you are not awestruck by me. Are you forgetting that you are the one who jumped over the precipice towards the sea, trusting in me? And that then you saved Angharad's baby from Vortigern? I am in awe of you!"

"I am not going to let you win this contest, Merlin, because of what you did today." And I held my breath; surely, I thought, my love-making was not that good? "You did what every single person in Britain, every February of every year, wishes they could do... Do you know what that was?"

She had me baffled. "What, my lady, can you mean?"

"You banished winter. How good is that!"

Feeling bereft, I changed the subject.

"Will you write to me when I am in Gaul?"

"That is a funny thing to ask! If I knew there was a postal service across fifteen hundred years, I would have written to you already."

"I am trying to think of a way and a place where we could leave letters to exchange them safely. It would have to be on a point of power, near a portal that a gryphon could safely reach."

"Why won't I just be able to think of you and send you a message like I did earlier today?"

"Because this space here is sacred and you can talk to me mind to mind whenever we are here, but from tomorrow we will not be in such a space any more, and my mother cannot meditate to keep the connection between us clear."

"Have you found anyone else to help?"

"The only one I have thought of is Arianrhod. She has offered but..."

"She is high maintenance."

"What does that mean?"

"She is emotionally needy. She is very demanding of your attention and she wants to be in everything and thinks she knows everything."

"What else would you expect of a goddess? I assure you, she knows a great deal!"

It was then that I realised how much Arianrhod did know. She had encouraged me to find out how love could raise us both above misfortune, transcending it.

"Would my Fairy Queen Emilia like to watch my final act?"

"That depends on what you and Ingraine were discussing very loudly outside the door—and let me warn you, I heard some of it... I thought when Jack attacked me and you stood back, you thought I had encouraged him..."

It was only when I had wrapped her tightly in my arms that I found the courage to recount every word of my discussion with my mother, repeating it gently straight into her ear. Have I told you how I can remember what people say to me and how I can say it back almost word for word? I told her how I was an arrogant fool and a show-off, a trickster who had been tricked—and tricked utterly— by a darker magic. I described my miscalculation and my underestimation of the cunning and treachery of Morgana. I told her about what we believed were her real intentions and how they perverted the actions of Jack. I described how my jealousy of her turned me into a stone and rendered me useless. Finally I raised the purpose of Jack and what we thought Morgana had done to prevent him achieving it.

I expected her to protest and argue with me about his destiny with her, but she looked at me when I finished my confession with gentle knowing. She smiled at me, a smile of extraordinary sweetness and compassion, and I knew that she accepted me exactly as I was. Although she had thought to say no, that she would not attend my entertainment, she said her shame and embarrassment were now somewhat diminished by my declaration of love, and for the moment her anger was under control and she did not want Morgana to see that she had triumphed in any way.

"But I don't want any of this talked about except between us, nor do I want anyone to see me. If I go out there I want to be invisible!"

And I breathed, "You will be invisible so only I can see you. Well, all the people from your realm will see you, and those with the sight from here."

And then she smiled again. "Either way, Merlin, I don't have anything to wear!"

"I thought you might say that because the goddess 'who thinks she knows everything' told me so!"

And I bounced from the bed and opened the door. A beautiful woman with pale hair strung with pearls was standing there, holding a froth of gold and silver.

"Come in, Lady Silver Wheel," and with a beaming face I told Emilia, "This is a robe for a fairy queen!"

"Greetings, Sweet Pea," the familiar voice sang. "I just spun this for you," and she unfolded a cloud of subtle colours. "It comes from my castle in the Northern Lights. Up there silver and emerald, ruby and gold are spread across my sky, and I caught their light and wove them into a robe for you. After your bath, when your wounds are *salved, I will help you dress. This time only those you want will be able to see you."*

I bent over the bed to kiss Emilia's hand, but wrapped in a sheet she scrambled up and reached her arms around me and pulled me down in a passionate kiss.

"Do you two want to be alone?" The Goddess stamped her foot. "Can you not see me? I am right here and I am the one who gives all the advice and does all the work. For once I am fang-free, so Myrddin, you can kiss me too. Come on, I won't bite!"

I kissed her on the cheek.

"Ah... ah... You know you could have had any of my..."

"Thank you very much, Lady Silver Wheel. I will see you both outside. Keep an eye on that Arch-Druid for me, Emilia, and if you suspect any trouble, let me know." And I rushed out, pulling on my robes, leaving the rooms of the villa unprotected; but Emilia, at least was under the care of the Goddess.

Trumpets and horns called everyone to return to the spectacle while the bagpipes blew hard to settle them down. The star-lit sky was mirrored below in a backdrop pierced with tiny licks of fire. Traced across the scenery was the outline of a tall hill moulded around the shape of a dragon. A few in the crowd recognised the scene and murmured: "Avalon."

The scene changed slightly when an outline of a wattle and daub building emerged in the foreground, followed by a sketch of a thorn tree some distance away. The Church of the Mother and Joseph's thorn tree were both well-known and recognised immediately. Arianrhod gave the signal to Tobias first; I followed, springing from the roof of the villa to land on a tall, drum-like stand.

"Greetings!" I called out. "My elf friend Tobias and I are going to sing a song of reverence. We dedicate it to our Lord and to those

who have lost their lives through the evils of Vortigern. This song
is especially for the great Constantine."

At a signal from Tobias, a pan flute played the introductory notes
and he sang the first verse in his pure tenor voice:

> "And did those feet in ancient time
> Walk upon Britain's mountains green?
> And was the holy Lamb of God
> On Britain's pleasant pastures seen?"

I joined Tobias for the second verse.

> "And did the countenance divine
> Shine forth upon our clouded hills?
> And was Jerusalem builded here
> Among those dark satanic mills?"

The next verse I sang alone, and as I sang, Arianrhod sent my
bow and each of my arrows and my spears flying through the night
into my hands.

> "Bring me my bow of burning gold,
> Bring me my arrows of desire,
> Bring me my spears, oh clouds unfold,
> Bring me my chariot of fire."

When Bruto's chariot arrived ablaze with the Northern Lights,
Tobias and I climbed into it to sing the last verse.

> "I will not cease from mental fight
> Nor shall my sword sleep in my hand
> 'Til we have built Jerusalem
> In Britain's green and pleasant land,

'Til we have built Jerusalem
In Britain's green and pleasant land."

The crowd was silent. They had never heard or seen anything like it. Aurelius stood up and began the clapping. He had not taken his eyes off Tobias because he knew he was not an elf but an angel, and everything he heard tonight convinced him he was right. He went up to Tobias and offered his hand, rigid like a sword.

"Tobias? We have met before. Greetings, I am Aurelius."

"My condolences, sir," Tobias said, bowing to him, "on the loss of your father and your brother."

"Thank you. Will you come and fight with us, noble sir? Uther and I are going back to Lesser Britannia to raise an army there, and with that host behind us we will reclaim the northern lands of my father. After that we will move south and rout the Saxons from all of Britannia. Once we have driven out the Darkness, we will create a New Jerusalem here. Will you fight with us?"

And when Tobias gently shook his head saying, "Sorry, but I cannot," Aurelius added,

"Well, Sir, if you are a Druid and cannot fight, will you be our bard and sing for us?"

"Thank you for your kind invitation. The bard you need is Merlin, but I will discuss your offer with him and let you know if I am allowed."

It was then that Tobias saw this beautiful woman who looked like a fairy queen, but it was not until he was a few steps from her that he realised it was Emilia.

"Hey, you look like you've had a total makeover, Em!"

"Hey, I suppose I should take that as a compliment, Tobes. Arianrhod did it. The makeover is only on the outside... Inside... I still can't talk about it." She looked away and bit the lip that had started trembling. "You two, you know, did wonders with that song! Thank you, Merlin, for learning it so fast."

And she managed that beautiful smile. "How's Jack?" she asked Tobias.

"Bad. Sooner we get him back home, the better he'll be. But I'd like to stay here, Em," he said. "I've just been offered a job as a bard."

"I'd like to stay here too," Emilia agreed, "but you know we can't. We have to be home by midnight. Our protection runs out then."

"Then I will see you later. I want to say goodbye to my Rat-face before I watch Merlin."

54

How to Outwit an Arch-Druid

8.30pm, Friday September 10th, Merlin's time

A FIERCE WIND WHIPPED OUT OF NOWHERE that gutted the lanterns, ripped the flags and tore down the bunting from the roof tops. But none of the country folk seemed alarmed at this because it was, after all, what they had come to see.

"There is our birdman! Look, this is our Myrddin, he is back!" one cowherd whispered to his children, while another countered, "This is the man who is the Master of the Winds," and their children shivered and called out to me:

"Myrddin, Myrddin, please scare us. Conjure up something very creepy and horrible!"

"Can you not fly over us like an eagle?" a young girl implored. "Please, Myrddin?"

"Bring the dancing fairy and the green elf back," an old woman begged. "Is she the one? Is she the sorceress, Myrddin, who has captured your magician's heart?"

Hearing her, I nodded with a smile that stretched up into my scalp. "Yes, Dame Bronwyn, that fairy has captured my heart!" It was then that I took a deep breath to empty my mind.

From the darkness, in front of me, a small flame grew. Slowly it illuminated the outline of my flowing robes and the screeching jackdaw on one shoulder and the silent falcon on the other. As the wind puffed my raven hair, my Druidic robes billowed out a ghostly white, and raising my staff over my head I cried out: "Silence!" Instantly the wind dropped and Crook went mute and even the wolfhounds of the kings settled.

And my Emilia gasped when she saw me because I appeared to them as a figure who towered more than a hundred feet over the courtyard. 'You look like Moses, the ancient prophet,' she said to me in our secret way of talking, 'about to smash the stone tablets. Are you as fierce and forbidding as that wind you just banished?' Her voice changed to the merest whisper, 'Do I know you, Merlin? Are you my gentle lover? Your voice echoes in me like it is in Westminster Abbey.'

And when again I bellowed, "I have memories of the future!" the crowd and the kings shivered, expecting wonders. And, for a moment, I thought I should cut off her small voice because those with the power may overhear it, but I loved the comfort and delight of her whispers. So I did nothing.

Emilia glanced at the Arch-Druid who watched the audience with his back to me, and when he moved his hands just like I do whenever I enchant, she knew he was interfering and trying to interrupt my magic with his own. She quickly closed her eyes again to shut out his craft and silently warn me,

'Powyll countermands you.'

I replied, 'Help the spider.'

"What spider?"

'That's me, Sweet Pea.' Emilia shuddered. 'Here I am, on your shoulder.'

'Arianrhod?'

'It is still me but I have grown back a few more legs. Pull your hair out over your face to cover me and listen to my instructions.

Nod your head if you can hear me. Good, now move very slowly through the crowd towards Ingraine until Myrddin, you and Powyll make up a triangle with equal sides. And then stop.'

Keeping her head down and biting her lip, and although she knew few people could see her, Emilia tried to look inconspicuous. Perhaps it was too soon to involve her in fighting this darker magic. But Arianrhod, who knows all, continued.

'Now, Myrddin will bounce his anwen off you to Ingraine and then to me, allowing it to pick up from each of us much of our power to intensify his own. Keep calm and watch how he will quell the Arch-Druid's interference. That bastard will not know what has hit him!'

Expecting a bolt or at least a bang, Emilia tensed, but when my energy came, all she could feel was its gentle warmth. It was merely a tremble.

'Is that all, Arianrhod? Surely there is more power to it than that?'

'Wait, it is coming.'

There was another tremble, then another, followed by a loud shriek.

'Oh no, Sweet Pea,' the spider murmured, "Can you believe it? The poor Arch-Druid just collapsed, and out of him pours forth his Spiteful Ones, his Angry Ones. Tch, tch, tch! What are we going to do now?' Changing her tone, she spat out, 'Isn't he a nasty piece of work! The shadows leap out of him seeking vengeance, and our Myrddin, who has opened himself up for prophecy, is now vulnerable to their attack.'

The instant I sensed the terror from Emilia, I was warned. I closed myself down, and throwing my birds into the air, I spun. That meant when his fifty blazing arrows screamed towards me, I did not see them as Emilia did, because my eyes were closed against all enchantments, although I did see them with my inner sight. I felt the gall of her anger rise as bile in my chest.

'Myrddin, you can leave them to us!' Arianrhod cried. 'You keep spinning, and Tobias will chant from the sky.'

It was not until Mot squeaked that I heard the green elf Tobias singing and the crowd whistling and clapping him. I am sure they thought this deadly display was all for their own benefit and delight. I could not bear to keep my eyes shut for another moment. When I opened them cautiously what I saw was chaos. Some of the Angry Ones attacked my father, some flew near to Emilia, others were taunted by Crook, but the rest were buzzing Tobias. He rode Mot bucking like a heifer, but every one of them had been redirected away from me. Not one of Powyll's arrows had touched me.

'Watch me, Sweet Pea, watch me. I will show you how to set fire to the Dark.'

The Goddess of the Silver Wheel who resides amongst the summer stars shook off her spider disguise, and spinning out her white hair into a full circle around her head, rose into the sky above me. The brother of Ingraine, King Caradoc, recognised the Welsh goddess immediately and cried out,

"It's Arianrhod. It's Arianrhod from Caer Siddi!" There were squeals of excitement…

"What can she be doing here?"

"How are we so blessed?"

"Our dreams will be full of wonders tonight!"

From her clenched hands fell a curtain of emerald light which billowed as if caught by a great wind. When the Angry Ones, the dark shadows with flaming red eyes, raced towards me again, the emerald light swept them up in its net. And Arianrhod trussed them up with her spider's silk, spun them around the sky and flung them to her castle in the Northern Lights.

"Hey that scene in the sky is pyrotechnically amazing!" I heard Tobias exclaim to Emilia. The crowd, however, was silent in awe, trembling from the vision and so very anxious about what could

come next that they asked one another whether it was now the time to take their children home.

Using my staff to navigate, I rose in the air and then, like a swallow I swooped and dived joyously above the heads of the children until I landed beside Hu Powyll. My father, however, had reached the fallen Druid first. There, shaking his head with mock sympathy, he clucked:

"Somehow, Ambrosius, he's had a seizure," and Marcus Cotta looked at me in way that implied he knew exactly what had been the source of the Arch-Druid's collapse. "Can you do anything to help him?"

After feeling his pulse, lifting his eyelids and checking his tongue, I assured myself Powyll had not had a stroke or a seizure.

"Can you pour this in his left ear," I asked my father, "and wait until it takes hold? It was a vial of salted water that I always carry to bring shaken people back to their senses. "When it works his eyelids will flutter open; at that time ask his servants to carry him inside. He will recover completely in an hour or so. I must return to my demonstration quickly or I will lose all that is left of my trance."

I now knew there was something very wrong. There was something I was not seeing; there was something I had not discovered or something I had forgotten. There had been four incidents in less than two hours and they happened despite the triple layers of protection coming from the Arch-Druidess Ingraine, the Goddess Arianrhod and myself, a magician. There was a darker magic that had crept into the house of my father and it had been carried in there by men of honour: an Arch-Druid and Emilia's friend, Jack.

I took a moment to take stock and opened my mind up to my master. But my thoughts scurried back to whatever remained unexplained: the Arch-Druid's threat to Vortigern in Moloch's voice, Jack's attack on Emilia, Powyll's attempt to manipulate my own enchantment; and now there were the Angry Ones that rose from *the body of Powyll to attack me. How could the defences of our household have been so breached? Who was doing this?*

It was not the Arch-Druid because his power alone, despite his posturing, was so much weaker than my own. It was not Moloch because I personally had enchained him. That only left Morgana. But Tobias had splendidly dispatched her to the Otherworld and from there, I knew, she would have to wait until she returned as the daughter of Ygern. And it was still five years to her birth. Yet somehow it could only be Morgana because only Morgana would have sufficient power. But how was she doing this? How could she have found another way back?

It was a bird that brought us the answer.

"My lady, my lady," Gaius, the pigeon-keeper called out, "there is another message."

My mother, thinking it was from the North about Constantine, called me back and beckoned my father towards her to hear the news. Carefully she unwound the message from around the pigeon's leg and the colour of her face changed.

"This is for Gorlois, the warlord of Cornwall," she said grimly. "Fetch him, Gaius."

"Careful, Princess," Bruto whispered. "Do not just give the message to him. He cannot read."

Sweating and purpled-faced from his exertion of hurrying and anxious about any new uncertainty, the war lord demanded, "What is wrong?"

"This message was sent by your wife only three hours ago. It has just arrived here. Would you like me to read it to you?" And Gorlois nodded in relief.

"Dearest husband, I send my greetings and good tidings. You are the father of a baby girl. She has your dark colouring, your bright green eyes and your lusty voice. The sea was raging tonight and I will call her Morgana after the sea goddess. She is early by many weeks but we are both well. Hurry home soon."

"Well, Morgana must have been in a hurry for she is at least six weeks early," Gorlois said, very pleased with himself. It was widely rumoured that Gorlois would never be able to father a child because of his war injuries. "She was not due until All Hallow's Eve," he announced laughing. "I wanted a boy, of course, who could fight beside me, but if my daughter has the beauty of her mother, I will be able to trade her to one of the guests of Marcus Cotta, for gold and influence."

In an effort to silence Gorlois before my mother flung him into the air with one of her expulsion spells, my father grabbed the warlord's arms and raised them up in victory.

"He is a father!" he called out to the crowd. "Congratulations!" And the kings, knowing of Gorlois' handicap, cheered and immediately wondered who the father could really be. Bruto added quietly to Ingraine, raising his eyebrows and turning his head to one side,

"And there I was, Princess, fearing we had more bad news," and he said it in a way she knew he was being ironic.

"Good news indeed," I replied and signalled to my mother to step into the shadows with me. "Yes. Yes. I must confess I miscalculated, she is not predictable! One dark face of Morgana conceals another darker one underneath it, and there is yet another hellish one underneath that. Now, at least, we know who is behind the incidents here. Yet I fear there is an artefact of hers somewhere and she is using it as a way in."

"I can see that the Arch-Druid"—Bruto interrupted us as the eyes of the Arch-Druid fluttered open—"is returning to the land of the living!"

Hu Powyll sat up. "What is happening?" he demanded of Bruto.

"You passed out," Bruto replied in a way that conveyed his stupidity at doing so.

"Has Myrddin prophesised yet?" he asked, in a way that conveyed he knew I could not prophesise.

And Bruto, sensing the overweening malice in this man, murmured,

"No, he is about to begin. Fortunately, you have returned to living in time to hear him," and his craggy face hardened as he drew his gladiolus and pointed it at the Arch-Druid's throat.

"You are here at this villa, you smarmy prick, because I invited you, and you have been interfering in the business of this household. You look crooked again at my son or my wife or try to interfere in anything that they are doing and you will not simply pass out." With the point of his sword, he sliced the Druid's robes. "I will slit you one hundred ways from your arsehole to your honey hole and then, like a true Briton, I will trophy your head for my gate-post. Have I made myself clear?"

"Yes!" he gulped.

"Good. So sit there on your hands and do not move until I tell you when my Ambrosius is finished."

While my father straightened out the Arch-Druid, my mother and I discussed how to stop Morgana interfering with me when I opened yet again to prophecy.

"Now she is back we will have to build a cone of power to protect you, Myrddin," Ingraine warned. "Otherwise Morgana will attack you just like the Angry Ones tried to. She will aim them through your crown when you open it up to go into trance."

While I agreed, I added, "We need five people for a cone of power."

"Yes. Well, there is me," Ingraine counted, pointing to herself first. "And there's Arianrhod, Angharad, Emilia and there's Aurelius."

"Aurelius—no, not him!" I protested.

"No. Sorry, I meant Tobias. I think he is ready. I have seen his light and it is pure gold, and we must have the energy from a man for balance."

"If you could get them together now, I will return to the platform and quieten the crowd down with some wonder and meditate with *you. We will have to search the villa later and find if there is any-thing of Morgana's in there that she could be using as a gateway to cause trouble. But the cone of power will give me all the protection I need for now for the prophecy."*

Like a mother hen gathering her chicks, Ingraine brought together the four people and showed them into the granary. There she had them sit in a circle with her and hum a tune in unison to gather their energies together before they went quiet. Three minutes later I was ready.

55

"I have memories of the future and predict this will be truth"

9.00pm, Friday September 10th, Merlin's time

ONCE I KNEW I WAS PROTECTED in the cone of power, I was safe to prophesise and give them all a good scare. But first I looked for my parents. I never tired of watching them, their hands entwined, whispering softly into one another's ears. Was she telling him what she just did for me? Or did she keep her magic as our secret? I tossed my head in a salute to them before I bellowed again, "I have memories of the future!" Shutting my eyes I raised my staff to swing it in a circle, then putting my thumb in my mouth as the sign to everyone that I was ready to speak of what is coming, I began:

> "Heed the words of Myrddin;
> I predict this will be truth.
>
> Below the place where my uncle
> The King of Davydd reigns,
> Beside the oak where my mother

Ingraine was born, from there
A red dragon hatches from his egg.
His body is covered in crimson scales,
His liquid eyes grow larger
To see through the darkness.

Slowly he unfolds his bat wings
And dashes through the caverns.
He leaps the Hafren.
He flies to us here.

Can you see him?"

"Yes, Yes," the crowd respond, pointing with delight at the red dragon that stretches longer than our path to the river. He flies into our courtyard with Arianrhod and slowly circles, flicking his tail and barring his fangs to demonstrate all his might before he perches behind me on the wall. When I swirl my cape and point my staff in his direction, the dragon reaches down and, like a kitten, playfully paws with the tip of my staff. The crowd hoots. Unsmiling, I continue:

"Sh, sh!" I sing out, and close my eyes.

Sh, sh! He hears you murmuring.
Beware.
The hearing of the red dragon
Is so very sharp
He can hear everything
That the wind catches.

Sh, sh! Give me your ears.
He hears the splash of the oars,
The sculls of the long hairs.

"I have memories of the future and predict this will be truth"

Can you hear them too?
Our dragon stands on his hind legs
And watches while a white dragon
Slithers ashore onto our island.

Can you see him?"

"Yes, Yes!" the crowd calls out. Beside the red dragon stands Arianrhod, disguised now as Vortigern, who beckons the white dragon up the wall. Once it settles, its immense talons and razor-tooth mouth shine through the light of the oil lamps at us. This dragon could easily swallow a man and his woman and still have room for their children. It is far more ferocious than anything else in the whole of Britannia.

A look of horror sweeps through the crowd. The dragons circle one another until a crack of lightning splits the night and the red dragon, sparking with its fire, screeches and leaps on the invader's back and sinks his teeth into its neck.

"Where is our strong lord?
Does he not hear my prophecy?
Is the honey-tongued lord here?
Is he full of vengeance for his slain kin?

From his grief, spears will shine with blood.
We see him at the Giants' Stones.
But where is the red beard
With his sword worked in the Angel's blue enamel?

Where is our glorious dragon king?

Where is the Goddess of the Gaels?
She of the smith's skilled hammer,

Of bards' poetry and sweet medicine?
Her fire will scorch the Darkness
Of the kin of the Bear.

A bear cub will come leaping
Bright and bold
From the concealment of the forest.
Merry Coel will teach him
The craft of kings.

His sword will slash like no other.
The Saxons will be slaughtered
By his host of ashen spears.
The young bear will grow into a lion,
The Saxons will cower at his might.

When the long hairs are tamed
The bards will flourish here.
The red dragon will roar
For a hundred years.
It is a triumph for the Britons!

Let my words be heard
As truth."

*Everything is quiet while the dragons circle the courtyard again
until, together with Arianrhod dressed as Vortigern, they disappear.
The lights blink out. I just stand there, my eyes closed, absolutely
drained. Ingraine asks her friend,*
*"Can you bring him back, Lady Silver Wheel; he is still in a deep
trance."*
With her help, I stutter back into awareness.
Once the small oil lamps are lit and the crowd, giddy from my

effects, is dispersed, Aurelius and Uther stand in the centre of the courtyard discussing something with great animation in that peculiar language they share. The only word I catch is in Latin, cried indignantly by Aurelius, and it is 'caelibatus'. I took it to mean 'celibate' as in 'a vow of celibacy.'

They approach my mother, and going down on one knee, Aurelius takes her hand as if he is about to propose marriage. It is very strange. I moved into the shadows to overhear.

"My dearest lady," Aurelius began, "I know that you and my mother often shared confidences about the future of your children. Whenever you did, did she ever raise with you how she planned to find a suitable wife for me?"

It took Ingraine a moment to realise what may have prompted his curious request. And as soon as she recalls that my prophecy implied that Uther will replace Aurelius as king, because presumably Aurelius is dead, she realises that to influence such a future Aurelius will have to act now to produce his own son and heir. He will have to marry and he will have to marry soon. And, as Ingraine has often said to me, 'What else is there for mothers to discuss other than how their sons will give them honour and many offspring?' I noticed Emilia move closer with that slight frown of concentration that closes her face.

"It moves me that you would ask me this," Ingraine replies. "Please rise. We did indeed discuss some prospects for you. Your mother, Elen, was anxious that you should follow your father's example and marry into the royalty of Wales. As you know, her first cousin Blodwyn married my brother Caradoc. Elen, before her untimely death, was going to raise your prospects with her. She might even have done that before she died. I do not know. But as you know, Caradoc and Blodwyn have a daughter who is, of course, Myrddin's first cousin, and while she is a little older than usual for betrothal at fifteen, she is very bright and comely. Would you like me to raise it with her mother on your behalf? I could do so tonight before they retire to their room."

*"I never doubted that if I ever had to marry it would be to…"
Aurelius' voice broke when he changed into Latin "mulier mollis
serenissima, to someone like my mother." Aurelius seemed close
to tears. Whether it was the prospect of marriage that grieved
him or his shock at losing both his parents and a brother within
a year, I would never know. Uther pats him on the back and offers
quietly:*

*"Let me look after it all for you." And once he had tenderly helped
his brother to a bench and settled him there, he turns again to Ingraine.*

*"Dearest lady, Aurelius will go tomorrow to Lesser Britain to
raise an army, and before I join him, I will appraise any prospects
you may have found for him. You may not know that before my
mother died she finalised a marriage for me with Narathew from
Lesser Britannia."*

*He lowers his voice and continues in almost a whisper into her
ear while his long bony fingers skitter in the air around her like
water spiders.*

*"I think it was a very bad choice. I have never even bedded her be-
cause she has yet to stop crying. So any girl you may find, my dear
lady, must have bled, because we do not want another child bride.
Your niece, Blodwyn, at fifteen or sixteen should be safe. I, myself,
will negotiate her maiden fee; and if it pleases you, do not propose
anything cheap to us; the price must honour the standing of my
brother and the nobility of the house of Constantine. And there must
be more than one bride on offer so that the chosen one will know how
deeply honoured she is by his choice.*

*"I will visit each prospect before Aurelius meets her. As our
father's heir, he is wealthy, and someday he will be king, and I can
assure you he is the dearest soul on earth who will be a devoted
husband to her."*

*"Thank you for your confidences, Uther. With your agreement I
will speak to Blodwyn now before I turn in for the evening and let*

you know what she says after the execution tomorrow. Come, Ang-harad, we have a potion to make."

She took her leave and went towards Emilia and Tobias who were standing aside but intently observing the marriage negotiations.

"It's time for me to return to my room and provide for the safety of your passage," Ingraine says to them, "It has been a pleasure getting to know you both. Thank you for all you did tonight to protect my son."

She kisses Tobias on both cheeks, and when she hugs Emilia, she whispers, "We have not found a way yet for you and Myrddin to meet again, but we are still trying."

And, for the first time, Emilia wonders whether Ingraine will really try hard. How will it be in her interests to help her son spend time with a girl whom he will not be able to marry and have her grandchildren with? Will she not be wasting her time and adding confusion to her plans for his life?

56

In a Dark Corridor

10.00pm, Friday September 10th, Merlin's time and Our time

ANGHARAD KNEW IT WOULD BE AT LEAST MIDNIGHT *before I re-turned to release her from her vigil and Ingraine from her trance. Behind the villa in a deserted place, I organised four departures. In thinking through my plans for the journey home of Jack and Tobias and Kelso, then of Emilia's at midnight, the only weakness I could see was in leaving Emilia alone while I returned with the others to Dartmoor. I was confident, though, that as long as my mother was in a sacred trance and my father and nurse were vigilant, the protection of Emilia should be assured. But should I burn that broken arrow I took from Jack? No time, I concluded. We are almost there. Everything is going to be fine.*

Quietly guiding Jack to the gryphon, I said,

"Time to go; and Jack, because you still look poorly you must come with me. Tobias, you ride Emilia's gryphon holding Kelso."

"Actually, I'm staying here, Merlin," Tobias protested. "Aurelius is soon to be crowned king and he has offered me a position as his bard, and living in your alternative reality suits me just fine. It's

awesome!" I smiled as I knew he had already refused Aurelius' offer, but I could not resist a little sport with him.

"Tobias, you cannot work for him because he thinks you are from the Otherworld."

"Well I will do, because that is, indeed, where I am from."

"But he thinks you are an angel, a Divine Being."

"Well, even that had to come out some day." He pulled me aside and whispered: "Seriously, Merlin, can I not continue training with you as a sorcerer's apprentice?"

"No, because as you know I am a magician and I work with science and the Light, I am not a sorcerer. Sorcerers work with the Dark Arts."

"Sorry! I am so sorry. I've still got a lot to learn. Can't I continue my training as a magician?"

"Your training will take up to sixty years and we can resume it at any time." And I grabbed him by the elbow and brought him back to Jack.

"Could I be someone, then, who carries your goods and chattels?"

"I have a gryphon for that."

"I guess all your answers are 'no'. But it was worth a try. If you are ever Exeter way, here is my address," and Toby handed me the card of the man from *The Battle of the Bands* with his own address scrawled across the back. "If you are flying in I am just near the hospital. It is the fourth house down on the right hand side. Well, how does this gryphon work? Its front end's a bird and its rear end is..." He looked puzzled and scared at the same time. "What is it, again?"

"A lion."

"Shit, Merlin! Do you think it's wise to ride it? Can't I borrow Rat-face?"

"These creatures are the only ones that work across time. They live between your time and mine, in that abyss we cross, and they *will hunt down anyone who should not be there, and unfortunately they would make a feast of Mot."*

"Merlin, I think you should come with a health warning," Tobias quipped, grinning, "because danger swirls around you. Anyway, in the event of my death, notify the Pope."

I knew it was all supposed to be witty, and although I seldom understood his jokes, I also knew that becoming a magician was a serious business, and as his master I have to speak the truth about a student's conduct and demand respect from him. So I began my response to him sternly.

"Tobias, I think it is time for you to give up pretending you are a coward. You are not." I paused to give him time to absorb my rebuke. "Tonight you will be flying home on eagles' wings and landing on lions' paws, and who could ask for a safer journey across time than that?"

"While you are away, what should I be doing?"

"As your friend," and I spoke to him in such a way that he would understand I was speaking as his master, "I will ask you some questions." And I told him to think for as long as he needed before answering them. I asked what made him happy, and what calling he was going to follow, and whether his answers to those questions had anything in common; and if his answers were not identical to keep working on them until they were.

"My question is, Merlin," Jack almost whined, "why can't Emily come with us?"

"Because there is much hurt spread between you two." I spoke to him as gently as I could, and patting him on the back, I added, "And I promised to take her to Avalon."

"Merlin, if ever I was Uther..." I tried to hide my amazement that Jack could even contemplate such a thought. He took a deep breath before he continued, "Then you would be my Prime Minister, wouldn't you?" When I nodded him encouragement, he continued: "And as such, you would be my closest advisor. Could you give me some advice now before we leave?"

I looked at him and sighed and somewhat reluctantly replied, "Of course. How can I help?"

"What am I going to do about Emily? She won't talk to me. She won't even look at me!" And as he spoke, he choked close to tears. "I know I have bruised her and shamed her and I have betrayed my honour, but I feel desperate that I am caught up in something here I do not understand."

Tobias moved back next to Jack and gazed up at me as though expecting me to deliver the commandments. I decided there and then I would not disappoint him, but I would not announce ten. I would only go half way.

"Any sane person, Jack, would not answer your question. But because you are a good man, and Emilia is a good woman, I will offer you some advice in the Druidic manner. It is composed of five remarks in few words, and each time I mention a point, I will raise a finger of my right hand as the Druids do when they are teaching.

"First of all: Listen. You assaulted her and tried to ravish her. Do not defend yourself or blame others. Second: Listen. Let Emilia know how much you respect her because she feels full of shame and she thinks, despite our reassurances, that she brought this on herself. Reassure her she did not provoke your attack in any way. Third: Listen and do not apologise, instead beg for her forgiveness. Fourth: Listen, and there may be some restitution you can make." Finally, I held up my thumb. "Be patient, Jack, because this could take a long time."

"Thank you. I hope we meet again."

"We will. And get well. It is good you have finally acknowledged your connection with Uther. The more you think about that link the more you will understand your present predicament. You would not have been given this insight if you were not capable of understanding its consequences.

"We are all concerned about your wellbeing and my mother has made a special herbal medicine for you to counteract any future ef-

fects of Morgana's poison. I will stand by you while you take this bitter stuff. Be assured she gave me something for the after-taste."

As he swallowed Jack pulled a face, screwed up his eyes and jumped up and down crying out:

"Yuck, yuck, yucketty yuck!"

We smiled at his performance.

"Here is the honeycomb to suck. Now, let us leave."

We landed outside Belstone at the Stone Maidens. Casey was there waving at us and looking very worried.

"Where have you been?" she demanded. "Where's Emily? Where did her dog come from? What the hell are those things?" she pointed to the gryphons. Next her eyes fell on Jack. "You look like shit, Jack. What's wrong?" But before he could answer, her eyes focussed on me. "Wow, and who is that?"

"Greetings, I am Merlin," I answered and bowed, all charm. She was not impressed. She did not believe it was the right time for jokes.

"Greetings," she snapped, and added sarcastically, "Pleased to meet you, and I am Guinevere!"

"Casey, this is the Merlin," Tobias said, "and he has come to you through a time portal."

"I am honoured to meet you finally!" I bowed again and kissed her hand. "I was here yesterday and watched you dance with great athletic grace with my foxes."

Casey was speechless, a very rare event I am told.

"We'll tell you all about him,"—Tobias rushed in to fill the silence—"Merlin has to return to bring Emily back. Why don't we walk back to the car? Jack may yet need to go to hospital. What time is it, by the way?"

"Eleven forty-five," Casey answered.

"And what day?"

"What do you mean… what day?" She sounded exasperated. "It's just before midnight on Thursday September the ninth, and tomorrow, remember, is Em's birthday."

"Our time is totally out of synch with your time, Merlin. But you know that, don't you, because I'll bet it is your work?" Tobias stretched out his hand and I grabbed it and pulled him into a hug, patting his back. "If ever I can be of service to you, in any way," Tobias said, "you just call and I will come running. I have just had the very worst time of my life and the very best time of my life!"

"Knowing you, Tobias, has been akin to knowing a most noble lord. Look after Jack, if you please, and let the parents of Emilia know she is safe and will be home soon. I can assure you, after I get back from Gaul we will work together again to progress your training."

As I climbed onto my gryphon I thought, 'I am taking Emilia to Avalon in a few minutes!' And despite all that had happened that day, I do not know when I have ever felt so happy.

10.30pm, Friday September 10th, Merlin's time

In a dark corridor outside Ingraine's room, Angharad sat on a stool guarding her mistress while Ingraine was in trance. Her daughter was slumbering in a wicker basket at her feet and her hands were busy unplaiting her hair to ready it for sleep. All was silence.

She cried silently, grieving for her Doone and for the loss she already felt anticipating the departure of her from Myrddin. Angharad envied Ingraine's ability to go quickly into her deep inner silence that seemed to fill her with peace and restore her tattered spirit. She had tried for years to learn from her how to go into that ocean of love, but she had never been able to still her active mind. A woman, she always said, is never still.

When she heard the noise down the corridor, she thought it was Myrddin's animals settling in for the night. Earlier she had heard him leave as he shepherded Jack and Tobias and Emilia's dog outside to the gryphons, and later she had heard him return for Emilia.

A shriek, like one of Myrddin's peacock calls, split her silence. But it was not a human sound. Shocked, she clutched her child to her and, lifting up the oil lamp, raced down the corridor towards the bellowing and barking in his chamber.

There was a spot in the stone paving where no one had ever stumbled before, but it was there where she slid suddenly and almost dropped her child. The floor was slippery with crimson blood like that in a slaughterhouse. It had the stink of fear. She wanted to run back and get Bruto but her terror sprung its iron trap and pinned her to the floor, and bile rose into her mouth. Something was on the door of Myrddin's chamber; she raised the lantern.

"Oh God!" she groaned. "No, no! Who could do such a thing?"

Dolossus, Myrddin's beloved fox, his eyes open in horror, his head lolling from a cut throat, was nailed to the door. Above him flapped Myrddin's falcon, shrieking in pain, caught by a single nail through its left claw. Who had breached their protection? Who had done this? Where was Arianrhod? Where was Ingraine? Was she safe?

It was the thought of a possible threat to her mistress that freed up Angharad, and she hurried back down the corridor to reassure herself of the safety of Ingraine.

A shadowy presence stood listening at her door. It was Bruto.

"My Lord, my Lord, help me!" she cried. "Someone has crucified Myrddin's fox to the door of his chamber!" Her voice caught in distress as Bruto's arm went around her. "His merlin is trapped too and nailed through her claw, and she is screeching in great pain! Can you help her? Is Ingraine safe?"

"Yes. She sits in peace while her hounds snore at her feet." His eyes flickered in the light. "Did you see anyone?" he demanded as he took Angharad's arm and hurried towards his son's chamber. "Anyone at all?

"No one crossed my path, my Lord. They must have come in through the back door, and only a few minutes ago because it is not that long since Myrddin left with Emilia."

"I warned that Arch-Druid!" Bruto growled. "Now, give me your shawl!" And Bruto flung it over the falcon and bunched it around her legs. Then using his short sword, he prised the nail from the wood. He expertly tied the shawl around the bird to stop its panic.

"There, my pretty one, Ambrosius will soon be here."

Unused to disagreeing with her master, Angharad said timidly,

"I do not think it was the Arch-Druid, my Lord. No Druid would risk such a desecration. Will you look at that poor beast? The guardian of the foxes would pursue a Druid until his life was forfeited if he committed such a crime. No, I fear it was one of the kings that did such a foul act!"

"Are you sure? I think it is Morgana's work. I can smell her musk; her scent is faint but it is still distinctive."

Angharad was shocked. 'How could he know about the Otherworld?' she asked herself. 'And Morgana? She was from our world, the world of the Welsh and the other Britons, the world that we hide from the Romans.'

He answered her question himself, and very gently.

"Your Doone was my Doone too. He was my spy," and he leant over and kissed their sleeping child on her head. "I used to run intelligence in Gaul, and my spies in Britannia are everywhere. I know many secrets. Not the pillow talk that Arianrhod specialises in, but the bigger secrets.

"Did you know, Angharad, that whenever Doone met with the Dark Ones, I knew? I was the first person he discussed their activities with. How else could I protect the innocence of my goodly wife and my Otherworldly son?"

"No, I did not know anything about his secret work for you."

"Everything Doone spoke about with them, whether it be the digger, Emilia's mother or about Emilia herself, or about the stench of Morgana or the malice of Moloch, we discussed. Morgana is the problem. She is a stalker, a woman of insatiable and perverted appetites. Who could not recognise her smell? Her desire is for my son, a virtuous and brilliant boy who today became a man, but not with her. And that, Angharad, is what has fanned her anger and her desire for revenge. Now, here it is with his beloved fox.

"Earlier she poisoned our food, and poisoned the friend of Emilia to get him to defile her and so wound Ambrosius. Now she has taken human form but her spirit is still not fixed in her body. It roams about, and she crucified the fox of my son to warn him. By this act she has said to him: 'You will never be safe because in the chamber where you sleep I can cause assault and I can cause slaughter, and I will stalk you as long as I exist.' Today we tried to form a plan to defeat the Saxon invasion, but the real battle for Britannia is being played out between these two, and will continue with others not yet born."

And Bruto walked out the back door cradling his son's merlin to wake Gaius, the pigeon-keeper.

57

The Church of the Mother

10.30pm, Friday September 10th, Merlin's time

"COME ON, COME IN," MERLIN COAXED. Instead, Emily stood there rooted in the earth and examined the squat wattle and daub building in the shape of a cross. She was unsure where Merlin's enthusiasm for this ramshackle building came from. But it was the eerie howling of hundreds of animals that was unnerving her: barking, howling, baying, and snarling. How could there be an abattoir so close to a Druidic centre?

"What is that horrible noise?" she asked.

"That is the wolfhounds and hunting dogs in the warehouse nearby. They are going to be picked up by traders and sold right around the world. This is a trading port. The glass ingots come in here from Phoenicia… Did you see the inkwell I used today? It was made here. What do you call this place? Glastonbury? Well there is the 'glass' in its name, and while the ingots come in here, our tin, silver and woad and dogs go out to the world.

"Strive to shut their noise out of your head. They are not being ill-treated, I promise you," and he tried again to coax her

429

into the building, this time by taking her hand. He ducked his head below the squat doorway and shielded her head from any bumps. "There is always an oil lamp burning in here."

Once she was inside he said proudly,

"We believe it is the first church in Christendom, the oldest Christian church in the world."

The inside was dingy, covered with soot. A carved oak table stood at one end for an altar. She could smell the mice that skittled on the stone floor where a ragged family with four small children slept in the rushes. She searched for something reassuring to say to him. Eventually she whispered so as not to wake them,

"Merlin, this place does look very old. When was it built?"

"It is over four hundred years old. In your counting it was built in the year 42."

"But that's even before Emperor Claudius invaded Britain!"

"Yes. One year before. Can I tell you the story? I will move these bales of hay because I want us to sit in the same places I sat with the Abbot when he told this story to me."

Once Merlin had reorganised the seating and allowed a colony of mice to run up his arm, he began.

"Tonight when you were bathing, Tobias and I sang Jerusalem just as you planned. And the bard who wrote it asked many questions in his song. Listen to what he asked." And Merlin sang the first verse.

> *"And did those feet in ancient time*
> *Walk upon Britain's mountains green?*
> *And was the holy Lamb of God*
> *On Britain's pleasant pastures seen?"*

"That was so good, Merlin! I wish I could've heard you sing it all!" Emily smiled for the first time since they came there. "I have a sense you're going to answer all of the poet's questions with a 'yes'. Jesus was here."

"Yes he was, and you are sitting exactly where he sat!"

And Emily started and stood looking around to see if he was there now.

"And he sat there not once but twice. But there I am jumping ahead. He was brought here when he was fourteen by his uncle, Joseph of Arimathea, who owned a share of a tin mine in Cornwall near Redruth. Later he sailed up here to collect silver and lead from the Mendip Hills, as the ballast for his trading vessel. Joseph wanted his nephew to see exactly what I am about to show you tonight."

"You're sure it was this spot?" And when Merlin nodded, she shuddered and said,

"I've just got goose-bumps," and her eyes teared up. "And what did Jesus think of Glastonbury?"

"His mother Mary had told him about it because she too had come here as a girl with her uncle, so when he saw it for himself he loved it; he loved the whole of Britannia. He had a good ear for languages, and Joseph taught him our trading Greek and Romano-British on his boat coming here so he could argue with the locals. We now call this place Yniswyrddn, the Isle of Glass, because, as I said, this is where the ingots and sheets of glass come in. Sometimes Joseph would bring them here. It was then, and still is, the spiritual centre of Britannia, and Jesus debated with the Druids on this very spot. He demanded, 'Why did you make a hollow man from willows and burn people alive in it?' 'Because they are rapists and murderers,' the Arch-Druid explained to him.

" 'God, the Father, gave them life. Why do you think you can take it away? Do you burn your prisoners of war as well?' he asked.

" 'Sometimes we do that because they have burnt our sacred trees and ravaged our land, but most of our prisoners are not burned. We honour our captives and set them free.'

"Yet Jesus stood his ground and condemned all practices of human sacrifice and criminal execution. He was fascinated that the Druids' eyelids were painted a brilliant blue and tattooed, just like Doone's. Jesus could see they were holy and sainted men, and he followed them around to observe how they taught their philosophy. He watched them arbitrate a case like you saw Hu Powyll doing this afternoon. Our concept of fairness gives all men and women the right to appeal over their chieftain's head to their king, to petition him personally and have their disputes resolved; and when he watched it all in action he understood how very different it was from Judaic law.

"The Druids also told him that everyone had the right to talk independently and directly to God, and their role as priests was only to formalise ceremonies like betrothal, marriage and passing, and not to intervene between anyone and God. Jesus took away two important ideas from us about fairness and individual independence and they buried themselves in his mind, only to emerge later in his teaching."

As Merlin spoke, Emily realised he was teaching her, instructing her in a way he had not done before, and she loved listening because she, too, was strongly against any form of capital punishment, and she liked all her priests at arm's length. When her mind flashed back to his earlier prophecies and she blended them with what he'd just been saying, she realised that he, too, could have been a priest. Maybe he was, in reality, a priest, but he just hadn't told her yet.

"You said Jesus was here twice. How did he ever come back?"

"After his resurrection, Jesus appeared to Joseph in a dream and asked him to bring his teachings to Britain. But later, face-to-face, he asked Joseph and Mary Magdalene to found a New Jerusalem... Joseph in Britannia and she in the Roman province of Gaul. So we are in the church that Joseph built, right here, and he called it the Church of the Mother, after his niece Mary, whom he brought here when she was eleven.

"One night, Joseph was praying on the very spot where I am sitting now, with a jackdaw on his shoulder…"

"Just like you?"

"Yes. It was considered by the Druids very odd because a jackdaw was a bird of ill repute among them. They believed it was an omen of ill tidings, but Joseph believed, as I do, that it was unfairly maligned. So yes, that is why I have a jackdaw."

"And Joseph is your hero?"

"He is. And when I talk to him in prayer I can see him. He is a big, muscular man like my father—but not as tall as Bruto—but with sweetness in his smile and in his manners, and I can always hear the poetry in his speech. Anyway, Joseph was praying here, and Jesus appeared right where you are sitting now, in all his glory—a shining cloud of gold—and Joseph nearly had a seizure. And what does Jesus say? 'It's all right, Uncle, it's only me, Jeshua.' I'm sure if Jesus knew your word 'okay', he would have said, 'It's okay, Uncle.'

"Joseph was, as anyone would be, speechless, and Jesus continued, 'I have come to bless this Church of the Mother,' and with that he consecrated this place. No more was spoken and he just faded from view. Now this was in the year forty-six, six years after Joseph came here."

"So the poet William Blake was right! But I thought the first Christian churches were built in Greece or Rome or in the Middle East… in fact, anywhere else but Merrie Ole England."

"The earliest Christians were still using and building synagogues or meeting in private homes or catacombs. This was definitely the first in the world."

"You know, I feel so humble to be here that it sends shivers running through me. It's a bit of a shocker, though. I go to a Jesuit school in Exeter and they don't believe anything about

Joseph of Arimathea, despite the fact that we sing 'Jerusalem' at every football game."

"And you know why they sing it? Because everything I have told you lives in the folk memory of the British people, and they know in their hearts it is true, whatever your official version says. And there is a lot more; but here is one for your mother. Can you see through that window there is a mound? It is a barrow grave, and that is where Joseph rests."

"How do you know these things?"

"It is the tradition taught by the Abbot. All the Abbots here are descended straight from Joseph himself."

"So if I was standing in my time in the ruins of our Lady Chapel, whereabouts would Joseph's grave be?"

"Just a minute... I am looking. Your Lady Chapel is built on top of the Church of the Mother. If in your time you are downstairs facing its altar, it is on your left. Why?"

"As you know, Mum loves digging up graves, and she says all lies will dig their way out of graves sooner or later."

"You can tell her this from me: Joseph is really buried there, and near his skeleton there is a tablet of lead. I can see that a corner of it is broken off. What a shame—it had the date on it! The tablet is inscribed in Latin and it says: 'Here are the mortal and sanctified remains of Joseph, Episcopus Primus Britannia, (First Bishop of Britain) Sent by God.' He was nearly ninety when he died...

"And we will have to go now."

She grabbed his hand saying: "I've one more question." Of course, she was playing for time, but it was still a genuine question and his answer would surprise her.

"It seems that Joseph was a special man, and with his staff and his jackdaw your hero, but was he a magician like you?"

"He could turn his staff into a snake, if that's what you mean, using enchantments. He could navigate by the stars. He was adventurous and schooled by nature. He was Jesus' confidant, probably the only one he ever had. Joseph knew Jesus was going to die and Jesus revealed to him how he was going to die, and how he would have to leave his body for many hours, even days, and then re-enter it to use it again.

"The way that works is very complicated. I know because my mother sometimes leaves her body when she's in a trance, and she needs someone to guard over her to keep her safe, just as Angharad is doing for her at this moment. But when Ingraine leaves her body, she is alive, not dead. Therefore what she does is very easy compared with what Jesus was planning to do.

"So Jesus commands Joseph: 'Buy my body from that corrupt Pilatus as soon as possible. Pay whatever you have to, but get my body back quickly. Put me in a safe place that is guarded by Antonius to keep it from any attack, free from rats and vermin, and cool and constant in temperature to protect my body from corruption.' So Joseph does that and puts him in his own sepulchre.

"And when Jesus returns to his body, he asks Joseph, 'Will you go back to Britannia? He does not say Iberia or Gaul or Cartagena or Egypt or any of the other half-way civilised places they had visited together. He asks him to come here into our wild mists, to the place that Julius Caesar himself was not able to conquer the first time with his twenty thousand soldiers, and where our people still ran around in wolf-skins, their own skin covered with woad. And Joseph does it. And I think of him every day and thank him for coming here.

"But now I have spent so much time talking, we cannot walk, we will have to fly."

"Thank you!" she breathed. "Do you know our Church made Joseph the patron saint of undertakers?" And when Merlin looked puzzled at what she meant, she repeated the word in Latin: "Vespillo!"

Merlin threw back his head and laughed: "Oh, he would love that title, because to be known everywhere as the only undertaker to a man who never died is a great laugh!"

"I am missing you already, Merlin. I have so much to learn from you," and they stood holding one another's hands, lost in the beauty of each other's eyes, until Emily asked, "Where to next?"

From nowhere her answer came as a screech of pain. It came from Merlin, and the force of his scream hit her so hard in the face that she clutched his arm in horror.

"What's wrong?' she gasped. "What's wrong?"

He could not answer; a tide of misery swept through his frame. It engulfed him. And after a while Emily herself knew what was wrong with him, because she could see what he could see through the eyes of his merlin. But it was weeks later before she realised how significant this revelation was.

"Oh, Myrddin. It's Mr Fox? And it's your merlin, too. Isn't it?" He nodded slowly, and tears ran down her cheeks. "I loved Mr Fox. Do you want to talk to me about it?"

He shook his head, simply unable to speak. He rested his forehead on hers before he jerked to attention, saying,

"No. My father and my nurse are looking after it. If I go into my grief any more, a grief that lies already on top of my grief for Doone and Constantine and Jack's assault on you, Morgana will ruin our last moments together, because I am sure that is her plan. You asked me, 'where to next?' My answer was going to be the sacred well and thorn tree. But now we will go to talk to Joseph first."

58

"And your destination, you don't know it..."

Friday September 10th, Merlin's time

As Merlin strode towards the barrow grave, Emily had to run to keep up with him. He knelt beside it and bowed his head and gestured to her to follow.

"Keep us safe, Joseph!" And reaching for Emily's hand, he continued, "And bless our union. I will be gone for many years. Watch over me and my beloved like you guarded Jesus, and watch over our Britannia while we are gone. Let me find a way to bring Emilia back here. Could you comfort Dolossus, my fox, who was crucified tonight? Can you ask him to wait for me?" Slowly he bent down and kissed the ground of the grave. "God willing, so be it."

He scooped Emily in his arms, saying, "Now let us drink at the red well."

In the dark it was hard for her to gauge the distance, but she thought they flew for a mile to the foothill at the base of Glastonbury Tor. They landed in an apple orchard in a cleared space where metal and pottery beakers lay scattered among the windfall apples on the grass.

"Is this the Chalice Well?" she asked.

"I do not know. I will look." Moments later he said, "It is the same water but it springs to the light from a different place. This is the well that Joseph and Jesus drank from when they came here from their ship. It was their first stop before they climbed up the Dragon's maze. See the Dragon? See how it encircles the hill seven times before it rests its head on the top? When Jesus stood here the Dragon looked very different. His toes were in plain sight over there, and Jesus was full of delight and bubbling with mischief. And he grabbed Joseph's staff—his magician's staff—and planted it beside the Dragon's toe and, being a clever mimic, he made the Dragon howl, 'Ouch, ouch! Someone just stood on my corns!' He was copying Joseph's voice, who complained whenever Jesus, before he got his sea legs, trod on his corns. 'I want to leave a mark here to celebrate the mystery of this place,' Jesus said, and prayed over Joseph's staff. It immediately sprouted leaves.'"

"That must be our Glastonbury thorn. We've moved the thorn from here nearer to the Lady Chapel. It's a wonderful story, Merlin. Very different from the one I know. Only last month I was on the Tor with my Dad to watch the Perseid meteor shower stream across the sky, but we never knew we were standing on a dragon. Did the Druids build it?"

"No. It was built thousands of years ago by the same people who built the Giant's Stones and the wonders on the Orkneys... Let's drink to Dolossus," and he handed her a beaker of reddish water for her to sip.

"I am so sorry about Mr Fox. He was a beautiful, elegant animal and I enjoyed dancing with him." And she hugged Merlin and kissed his cheek. "Urrr, this water tastes of iron."

"Just like blood," he replied grimly.

"Are we going to the top?"

"Let us go to the Dragon's head,"

He spun her around into his arms until they faced the same direction, and they ascended the five hundred feet so rapidly that Emily's ears popped. When they landed Merlin he continued,

"It's a wingless dragon. It keeps its back paws down there near the well and its front paws are up here," and he pointed with his staff. "This is where his paw holds the golden apple—a treasured orb. All this is the isle of the apples… Avalon."

"At last."

"And your destination," Merlin sang, smiling again, "you don't know it, Avalon."

"I wouldn't know this countryside," Emily said looking down and turning around in a circle. "This looks like an island surrounded by an inland sea that has hundreds of smaller islands in it. There is water on four sides of us. Where do I live? Can you orient me?"

Standing behind her, he put his arms around her again to guide her.

"Let us start backwards. First, can you see those beacons on the high hills over there?" She nodded.

"Are they for signals?" she asked.

"Yes, and they are navigation points for night travellers like me. That is the north, and those are the Mendip Hills above those watery marshes. Turn right with me to the east. There's Mere, a very old place. Now turn to the south-east: there's the old hill fort at Hamelot, where the Carthaginians kept a leprosarium. Now move your eyes to the right again. There! That's the very faint beacon on the hill near Isca. Is it anything like this in your time?"

"No. There's no water. It's been all drained away by the Dutch and it's now called the Somerset Levels. There are rivers, of course, and large towns like Wells to the north, and the night sky still drips with stars, but our sky seems much further away than yours."

"I brought you here because this is one of the best gateways to Annwfn, the Otherworld, where you come from. I travelled once to another time from here to meet Britga, the Trojan, who founded this place. He is the man after whom Britannia is called."

"I thought his name was Brutus!"

"We Romans Latinise everything, just like I did with your name, otherwise we cannot get the cases or the endings right in our language—which makes them easier for us to say. Anyway, I have written you some star charts that show certain alignments. In your time there is a tower up here, is there not?"

"Yes, dedicated to the Archangel Michael, the dragon slayer. No wonder the dragon disappeared!"

"Sometimes I talk with Lord Michael and he too will be looking after this country while I am away, so this would be a perfect place to leave me a message. At each of these alignments," and Merlin handed her a small scroll, and when she unrolled it she saw the algebra of planetary alignments, "I will leave you a letter brought by my gryphon and he will be able to pick up your response. Would you, Emilia, do me the honour of leaving a message for me?"

"Of course I will, but whereabouts? I'll be living back in Exeter soon, but I often come here with my dad when he plays with his band. But it's at least sixty miles away."

Now he held her very tight and whispered in her ear, "Let us draw an airy line from here through the south-west to Isca. It takes six days on foot because I walked it once." Emily knew Merlin was dragging this out. Like her, he did not want to say goodbye.

"Now it's only an hour and a half to Exeter?"

"If we went straight south to the Temple of Bacchus..."

"Mum has dug there. It's not called that now. It's called Maiden Castle in Dorset."

"And then due west from there to Isca. So that means this will be at this spot then."

"So I leave it here, in our ruined tower, in a direct line with Exeter?"

"Yes. But listen, here is your first letter, hand delivered." His voice broke and he spoke hoarsely into the back of her hair and Emily knew he was very upset. "Do not turn around. Please take it but do not read it until you get home." Emily stuffed it into her jean's back pocket. "I wrote this to you after the first time we laid together. I found I could write things on parchment I could not say facing you. It is like now when my speech deserts me, my tears wash my face and my mind tells me not to try to put into words what I am feeling. But tomorrow when you are back in your world, my words will gush forth and pour into my next letter."

For a while Emily could not speak because she, too, was lost in a crushing sadness of goodbye. When she had composed herself, she turned around and said very softly,

"Thank you! I wanted to give you something too," and she pulled out a small ornate jar. "This is a box of kisses—there are one thousand kisses in there—I counted each one and sealed them in this little pot." She pressed her lip gloss into his hand. "How can I let you live in kisslessness for four or five years?"

"Thank you! For something laden with a thousand of your kisses, it is very light."

"Well, if I freed your hands I could give you big heavy kisses all the way home?"

Now that Merlin's mood had lifted he could laugh.

"And how would I concentrate on our navigation?"

"Isn't that what our gryphons are for?"

59

Dancing

Three minutes to Midnight,
Friday September 10th, Timeless

"WE MUST GO, EMILIA. The gryphons are ready."
But Emily wasn't. The baying of hounds, the aroma of apples, the taste of iron, the spring of the Dragon underfoot, the tears of Merlin, all of them held her and she did not want to leave Avalon.

"I want to stay with you, Myrddin!" She held him so tight he gasped for breath. "Can't you look into the stars and see if there is any future for us?"

"I have strained to remember our future but the vision that comes to me is of a dream. In it I am very, very old; and you are very, very young and we are telling someone our story. There is nothing else."

Suddenly her mood lifted. "So there is that faint hope!" and laughing she added, "I suppose you magicians, you just get older and wiser while we fairies, we never age. Actually it is a kind of a rule we fairies have." And she pirouetted with joy. "Now, you tell me the truth, you old trickster man!" and she pulled him close to her again. "In this dream, do we still love one another?"

"I love you more than ever, and whenever I look into your eyes I see the love light shines there too."

"Well if your dream is our only possible future I will snatch it because I will be with you, and now that there is some hope that I will see you again, I can go home. But do we have to ride those animals?"

"They could just fly beside us! Why?"

"I loved it when you danced with me on the ceiling of our kitchen. Come dance with me into the future!"

He took her in his arms and they leapt off the Dragon's head into a swirl of purple light with the gryphons behind them. "This is my colour," and at once the purple and violet faded into a blue mauve, "and this is yours." It was the colour of wisteria.

Merlin sang:

"Would you have me dancing out of nowhere, Avalon?"

And she responded, her voice a strong soprano which brought a joyous laugh from Merlin. He had never heard her sing before.

"Avalon
Avalon
Avalon
Without conversation or a notion, Avalon
Where the samba takes you out of nowhere."

And together, spinning through dark space, they sang:

"And the backgrounds fading out of focus
Yes, the pictures changing every moment
And your destination, you don't know it Avalon."

Giddy with delight, Emily sang first and Merlin answered:

"Dancing
Dancing
Dancing
Dancing."

"I almost forgot, Emilia. What is the Perseid meteor shower?"

60

The Grace of Vengeance

Dawn, Saturday September 11th, Merlin's time

A COLD WIND TASTING OF WINTER *fanned the bonfire in the courtyard. Behind the fire, in the grey shadow, Uther placed a shallow vat of ale. At the very moment when the dawn light hit the battlements, the bagpipes droned and Marcus Octavius Cotta, dressed in the uniform of a Roman general, marched through the open doors of the villa.*

Despite his sorrow he was satisfied. The Moot was one of the best gatherings of powerful men he had ever experienced. The petty kings' attention had never flagged, everyone had had their say, both Aurelius and Uther showed that they could persuade and lead, everyone agreed on both Vortigern's guilt and his punishment, and they had made sound plans to raise an army. I shadowed him in my new military dress carrying a coronet on a small cushion.

"It is dawn!" the general proclaimed. And in a quiet and solemn procession, the kings followed him through the door before fanning out below the steps of the villa to witness the threefold execution of Vortigern.

"Sound the trumpets!" His command was taken up immediately by the soldiers on the battlements.

"The sons of Constantinus Maximinius, advance!"

The sons of the Dux of the Fifth Legion came forward and knelt down on the step below my father.

"Behold this ceremonial sword that was given to me for safe keeping by your father because he feared for his life." And my father held the jewel-encrusted sword over his head and slashed the air with it. "You will take it, Ambrosius Aurelianus Maximinius, to avenge the death of your father and your brother and please them by rinsing it red with the blood of their murderer.

"I call forward Ambrosius Marcus Cotta, who only a few hours ago prophesised the coming of a new king. I ask him to remind us of your memory of the future."

I sang again, smiling at Aurelius:

"Is the honey-tongued Lord here?"

And the assembled kings cried "Yea!"

"Is he full of vengeance for his slain kin?"

And the assembled kings cried "Yea!"

"From his grief, spears will shine with blood.
We see him fighting at the Giants' Stones."

And the assembled kings cried "Yea. We will be with you!"

The brothers arose as one and bowed to my father and to the kings on his right hand and then to those on his left. Aurelius, stepping into the centre of the courtyard and brandishing the sword above his head, called out,

"We are ready. Bring forth the man who murdered our kinsmen and stole our lands!"

A trapdoor sprang open under the wall of the villa and Vortigern, manacled in an iron bracelet, was pushed up the steps by soldiers. They unlocked his wrists and gave him his only weapon of defence, the athane. He crept forward blinking and cringing like a mole into the light.

'A coward to the end,' I thought, and I ensured again our villa was shielded from the intervention of his cronies of the Dark who hovered above us looking for any opening to rescue him.

Uther, long and lean and muscular, was also dressed as a soldier. He wore a leather gauntlet on one hand and in the other he carried a gladiator's net; he stalked his quarry by goading and pushing Vortigern towards the sword of his father. The kings cheered his every move Almost immediately Aurelius sent the athane of the condemned man flying through the air and its loss caused Vortigern to let out a piteous cry: "Oh wicked blade!" and the kings to applaud in anticipation.

"Shame, Vortigern, shame!" Uther called out over the acclaim. "Die like a man!"

Enraged at the insult, Vortigern raced towards Uther screaming, "Sons of Constantine, hear me! I curse you!"

Both brothers instantly fell to their knees and crossed themselves.

Raising his hands to those unseen above us, Vortigern continued: "I invoke the demon powers of Moloch to curse you and scatter your armies and crush forever the spawn of..."

Just as I raised my staff to release a bolt of lightning to scorch Vortigern's mouth and blister it shut, my father bellowed, "That is enough!"

Vortigern staggered backwards. Aurelius, lithe and graceful, sprang to his feet to prowl like a wolf around him. Maybe, but only for a moment or two, Aurelius allowed himself to enjoy this dance of death until, signalling to Uther, he cried out something in their special language before lunging forward and piercing the neck of the man who cursed them. The blood of Vortigern sprayed around his beard but it did not arc as it would have if Aurelius had cut the main highway of his blood. I tossed my head at him to acknowledge the dexterity of his placement of the blow. After all, this was only the first death of Vortigern.

With the utmost care and deliberation, Aurelius raised his boot and pushed Vortigern backwards into the fire. There were loud cheers from the kings. It only took a moment for his hair and his kilt to catch alight, and as his flesh burned I gagged on the stench of his scorched meat. His screams were distorted by the blood gurgling in his throat. 'Thank God, Emilia is not here to witness this. It is vile!'

It was now time, Uther decided, for the third death, and with his left arm sheathed in his leather gauntlet against the flames, he yanked Vortigern from the fire and tossed him face down into the vat of ale.

"Your last drink is on us, Vortigern!" he bellowed, and roaring with laughter Uther stamped his boot on the head of Vortigern until his gurgling stopped.

All was silence.

There was not a sound from the kings; they held their breath because they were waiting for something, something very British. And their hopes were soon realised. The drums began a slow beat as the older brother handed his younger brother their father's sword, and with his freed hands he held aloft the dead man by his ankle, and Uther with one slash beheaded him.

Uther picked up the head of Vortigern and carried it with pomp and grace to his brother who, in turn, carried it ceremoniously to my father. Bruto held the head high to the loud acclaim of the British kings. When the trumpets sounded, I smiled grimly to myself because I was very pleased with all the dramatic flourishes I planned.

I hope you can appreciate that this is how one creates legends. One suggests every gruesome detail and, as they play out before one's eyes, the spectacle appears spontaneous and that ensures it will be remembered and retold by every king here who saw the triple death of Vortigern the Betrayer. And many of them agreed with Coel, that in Vortigern they executed a rare man, a man who died without one single virtue.

And the kings will cross themselves and repeat the curse of Vortigern that jinxed the brothers; before they smile saying, 'I was there at the coronation of Ambrosius, the new king, and heard Myrddin, our new bard, sing and foresee that after red-sworded battles, we will be free.'

My father interrupted my thoughts.

"The head of Vortigern will be displayed on our gatepost until the ravens have picked it clean. Then it will rest in our granary with his decaying body as a warning to any other rats that try to usurp a throne that only God can give. May he rest in peace!"

He would place the skull above the trapdoor that concealed our small vault where our treasure lay.

Marcus Cotta handed the head to a soldier to carry out his orders, and his slave Maroc, smiling his approval, brought him a silver bowl of water with a heated stone in it to wash the blood of the Betrayer from his hands. After drying them, he walked into the centre of the courtyard and beckoned for me to follow. Maroc, carrying a salver of silver cups, followed us.

"Ambrosius Aurelianus, son and heir to Constantine," the general boomed, "come forward and kneel."

He placed the cushion I had been holding on the ground for Aurelius.

"Ambrosius, son of Constantinus and Elen, princess of Powys, I, Marcus Octavius Cotta, Legate of Rome, and with the power vested in me by the Emperor Honorius, crown you, Ambrosius, king of the north of Britannia.

"Hear ye, all kings present, what I proclaim Ambrosius will inherit. He will govern the land of Constantine. His land will reach from Petriana (Carlisle) at the wall's end in the west to Eboracum (York) in the east, and include all of Petuaria and Lindum Colonia (Lincoln) to the south."

And then, taking the coronet from my hand, my father placed it on Aurelius' bowed head.

"May Our Lord bless you and keep you safe and may your reign be long and honoured by God. Pax vobiscum!"

When the new king rose, he slashed the air with Constantine's sword and, acknowledging the cries of 'Long Live the King!' he grabbed two cups from the slave, and he and Uther dipped them into the death pool and drank its ale. Courtesy demanded that my father and I follow them.

"Long Live the King!" I called out as I tasted but did not swallow the bitter iron of the blood of Vortigern in my mouth. For an instant, only long enough to spit out every drop of him, I made myself invisible. I wanted no part of him to desecrate my body or spirit.

And Uther bellowed:

"Down with the invaders, be they Saxons or Danes, Angles or Jutes, they are not welcome here and we will fight them all to the death!"

"But first," the new king said, "we will hunt down the so-called Vortigern of the north, and take our restitution as ordered by the Arch-Druid, and Vortigern will die not once, not twice, not thrice but four times: one death for every murder we know he committed. May God rest his soul!"

The battle of Britannia had begun.

List of Characters

Merlin's Time

MERLIN: born early November 433, about 30 miles from Exeter (Isca) near Okehampton in his father's village. Extremely tall at 6 feet 3 inches, in a time when few men were more than 5 feet 4 inches, he is raven-haired with intense blue eyes, and called Ambrosius Marcus Cotta by his father but Myrddin by his mother. As a Roman soldier, he will change his name again to Ambrosius Merlinus. A child prodigy with 80 percent recall of everything he reads and hears, as a young adult he matures into an accomplished poet, linguist, engineer, mathematician, scientist, architect and astrologist. He is able to unlock the future, to fly the pathways of the air, and has been schooled by a Pictish shaman in the Wyed ways of the wood. His Welsh mother trains him in shape-shifting, in complex spells and enchantment and Michael, the Archangel, trains him in aerial display and combat with the Darker Magic

MARCUS OCTAVIUS COTTA: born 405, is Merlin's father. He is from a noble Roman family and was Dux of the Third Legion stationed in today's Regensburg, Germany. He inherited wealth and became wealthier from selling the booty of war and investing in Spanish gold mines. Married Ingraine, a Welsh princess, whom he suspected was a goddess such were her powers. Intensely ugly, tall and strong and known affectionately by his soldier's name of Bruto, he is more cunning than intelligent. He fathered one child, a son, whom he calls Ambrosius, of whom he is in awe.

INGRAINE: born 418, Cotta's dark haired and blue eyed wife is an intelligent and gifted woman of extraordinary beauty, the only daughter of Lunedda, King of the Silures. She is an Arch-Druidess and enchantress. She is Myrrdin's mother, and renowned for her gifts as a physician, herbalist and musician.

ANGHARAD: the daughter of Ingraine's childhood nurse, she comes to the Cotta household to be nursemaid to the baby Myrddin. She loves him as a mother and teaches him the healing power of plants and how to play the harp.

DOONE: a slight, black-haired, dark-eyed Pict from near Oban in today's Scotland. He is an inventive man and a master of Wyed or the ways of the wood, and as a shaman he is able to fly the pathways of the air. Captured by Constantine's legionnaires outside their military camp, he was shackled and sold as a slave to Marcus Cotta as a woodsman. He becomes Merlin's teacher and Bruto's trusted servant.

ARIANRHOD (pronounced Ahr-ee-ahn-hrod): is a Welsh goddess who resides at Caer Siddi, a revolving castle in the Northern Lights. As a spider she is a master spy who observes in secret events from cracks in the ceiling. Arianrhod as Lady Silver Wheel is the goddess of the moon and the weaver of dreams; she can spin strong spiders' silk into wondrous garments. Her best friend is Ingraine.

CONSTANTINE: Dux or Field General of the Sixth Legion stationed in north Britain guarding Hadrian's Wall. He is a civilised Roman, an inspiring leader and a close friend of Marcus Cotta. He married Elen, the daughter of a Welsh king and they had three sons. Just before his death he drafted the Groans of the British.

CONSTANS: Eldest son of Constantine. At 14 he enters a monastery in York where he dies mysteriously in his early twenties.

AMBROSIUS AURELIANUS: Assumes the role of eldest son and is sent by his father, Constantine, with his younger brother, to Lesser Britain in Gaul (Brittany in France) to live under the care and protection of their uncle, King Audren. He is known as 'Aurelius' for his golden tongue and his peaches and cream complexion. He is an inspiring leader and a strong, although sometimes squeamish, warrior. He is less than a year older than his younger brother and although they look nothing alike, they behave as twins, speaking together in their own language and completing one another's thoughts. The two brothers served together in the Roman Army in Gaul for two years. Aurelius is a deeply devout Christian and would have preferred to have served God as a monk.

UTHER (pronounced Oota) formal name is Eustucius: the youngest son of Constantine, is red-haired, bearded and a fierce fighter. Very tall, at 6 feet 2 inches, he is the only man besides Bruto who can look Merlin in the eye. With a great ear for music and languages, he speaks Latin, Greek, Gaulish, Pict, Saxon, Romano British, Welsh and Cornish. He will father King Arthur.

VORTIGERN THE BETRAYER: Vortigern is the son of a petty king from Petuaria on the Humber River. He murdered both his parents, poisoned Constantine's eldest son and in his hunger for soft fat land in the south he brought Saxons, Jutes and Angles from northern Germany and Sweden as mercenaries to protect his back from the Picts as he marched south to Lincoln. He was, according to Merlin, a handsome man beyond belief, a golden dandy, manicured and perfumed and a violent rapist of his own daughter. His success comes from the Dark.

YGERN: born 433, some say she is the most beautiful woman in Britannia with long hair the colour of crushed ice. She is sweet, natural and treasures her reputation for faithfulness to her violent husband. Merlin's childhood friend, Ygern was married at 14 years old to the forty year old Gorlois. She will be the mother of Morgana, the sorceress and Marguese and will five years later become the mother of Arthur.

GORLOIS: Duke of Cornwall, an elected nobleman in charge of Cornwall's armed forces. He is husband of Ygern, and father of Morgana and Marguese.

HU POWYLL: Arch Druid, a powerful and manipulative Druid from the Sanctuary at Yniswyddin, today's Glastonbury. Merlin suspects he is working with the Dark, but his father, Bruto knows he is!

MOLOCH: a prince of Darkness with blazing vermillion eyes, has no form or substance, and moves like a wraith. His purpose is to suborn all those who work for the Light, enslave Britannia and place Morgana and her progeny on the British throne.

MORGANA: as yet unborn as Ygern's daughter, exists in this novel as a shape-shifting spirit. She is called by her future name and keeps her real name as a secret, believing if it was revealed it could affect her power. She is an evil, voluptuous sorceress.

Our Time

EMILY CHARLOTTE HUGHES: born 10 September 1996, only child of Professor Julia Hughes and Dr Rhys Hughes, attends the Exeter Academy, a Jesuit school in Exeter, Devon. She started learning ballet at three around the time she rode her first pony. She hides her considerable intellect behind a smile and a wonderful laugh, but she cannot hide her grace, beauty and easygoing nature. Besides dancing, riding, swimming and surfing, she loves studying the stars. Emily has the tawny look of a Celt.

TOBIAS LAWLESS (Toby): born 13 March 1996; has spiky blond hair and diamond stud earring, he is Emily's school friend and dancing partner and her mother's godson. He is active in the Young Archaeologists Club. He is the only child of Karen Kirk and Richard Lawless, an archaeologist who died as a result of a cave-in at a dig in Egypt when Toby was three. He inherited his father's love of horses and is a champion show jumper. He plays the guitar and sings in a band called Brick Road, with Jack and Casey.

CASEY MADIGAN: born 15 August 1996, she is a school friend of Emily and is tall, blond and athletic and a talented singer. She sings in Brick Road with Toby and Jack.

RHYS ANEURIN HUGHES MA, DPHIL: born in 1965 in Barry, Wales and educated at the University of Oxford. He is a Senior Lecturer in Classical Languages at the University of Exeter. Fluent in Latin and Greek, he reads Sanskrit. He is passionately Welsh and moonlights in Glastonbury singing folk and songs of the seventies and eighties.

JULIA VERA JONES HUGHES BA, MSc, D PHIL: born in 1968 in Kinmel, Wales. Julia is tall, bronze-haired and brilliant, now a Professor of Archaeology at the University of Exeter. She is an authority on the re-use of Iron Age forts and Roman villas. She met Rhys at Oxford when she was 17. They lived together and eventually married when their only child, Emily, was born.

JOHN HENRY ARTHUR DEVONPORT: born 30 January 1996, Marquess of Exeter, known as 'Jack'; eldest son and heir of the Duke and Duchess of Dartmoor. Very tall at 6 feet 4 inches, golden-haired with fair skin and ruddy cheeks, he is an accomplished horseman, trainee pilot, budding artist and a gifted musician who plays the cello and the drums. He adores Michael Jackson and heavy-metal bands. He has his own butler, Alfred, who dresses him and drives him around. His mother is the heir to a fortune made in chocolate and he shares with his parents a passion for nineteenth century and pre-Raphaelite paintings of the Arthurian legend. He will attend Sandhurst Military Academy, despite his mother's Quaker beliefs. He told his mother when he was eight he would marry Emily, and that she and the Duke had fifteen years to get used to the idea.

Animals

ROGET: Emily's Australian long-necked turtle who lives in a terrarium at night and spends the day in her bra.

WINSTON: Emily's second turtle who lives mostly in the terrarium.

JERRY: a retired white polo pony that Emily rides on Dartmoor.

KELSO: a bird-obsessed, orange and white Brittany spaniel who is totally faithful and protective of Emily.

SQUEAK PRIMO & SQUEAK SECONDUS: a pair of mice who live, most of the time, somewhere below Merlin's shoulders, but above his feet.

CROOK: a male black and grey jackdaw who resides on Merlin's left shoulder. Despite his crippled leg, he works constantly with Merlin.

MERLIN: a large female falcon, a merlin, who resides on Merlin's right shoulder. She has strange orange eyes and Merlin is, of course, called after her, rather than the other way around.

DOLOSSUS: a male fox whose name means 'crafty'. He is Merlin's friend and Merlin hand-raised him since he was a pup. Merlin sends him on special or dangerous assignments and as with all of Merlin's animals, Merlin can move into his consciousness and see the world as he sees it wherever he is on assignment.